ANN

The Hardie
Inheritance

GraftonBooks
A Division of HarperCollins*Publishers*

Grafton Books
A Division of HarperCollins*Publishers*
77–85 Fulham Palace Road,
Hammersmith, London W6 8JB

Published by GraftonBooks 1991

First published in Great Britain by
Grafton Books 1990

Copyright © Margaret Potter 1990

The Author asserts the moral right to
be identified as the author of this work

A CIP catalogue record for this book
is available from the British Library

ISBN 0-586-20706-6

Printed in Great Britain by
Collins, Glasgow

Set in Goudy

CONTENTS

The Hardie Inheritance

PROLOGUE

On a summer morning in 1932 Grace Hardie rose early, as usual. For a few moments, stretching herself, she stared out of one of the windows of her tower bedroom, enjoying the stillness which surrounded her. No breeze rippled the trees; no clouds drifted across the sky. The sheep in the meadow were still asleep and even the birds were not yet on the wing.

All the land she could see was her own. The stone spires of Oxford and the ever-expanding factories of the Morris works were not far away, but were obscured from her view by a screen of mature woodland to the south and west. In terms of acres to be kept under control, the size of the estate was an anxiety; but at five o'clock in the morning it could be thought of simply as space: a guarantee of peace and solitude. She breathed deeply, savouring the silence.

Then it was time to throw off the mantle of a landed gentlewoman and prepare for a day to be spent in manual labour. She plunged her face into a bowl of cold water, pulled a comb through her short black hair and dressed herself in dungarees which were intended for a man but fitted her tall, straight figure well enough. It would have been true to say that she didn't care what anyone thought of her appearance; but there was a simpler truth than that. She didn't expect anyone outside her family to see her on what she assumed would be an uneventful day: a day like any other.

Few visitors came to the house which Grace shared with her mother and brother. No neighbours called to leave cards; no friends arrived by invitation for luncheon or dinner.

Greystones, the mansion on Shotover Hill which an elderly marquess had built for his great-granddaughter, contained a dining room in which a butler and full complement of footmen might serve twenty guests with a meal prepared by a cook and her kitchen maids. But the last indoor servant had left in 1922, and the three resident members of the Hardie family ate in the kitchen.

So no longer did any ladies withdraw after dinner to the large, light drawing room. No gentlemen retreated to the smoking room or chalked their cues in the billiards room. All the main entertaining rooms and most of the bedrooms had been covered with dust sheets, in order that pretty chintz covers and embroidered bedspreads should not fade, nor polished mahogany surfaces become scratched.

Yet the house, although for most of the time silent, was still alive. Only the top storey, where once servants slept, had been abandoned to damp and dirt. Each member of the family had chosen some part of Greystones to be converted into a private kingdom. Grace had taken over the large studio originally designed for her mother. Mrs Hardie herself nowadays painted her watercolours mostly out of doors, using for indoor work one of several pantries which led off the kitchen. Appreciating its north light, she ignored the lack of comfort.

For her private sitting room she used the boudoir which was part of the main bedroom suite. Her own paintings, covering the walls, provided memories of her husband, who had inherited his family's business but escaped to become an explorer. As she sat sewing or knitting she could rest her eyes on the scene of his grave in China, with the Himalayan mountains rising in the background; or enjoy the more cheerful picture of the valley of lilies which had made Gordon Hardie famous as a plant-hunter and had given his name to a new species.

Philip, the only one of her six sons who still lived in his childhood home, had inherited his father's interest in new plants, and so had appropriated not only the panelled library which adjoined the drawing room but also the plant rooms which stood a little way away from the house. In these he continued practical experiments in grafting and hybridization, before planting out his experimental seedlings in the cold glasshouse or the walled garden.

In a manner which the architect who designed Greystones could never have intended, the kitchen had become the new heart of the house. It was here that the three Hardies assembled whenever they did not want to be alone, for it was always warm and cheerful with the smells of newly-baked bread or nourishing soups made from home-grown vegetables. Lucy Hardie had been born in a grand country house and brought up in an aristocratic family which hardly knew where its own kitchens were to be found – certainly never venturing inside them. But on finding herself widowed and almost penniless, unable any longer to afford the staff which all her life she had thought to be indispensable, she had set to work to acquire new skills. No longer was food always brought to the table tepid and overcooked. With no more ceremony than a good washing of hands, Philip and Grace could sit down at the scrubbed kitchen table and know that they would be sustained through days of hard physical labour by generous and tasty meals.

The three inhabitants of Greystones were not ashamed of their change of fortune. It was not through any conscious choice of their own that no visitors – except of course Jay, the youngest of Mrs Hardie's surviving children; and Midge, her sister-in-law – ever came to the house. None of them was by nature unfriendly. It was just an accident of life that they lacked friends outside their own family.

Grace, who was thirty-five years old, had no schoolfriends with whom to keep in touch because she had never been to school. She was educated – after a fashion – by a governess at home, and her brothers and the son of the head gardener had provided sufficient companionship during her childhood.

In normal circumstances she would undoubtedly have been introduced into a wider social life when she reached the age of eighteen; but by that time the war had started. The young men who should have been partnering her to dances were dying on the Western Front, and the mood at home was sombre. It was no time for parties. Grace had made a way of life for herself in which she was happy and had not allowed the coming of peace to change it. It was a solitary life, but she had adjusted herself to it so well that she never felt lonely.

Her brother Philip became solitary for different reasons. The end of the war in 1918 found him still shell-shocked and with lungs damaged beyond repair in a gas attack. The fourteen years which had passed since then failed to heal either his body or his spirit completely. He spent most of the daylight hours out of doors, because every shallow breath he took must be of the freshest air, but the impression of good health created by his sun-tanned face was a deceptive one.

Although by now he had recovered well enough to converse normally if he chose, the first years of convalescence, spent in a silent community, seemed to have robbed him of any wish to speak. Smiling and nodding, he listened to the conversations of his mother and sister, but rarely contributed to them. The friends he had made at school or in the army had for the most part died in battle. Those few who survived understood his need for silence: they wrote letters from time to time, but did not intrude on his privacy.

Their mother's approach to self-sufficiency took a more individual route. Her pedigree – for she was the granddaughter of the eleventh Marquess of Ross – should have opened the doors of county society to her; and Greystones would have provided a suitable setting for her skills as a hostess. But she had married into trade. The highest class of trade, admittedly, for there was a difference between a vintner and, say, a butcher: but trade nevertheless. The county stayed away and Lucy Hardie, rearing her large family and running the household during her husband's long absences, held her head high and refused to notice its coldness. At the same time, the grandeur of her connections perhaps daunted those members of Oxford's other family businesses who might otherwise have welcomed her into their own circle.

Whatever the reasons, she had never since her marriage enjoyed much social life. In the prosperous days before 1914 she was content to live surrounded by her family; and when, after the war, The House of Hardie came near to bankruptcy and her income disappeared almost overnight, she was too proud to look for any sympathy or company except that of her children.

They had settled down together, Mrs Hardie and Grace and Philip, in a manner which brought them satisfaction. They each had time in which to indulge their different enthusiasms, whilst contributing equally to the care of the house and the cultivation of the land around it – working as their own domestic servants and farm labourers in the interests of self-sufficiency.

So it was that as Grace ran down the spiral staircase from her round tower bedroom that morning, her mind was on nothing more exciting than the list of jobs to be done. Waving a cheerful hand at Philip, who was already milking the goats, she carried buckets of swill and scrap towards the pigsties and the henhouse. She was a tall, strong woman, accustomed to carrying heavy loads. Later, after breakfast, she intended to pick many pounds of raspberries: some for her mother to preserve; some for Philip to use in wine-making, a few for the family to eat, and many more for Frith to carry down to a greengrocer to be sold as local produce.

Frith had been the head gardener at Greystones in the days of the family's prosperity, ruling over his own staff of journeymen and boys. Rather than lose the lodge cottage as well as his job when Mrs Hardie found it no longer possible to pay staff, he had agreed to continue working without wages in return for the right to sell surplus produce and keep a proportion of the profit for himself. It was only as she started picking the fruit that Grace noticed the gardener's absence and remembered that he had not been in good health for the past few days. Later, she promised herself, she would go down to the cottage and make enquiries. But there was no cause for anxiety, so far as she knew: his non-appearance was worthy of note only because it was so rare for there to be any variation on the day's usual routines.

And so, as she picked and tasted the juicy ripe berries, Grace allowed her mind to wander to the work she would do on her own account once her day's chores were accomplished. Not that she thought of it as work, for her all-absorbing activity brought her nothing but satisfaction. She was a maker of shapes.

Sometimes she carved wood and sometimes stone; sometimes she modelled clay; but always the work which emerged deserved no name except that of a shape. People, animals, flowers, objects of any kind – none of these things inspired her to copy them. The forms she created came out of her own imagination and satisfied her own eye: that was all she cared about. This afternoon, since the weather was fine enough for working out of doors, she would return to a piece that she was making from stone. She allowed her thoughts to dwell on curves and planes and spaces. More than anything else Grace enjoyed creating spaces.

Each of the leaf-lined trug baskets which she carried into the walled garden was in turn filled with fruit and set down between the rows to await collection when the task was completed. She had no reason to expect any interruption in her daily routine. No visitors were expected today, because no visitors were *ever* expected. There was no way in which she could have guessed that before she went to bed that night not just one caller, but four, would have made their way up the long drive towards Greystones. Nor could she have foreseen the dramatic consequences of each of those visits. As

14

the sun rose higher in the sky there was nothing to suggest that 23 July 1932 was to be anything other than the most ordinary of days.

PART ONE
Grace

1932–1933

ONE

'Are we going to look at another house?'

Ellis Faraday smiled sympathetically at his daughter's question. Of course they were going to look at another house, and Trish knew it as well as he did. They had been looking at other people's houses ever since the summer holiday began.

On the first occasion the six-year-old had been excited, probably hoping that her father planned to buy the house and take her to live in it. Later, realizing that he had no plans of this kind, she became bored. But by now she had been told the reason for all these visits and was interested again.

'Yes, we are,' said Ellis, taking hold of the little girl's hand to help her along. 'This one's called Greystones.'

'How old is it?'

'It was built in 1900. So you tell me how old it is.'

'Give up,' said Trish without even trying. She was no good at sums.

'Thirty-two years old. Twenty-six years older than you. And there it is.'

They had been walking along a narrow lane, bounded by stone walls. Now he lifted Trish on to the top of one of the walls so that she could get a better view; because the house was still a considerable distance away, almost at the top of a hill. 'What do you think of it?'

He waited patiently while she stared at the mansion and considered what to say. Ellis was not too bothered about his daughter's slowness in coming to terms with figures, because he was not a great one for making calculations himself. But he had been patient in teaching her that it was never good enough to announce simply that she liked or didn't like something. She was expected to give reasons for her opinions; and she did so now.

'I think it's lovely,' she said when she had thought about it. 'Because of the tower.'

The front of Greystones was wide and comparatively low, its third tier of windows, for the servants' bedrooms, being concealed behind the parapet. But in one corner a round tower rose two storeys higher than the rest of the house. The lack of symmetry, and the contrast between the curve of the tower and the angles of the main building might have created an odd impression but in fact gave the house its individual character. Ellis approved of it himself, and was interested that his daughter should react in the same way – although for different reasons.

'It's a fairy-tale palace for a princess,' she announced. 'Like in the story where the princess has to let down her long golden hair to make a ladder. I should think everyone in that family wants to live in the tower.'

'Let's go and ask them, shall we?'

He lifted her down, and together they walked along the lane before turning into the drive which led up to the house. In order to make the ascent of the hill less steep for the horses which would have carried guests to the house when it was first built, the drive zig-zagged in wide curves through grassland on which a flock of sheep were grazing, but a straighter track had been worn down by the feet of walkers, cutting off all the corners.

'Do the people at Greystones know we're coming?' she asked.

Ellis recognized a note of anxiety in her voice. When they arrived at a mansion by invitation, they drove right up to the front door in the van which was necessary to carry all his equipment. It had not taken her long to learn that whenever they left the vehicle before they even reached the gates, as had happened today, it was because they weren't expected.

'No, they don't,' he admitted. 'I thought we'd give them a surprise.'

'Why?'

'This house may be in a rather different state from some of the others we've seen; the grand ones,' he told her. 'The family must have been well off at the time when it was built, but from what I've heard, it sounds as though they've come down in the world since then.'

'Do you mean they're poor?'

'That's not a word to use when we're talking to them.'

'I know *that*.' Her voice expressed indignation.

'I don't suppose they're poor in the way that ordinary people are poor. I don't even expect that they have to tell their children, if they have any, that they're not allowed new red sandals until their feet have grown out of horrid black strap shoes.' This was a subject which had been much discussed between Trish and her father recently. 'But a big house like Greystones costs a lot to keep up, if it's to be done properly. The Hardies may not have been able to manage that. If I'd written in advance and asked permission to call, they'd probably have said No.'

'Why?'

'When a house has grown shabby, its owners often don't want people to come and look at it. Or if they do say Yes, they feel that they ought to do something about it before they let us come – you know, clean it and make it tidy. That would mean that we'd be giving them a lot of hard work. So we're just going to turn up. Then I can explain what I want. They're more likely to let us look round this way.'

'They might think we're burglars.'

'That's why I've brought you with me. I may look like a burglar, but you don't.' He squeezed her hand affectionately. 'You're a very useful companion.'

Trish grinned and began to skip along the path, pleased to feel that she was useful to her father by not looking like a burglar. Watching her, Ellis felt himself overcome by love. He had embarked on her upbringing, four years earlier, in a mixture of rage at the rotten hand which life had dealt him and terror

21

at the thought of his own inadequacy as a father. But almost from the start she had seemed to know how to bring herself up, leaving him only the task of translating her instructions into practical arrangements.

Today, for example, she had decided which of her summer dresses would be most suitable and had given two days' notice that it ought to be washed. Her long white socks and the straw hat, with a red ribbon tied under her chin, proclaimed her to be a well-behaved little girl, which she was, and a demure little girl, which she most certainly was not. Only the hated scuffed shoes spoiled the neat picture she made, and it was Ellis's own fault that he had refused to accept the need for new red sandals. Trish was a bundle of lively energy, but the bundle came in such a neat and pretty package that her father longed to pick her up and hug her every few minutes. If only she could stay like that for the rest of her life and never grow into a woman!

Trish's attention was no longer on her own appearance, but on the grounds through which they were walking.

'Do the sheep belong to the Hardies?'

'Might. Might not. Most likely thing is that a farmer pays them for grazing rights.' Ellis always tried to give his daughter a serious answer to her many questions. 'The farmer gets more grass to fatten his sheep, and the owners get a bit of money and don't have to mow the grass, so it suits everyone.'

But although Trish had asked the question, she was no longer listening to the answer. She had come to a halt, staring. 'What's *that*?'

The object which had caught her eye was indeed strange. Immediately in front of Greystones was a circle of lawn surrounded by the turning circle of the carriage drive. Unlike the rough parkland which was kept short by the nibbling sheep, this area of grass had been smoothly mown, and in its centre was an object made out of stone.

'It's a hole,' said Ellis. Someone had hollowed out a large block of stone so that what faced forward was indeed a hole.

22

It had a roughly rectangular shape, but because the stone around it curved backwards like the tyre of a motor car, the effect was round rather than angular; and a knob, curved again, which rose from the top right-hand corner prevented the shape from being dull.

'It's –' Trish ran forward across the grass. Bending down, she stepped through the hole. Ellis, following, saw that she was now standing in a second hole cut from the same block and lying flat on the lawn. 'It's the house!' she exclaimed. 'It's Greystones!'

'Full marks for imagination, but I hardly think –'

'But look, Daddy. That's the tower. And this is the space for living in.'

'Then I don't think you ought to scramble about in other people's houses.' He was laughing, not pretending to agree with her understanding of the stone. Reluctantly she stepped out of the hole and allowed her father to take her hand again, for now they had arrived at the house.

He rang the bell beside the front door, but frowned to himself as he did so. It must have been a long time since the door was last opened, for cobwebs stretched across all the cracks, and some of last year's dead leaves lay undisturbed on the threshold. 'We'd better go and look for another door,' he said, without waiting long for an answer.

The windows of the rooms they passed were large and long, but the curtains inside had all been drawn across.

'Do you think someone's dead?' asked Trish.

'They probably just want to keep the sun out, so that their pictures won't fade.'

'I don't think anyone's living here.'

Ellis, who had made enquiries in the village, knew better and took his daughter's hand again to lead her past the front of the house and round a corner. A few yards ahead of them a woman was sitting outside in the sunshine. She was grey-haired; but her face, which had once been that of a beautiful woman, was almost unlined, needing no make-up to cover it.

23

She looked very much at ease, comfortable and relaxed as she plucked a chicken.

'I'm sorry to intrude,' said Ellis. 'I did ring the bell, but . . .'

'I wouldn't hear it out here.' The woman smiled her thanks to Trish, who had run to catch some of the escaping feathers, and now approached shyly to press them down with the others.

'I'd like to have a word with the owner of Greystones,' Ellis said, phrasing the request vaguely because he was not sure whether he was addressing a servant or a member of the family. The woman's occupation – and the serviceable apron which protected her simple cotton frock – suggested that she was a member of the kitchen staff, but her calm, pleasant voice conveyed a different impression. She might even be the owner of the house herself – but this proved not to be the case.

'You'll find her in the stables. Go back past the front door to the other side of the house, and then through the arch. But if you're trying to sell something, you'll be wasting your time.'

'Thank you for your help.' Ellis turned to go, but paused for one more question. 'I'm correct, am I, in believing that Greystones is still in the possession of the Hardie family?'

'That's right. It's Miss Hardie you're looking for.'

'Thank you.'

Trish took hold of his hand again as they retraced their footsteps. 'Was that lady the cook?'

'Perhaps. I'm not sure.'

'She had a nice face. But I didn't know that chickens without feathers looked like that. Do you think there'll be ponies in the stables? Will they let me have a ride? What's all that hammering going on?'

'You know as much as I do.' By now they had reached the stable block. Over the arch the golden hands of a clock with a blue face pointed to twelve o'clock, although that was not the correct time. Hand in hand they walked through the arch and into the cobbled courtyard.

All Trish's questions were answered at once. There were no horses to be seen. And the hammering sound was coming from

24

the far side of the courtyard, where someone – facing away from them – was hitting a large piece of stone with a mallet and chisel. Could this really be Miss Hardie? It looked more like a man; a tall, thin man wearing workman's overalls. A strong man, as well; the hammering appeared to be hard work. Perhaps he was a mason, preparing to repair the fabric of the walls.

Ellis put a finger to his mouth, warning his daughter not to make any sudden noise, in case surprise might cause the chisel to slip. Instead, they moved together round the outside of the stable yard until they could be seen.

It was after all a woman and not a man who caught sight of them and, startled, paused with her mallet raised in the air for the next blow. She looked from one to the other, waiting for one of them to speak.

'I'm afraid we're disturbing you, Miss Hardie,' said Ellis. 'Your – your cook, was it? – told us we should find you here.'

'Cook? Oh, you mean my mother.' Grace Hardie smiled, and the smile transformed her face. Until that moment the concentration with which she applied herself to her work had given an absorbed, withdrawn look to her dark eyes; but now they twinkled with amusement. She set down her tools carefully in their flat wooden rack and pulled off the cap which had been protecting her hair from the stone dust, shaking her head vigorously as she did so as though to let the air in. 'How can I help you?'

'My name may not mean anything to you,' said Ellis. 'I come without introduction, I'm afraid. Ellis Faraday. And this is my daughter Patricia, who usually answers to Trish.'

'Hello, Trish. I won't shake hands, because I'm filthy.' But she smiled again in a friendly manner. Then, more seriously, she looked into Ellis's eyes.

'Faraday?' she repeated. 'Oh yes. The name Faraday certainly means something to me.'

Faraday! Grace looked with new interest at her unexpected visitors. The child, fair-haired and pale-faced except for a scattering of freckles on her cheeks, was standing quietly while the adults conversed, biting her lips to hold back the questions she was bursting to ask. The man, a few years younger than Grace herself, had the same fair hair as his daughter and a soft, crumpled face. He was tall and slim – though it was odd that she should use the word slim in her thoughts, rather than thin: that must have something to do with the grace of his movements and the charm of his smile.

That he was deliberately trying to charm her was obvious enough. In a moment he would be asking some kind of favour and making in return some promise that might never be fulfilled. She would have sent packing any other stranger who smiled at her like this, seeming to appeal for instant friendship, had his name not been Faraday.

He was presumably related to the architect, Patrick Faraday, who had been killed in the war; and Patrick Faraday had been of significance in her life not just once but twice. He it was who had designed Greystones as a house specifically intended to improve her health. If Grace had ever seen him while the plans were under discussion, she did not remember the occasion, for she was only an infant at the time. But she had met him once ten years later, in the home of her aunt, and that was an encounter she was not likely to forget.

It was because Aunt Midge, headmistress of a school for girls, had a lover whose existence must be kept secret that Grace had been deprived of the chance to go to the school and had instead been forced to continue doing all her lessons with a governess. Patrick Faraday was to blame for that. No longer now did Grace mind about the defects in her education or her lack of companionship; but she had minded at the time. 'I met a Mr Patrick Faraday once,' she said cautiously.

'You actually met him! Oh, marvellous! I didn't think – because of course you can't have been born at the time when Greystones was built.'

'I was three years old when we moved in.' Grace never made any attempt to conceal her age. She accepted the fact that she was on the shelf: a spinster. It was a life she had chosen for herself, and she was happy in it. Had she believed that Ellis Faraday was trying to flatter her by misjudging her age, she would have been scornful. But as a matter of fact and observation she recognized that her appearance had hardly changed at all in the past ten years. Her pale skin and dark hair shone with health and apparent youth, and her tall, slender body was in its prime. If someone meeting her for the first time claimed to believe that she was younger than her thirty-five years, he was not necessarily being insincere.

'Patrick Faraday was my father,' said Ellis. 'Though I must confess that I hardly knew him. My mother ran off to Ireland with another fellow when I was only a young boy, and took me with her.'

'And are you an architect too?'

'No. A photographer. I'll come straight to the point of my visit. I earn my living taking misty close-ups of débutantes. But for my own pleasure – and to honour my father's memory – I'm compiling a book about his work. Mainly photographs, with just enough text to explain them. He died too young, of course. Another twenty years, and he might well have been recognized as one of the giants of his profession. But he was only forty-four when he was killed.'

'I remember,' said Grace softly. Aunt Midge had come to Greystones to mourn, weeping with anger and misery at the waste of a life.

27

'All the same, he had time to achieve a good deal, especially in domestic architecture. Greystones was his first really important work. A turning point in his life, you might say, because its success brought him other major commissions. So I've come to ask your permission to photograph it. Not just one flat-faced view, but from as many different angles as possible. And interiors of the main rooms.'

Grace considered the request for a few moments,

'I'm not sure about inside the house,' she said at last. 'I'll have to think about that and have a word with my mother. But the outside – yes, certainly you can put that on record. Have you brought your equipment with you?'

'It's not far away. But I didn't arrive here expecting to get straight to work.' He laughed as he explained. 'In the ordinary run of things my sitters come to my studio by appointment and at their own request. The more clutter there is in the studio, the more they feel they're getting a professional service. It's only since I embarked on this project that I've realized that someone who drives up in a van and starts to unload a selection of tripods and umbrellas and all the rest of it, without an invitation, is most likely to have the dogs set on him. This visit is purely exploratory.'

'Then perhaps you'd like to walk round the outside. See what the best views might be. Shall we all go together?'

She felt a small hand tugging at hers. The little girl had kept quiet whilst her elders were talking, but was longing to ask a question.

'Please, did you make the hole?'

'The hole?' Grace was puzzled.

'I think Trish is talking about the piece of sculpture in front of the house,' Ellis explained.

'Sculpture! I should hardly call it that.'

'What *do* you call it, then?'

'Oh, just a shape. It's a hobby of mine, carving and modelling. But I wouldn't be capable of creating a piece of work which actually looked like anything real.'

'Well, whatever you call it, I thought it was a hole but Trish said it was Greystones.'

'Then Trish is a very observant little girl,' said Grace, smiling down at her. 'Yes, I did make it, and of course it isn't anything more to look at than a pair of holes in different planes. But I carved it at a time when I'd just learned that my father was dead and yes, Trish, it *is* Greystones in a sort of a way. My home with a big gap in its life. I don't think anyone else has ever recognized that before, though.'

'I wish I could make a hole,' said Trish, looking longingly at the row of tools set neatly in a rack.

Grace followed her glance and spoke firmly.

'You mustn't touch any of those tools, Trish. They're very sharp; very dangerous. But –' She took the lid off the old dustbin in which she kept her modelling clay. She had been using it on the previous day to make a small maquette of the piece which she proposed to carve from the stone. Now she broke a little off and handed it to Trish. 'You could make a hole for yourself out of this,' she said. 'And if it's the right size you could put it on your finger to be a ring.'

Trish stuck her finger through the lump of clay she had been given, but shook her head in disapproval at the result. Grace watched with interest as the six-year-old decided what to do. First of all squeezing the clay between her hands to see how soft it was, she broke off a very small piece, rolled it again into a thin sausage and pressed the ends together to form a circle. It was too large to be a ring. She repeated the process, this time fitting the sausage of clay round her finger before sealing it. Beaming with pride, she held up the finger to show her ring to the grown-ups.

'Please may I make something else?'

'Of course.' Grace broke off a larger piece of the clay and handed it to her before pressing the damp cloth back in place. 'What would you like to make?'

'I'll tell you when I've finished. May I stay here to do it, instead of looking at your house?'

Grace was about to say No, although in a kindly fashion, when Ellis interrupted.

'If you're worried about your tools, Miss Hardie, you can trust Trish to do what she's told. If she promises not to touch anything here except the clay, she won't.'

'Do you promise?' asked Grace.

The little girl nodded. 'Trust Trish.' She enjoyed the sound of the words and repeated them fast several times until the sounds became muddled. 'Trust Trish, trush Trish, trush Trist.' They all laughed together at the muddle.

'This way, then.' Grace led Ellis out of the stable yard, but instead of turning towards the house she indicated that they should walk in the opposite direction.

'My own favourite view is from higher up, up the hill,' she told her companion. 'You can see the design of the house particularly well from there. It may help you to choose the positions you need for your photographs. We'll go through the walled garden: it's a short cut.'

Philip was hoeing between the rows of French beans, taking over one of Frith's usual tasks while the gardener was confined to bed. He paused for a moment to rest as Grace pushed open the wooden door.

'This is my brother Philip,' she told Ellis. 'Philip, this is Mr Faraday, the son of the Greystones architect. He wants to take some photographs of the house.'

Philip smiled, nodding in a friendly way at the visitor. With exactly the same movement used by Grace herself earlier to demonstrate that she was too dirty with stone dust to shake hands, he turned his earth-stained palms towards them before returning to work.

Beyond the walled garden, which was used solely to grow food, was the serpentine garden which Philip had created when he first returned to his childhood home after the war. Still suffering the effects of shell-shock, he had discovered his own therapy in designing and planting an area which was almost, but not quite, a maze. A wide grassy path twisted and spiralled and turned back on itself; but it never in fact offered choices. Evergreen shrubs and trees sometimes lined the path closely and at other points curved away to enclose circles of earth, each devoted to a single species of flower. Other curves in the line of evergreens formed alcoves which framed examples of Grace's own work. Ellis, catching sight of the first, came to a halt.

'Did you make this? Another of your – what did you call them? – shapes?'

'Yes.' Grace laughed. 'What other name could you possibly give it?' The wood carving which had caught his eye resembled a vertical figure of eight whose lines, instead of merely meeting at the top, had crossed over as though lifting hands to heaven. 'More holes, you see. This is my brother's garden really. But one or two of my earliest efforts seemed to suit it, and so I went on to make some more specially.'

'Where did you train?'

'Train?' Grace was amused by the idea. 'Well, the village of Headington Quarry has that name because the masons who built the Oxford colleges took their stone from there. The tradition is still alive, so I persuaded an old mason to teach me how to tackle stone. For the wood, I found carpentry equipment in an outhouse and borrowed some carving tools that had once belonged to one of my brothers. I have a good many split masterpieces, I can tell you, to show that I've never had any proper training. It took me a long time to learn that wood must be seasoned. Now, we'll go straight up this hillside, unless your shoes are too slippery to grip.' Grace herself was wearing a pair of moccasins which her mother had made from rabbit skins and given her for Christmas. Shop-bought shoes were a luxury in a household which never went hungry but rarely possessed very much actual cash for shopping; they were worn only on special occasions.

Ellis made no further comment on her work. No doubt he needed all his breath for the climb up the steep slope. Grace

31

herself, who was used to it, did not pause until they had almost reached the band of trees which crowned the hill.

'Now turn round,' she said.

THREE

Touched by the note of pride and affection in Grace's voice, Ellis turned and looked down at Greystones. From here, as she had promised, it was possible to appreciate the design. The front of the house faced south-west, and behind it two wings extended at right angles. The courtyard thus formed was further enclosed by the ends of the two wings, which turned inward at an angle of forty-five degrees. Ellis, who had studied the plans before embarking on today's expedition, knew that this was in order to give a true north light to a large studio. The kitchen had been angled in a similar way merely to balance it. Patrick Faraday had believed in symmetry.

It was that fact which made the placing of a round tower on one corner so surprising. Ellis studied this corner now – not entirely with approval.

'Oh, Miss Hardie!' he exclaimed. 'What has happened to the tower?'

Grace laughed. It was an attractive laugh, full of genuine amusement. 'You mean the tree?'

'I certainly do mean the tree.' A large oak was growing within a few yards of the tower. 'I can't believe that was part of my father's landscape design. And the roots could prove dangerous to the structure.'

'Yes, I know. And my reason for not having cut it down years ago is shamefully sentimental. The son of our gardener was my best friend when I was a small girl. He planted an acorn beneath my bedroom window as a surprise present. Watching it grow was a great delight to me when I was young. I've only recently realized that something ought to be done,

33

and now, of course, it's become rather a large and dangerous task. I suspect that I shall continue to feel sentimental about it, and hope that the structure will last my time out. Shall we go down again?'

'Have you thought any more about allowing me to take some interior shots?' asked Ellis as they half ran, half slid down the slope.

Grace came to a halt and turned to face him. For a moment she seemed to be considering what she should say. When she did speak, it was with an honesty which Ellis found as touching as her earlier pride of ownership.

'You probably realized as soon as I told you that the cook was my mother that we can't afford the domestic staff needed for a house this size – or, indeed, any staff at all. So I'm afraid the reception rooms, which I imagine are the ones which interest you, are out of use.'

'I appreciate your candour, Miss Hardie. But an architectural photograph is quite a different matter from the sort of photograph illustrating interior design. It might even be an advantage to me if the rooms are empty.'

'They're not empty. Just – well, neglected.'

'Would you let me take a look?' he asked. 'I could promise complete confidentiality.'

She continued to hesitate. 'It's not that we're ashamed of the way we live,' she explained. 'But I do recognize that the house deserves to be better treated. I feel I'm letting it down. Letting your father down, as well. This can't be how he expected his creation to look.' She began to walk forward again, her head bowed in thought. 'The funny thing is that it's because I couldn't bear to part with the house that we're so short of money. In my father's lifetime, the property was financed by the family wine business. The House of Hardie; you may have heard of it.'

Ellis nodded. His modest home in London did not require the services of a firm which specialized in filling the cellars of gentlemen of good taste and deep purses, but he had read his father's notes on the family for which Greystones was to be designed. He even knew the names of all the Hardie children who had been born before 1900, and the fact that two of them, David and Kenneth, were twins and would choose to share a large bedroom rather than to sleep separately. From studying those same notes he was even aware that the strong, healthy woman who had just raced him up the hill had once been a sickly child whose chronic ill-health was thought to be caused by Oxford's marshy setting. It was for her sake that the house had been built on a hill and for her sake, as well, that the tower had been designed to give her an airy bedroom. But none of this had anything to do with her present lack of money. He listened with interest to her explanation.

'Well, you see, after the war one of my brothers wanted to use Greystones as security for a large loan to set the business on its feet again. Neither of us realized to begin with that the house belonged to me personally. But when I did find out, I refused to let it be put at risk. I'm very fond of Greystones, and I was afraid that if anything went wrong I might lose it. It made my brother very angry. He cut off our income just like that, as a sort of revenge. So I've held on to the house, but it does worry me that I'm not keeping it up properly.'

'There's some damp on the roof,' said Ellis, who had noticed the tell-tale signs from the higher viewpoint.

'I know. It's all a bit of a worry. There's enough land to sustain the three of us in a way that suits us, although it might seem odd to other people. But it doesn't enable us to build up the sort of fund that's needed for repairs. Still, to answer your question, there's no reason, since I've admitted all that, why I should prevent you from seeing the consequences for yourself. Yes, you can look round inside. We'll pick your daughter up first, shall we?'

They found Trish sitting on the cobbles of the stable yard, staring at her handiwork.

'That's a fine animal to be sure,' said Ellis, not risking any more specific identification.

35

'It's a cat,' Trish told him.

'It's good.' Grace picked up the clay figure and stroked it under the chin before giving it back. 'Would you like to take it home with you? Or if you leave it here I could put it in the oven next time I fire my own things, and then it won't crumble away.'

'I don't want to keep it.' Trish squashed the cat between her two hands and rolled the clay back into a sausage.

The two adults stared at her in surprise.

'I can make another one,' she told them. 'The next one will be better. It's more fun making things than having them.'

'But it's more fun making something that's going to last than making something which is going to be thrown away,' suggested Grace.

Trish shook her head in disagreement. 'If you're going to keep it, you've got to get it right. But if you know it's going to be thrown away it doesn't matter if the ears are too big.' Already she had begun to model another cat, while Ellis laughed.

'I can see we have a basic difference of philosophy here,' he said. 'Trish, Miss Hardie is very kindly going to let me look inside the house. Would you like to come?'

'Yes, please.' Trish scrambled to her feet and the three made their way out of the stable yard and into the larger courtyard enclosed by the wings of the main house. Grace opened a door into the back hall and led the way along a corridor and into the drawing room. She drew back the curtains from one of the five windows which reached very nearly from floor to ceiling.

'My mother comes in here to play the piano, that's all,' she said, and waited in silence while Ellis looked around. Except for the grand piano, which had a cared-for and well-polished look, everything in the room was covered with dust sheets. Even the carpet was hidden under a drugget. But the plaster-work of the ceiling and cornices was in good condition and the wall coverings, although faded, were not tattered: they would not show their age in a black and white photograph.

Without making any comment he moved on through the library and billiards room: Grace pulled open one pair of curtains in each, but the rooms remained only dimly lit. So the contrast was great when, after returning to the corridor, he was shown into the high-ceilinged studio.

They had turned two corners as they walked, so that it was a clear north light which reflected off the white walls from a skylight. And this was clearly a room in constant use. At one end was a wide work bench, with shelves on the wall behind it and a row of oil lamps hanging above. A potter's wheel with a foot tread stood near to the bench, and another free-standing table in the middle of the room was fitted with a clamp which would hold a piece of wood steady while a carver moved around it. There was a brazier in the middle of the floor as well, suggesting that his hostess did not allow winter's cold to interrupt her work.

With a cry of pleasure and interest, Trish ran towards the far end of the room.

'You're not to touch anything,' Ellis called after her. 'Not anything at all.'

'Trush Trist.' The phrase seemed set to become one of her long-running jokes. Ellis, although keeping an eye on her, turned towards Grace.

'This – the state of the other rooms, I mean – is simply the way houses used to be left when a family moved off on holiday in the old days,' he said. 'If you would trust me to deal with it, I would be very happy to uncover them, take my photographs, and put everything back exactly as I found it.'

He looked steadily into her eyes. Two hours ago they had been strangers, and yet there was a feeling of sympathy between them. It had something to do with honesty. Grace Hardie was a straightforward person. But there must be something more than that to make him hope so strongly that she would agree to let him return and do his work at leisure.

It didn't very often happen that Ellis liked a woman at first sight and felt a wish to make her a friend. Some women frightened him; others he scorned. This one, whom most men might have dismissed as eccentric, was curiously to his taste. Perhaps it was because with her cropped hair and her boiler suit she looked and behaved more like a man than a woman. And yet there was nothing unfeminine about the smile she gave him as she made up her mind.

'All right,' she said. 'When do you want to come?'

'I could do a little preparation today and come back tomorrow. Not because I want to hustle you, but to be sure that you really do leave all the uncovering to me, and don't start rushing around yourself. And I have got all my equipment in Oxford with me, though I didn't want to startle you by turning up on your doorstep with a full load.'

'How long will you need?'

'I shall need a whole day of good weather to do the outside, so that I can move round with the sun. And a second day for the interiors.'

'Would you like to stay here for a couple of nights, then, with Trish? Not tonight, but after you return. If your wife can spare you.'

Ellis glanced towards the far end of the studio and saw that Trish was still there, out of earshot.

'My wife – well, we're divorced – lives in Ireland. I haven't seen her for four years,' he said and then paused, amazed by an unexpected wish to confess to something he never normally talked about. It must have been Grace's own candour about her poverty which made him wish to offer a confidence in return. 'We only married in order that the child should be legitimate. It was a mistake even before the wedding day.'

Even to someone whom he would like as a friend he was not prepared to give further details of the seduction – very nearly the rape – in which he had been the victim and not the aggressor. He had been mistrustful of women even before that appalling night, and ever since had felt nothing but disgust at the thought of their sexual avarice, their hot, fat, damp bodies, their possessive attempts to control the time and the actions

38

and even the thoughts of any man who fell into their power. Grace Hardie seemed to have little in common with Moira Murray, who had been so determined to become Moira Faraday; but she was a female and would take the female side of the argument if she were to be told the details.

'I'm sorry,' she said. 'I didn't mean to pry. I only thought – well, if you're free to do so, please do stay. All these bedrooms, and nobody except my youngest brother ever comes. All we need is a little time to see that they're aired.'

'You're very kind. We shall be delighted. And now we've kept you from your work long enough. Trish! Come along, my darling. We're off now.'

'There's one more thing,' Grace said as they made their way outside. 'I don't know if it showed on the plans you've seen. But as part of the landscaping of the site your father designed a lodge cottage to provide a vista. I'll walk down and show you. I mean, it's a perfectly ordinary gardener's cottage inside, but there's a false wall on the north side, so that when you look from the house you'd think there was a kind of monument there. More like a temple than a lodge. You wouldn't have noticed it coming in from the road.'

How curious it was, thought Ellis as they once more took the short cuts between the curves of the drive, that a woman should be so completely lacking in self-consciousness. If she had felt the slightest awareness that she was oddly dressed in her overalls and rabbit-skin moccasins, she would have become ridiculous at once. It was because she was wholly at ease as her long legs strode down the path that her appearance seemed unsurprising. He had interrupted a workman – or rather, a workwoman – at a task for which she was appropriately dressed. No doubt she could dress the part of mistress of a grand mansion if she chose. It would be interesting to discover whether in fact she *did* choose to do so when he returned by invitation instead of appearing without warning. He rather suspected that she would not.

But even as these thoughts passed through his mind he

39

became aware of a change in his companion's attitude. Unexpectedly she *had* become self-conscious. Had she become aware of his appraisal, or had something else changed?

They were close to the lodge by now. Ellis could already see how its north wall had been designed to give a distant impression of pillars. He could also see that someone, a man, was sitting in the tiny garden with his head buried in his hands.

In that position, all that could be judged of him was that he had curly red hair. But as he heard footsteps approaching he first of all lifted his head and then raised himself slowly to his feet. He was a strongly-built man in his late thirties, with a freckled, worried face. He wore a suit so dark as to be almost black, but very much lighter in weight than was usually to be seen in England, even at the height of summer, so that he gave the impression of being foreign but at the same time at home.

'Hello, Andy,' said Grace.

Ellis glanced at her in surprise. In speaking those two words not only her voice but her personality had for some reason changed. For the past two hours, as they talked, Grace Hardie, the mistress of Greystones, had been confident and happy. Now, for some reason, she was uncertain of herself, and embarrassed. The man, Andy, was embarrassed as well, if the flush on his face was a true sign. Yet as Ellis, although holding himself and Trish back out of the way, listened to their conversation, it appeared only that Andy had been sent for by his mother and that his father's condition had been described as very serious by the doctor who had called an hour earlier. There was nothing, surely, that either party to the conversation needed to blush for in that.

There was something between them, though – some exchange of emotion which could not be explained simply by a surprise meeting or a dying father. Earlier in the day Ellis had been affected by Grace's aura of straightforward friendliness and felt with pleasure that an immediate sympathy had been established between them. But the link between these two was clearly of a different nature. Could it be that Grace Hardie was not quite as unfeminine as she had appeared at first sight?

Well, that was none of his business. Ellis apologetically interrupted the conversation for just long enough to say good-bye, thank Grace for her co-operation and confirm the arrangement they had made for his return. Then, taking Trish's hand, he went past the lodge and turned down the lane. But he could not resist glancing into the garden as he passed it from the other side.

They were no longer talking. At any moment the woman would extend her hand, to rest it on the back of the bench, and the man would touch it with his own. Yes, there was definitely something between them. There was a gossipy side to Ellis's nature which made him curious about other people's relationships and eager to hear or to make up explanations. He wondered if he would ever learn the truth about this one.

FOUR

'It's been a long time,' said Grace; and indeed it had. She had been only sixteen years old when she fell in love with the head gardener's son, and not yet eighteen when he left to fight in the war. She knew that from time to time since then he had returned to visit his parents, because once she had glimpsed him from a distance and once his mother had mentioned his presence. But he had never come up the drive to see her. He was too greatly ashamed, no doubt, of his broken pledge. When the young Frenchwoman who hid him from the Germans while a battle raged became pregnant with his child, he had done the right thing by her, but at Grace's expense. Ever since his marriage he had lived in France.

He had stuck by the Frenchwoman, too. It was a curious coincidence that her unexpected visitor, the architect's son, should apparently have been trapped into matrimony in exactly the same manner. But Ellis Faraday had freed himself from the trap. Andy was less ruthless – and presumably had grown to love his wife, for there had been other children. He had always had green fingers and must have found congenial work on his father-in-law's vineyard. He was comfortably settled – and Grace was a realist. Many years had passed since she first fell in love with him and it was a long time, too, since she had wept for her lost love. There had never been any need for him to be afraid of meeting her.

'Yes,' said Andy. 'I'm sorry. Sorry about everything. I should have said that years ago, not left it till now.' He was silent for a moment, perhaps recalling the events of 1914. 'But they –

your parents, I mean – they'd never have allowed you to marry me.'

'They might not have been able to stop me,' said Grace. 'Still, no point in churning over past history.'

'No. My mother did tell me – this is a long time ago as well – that you were engaged to be married. But that it didn't happen.'

'That's true.' But she was not prepared to discuss that old story either – and at that moment Mrs Frith, looking distressed, appeared in the back doorway of the cottage.

'Your mother needs you,' Grace said. 'I hope your father's condition isn't as bad as you fear. Give him our best wishes. And why don't you come up to Greystones later in the day, Andy, if you can be spared for an hour? Have tea with us, tell us all your news – and let us know whether your father would like to be visited or prefer to be left in peace.' After the first surge of excitement at finding herself in Andy's presence after so many years, her emotions were by now completely under control.

Nevertheless, the meeting – and the possibility of a visit – prompted a change in her usual routine which caused Philip to look at her in surprise and Mrs Hardie to tease. At three o'clock that afternoon she took off her working overalls, in which she normally spent the whole day, and dressed herself in a clean cotton frock. Andy must not be allowed to feel that he had had a lucky escape from an eccentric slut. She would prefer him instead to experience a moment's regret for what he had lost. 'Petty!' said Grace aloud to herself as she brushed her newly-washed hair into shape; but to indulge in a little harmless flirtation would be an unusual form of entertainment. Her eyes sparkled with pleasure and amusement as she made her way from the tower bedroom to the kitchen.

'Let's have raspberry scones for tea,' she suggested – without giving a reason, in case Andy didn't come after all. 'Is the oven hot? I'll make them.' Although Mrs Hardie was in charge of the kitchen, Grace had insisted on being taught to cook in

43

order that her mother could have a day off from time to time.

'Put an apron on, then.' It was only Grace's tidy appearance which caused surprise. Throughout the summer and autumn there was always a glut of one crop or another from Philip's fruit and vegetable gardens, and at the moment it was the raspberries which must be used in as many different ways as possible.

She made a cake as well while she was about it, and while it and the scones were baking she began to carry deck chairs out of the room which had once been a schoolroom but which these days held all the garden clutter: everything from Wellington boots to croquet mallets. By now the sun had gone from the area near the kitchen. The favourite place for tea in the summer months was near the tower, where Mrs Hardie could sit in the shade of the ill-sited oak tree while Philip and Grace enjoyed the sun.

By a quarter to four all preparations were complete. Grace took off her apron, washed her hands, ran her fingers through her hair and glanced into a looking glass, able for once to approve what she saw instead of laughing at herself. She had never been pretty – and certainly not beautiful – but her strong features and the dramatic contrast between her white skin and black hair gave her a striking handsomeness whenever, as now, she chose to make the best of herself. And so it was that when the next visitor on that day of surprises arrived at Greystones he did not find himself greeted – as Ellis Faraday had done – by someone who might have been an assistant gardener or handywoman on the estate. The mistress of Greystones was clean and neatly dressed, confident in manner and with lively eyes which sparkled with interest and curiosity. That next visitor, however, was not Andy Frith.

Grace heard the sound of the approaching motor car long before it came into sight. It rattled up the potholed lane, hesitated beside the lodge gates and changed gear to tackle the steep drive. Although she knew nothing at all about cars, she felt sure as soon as it came into sight that this must be an expensive model: the length of its bonnet and the high polish of its fittings both spoke of money. It was an open model, suitable to the heat of the day. As it came to a halt in front of the house, the driver tugged off the scarf he had wound around his mouth to keep out the dust and jumped athletically out of the car before the uniformed chauffeur had time to move from the passenger seat to open the door for his master. Grace took a few steps forward and then waited for him to approach.

Without the scarf and cap he was revealed as being a young man, no more than eighteen years old. His blond hair was clipped close at the back and sides and his cheeks were smooth, although the beginnings of a moustache showed on his upper lip. From the deference shown to him by the chauffeur, and the easy friendliness with which he took it for granted, Grace suspected him of being not merely a rich man but an aristocrat. His assured voice turned her guess into a certainty.

'Afternoon,' he said. 'I'm looking for Mrs Gordon Hardie.'

'My mother takes a rest at this hour, but I expect her down at four o'clock. If you don't mind waiting a few minutes, I'll tell her you're here. Who should I say?'

'Your mother? So you're Miss Hardie? Jolly good. We're cousins of a sort, you know. Haven't bothered to work it out exactly yet, but we've got an ancestor in common. The eleventh Marquess of Ross.'

'So you are?'

'Rupert Beverley, at your service. Here's my card, for your mother.'

Grace glanced at the card as she took it. *Lord* Rupert Beverley. For a moment she stared at him, taken aback, before remembering her manners. Some of them, at least – for of course he ought to have been invited at once into the drawing room to be waited on by a parlourmaid while a footman carried his card on a silver tray. 'Won't you sit down and enjoy the sunshine?' she said instead, indicating the shabby chairs which she had already arranged round a small table. 'I won't be a moment.'

As she ran upstairs to her mother's boudoir she tried to work out the relationship. It was the Marquess of Ross, her mother's grandfather, who had provided the money to build Greystones and had insisted that the house should be the personal property of an asthmatic baby, Grace herself. But that was thirty-four years ago, and the marquess had been in his eighties at the time. The present holder of the title was probably his grandson – or even great-grandson. Lord Rupert must be a younger son. Her second cousin, then. She handed the card to her mother with a quick explanation before returning to do her duty as a hostess.

'You must think us an unfriendly lot,' said Lord Rupert, accepting her invitation to stroll in the gardens. 'Never coming to call on you, or anything like that. Speaking for myself, I never knew of your existence until Cousin Archie died. That's why I've come here today, to tell your mother that her brother's dead. Well, that's my excuse, anyway. Curiosity about my unknown cousins is a truer reason, I suppose. But I'll start by passing on the news. Don't imagine it's going to break her heart if they haven't seen each other for forty years, but someone has to go through the motions, don't you agree?'

'Yes, I suppose so.' Should she address her companion as 'my lord' or 'Cousin Rupert'? The rules of etiquette had not figured greatly in Grace's education, so she did neither. 'I never met my uncle, of course. He quarrelled with my mother long before I was born.' Did her visitor, she wondered, know what the quarrel had been about? Probably not, if he had only recently found out about this branch of the family. Although he spoke with the confidence of a much older man and seemed to take it for granted that he should speak as a representative of his family, he was hardly more than a boy. There might not be anyone, except Lucy Hardie herself, who still remembered how a beautiful young Beverley had disgraced herself and the family by marrying into trade.

It would be for Mrs Hardie, not Grace, to discuss past history if she chose. For the moment the conversation could be safely confined to the gardens through which they were walking. Although the house was shabby, the grounds which immediately surrounded it were well-kept: there was nothing to be ashamed of there. Only when the visitor came face to face with one of Grace's carved shapes did he appear to be taken aback.

'I've heard about this sort of thing,' he said. 'Modern art. Causing quite a rumpus, the shows in London, according to the pater. First time I've met anyone who's actually bought a piece, though.' The lack of enthusiasm in his voice made it clear to Grace that if she were to confess that she had carved it herself he would be apologetic about an impoliteness, but not impressed. Yet Mr Faraday had seemed to like her work. Her interest in the two contrasting reactions made her slow to realize the implications of this latest comment. If her cousin thought she had bought it, did that mean that other people were creating shapes of a similar kind? She would have liked to ask questions, but he had moved on to another topic as they turned to retrace their steps.

'Good-looking house. Lutyens?'

'No. Faraday.'

'Never heard of him. But I suppose there's a lot I haven't heard of. It does you all right, does it?'

'Yes, very well, thank you. Ah, here's Mother.'

Grace could not resist a smile as she performed the introduction. Lucy Hardie had changed into a tea gown of a style which had been fashionable fifteen years earlier. It could hardly be in fashion still, and yet it was so well cut and so confidently worn that it gave an immediate impression of elegance. Grace's mother was tall and slender and she had used the time since her relative's arrival to put her white hair up in a more formal style than usual. Grace grinned in approval, and saw her mother's eyes twinkle with amusement in response.

Excusing herself, Grace went first into the walled garden to tell Philip what was happening and then hurried into the kitchen to fill the newly-baked scones with the raspberries and to prepare a tray with the best china and the silver tea service.

'A picnic!' exclaimed Lord Rupert. 'Jolly good!' He had a young man's appetite and tucked into the scones and the home-made cake enthusiastically as he apologized for the fact that the Hardies had not been notified of Archie Yates's death before the funeral.

'I was away at Eton,' he explained. 'And Miles – that's my elder brother – is in India, in the army. But my mother's a great one for pedigrees. I'm surprised she didn't manage to track you down.'

'Oh, I'm sure I was crossed out of the family Bible years ago,' laughed Mrs Hardie.

'No. Matter of fact, that's where I found your name. I like keeping up these things, so I went to write in Cousin Archie's death, and there you were.'

'I don't suppose Archie himself ever mentioned my existence.'

'I didn't know him all that well either. He lived a jolly sort of bachelor life. Didn't come down to Castlemere much. Chambers and clubs in London and a lady-friend in Nice. Died in France, as a matter of fact, and wanted to be buried there. So the lawyers in England have only just got to work. No children of his own to leave anything to. But –'

'Oh, he wouldn't leave anything to *me*, Rupert.' Mrs Hardie smiled at the very idea. 'And he never met any of my children.'

'No great fortune anyway, as far as we know. But look here, now that we've discovered you at last, you must come and visit Castlemere. I'm sure none of us believes in carrying on family grudges. And you must have been brought up in the house, Cousin Lucy, like your brother.'

'Yes, I was,' said Mrs Hardie. 'I had a very happy childhood there – and loved the house very deeply. But – I'm not sure, you know, that I want to go back. I very much appreciate the invitation, but – I wonder if you can understand how I feel. There are so many memories, but they may not all be quite true after all these years, and naturally some things will have changed. I can remember, just before my elopement, riding with Archie early one morning and looking down on Castlemere. With the mist rising round it, it looked like a fairy palace, an enchanted place. It can't ever look quite like that again to me, and I might be disappointed. I think, if you don't mind . . .'

'You eloped?' exclaimed Lord Rupert. 'That's another story nobody's ever told me. What happened? I thought that sort of thing went out a hundred years ago.'

'It feels almost as though it *was* a hundred years ago.' Mrs Hardie's smile showed how well at ease she felt with her young kinsman. It sounded as though she was just about to confess to the social misalliance which was the cause of the family quarrel – and perhaps even admit to the reduced circumstances in which she now lived. But Grace's attention was no longer on the conversation. She had noticed Andy standing on the far side of the oak tree, watching the scene.

She had asked him to tea, and he had come. But it was clear that he did not intend to interrupt the family group. Nor would it be an appropriate moment for Grace to invite him to join them. She was well aware of that; but nevertheless felt a pang of regret as, after catching her eye, he turned and walked away. Would he come back later? She was surprised by the intensity of her wish to see him, to have time to talk. It was because her brief girlhood romance had never had time to work itself through to a natural end but had been too violently disrupted by war. She felt as though she and Andy still knew each other intimately, although common sense told her that their separate lives during the past eighteen years had made them strangers. When he paused to look back for a moment now, she raised a hand in a gesture which she hoped he would understand.

Then it was time to be polite again. The invitation to visit Castlemere, which Mrs Hardie had declined, was being pressed upon Grace, and curiosity made her eager to accept. A day was fixed when Lord Rupert would call to drive her over in person. What a day of excitements this had become!

FIVE

Andy returned, as Grace had hoped, soon after Lord Rupert's Lagonda had passed the lodge and turned out of the drive. Tea by that time had been cleared away, but Philip produced a bottle of his home-made wine.

Andy did not disguise his astonishment that the family of a vintner should choose to drink anything but the best French wines, but he was offered no explanation. The House of Hardie was run now by Grace's brother David – the brother who had asked her to pledge Greystones as security for a loan and who had never forgiven her for her refusal. The days when cases of wine were sent up to the house whenever requested were long since over. It didn't matter. Philip enjoyed putting weeds and surplus crops to good use, experimenting with different blends and laying the results down for several years. Had Andy arrived later in the evening, he might have been offered the 1927 apple and raisin wine which in maturity had become as dark and creamy as a sweet sherry. But instead, Grace's own favourite was produced: the young nettle wine whose sharp bite was particularly suitable for a hot day.

Although Andy was taken aback by the refreshment on offer, Grace was amused to see that her mother showed no surprise at being expected to entertain socially the gardener's son – someone whom she had last seen acting as a junior member of her outside staff.

Some of the credit for her relaxed manner must go to Andy himself. He, like Philip's wines, had matured with age. He was thirty-eight years old, the father of a family, a man of standing, no doubt, in his own community. His freckled face had changed very little since he was eighteen, but he had lost the lean look of his youth, and the foreign cut of his suit helped to emphasize the fact that he could no longer be neatly categorized inside an English class system. Besides, over the past ten years his father had been not so much the Hardies' head gardener as their partner in a market gardening enterprise. Mrs Hardie no longer – as had happened in pre-war days – ordered peaches or pineapples or asparagus out of season to be picked for the dinner table, but instead asked what she could have to cook for the evening meal. Andy would certainly have learned from his parents how much the old order had changed.

He himself, although certainly much altered, was still the same person as the boy with whom Grace had fallen in love. As she watched him, at once earnest and polite, conversing with her mother, she felt a small glow of satisfaction. Unsophisticated as she was at the age of sixteen, her judgement had been sound enough to fix her affections on a man who would have proved worthy of them. There was nothing in her behaviour then of which she need feel ashamed – and she had long ago forgiven Andy for his betrayal of her trust. Now that the barrier of fortune had disappeared, they could be friends again – and friendship, in Grace's solitary life, was a most precious gift.

Andy was at ease too. As he set down his glass after sampling the brown, tangy liquid, he addressed Philip on equal terms: a man who grew grapes questioning a man who made wine without them.

'What is this made from?'

It was Grace who answered. She and her mother were both accustomed to spare Philip the effort of talking.

'We pick young nettle tips in spring and boil them like spinach. I can tell you, the smell is disgusting. Philip does all the skilled work; the fermentation.'

'Do you sell any of it?'

'Not the nettle wine. Not everyone likes it. But elderberry wine, yes. Your father takes some of that down to the market

51

for us.' Grace flushed a little as she admitted it, although it was foolish for someone whose family had in earlier generations prospered by selling wine commercially to be ashamed of this small-scale activity. The cash it brought in enabled them to buy the sugar needed both for the wine they consumed themselves and the preserves of fruit which Mrs Hardie stocked up for each winter. Sugar, like shoes, was something which could not be produced on their own land, but must be bought for money.

'Do you never use grapes?'

Grace shook her head. 'The vine that you probably remember was in one of the glasshouses. We don't heat those any longer.'

'But you could grow vines out of doors.'

'Surely not. They wouldn't ripen in an English summer, would they?'

'Romans,' said Philip. On the rare occasions when he spoke, he was economical with words; but Andy, understanding his meaning, nodded.

'That's right. The Romans had vineyards in England – even further north than this. I was walking about earlier on, while your visitor was here. The ridges on the lower pasture, you know, below the house – I reckon that's old terracing. Facing south-west, sheltered from the north, draining down well. There could have been a vineyard there once. Could be again. Though nowadays anyone who wanted to plant would take the rows north to south. Let me show you.' He stood up, eager to lead the way down the hill.

Both Mrs Hardie and Philip shook their heads smilingly. The visit of their young relative had interrupted their usual daily routine and they were anxious to return to work. Only Grace, who had abandoned her carving for the day when she took off her working clothes, was prepared to walk down through the upper meadow and stand with Andy on the highest of what must certainly have been a series of terraces long ago.

'A row going north to south would cut across these lines,' she pointed out; for the meadow, like the house itself, had a south-west aspect.

'All the better,' said Andy. 'The extra height would allow more sun to reach the end of the rows. It would be more difficult to plough the land for the first time, I suppose – but you wouldn't need to use the whole meadow. An acre would be quite enough to start with to see how it went. About three thousand vines, say.'

'Three thousand!' Grace had thought they were discussing only a small test area: half a dozen vines, perhaps, from which an experimental wine could be made by the same method which Philip applied to raspberries or redcurrants. 'You're not suggesting that we should attempt to start a proper vineyard here!'

'It's easier than you might think. In France –'

'We're not in France,' said Grace. 'And we have no labour. Who is going to dig out three thousand holes and drive in three thousand stakes and plant and prune and hoe for three or four years, I suppose, before the first fruit is seen? And all for nothing, perhaps, if the soil proves unsuitable or the summers too cold.'

'The soil's all right. And it's autumn that matters, not summer. I remember some good Septembers and Octobers here. Five years out of six you'd get a good ripening.'

'Anyway –' Grace hardly listened to his interruption – 'we couldn't possibly afford to buy vines on such a scale.'

'Well, you could cut the number by half and plant them at six feet instead of three. Or even fewer to start with, and root the prunings to build up stock.'

Grace shook her head. 'Your mother must have told you about the change in our circumstances,' she said. 'We're very content with the way we live; and thanks to Philip's war pension and your father's help in selling produce as well as growing it, we have as much money as we need, just about – but nothing extra that we could possibly risk in such a way. I mean, it would be far too much for your father to undertake on top of his present work, wouldn't it?'

'That's something I need to talk to you about,' said Andy, his enthusiasm fading into gravity. 'Doctor's not too cheerful about Dad. Not to beat about the bush, he's dying.'

'Oh, Andy, I'm so sorry.' Instinctively Grace put out a hand and felt it firmly taken. 'Is it his chest? I've heard him coughing in the mornings.'

He nodded. 'Nothing to be done, doctor says. So I have to ask you about my mother. Would you let her stay on in the lodge, after? She'd be miserable living with us, not speaking the lingo, and she can't be doing with my wife at all. I could pay a bit of rent, what you thought was right. And I could send one of my boys over. Not the eldest, because he's got his eyes on the family land. But the next one, Jean-Paul, he's a bright boy. Learnt a bit of English from me already. He'd be company for my mother. And he could be useful to you on the land. He's thirteen. Not got his full strength yet – and none of my father's know-how, of course. But you'd find him a good worker if you showed him what to do. You could pay him in food, with a bit of pocket money. He wouldn't expect the market proceeds, not till he was old enough to be useful.'

Grace, troubled, was silent – not considering Andy's suggestion, but thinking about his father, who had been part of her life at Greystones ever since she could remember. While aware that he was ill, and sorry on his account, this was the first moment at which it was brought home to her how much the Hardies depended both on his work and on his willingness to sell their surplus produce. Philip possessed all the necessary gardening skills, and Jean-Paul certainly could be useful in the steady labour of keeping the gardens tidy, but none of the family would enjoy acting as a salesman. If only Andy himself . . . but there was no point in day-dreaming.

'Of course your mother will be able to stay on,' she said at last. 'And we'll be glad of your son's help. But –'

'But I see what you mean, yes, you can't be tackling a

54

vineyard, not just now.' Andy was changing the subject with a deliberate briskness; and releasing her hand as he did so. 'Tell you what, though. Suppose I were to send over just half a dozen roots with Jean-Paul when he comes. Just to try out the soil and the weather. Your brother could take cuttings in a year or two, if they settled in well. Wouldn't commit you to much in the way of work. But might be interesting?'

'I'll ask Philip what he thinks. Thanks for the offer, anyway.' They began to stroll down the terraced meadow, its grass kept short by the grazing sheep. But almost at once Andy came to a halt again, looking down at the flatter land which lay between them and the centre of Oxford.

'Have you thought of selling any of your land?' he asked abruptly. 'Must be more'n you can manage. And would put a bit of money in your pockets.'

Grace shook her head. They had moved round the side of the hill as they talked. The view from here was no longer obstructed by the wood, as it was when she looked from her bedroom window. Instead it offered – or rather, had offered once – a vista of open countryside, broken by the villages of Cowley and Temple Cowley, with Iffley in the distance. Even when she was a little girl the barracks had already been in evidence at the foot of the hill, but only later had the sprawling buildings of the Morris Motor Works begun to spoil the view. They were still spreading. She could see from here the unfinished building which would contain a new production line – and between the spokes of the roads which stretched from Carfax was growing a grid of narrow streets to house the workers who were swarming to Oxford to take employment in the motor car factories. The bricks and concrete were creeping towards Greystones. At all costs she must preserve her own land as a buffer; a no-man's land on which no builder could set foot.

'The villagers would lynch me if I let the wood go,' she said laughingly. The inhabitants of Headington Quarry claimed old-established poachers' rights on the strip of woodland which bordered the stream. They took furze for their fires and acorns for their pigs and rabbits for their pots. There were plenty of rabbits left to be eaten at Greystones itself and, in return for the Hardies' forbearance in respect of the lower land, it was tacitly understood that no one would trespass or steal from the cultivated ground higher up the hill.

'Do you remember how we used to play there as kids?' Andy asked her.

'I remember how you planted a forest once. Acorns and conkers and sycamore wings. All in about a square yard of ground. Shall we see how it's grown?'

She felt once again like the little girl she had been when nine-year-old Andy first showed her his plantation as she led the way into the wood – although the shoes and stockings she was so unusually wearing were inappropriate for such an exploration. Andy needed to take her hand as she made an unsteady crossing of the stream by means of a fallen tree trunk, and he did not let it go. She thought nothing of it. It was as if they were children together again. Only when they reached the boulders was her heart pierced by a memory of the day when she had ceased to be a child.

The two huge boulders stood in the silent heart of the wood, near the place where the stream fed a deep pool from which it emerged both invisibly and inaudibly on the further side. Grace knew now that the stones must have been smoothed and rounded by a glacier many thousands of years earlier; but as a little girl she had thought of them as a giant's playthings, for each was indented in one place only, the shape resembling a handhold.

As she grew older she had brought her anxieties and hopes to the boulders, using them as both comforters and confidants. But it was not the emotional crises of her early years that she remembered now. It was here that Andy had kissed her for the first time. It was here, a year later, that they had said goodbye.

'Do you remember –?' she began; but quickly bit back the words. It was the wrong thing to say – the wrong thing at any time, but especially now, when Andy was holding her hand so tightly.

'Of course I remember. I wish –' Andy in his turn left words unspoken, but it was because he was already pulling her into his arms, pressing his lips against hers. Not, as on the occasion of that first kiss, with a boy's shyness and joy, but with all the force of a man's passion. Grace felt her lips bruising against her teeth as her head was forced backwards. Andy's body pushed her own against one of the boulders. One arm was round her waist, holding her close, while the other groped underneath the skirt of her dress. Between kisses, his breath emerged with a noisy shuddering and he muttered something which she could not hear or understand.

Grace, for her part, was faint with excitement and wonder. She was not sure what was happening – what Andy was going to do or what she herself was supposed to do; but with all her heart and all her body she wanted it to happen. She must tell him, though, lest he should think her unwilling when she was merely ignorant.

'I don't know – I never have –' How difficult it was to say the words. But it seemed that he understood at once. He drew a little way away, swallowing the lump in his throat as he looked into her eyes and then pulled her by the hands away from the boulders and down on to the mossy ground. Stroking each inch of her skin as he exposed it, he was for a little while gentle again; but before long his body once again began to beat against hers. Grace felt herself being battered, pierced. It should have hurt, but instead only took her breath away.

'I love you, Andy,' she panted. 'Love you, love you.' They were moving together and then lay still together.

Afterwards came a sense of anti-climax. As Andy helped Grace to her feet she could not help staring at him. She had often enough noticed Philip stripped to the waist as he worked in the sun, but this was the first time that she had seen a man without his trousers. His vulnerability should have increased her love, but instead she found the sight interesting but

57

somehow ridiculous. No doubt she looked equally absurd to him, with the skirt of her dress rucked up around her waist. Tugging it down, she saw with dismay that her petticoat was stained with blood and her dress with streaks of green from the moss. Her skin was sticky and she found herself walking awkwardly. Anyone who saw her would guess at once what had happened.

There was an awkwardness, too, in wondering what she should say to Andy. She put out a hand to touch him in a gentle gesture of love and thanks, but almost at once picked up her stockings and knickers and hurried away through the wood – because already, as the excitement faded, she knew that this was something which ought not to have happened.

Philip would be back at work in the walled garden while Mrs Hardie prepared supper in the kitchen. Grace made for the stable yard and wrapped herself in the rarely-washed overall which she wore when making up glazes for her pottery. If her appearance caused raised eyebrows now, it would only be because she normally stripped off such a covering before going into the house.

Nor would it come as any surprise that she should take a bath before the evening meal, for this was her usual habit whenever she had been carving stone. And only a few hours earlier she had indeed been carving stone, with no possible way of guessing that so many visitors were on their way. What an ordinary start it had been to such an extraordinary day!

SIX

Grace was dreaming of Castlemere. Rupert Beverley was driving her round and round the house in his Lagonda whilst Ellis Faraday dodged out of the way, doing his best to take a photograph of a blonde six-year-old who was waving from a window. A peacock perched in a tree with its long tail dangling, emitting a raucous shriek every time the car passed.

It was the shriek which aroused her at last, for of course it came from the roof of the henhouse at Greystones, where the cock was announcing the start of a new day. As a rule Grace was quick to rise as soon as the sun touched the east window of her tower bedroom. But it had taken her a long time to get to sleep on the previous evening as questions and doubts and excitements swirled through her mind; and now, in a half-waking state, her uncertainties returned.

She felt little guilt about what had happened. Andy, who was a married man, had behaved reprehensibly, but she herself had not. She had not deliberately excited him: indeed, the events of the evening had taken her by surprise. If she were to be honest with herself she must admit that she had hoped for some expression of regret and love – a word, a look – but her very inexperience had made it impossible for her to foresee what might happen.

Was she glad that she had lost her virginity? Had she enjoyed it? Odd, how difficult it was to answer what should have been simple questions. There was a surprising satisfaction in knowing that she would not after all grow old and die without ever understanding what it was that inspired poems and novels, betrayals and murders. What was to her an extraordinary experience had made her for a moment ordinary: that must be good. And the gasping happiness with which she had surrendered both body and spirit was a memory to be cherished.

But not necessarily an experience to be repeated. She had decided many years ago to keep control of her own life instead of surrendering it to a husband; and the way in which that control expressed itself was in her domination of inanimate materials: wood, clay, stone. Was she prepared to put at risk her contentment with the routines of her daily life by allowing herself to hope for an occasional invitation to delight?

The peacock – no, the cock – shrieked again impatiently. Although she must decide before too long what she should say and do at her next meeting with Andy, for the moment there were more urgent tasks to be performed. But she felt stiff and heavy, reluctant to leave her bed.

'Come on, now,' she exhorted herself. 'Work to be done.' To start with, the hens and pigs must be fed. And then a bedroom must be prepared for Mr Faraday, and its dressing room for his daughter. She had already opened the necessary windows to begin the airing of the room, but the events of yesterday afternoon had allowed no time to sweep the floors or make up the beds.

What should she wear? Yesterday she must have looked like a labourer when the first of her unexpected visitors arrived. Mr Faraday had not seemed disapproving, nor even surprised; but since he was returning by invitation it seemed only polite to disguise herself as a conventional hostess. Even so, he and Trish were unlikely to arrive before nine o'clock. She would have time to change out of her working overalls after breakfast, when the dirty jobs had been done.

So there was nothing unusual about her clothing as she passed through the kitchen to pick up the bucket which was waiting outside for the pigs. Nor was there any way, surely, in which her appearance revealed that she was no longer the same person that she had been twenty-four hours earlier. And yet she was conscious of her mother glancing at her with what seemed like curiosity, although it could only be concern.

'Didn't you sleep well, Grace? Your eyes look tired.'

'All that coming and going yesterday. I'm not used to it. What vegetables would you like me to pick for lunch?'

'I suppose a child expects her main meal in the middle of the day? I can hardly remember – it's so long.'

'Don't pretend that you ever cooked for any of us when we were children,' laughed Grace. But she shared both the excitement and the slight nervousness which Mrs Hardie was exhibiting. Since the days when preparing for a visitor required no more exertion than the giving of instructions to the servants, no one outside the family had ever been invited to spend a night. Grace was amazed at herself for having issued the invitation, and realized that she must take responsibility for her guests while they were at Greystones. She was glad to be distracted from thoughts of Andy, and set to work with all her usual vigour.

By the time the two Faradays arrived she had changed into a cotton dress. The day promised to be too hot to make the wearing of stockings tolerable, but she had put on a pair of shop-bought sandals instead of the home-made moccasins in which Ellis had caught her the previous day.

'What a lot of equipment you need!' she exclaimed, going out to greet them while Ellis was still unloading it all. In addition to the cameras – larger and heavier than she had expected – there were tripods and reflectors and umbrellas and heavy wooden boxes.

'The old-fashioned stuff is the best,' Ellis told her. 'And I can rely on a house not to blink or fidget through a long exposure. Unlike débutantes. But you can see why I never feel I can simply arrive on someone's doorstep with all this. What a cracking day I've got for it! I'll get on with the exterior views straightaway.'

'Is there anything useful I could do to help?'

He shook his head. 'I've got everything I need, thank you.'

Grace turned to leave, but felt a tug at her hand. Trish was looking up at her. Her pale, oval face, lightly freckled beneath the eyes, was framed by the blonde hair which fell straight to her shoulders. Beneath its fringe, her blue eyes were appealing.

'Please may I make something with your clay again?'

'Certainly you may. Let's go and find it.'

The demure expression with which Trish had asked her question was banished by a grin of delight as she skipped happily into the stable yard.

'What do you want to make this time?' asked Grace, digging into the old dustbin for a handful of clay.

'A house.'

'This house? Or your own house?'

'We haven't got a house of our own. We live in a flat with no stairs and no garden. I want to do a make-believe house, with trees round it.'

'I'll give you a board to build on. And –' Grace hesitated before offering any kind of implement. She had made most of her own pottery tools out of wire, but small fingers might be cut by them. She looked instead for the shaped piece of bone which could be used as a knife and offered an old rolling pin as well.

'You can roll it out like pastry, and cut out walls or bricks. Do you think you might want to keep what you make this time? Because if so, I'll show you what you have to do to the clay before you start.'

'No, thank you. I don't like keeping things.'

'There you are, then. You won't touch anything else, will you?'

'Trush Trist.' They laughed companionably together. Then Grace left the young potter to her work and went to watch the photographer at his.

'I *could* be useful,' she said to Ellis, realizing that he would need to make at least three journeys in order to move his equipment to each new position.

'But why should you? You have your own work.'

'I'm taking a day's holiday. Acting the part of lady of the manor. A hostess.'

As though the word 'acting' had put a new thought into his mind, Ellis looked up at her questioningly. 'Hardie,' he said. 'Jay Hardie, the actor – is he any relation of yours?'

'My younger brother. Do you know him?'

'We have some friends in common.' Ellis seemed to be regretting that he had asked the question as he busied himself with the camera. 'Would you like to have a look?' He held up the heavy black cloth so that she could put her eye to the viewfinder.

'How extraordinary!' she exclaimed. 'All the proportions look quite different.'

'It's because you're not seeing the usual amount of sky. I shall take more than one shot of each façade. One has to choose every time between good detail and a general balance. It's something that I imagine you must be aware of whenever you choose a position for a new piece of sculpture: how much space it ought to have around it.'

'Sculpture!' Grace laughed at the idea that her shapes could be dignified with such a professional word.

'That's what it is, you know.' Ellis took a last look through the viewfinder himself before lowering the cloth and starting the exposure. 'Have you had any art education, Miss Hardie? Or any contact with artists?'

'Does it look like it?'

'Yes,' said Ellis, 'it does. And that's what makes it so extraordinary – that you should be creating work which is so much in tune with what's coming out of the art colleges at the moment if you haven't been in touch with what's going on. I'm not saying that the shows of the modernists are popular. Far from it. The people who write letters to the newspapers protesting about them have a vocabulary range which goes from contemptible to disgusting.'

'Thank you for the comparison, then.' Not in the least offended, Grace laughed.

'I'm not quoting my own opinion. Although I confess that I do prefer representational art, I find this new work immensely powerful. Expressing emotion rather than depicting nature.'

'Yes! That's exactly right.' All Grace's favourite pieces of her own work had been inspired by some overwhelming emotion, whether of grief, fear or love, but she had never expected that anyone else would understand that. Absorbed in the conversation, she picked up as much as she could carry of Ellis's equipment as soon as he indicated that he was satisfied with the views he had taken from the south-east, and followed him to his next position.

'I was thinking last night,' he said. 'I would very much like to take some photographs of your sculptures. An album. As a token of gratitude for your co-operation over the house. There won't be time during this visit. But if I might be allowed to return, in five or six weeks, say . . . ?'

'I'd like that very much indeed. How very kind. Tell me about some of these modernist sculptors.' She still could not think of her work as sculpture, and certainly not of herself as a sculptor, but that might be only because she had no mental picture of what a sculptor might be. In the course of an inadequate education her governess had told her about Michelangelo but had never been able to produce any illustrations of his work. Now she felt enraged by her own ignorance, and passionately interested in whatever her guest could tell her.

No longer did she feel regret at giving up her own work for a day, or guilt at not doing more to help her mother. This was the first time in her life that anyone had talked to her in such a way – willing to instruct without showing any condescension to such an unsophisticated listener. Ellis even taught her some of the techniques of photography, allowing her to take a few exposures herself. She had expected her heart and mind to be troubled by thoughts of Andy throughout the day, but instead discovered when evening came that she had not given him a thought since the Faradays arrived.

For the first time in many years, the evening meal was taken in the dining room. Ellis had uncovered its mahogany furniture in preparation for the next day. Trish had already been given a high tea and put to bed, her father guaranteeing that she would feel no nervousness at finding herself alone in a strange room. 'It happens too often, I'm afraid, and she's learned to treat it as an adventure. My housekeeper in our London flat is always willing to care for her when I have to travel, but I feel easier to have her in my sight.'

'Your wife –?' asked Mrs Hardie.

Grace bit her lip in self-reproach. She ought to have mentioned to her mother in advance that Mr Faraday would not want to discuss his wife.

'We're divorced,' Ellis told her.

'Forgive me. I shouldn't . . . In such cases, I've heard, any child usually stays with the mother, so I thought . . .'

'My wife was adjudged to be the guilty party.' Ellis raised his chin to show that he was resolved to make the situation plain. 'In fact, though, the fault was mine. I had been inattentive, so it was hardly surprising that she looked for pleasure elsewhere. But the man she wished to marry had no desire to bring up someone else's child, so it seemed simpler for her to accept the blame in order that the custody of our daughter should be awarded to me. All past history now.'

Mrs Hardie hurried to make up for her tactlessness by asking her guest to describe some of the other houses which his father had designed, and the evening passed as pleasantly as the day. It was at a much later hour than usual that Grace made her way up the spiral stairs which led to her tower bedroom. Her mind was still on photography and architecture as she opened the door – which made the shock all the greater as she saw Andy standing inside the room.

'Andy! What are you doing here? You shouldn't –'

'I couldn't keep away.' He came towards her, his arms outstretched. 'All day I've been waiting to see you again. Couldn't think of anything else.' Now he was almost touching her, and with half of her mind Grace wanted to feel herself pulled into his arms. But the other half was stronger. She put up a hand to stop him.

'No. It's not right. We mustn't.'

'But last night . . .'

'You took me by surprise last night. It was wonderful. And I was glad . . . It was a proper finish, in a way, to something that was untidy.' Grace knew that she was incapable of explaining exactly what she meant. Andy had disappeared from her life all those years ago in an unsatisfactory way. Had he been killed in the war, she would have grieved over his death but without feeling that her own inadequacy was somehow responsible for it. But the knowledge that he could have returned but was held in France by a wife and baby had been harder to bear. She had not, at their last parting, said a proper goodbye; but she could say it now. 'You're married, Andy. It would be wrong.'

'She'll never know.'

'That doesn't make it less wrong. And anyway, think of it from my point of view. You'll be here for a week or two more, perhaps, and then you'll go back to France. I can't spend the rest of my life wondering when you're next coming to visit your mother – just hoping.' It was as the cock crowed that morning that Grace had realized that the decision must be her own. If she did what Andy wanted – whatever that might be – she was certain in the end to find herself not just lonely but guilty. Only by sending him away at once could she retain her self-respect, even though the price would be unhappiness.

Andy took no notice. Perhaps he thought that she wanted to be overruled, to be physically forced into a surrender which she could pretend was against her real wishes. Perhaps he was right! The shame of that thought spurred her to resist as he held her close, kissed her, pressed her back against the wall of the tower room, as yesterday he had pressed her against the boulder.

She was as tall as he was, and very nearly as strong. Strong enough, certainly, to show him that her struggle to escape

66

from his arms was more than a token. Pushing him off, she ran to the far side of the room and stood there, panting with the effort.

'Don't you see, Andy, we've got no right. We'd never be able to meet again, if . . . Oh Andy, I do love you. You know that. I'm glad about yesterday. But it mustn't ever happen again. And we must both *know* that it won't. Please go away. Go away now.'

It was a battle of wills, and Grace's was the stronger. Andy's freckled face paled with disappointment: perhaps with anger as well. For a few moments he seemed to be struggling to speak. But as though recognizing that no argument would change her mind, he turned abruptly away and went out of the room, closing the door behind him.

SEVEN

Mrs Hardie remained unwilling to return to the house in which she had been brought up, but ten days after Rupert Beverley's first visit to Greystones, his chauffeur returned to collect Grace for her visit to Castlemere. The rush of the wind in her hair as the motor car sped along the narrow lanes was thrilling enough to someone whose usual speed was that of foot or bicycle; and her excitement increased as they turned off the road through an entrance guarded by two lodges and a pair of high wrought-iron gates painted in black and gold.

A choice of two drives presented itself almost immediately. The chauffeur took the steeper and narrower of the two, climbing up the side of a hill until they were brought to a halt by a figure on horseback.

'Stand and deliver!' called Lord Rupert. Swinging himself off the horse, he tossed the reins to the chauffeur. 'Welcome to Castlemere, Cousin Grace. You're to see it first from a distance. I forgot to tell you to wear sensible shoes' – he glanced down at her feet as he helped her down from the motor car – 'but you have anyway. Jolly good. This way then. It's not far.'

Grace smiled to herself as she followed the bridlepath which her young host indicated. Only a few days earlier she had insisted in much the same way that Ellis Faraday should enjoy a view of Greystones from far enough away to appreciate the whole design of the building. But there was to be no other resemblance between the two occasions. As a little girl she had thought of Greystones as a palace; but Castlemere was a palace indeed.

Surrounded by a moat on which swans lazily floated, the house enclosed a courtyard spacious enough for half of it to be in sunshine even though the building was four storeys high. Around the central fountain a parterre was laid out in patterns outlined by box hedges and filled with herbs. At each corner of the house rose a turret whose grey slate roof was pitched as sharply as the point of a pencil. Grace, who had once spent six months in France, recognized the style even before she was given an explanation of it.

'The family had a Tudor home near here, on the river,' Rupert told her. 'This one's only about two hundred years old. The marquess of the time fell in love with a Frenchwoman. But she – the story goes – had heard terrible things about English houses. So my ancestor ordered a house to be built that was stone for stone the same as her father's. Monsieur le Duc was so delighted when he saw the plans that he handed over not only his daughter but cratefuls of Louis Quinze furniture to make the rooms look right. I'll show you. Would you like to get back in the car now and I'll join you there.'

Riding his horse by a more direct route across the deer park, Rupert had already handed it over to a groom before the car arrived at the bridge which crossed the moat.

'I expect you'll want to freshen up after the drive,' he said. 'And then have a cool drink to get the dust out of your throat.' Inside the house a maid bobbed in curtsy to indicate that Grace should follow her upstairs. By the time she was shown down again a footman was pouring ice and lemonade into tall glasses.

'My parents asked me to present their apologies,' her host explained. 'I specially chose a day when I knew they'd be at the races so that I could show you the house as though it were mine. If they'd been at home, we'd have had to waste hours in polite family chat. My mother's a great one for family trees. She would have explained to you exactly who your ancestors were, without stopping to consider that you might know already. So what I thought was, an hour looking round inside, a glass of champagne before luncheon, and a walk round the outer gardens – the ones outside the moat – afterwards. Then a rest, if you need one, before tea. But tell me first what most interests you. I mean, pictures, furniture, silver, china, that kind of thing. We've got special collections that could take a day each to study, but I don't want to bore you.'

'There's too much to take in,' said Grace ruefully. 'I'd just like to get a general impression of the house itself, and the rooms in it. Not looking in too much detail at individual items. Except perhaps family portraits: that would be interesting. And do you have any statues?' It was Ellis Faraday's claim that she was a sculptor which had made her curious to study what sculptors in other centuries had produced.

'Hundreds. Italian copies of Roman copies of Greek originals, mostly. They're in the gardens and the orangery, so we'll see them in the afternoon session. Right then, off we go. We'll start at the top.'

Doors opened silently in front of them as they made their way to the stone-flagged hall from which rose a double spiral staircase of extraordinary elegance and complexity. Grace felt her fingers twitching as she tried to work out its construction as though she were about to copy it in clay. But all her concentration was needed to keep up with her companion's flow of information.

'Some oddities, you'll find, in the way things are arranged. Beverleys never throw anything away. So of course they kept all the furniture and panelling and such from the Tudor house. Just tucked it away on the top floor of the new building to make way for the French stuff. There can't be many places where something that looks like a French chateau has an Elizabethan long gallery, I don't imagine. Now, let me introduce you to the family.'

The panelled walls were covered with portraits, of every period from the sixteenth century to the present day. Rupert took them in order, giving brief biographies of those who were particularly distinguished or profligate and identifying others merely by their number in the line: the third earl, the seventh marquess. Grace felt no great interest in them as individuals until they arrived at Rupert's great-grandfather – and her own.

He had been painted late in life. Grace stared at the heavy, expressionless face. She had met him only once, when she was a baby: the occasion had been described to her, but she had no memory of it. This large, white-haired gentleman had picked her from her cot and listened in dismay to the wheezing of her asthmatic chest, before giving orders that she should be moved at once from marshy Oxford to one of the hills which surrounded the city. According to her mother, he had saved her life. It seemed wrong that she should not remember him – wrong, too, that he should have been portrayed here with no sign of sympathy or affection in his expression.

'Nobody smiles,' she exclaimed in surprise. 'All these portraits, and not a smile amongst them.'

'It wouldn't be properly dignified, would it? And I suppose it's difficult holding a smile for as long as it takes to paint it. I mean, smiling alters the whole shape of the face, doesn't it?' He turned towards her, grinning in different, ridiculous ways until they were both laughing.

Next to the old marquess hung a portrait of a young woman. Tall and slender, she was wearing what in the eighteen-sixties must have been fancy dress, making the picture look like a Gainsborough – except that her hair was not powdered, but hung in golden ringlets. Her eyes were blue, her lips were rosy, her complexion fair. 'What a beauty!' exclaimed Grace: and Rupert answered, 'Your grandmother.'

Grace stared at the portrait for a long time without speaking.

'My mother was beautiful in just the same way when she was young,' she said at last. 'Indeed, I remember her very much like that when I was a small girl and she had had six children. It's always seemed unfair that I should inherit nothing from her or my grandmother except my height.' Grace's hair was black and straight. Her eyes were dark, her skin almost white. Although she was as slim as her mother had been, or the young woman in the portrait, it was a straighter slimness, lacking the curves which seemed essential to feminine grace. To prevent her cousin from feeling forced to produce a polite compliment, she turned hastily to another of the paintings. 'This looks more modern.'

'My brother on his twenty-first birthday. A gift from the tenants.' He shook his head sadly as he considered the handsome young officer. 'Family tradition says that the eldest son should stay at home and learn how to run the estate, ready for when it's his turn. The second son, which is me, should go into the army. But Miles could see that I was never going to be a soldier, so he dashed off himself. Reckons that the pater is good for thirty years or so yet – plenty of time to get in a bit of polo.'

'So will you be the one who learns to run the estate?'

'If I do, there won't be much future in it for me.' Until that moment his mood, ever since her arrival, had been light-hearted, but suddenly he was serious. 'Not much fun, you know, being a younger son. You're brought up in a place, get fond of it and then whoosh, you're out. Not your home any longer. You're supposed to make a new life for yourself from scratch. But there's a long list of professions which are reckoned unsuitable, and a remarkably short list of approved jobs for which one has any inclination or aptitude.'

'You won't need to earn a living, will you?'

'Don't know. There'll be an interview just before my twenty-first birthday when I shall find out whether I've given the impression of being a steady chap or a wastrel. But I doubt if there'll be a great deal to spare, either way. It's one of the things that nobody believes, and I hardly believe it myself. Of course the family's stinking rich in the sense of owning property, but as far as ready cash is concerned, almost everything that comes from the estate in the way of rents goes straight back into it again. The house costs a fortune to maintain. It's more of a worry than a privilege.'

'So you're well out of it, are you, being a second son?'

'Only in one sense. I can't bear the thought of being cut off

72

from Castlemere. . . . Coming back just for Christmas, that sort of thing. While Miles is still in the army, I could make myself useful here for a bit after Oxford if I chose; but that would make it even worse when I had to leave. It's such a marvellous place.'

She was touched by the strength of his feeling, and his pride and affection as he led her through one room after another in the morning, and one garden after another in the afternoon.

'My mother mentioned a herb garden,' she said, when it seemed that the tour was over.

'Oh yes. On the other side of the walled garden. A bit dull, in my opinion. But very famous. Everything in it is properly medieval.'

'It was where my mother first met my father.'

'Then certainly we must see it. Without the herb garden, clearly I shouldn't ever have had the pleasure of entertaining you here.'

Yes, it was dull. Grace needed all her imagination to picture the scene which her father had often before his death described to her: of the wine merchant's son bursting upon the most beautiful girl he had ever seen as she painted in the garden. Rupert, waiting until she had seen enough, was thinking of something else.

'Your uncle Archie, your mother's brother, had the same problem as me,' he told her. 'He wasn't even a second son. A grandson. But brought up here, because his mother was dead. Never any possibility at all that he could inherit: he'd always have known that. But all those years here as a boy before going out into the world – it made it hard for him to settle down anywhere, I think. So you see, I shall have to be careful.'

'I do see, yes.' It was time for her to return home. 'Did you say you were coming to Oxford?'

'In October, yes. To The House, to read history. It's not expected that I shall actually study any history, but as a matter of fact I'm rather keen on it. Here at Castlemere, for instance. Generations of the same family living in the house. And at the same time, you know, generations of farmers and craftsmen on the estate. We have an old carpenter who does repairs in the house, and it was one of his ancestors who fixed the panelling in the long gallery you saw this morning. I like thinking about that sort of thing. But talking of Oxford –'

'Yes?'

'Well, I did wonder. It's the Lagonda, you see. I gather there are lots of petty rules about undergraduates not keeping their own cars within so many miles of Carfax. I wondered whether it might be possible for me to garage her with you, and come up by cab whenever I feel like a run.'

A month earlier Grace would have said – and believed – that she had no wish for visitors and no need of new acquaintances. How unexpectedly the events of the past few days had changed her attitude! As she held out her hand in farewell, she surprised herself by the sincerity of her words.

'Of course. Then I shall see you again. Good.'

EIGHT

Grace saw Andy for the first time after the confrontation in her bedroom when she attended his father's funeral. It was an awkward meeting. She longed to make some gesture which would tell him how much she still loved him, but knew that her earlier decision was the right one: he belonged to another woman. Was there any way in which she could express a hope that they would remain friends? She searched for the right words, but failed to find them.

Andy, doubtless still puzzled and hurt by his rejection, avoided her eye as he supported his mother at the graveside. Only when Mrs Frith was expressing her thanks for the flowers which had come from Greystones, and for the promise that she could remain in the cottage, did he speak directly to the Hardies – and then it was merely to confirm that his son would soon arrive and be at their disposal. Grace told herself that everything had turned out as she wanted it, and tried to be cheerful about it.

In this she was helped by the arrival of her aunt that evening. Midge Hardie, after marrying at a later age than usual to become Midge Witney, had been widowed three years previously and returned to the annual routines of her earlier life as a schoolmistress. She was sixty-seven now, but her energetic nature made it impossible for her to sit idly at home. So she took private pupils for individual coaching during the three academic terms, and spent a month each summer in Switzerland. As usual, she came to Greystones for a meal soon after returning to her house in North Oxford.

For once, after listening to a description of her vacation,

the Hardies had news of their own to pass on. Midge had spent many holidays at Greystones, but it had never been her home; so the gardener's death did not touch her deeply. Of far more interest was the visit of Ellis Faraday. His father had once been her lover.

'I never met Patrick's family,' she said. Her illicit relationship had been a deep secret at the time, but the need for comfort after his death in action brought the subject into the open. 'Although there was no divorce, his wife had left him and taken the children to Ireland before he and I ever met.'

'The Faradays don't seem to be very good at marriage,' commented Mrs Hardie. 'This Mr Faraday is equally unencumbered – except by his daughter.'

'I wonder – thinking about his book of photographs – whether he knows about the school buildings which Patrick designed. Do you expect to see him again, Grace?'

'Yes.' Grace flushed slightly. 'He expressed some interest in my carving. He'll be back at Greystones in three weeks' time. Come and meet him while he's here.'

They continued to talk about Patrick Faraday and his work, and it was not until later in the evening, when Grace and her aunt were strolling together through the gardens, that Grace remembered a second piece of news.

'There's been another visitor while you were away,' she said. 'One of Mother's Beverley relations turned up to tell her that her brother Archie was dead. I don't suppose you knew him, though. Mother hasn't seen him for years herself.'

'Archie dead!' Midge gasped with shock and came to a halt. It was a moment or two before she could compose herself. 'Well, I haven't seen him for even longer than your mother. But yes, I knew Archie almost fifty years ago. We were both at the university at the same time. Both reading history. In theory, at least. Archie spent most of his time on the river or cricket field.' She paused for a second time. 'I've never told anyone this. Archie was my first – well, to put it in the language of the time, Archie ruined me.'

Grace could hardly believe her ears. 'Seduced you?'

'Yes. Mind you, I wasn't entirely unwilling. I knew it was wrong, but at the same time I wanted it, if you know what I mean.'

Grace did indeed know what she meant, but made no comment.

'Of course, I expected him to do the decent thing. To marry me, I mean. He was as much in love with me as I was with him, or so I thought. I'd overlooked the difference between middle-class and upper-class morality. The grandson of a marquess does not marry into trade. A matrimonial connection between the house of Beverley and The House of Hardie was unthinkable.'

'But Mother and Father —' began Grace.

'Yes. Archie's sister married my brother and that's why Archie never spoke to her again. Or to me.'

'How terrible for you.'

'It seemed so at the time. But only for a little while. Once I'd got my senses back I realized that for someone like me to marry someone like Archie would have been a fate worse than a fate worse than death. All the same, if there'd been a baby . . . ! I can tell you, the three weeks after the night of the great seduction scene were the worst three weeks of my life.'

Midge was talking as one mature woman to another. She would certainly not have spoken to anyone at all about an anxiety of this sort when she was young herself; nor would she have confided in Grace at an earlier period of her niece's life. She could have had no inkling of the effect that her words produced.

It was as much as Grace could manage not to faint with shock at a remark which — so long after the event — was made almost casually. For the moment she managed to conceal her distress, but when at last she retired to her bedroom in the tower she walked round and round it until she became breathless.

How could she have been such a fool! She was not thinking so much of her passionate hour with Andy when she threw that accusation at herself, but of her blindness to its possible consequences. It had not even occurred to her to worry – but she worried now. How long would she have to wait until she could be sure that there was to be no unwanted pregnancy? So uneventful was her life as a rule that she kept no diary. One day was very much like another, and she made no special note of her monthly cycles.

Sitting down on the edge of the bed in an attempt to calm herself she counted back past her visit to Castlemere to the day when Ellis Faraday and his daughter had arrived without warning – a day which at its beginning had promised to be remarkable only for the prodigious number of raspberries which were to be picked. And then before that . . . No, there was no need to feel anxious yet. In a week – or even a little less – she would know that she was safe.

The week passed, and another. Perhaps her own panic was having an effect on her body. Or perhaps this stage of her life was coming to an end. Surely at thirty-five she was too old to have a baby.

The days plodded on through August. This summer was proving to be a hot one. Normally she revelled in the sunshine, but now it became insupportable. Telling herself that the sickness which overcame her each morning was caused by either anxiety or sunstroke, she tried to deceive herself, but was bound to fail in the end.

The day came when she was forced to accept the truth about her condition. So what was to be done about it? Could any steps be taken to bring the pregnancy to an end? She was too unsophisticated even to know whether it was possible and far too ignorant to know what to do. Who would tell her? Was there anyone she could talk to? Not since she was six years old had she kept any important secret from her mother, but this one was too shameful and shocking.

Nor could she face the family's doctor, who was almost a

stranger and would need to be paid. Grace had no money and would have to ask her mother for his fee.

The only person who might understand would be Aunt Midge. She was not likely to be of much practical help; but at least she would be a confidante. As much as anything else now, Grace needed to talk. But even this small comfort was to be denied her, for by the time she had screwed up enough courage to approach her aunt, Midge had gone to visit a friend in Scotland.

The heat of the summer at least provided an explanation for Grace's lethargy and lack of appetite. It was too oppressive to continue with her carving. To remain on her feet for several hours, vigorously hammering at a chisel, was far too great an effort. Abandoning the piece which she had started in the stable courtyard, she retreated to the studio as soon as all her daily tasks in the house and garden were done. There she began to model in clay. The firm movements of her fingers as they pressed and smoothed the shape helped her to be less conscious of the passing of time.

During one of these modelling sessions she was interrupted by her mother.

'You should have given me warning, Grace. They're here, and I've nothing prepared.'

'Who are here?'

'Mr Faraday and his daughter. You agreed, he said, that he might return today to photograph your carvings.'

'Oh!' Appalled by her own forgetfulness, Grace wiped her hand on the trousers of her overalls. 'I hadn't realized – I'm sorry, Mother. I must have lost track of dates.'

After washing and changing as quickly as she could, she hurried down and made her apologies for not being on hand to greet the guests.

'Do you want to do some more modelling?' she asked Trish.

'Yes, please.'

'Come into my studio then. It's too hot outside.'

She settled the little girl down and then asked Ellis what he planned to do.

'May I walk round with you first, looking at the different pieces again?'

'Of course.' Grace could hear that her voice was not completely under control. She struggled to give an impression of calmness and normality, but recognized that she was failing. Ellis, though, spoke of nothing but the carvings until the moment when they reached the furthest point of the serpentine garden which Philip had created. Instead of turning to retrace his steps, he looked straight towards her.

'You're not well, I think, Miss Hardie.'

'Oh yes, perfectly all right, thank you. I find the heat a little trying, perhaps, but that's all.'

'Are you sure? You look worried. Distressed, even.'

'I'm quite sure. Perfectly all right.' But even as she spoke she could feel her bottom lip trembling. It was because she had had no time to prepare herself to face visitors. Clenching her fists, she willed herself not to cry. Ellis continued to stare at her in a serious manner.

'I don't want to be impertinent; but if there's anything I could do . . . ? Sometimes it's easier to talk to a stranger than to one's own family.'

'Kind of you to suggest it, but there's nothing to be done, thank you very much. Nothing to be done at all.' And then, to her great chagrin, Grace burst into tears.

'Do sit down for a moment.' There was a bench in the hidden centre of the garden. She felt his hand under her arm, supporting her as she sank on to it. For a few moments she cried noisily, her breath juddering as she tried to control it. Then she accepted his proffered handkerchief and blew her nose violently.

'Sorry about that. I've been bottling it up, I suppose. Trying to pretend nothing's wrong.'

'And what *is* wrong? I promise to respect your confidence. Is it your health?'

'Only in a way.' She bit her lip as though by doing so she could force herself to keep silence. But the need to talk to someone, anyone, overwhelmed her. 'I'm expecting a baby. My mother doesn't know, so please –'

'Of course not. Oh dear! Does the father –?'

'He's a married man. I shan't tell him. It wouldn't do any good, and I'm not likely to see him again for a long time. But I just don't know what to do.' Once again her tears began to flow, but this time she sniffed them back. 'It was only the once,' she said. 'It seems hard, when it was never going to happen again anyway.'

'I sympathize more than you might expect. My own experience . . . but in our case there was no impediment to a marriage except my own distaste for it. And to me professionally this is not an uncommon story. I take photographs of beautiful young women. Girls who are taken straight from the schoolroom and thrown into a whole summer of parties and dances. It goes to their heads, and chaperones are not always at hand. Accidents happen. The girls talk to me as they sit. There are doctors, Miss Hardie, if you know where to look. Doctors who –'

'I don't suppose their services come cheap. I haven't got any money, you see. None at all. Anyway.' She stood up, straightening her back and stiffening her resolve. 'I'm not like those girls, out in society and needing a good reputation to make a good marriage. I live here so quietly that really hardly anyone except my mother and brother would ever know that there was a baby on the premises. A reputation is only the opinion of other people, and we've never bothered about that.'

In a curious way, the act of making this statement helped her to believe it. Tomorrow she would tell her mother. Once she had confessed her sin and her predicament, this feeling of panic would surely calm itself. 'I shouldn't have burdened you with my problems; but thank you for listening.'

She was anxious now to escape. It had been a relief to tell her secret, but she needed to be private again. Leaving him to set up his apparatus, she returned to the studio.

Trish, seated cross-legged on the floor, was working with a concentration remarkable in a six-year-old, but looked up to ask for help. Grace showed her how to coil and smooth the clay – and then, to amuse her, gave a demonstration of the use of the potter's wheel. They were both absorbed in watching what they hoped would become a jug rise and fall as her wet fingers squeezed the clay or pressed it outwards when Ellis Faraday came into the room.

'I'm sorry to disturb you. If Trish can spare you for a moment, Miss Hardie, there's something I'd like to ask you.'

NINE

Grace followed her guest to one of her favourite stone carvings; a twisted figure of eight.

'Let's sit down for a moment,' Ellis said. He looked around to make sure that there was no one within hearing. 'I've been thinking about what you told me. And there are two suggestions I'd like to make. The first one concerns money. You said you didn't have any, but have you ever considered selling any of your carvings?'

'Who'd want to buy them?'

'I consider them very fine. Full of emotion, and most pleasing to the eye. Not to everyone's taste, of course, but it would only need one person to admire a piece. There's another woman – does the name of Barbara Hepworth mean anything to you?'

Grace shook her head.

'She's also experimenting with abstract sculpture, and selling some of it. There are others, as well. A group which calls itself the Seven and Five. And one or two of the London galleries are sympathetic to new ideas. If you would like me to, I could show some of my photographs to the Leicester Galleries and ask whether they'd include you in a show. And then, you see, if they sold something, you could afford to have your pregnancy terminated. Even if you decided not to, you would have had a choice.'

'I can't believe . . .' But it was stupid to challenge Ellis's opinion when she had no personal knowledge of the London art world. She concentrated instead on the secondary point of what she might do with money if she had it.

The answer was surprisingly clear. She was not like little

Trish, prepared to make something and then destroy it. The pleasure of creation had always lain in the knowledge that what she made would endure and outlive her. If she felt that so strongly about a lump of stone or wood, how much more must it be true of her own baby?

'I should be very grateful for any help of that sort you could give me,' she said. 'I shall need money. But to buy things for the baby, not to kill it.'

'So you're determined to go through with it?'

'I shouldn't be sorry if there were to be some kind of accident,' she admitted. 'But I'm not going to the sort of doctor you mentioned; no.'

'Good. Then I come to my second suggestion. Will you marry me?'

'What did you say?' She could hardly believe her ears.

'It's just as well, isn't it, that I made you sit down before I asked you. But it's a serious question. I would very much like to marry you.'

'You hardly know me, Mr Faraday.'

'Ellis, please. I agree that our acquaintance isn't a long one. But everything that I know, I like. I'm not pretending that this would be a love match. A marriage of convenience, I suppose you'd say – but the convenience on both sides would be very great.'

'I can see that you'd be nobly doing me a favour. Making a respectable woman of me, as they say. But I couldn't possibly allow –'

'Put yourself in my shoes for a moment,' he said. 'For you, marriage would have the one small convenience of giving your baby name. But for me . . . ! To start with, Trish needs a woman's care, so straightaway, you see, I'd be asking for more than you'd be getting. And just as your reputation would be helped by a wedding, so would mine. It's a problem I have to keep continually in mind. The society ladies who ask me to photograph their daughters would feel much happier dealing with a married man.'

'But you're free, aren't you, to marry someone you love. Not someone like me.'

There was a long silence while Ellis chose his words carefully.

'This will shock you, I'm afraid. Something that I've never admitted to anyone. I'm putting myself in your power, because of course it's against the law. I shall never be able to marry the person I love, because he's a man. He acts as housekeeper for me in London. I would have to make it clear – I'm making it clear now – that although I think you and I could live very happily together as friends, I shouldn't want to consummate the marriage. But that – let me assure you – has nothing to do with your attractiveness. You're a very handsome woman.'

'I really don't know what to say.' The arrangement he had in mind for herself was clear enough and the limitations he proposed were acceptable in themselves. She had taught herself to live without a man's love, and since her single lapse had had such disastrous results she felt no urge to repeat it. But that did not make the simple fact of his proposal anything but extraordinary, and she had no idea what he meant about his housekeeper.

'You'll be wanting time to consider it,' he said. 'I've been thinking about nothing else for the past couple of hours, but I must have taken you by surprise. And you do have to be quite clear that I'm asking for a great deal more than I'm offering. I'll leave you to think about it. There's no hurry on my part, although you may feel that there is on yours.'

'Not today,' said Grace. 'I can't possibly –'

'Of course not. Could I persuade you to come to London next week, say? We could do the rounds of the galleries, look at the sort of work I was telling you about earlier. You'd be interested, I do believe.'

'Yes. Yes, I'd like that.'

'And then we could have another chat.'

Grace nodded. She had no notion what her decision would be, but in Ellis she had found someone she could talk to.

85

Almost from the first moment of meeting him she had felt that. It was probably because neither of them would pretend to be in love that she felt sure they could discuss their future without embarrassment.

'Yes,' she said again. 'And Ellis – thank you very much. It's like your first suggestion, about the money. It's such a marvellous relief to feel that there's a choice.' It had not been merely terror that she had felt earlier, but anger that something alien had taken control of her body and that there was nothing she could do about it. Ellis had given her the power to make her own decisions, and she would always be grateful for that.

She soon discovered that he had taken the precaution of weighting the balance as heavily in his favour as possible. After he and Trish had taken their leave, Grace went into the kitchen to make herself useful and found her mother in a high state of excitement.

'Grace, darling, I'm so happy for you. What a charming man! And dear little Trish. I shall love having a child in Greystones again. I told Mr Faraday, Ellis, that a grandchild is just what I need. I see David's family so rarely, and the rest of you have been most remiss about producing a new generation.'

'What are you talking about, Mother?' asked Grace. She knew the answer, of course. But Ellis ought surely to have kept his proposal secret until it had been answered.

'Well, naturally Ellis told me that he wanted to marry you. In the normal way, it's a girl's father who is asked for permission, but –'

'I'm hardly a girl. Really, Mother!'

'So of course I told him that you would make up your own mind. I think he mentioned the matter to me partly to reassure me about money. Trish would go to school, so we shan't need a governess, but we shall be able to have some help in the house again. He'd like to see the entertaining rooms back in use, and –'

'Don't go too fast, Mother. We hardly know him. It's far too soon to make up my mind.'

'But you will accept him, won't you? I never understood why you broke your engagement to Christopher at the end of the war. But you've had plenty of time since then to realize that it's not easy for someone of your generation to find an eligible husband after so many men were killed in the fighting.'

'I decided that I didn't want to be married. I've never felt ashamed of being a spinster, on the shelf. I've been very happy living here just with you and Philip.' She paused, swallowing the lump in her throat. Was this the moment to confess that her way of life was about to be changed whether she liked it or not? It was not a secret which could be kept for long. But in the astonishment of hearing Ellis's proposal she had failed to ask a good many important questions. Her mother would want to know who the baby's father was. What should the answer be? Ellis proposed to claim paternity as far as the outside world was concerned, but would he want members of the family, and later the child himself, to know the truth? Probably not; but she ought not to risk making a wrong guess.

'I'll be going up to London next week,' she said instead. 'I'll see Ellis there. There's a lot to be considered. To start with, what should I wear?' The question, she knew, would divert her mother's attention from the larger matter – but it was a genuine one. There was nothing in her wardrobe which would look respectable in the West End, but she must try not to disgrace her suitor.

'A well-cut suit never dates,' said Mrs Hardie with a confidence which came from a lack of any interest in current fashions. 'What a good thing we're the same height. Let's go and see what I can lend you.' They went upstairs together.

Since Grace had as little idea as her mother whether the outfits she was offered would be considered old-fashioned, she allowed quality of fabric and unfussy styling to guide her choice. The peach colour of a wild silk suit did not suit her complexion;

but the tight-fitting skirt and loose jacket – for she was smaller in the bust than her mother had ever been – gave her an unaccustomed air of sophistication. Under protest she allowed herself to be bullied into wearing the matching hat and agreed that she would have to endure the discomfort of her only pair of smart shoes.

The effect was to make her feel a stranger to herself when she took the train to London, increasing the impression that this whole drama was happening to someone else. Perhaps it was a dream. But no; there was Ellis waiting for her at Paddington, and his look of approving admiration brought a smile to her own face. It was a very long time indeed since anyone had last noticed her appearance favourably.

'Where's Trish?' she asked, to start the conversation on a safe subject.

'I asked Alan to take her to the Zoo. I was afraid she might find our day too tiring. I do take her to look at pictures quite often, in the National Gallery mostly, but I only let her look at a few each time, so that it stays a treat. Now, let's find a taxi. Private shows before lunch, I thought, and the Tate afterwards.'

'Whatever you say.'

It was an educational morning. There was not a great deal of sculpture to be seen in the galleries clustered around Bond Street, and what there was proved to be small in scale. But it was interesting to discover how many modern figurative paintings were sculptural in style, depicting limbs so thick and solid that they might have been carved from stone. Even more interesting were the abstract paintings in which she could often recognize the same sense of movement that she was trying to create herself.

Most interesting of all, however, was the fact that all the gallery owners knew Ellis by name. When he introduced Grace to them, and mentioned her work, it was with the authority of a man who was already acquainted with most of the artists whose work was on show. He was in the swim of London's art world; and was offering her the opportunity to step into the current beside him.

Until a few weeks ago Grace would have said that she wanted nothing better than to continue in a way of life which most people would consider to be dull and solitary – and she was still not discontented with it. But Andy and Rupert and Ellis himself had converged on Greystones to jolt her out of a routine which for fourteen years had been pleasurable but unstimulating. They had opened the doors of her imagination on to different worlds – France, Castlemere and London – preparing her for the possibility of stepping out of her narrow rut.

In the excitement of today's new experience she was even able to forget for a little while the personal disaster which would shatter her existing routine whether she liked it or not. A meal in a restaurant was one of her rarest treats and her eyes were as bright as a child's as she pointed to her choice of hors d'oeuvres from the dishes which a waiter revolved on a trolley. Ellis's eyes were bright as well; but with amusement.

'This is only a first course,' he warned her. 'There'll be something more substantial to come.'

'Oh!' Aghast at what must seem to be her greed, she put her hand up to her mouth. 'What a real provincial you must think me!'

'What I think is that you mustn't ever change,' he said. 'These shapes that you're carving and modelling emerge from your own personality. It would be a mistake, in my opinion, for you to turn yourself into a metropolitan person. If you marry me, I hope you'll go on living in exactly the same way as before, boiler suit and all. I can handle any dealings with these people – gallery owners and critics – for you, to build up your reputation and get a bit of money. It's something I'd very much like to do. So that I could feel I was putting something back in return for what Trish was getting. Have you thought any more about it, Grace? Will you take the plunge and marry me?'

Grace looked up from her overloaded plate and stared into her companion's eyes. He was still little more than a stranger, but did that matter when he was not expecting intimacy? He was sympathetic and considerate, sharing many of her own interests with an enthusiasm which excited her. He was a man of taste, sophisticated but not snobbish – and he was more competent to manage business affairs than any of the present occupants of Greystones. She liked him; and she liked his daughter.

'Yes,' she said. 'I would be very happy to marry you. '

TEN

It was all over. On a cold Sunday morning in March 1933, Mrs Hardie collapsed at last into a chair in the kitchen, as exhausted as though she, and not her daughter, had spent the night in labour. Ellis was sitting with his wife whilst the midwife looked after the newly-born little boy. Mrs Hardie had made tea for them all, and gave Philip a tray to carry upstairs.

Her youngest son, Jay, who was spending the weekend at Greystones, came to join her, shivering but elegant in a silk dressing gown.

'Gracious, what a commotion!'

'I thought you were managing to sleep all through it.'

'Faint hope. It's just that I didn't see much point in adding to the confusion by appearing. No one is likely to ask me to portray a woman giving birth on the London stage, thank God. All well?'

'Yes. A dear little boy. Nine pounds.'

'Is that good or bad?'

'It's heavy, especially for a boy.'

'And especially for a baby who's supposed to be premature?'

Mrs Hardie refrained from making any comment. On the day when Grace returned from London to announce that she had accepted Ellis's proposal, she had confessed that she was already pregnant, but naturally enough had asked that the fact should be kept secret.

'Is Ellis up with her now?' Jay asked.

'Yes. She's very tired. Most women are much younger when they have their first babies, of course. But she'll be all right. Would you like a cup of tea?'

'Thanks.' But instead of enjoying it peacefully, Jay began to pace around the kitchen. 'How well did Grace know Ellis before they got married, Mother? The wedding was arranged in such a rush, while I was on tour, that I didn't have a chance to say anything.'

'Say anything about what, dear?'

'Well, it's just that . . . well, he and I have a good many friends in common.'

'I'm glad to hear it.'

'No, I mean . . . I didn't actually know him before I met him here, but I knew his name, and his friends.'

'So you just said.' What was it that Jay was trying to explain? As an actor he was accustomed to declaim the lines written for him fluently, but seemed to be having trouble in expressing his own thoughts. She waited patiently.

'I wouldn't have thought he was the sort of man to fall in love with Grace. In fact, I wouldn't have expected him to want to get married at all.'

'Well, perhaps they didn't fall in love in the way that two younger people might have done.' She paused for a moment, remembering the passion which had driven her at the age of eighteen to defy her family and run away from home without even being sure that the man she loved wanted to marry her. Grace had made no pretence of feeling anything like that. Indeed, she had retained the use of the bedroom in the tower which had been hers ever since the house was built, and had provided her husband with a room of his own some distance away. 'It's more of an affectionate friendship. Companionship. They like talking to each other. They admire each other's work.'

'You don't have to marry in order to chat. Still, I suppose it's a good sort of camouflage. As long as Grace realizes . . .'

'Camouflage? What does that mean? I don't understand what you're getting at, dear.' She would have pressed further, but at that moment there was an interruption. Trish came running into the kitchen.

92

'Grandmother, the baby's cold.'

'What do you mean, darling?'

'I thought I heard a kitten mewing, but it was the new baby crying. I went into the room just to have a peep. The window's open and the room's freezing cold and the baby hasn't got any clothes on.'

Almost unable to believe her ears, Mrs Hardie stood up so abruptly that her chair toppled backwards. Leaving Jay to pick it up, she hurried upstairs. She could hear Trish running behind her, but did not wait for the little girl to keep up.

Grace had moved into a guest bedroom in the last two months of her pregnancy, when she began to find the spiral staircase of the tower too steep and narrow. Mrs Hardie glanced quickly through the open door as she passed. The new mother, looking pale and tired, was lying in bed with her eyes closed, while Ellis, at the side of the bed, held her hand. The midwife was in a corner of the room, rolling stained sheets into a bundle.

The cradle which had been prepared for the baby was in the dressing room next door. Trish's story proved to be true. The window was indeed open, allowing the cold March wind to puff at the curtains. And the baby, no longer crying, lay naked, his hands and feet purple and his face a bluish white.

In a single gesture Mrs Hardie covered the baby with the blankets which had been put on a chair and picked him up, holding him close to her body so that some of her own warmth might pass into him. 'Nurse!' she shouted as with her one free hand she closed each window in turn, although as a rule she never raised her voice. More quietly, she said, 'Trish, tell the nurse to come here at once.'

The midwife came in response to Trish's message, with a lack of haste which made Mrs Hardie breathless with indignation.

'Surely you didn't just *forget* about him! What do you mean by leaving him to catch his death of cold like that? Your first duty –'

The nurse put up a hand to check Mrs Hardie's anger. 'Have

you looked at him, madam?' she asked. She had the slow, soft voice of a countrywoman; a voice which earlier had inspired confidence. And the doctor had been warm in his recommendation. It was impossible to understand why she should suddenly have become either inefficient or heartless.

'Of course I've looked at him. What are you talking about? Get him well wrapped up at once.'

'Have you *really* looked at him, though?' She reached out to loosen the blankets and free one of the baby's hands. 'Look at the fingers: the extra joint. And the shape of the eyes. It's a mongol baby.'

Mrs Hardie laid her grandson back in the cradle, tucking the covers tightly around him as she leaned over to stare at his face. The eyes were not round, but slanting and almond shaped. She felt a moment of sick disappointment, followed by distress at the thought of breaking the news to Grace. But none of this was any excuse for failing to take proper care of a new-born child.

'The mother's, what, thirty-five, thirty-six?' continued the nurse. 'Always a risk, it is, leaving a first baby so late. It's for the best, just letting nature take its course.'

'This isn't nature taking its course. What you're trying to do is to murder a human being. You've no right to take such a decision on yourself.' Mrs Hardie spoke with a passion which welled from deep in her heart. Her own youngest child, Felix, had been discovered to have brain damage, and had died at the age of twenty-five without ever really leaving childhood, but it was not Felix that she thought of now. Many years ago her first baby, born prematurely in a Chinese village, had been snatched from her while she was unable to move by an ignorant woman who took it for granted that she would not wish a female child to live. She had never forgotten the grief she felt then, and had no intention of allowing her only other daughter to suffer in the same way.

'With respect, madam, you can't expect a new mother to make such a choice when she's tired and emotional. And she

94

can't know what it's like to see such a child grow into an adult which still has to be treated as a baby.'

'Wrap him up!' ordered Mrs Hardie. 'And then get the fire going again. I'll fetch hot water bottles.' As she turned to hurry from the room she was startled to see that Trish was still standing there. Had she overheard the conversation? Well, there was no time to think about that for the moment. There was too much to be done.

Later in the day she discovered the answer to her question.

'Grandmother,' said Trish, painstakingly scraping out the bowl which had held a gingerbread mixture, and sucking the spoon. 'What does mongol mean?'

Mrs Hardie's face paled with shock. 'Did you hear –? Oh, Trish dearest, the midwife shouldn't have used that word, and you shouldn't have been listening. I want you to promise me now that you'll never use the word to anyone again. Not to me, not to Grace or Ellis, not to anyone. Will you promise?'

'Yes,' said Trish. 'But I still don't know what it means.'

'Come and sit on my lap for a moment. Well, it means that the baby will never be clever.'

'Can't we change him for another one if he's not good enough?'

'No, of course not. It's not like one of the clay animals that you make and then throw away. And not being clever isn't important. He'll be a smiling, loving little boy. You're his big sister, and he'll give you lots of hugs and kisses. But he won't be good at looking after himself. When he's nearly seven, like you are now, he'll still need to be helped with getting dressed, and he won't be able to read like you can. That sort of thing. Now then, Trish, I've answered your question, but you have to forget what I've told you. Every tiny baby needs to be looked after all the time, so we shall all take care of this one. The only difference is that the caring will have to last a little longer than usual, that's all.'

'Does Grace know?'

'Not yet, because she's very tired and she's having a good

95

sleep. She will soon. But she won't want to talk about it. So I can trust you, can't I, Trish, to keep your promise.'

Trish nodded, and was distracted at that moment by a new arrival. Rupert Beverley came, as had become his custom, to the kitchen door, although since Grace's marriage to Ellis there had been a maid to answer the front doorbell and all the entertaining rooms were back in use. Mrs Hardie had been glad to hand the housework over to someone else, but continued to do the cooking herself. She had allotted one of the many sculleries to be a special place in which Trish could make as much mess as she liked with the jars of poster paint she had been given for Christmas, so that in the late afternoon, when school was over and dinner was in preparation, the kitchen was as much of a family centre as it had been in the servantless days.

'Good afternoon, Cousin Lucy. Hello, Patricia. What a ripping smell! You must have been expecting me. Gingerbread is my favourite tea.'

'I'm Trish,' said Trish. This conversation took place at every encounter.

'Patricia is a beautiful name and beauty should never be cut short. One of these days you're going to be a beautiful woman and then you'll find yourself begging everyone to forget that you were ever called trish-trash-Trish. Any news of the baby yet?'

'He arrived early this morning,' said Mrs Hardie.

'Good for Grace. As soon as she's had time to recover, remind her that all the best families have to have first an heir and then a spare. Is she receiving visitors?'

'Not yet. She's still resting.'

'Give her my best wishes, then. I've come to pick up the motor, and I shan't be back for a few weeks, not till the new term starts.'

'Are you going on holiday?' asked Trish.

'I'm going back to Castlemere to do some work.' Laughing, he turned to Mrs Hardie to explain. 'So much goes on in

Oxford during term that it's quite hard to settle down to any serious reading. My friends would laugh at me if I suggested it, and even the dons don't seem to expect it. Beverleys have been keeping their terms at Oxford for generations, and I suspect that not one of them has thought of it as anything but a place to row and play cricket and get drunk. I'm actually quite keen to learn a bit of history, but I have to keep it to myself, or I should get terribly ragged. So. If I eat any more of this delicious gingerbread I shall get fat. Goodbye, Cousin Lucy. And beautiful Miss Patricia.'

'I like Rupert,' said Trish when he had gone.

'So do I.' Mrs Hardie had been hurt, when she was younger, by the coldness with which her family had punished her for making a misalliance. Rupert's friendliness was refreshing – but after a few moments the sparkle which he had brought to the atmosphere began to fade as she was left to face the realities of a depressing day.

ELEVEN

The day which in happier circumstances might have seen baby Tom Faraday's christening proved instead to be the occasion of his funeral.

In the twenty-four hours after the birth Grace had been too tired to understand why her mother had so adamantly insisted that the doctor must attend at once to examine the new-born child. Even later, after the news of her son's abnormality was broken to her, she had assumed that the visit was for the purpose of checking the midwife's opinion. But it seemed that Mrs Hardie's experience of childbearing – for she herself had given birth to eight children – must have given her an instinct that something else was wrong. Within four days of his birth, little Tom was struggling for breath through congested lungs. He was taken down to the Infirmary; but in three weeks he was dead.

Only a small family group gathered to watch the tiny coffin consigned to the earth. Besides the Greystones household, Grace's Aunt Midge was there; and a day had been chosen on which Jay had no matinée to play, so that he was able to travel from London with his elder brother, David, and Sheila, his sister-in-law. It was not thought necessary to keep David's three children away from school for the occasion.

Jay was a regular weekend visitor, but an appearance by David's family was rare. David himself, since abandoning the law to take charge of the family business, called regularly at the shop in Oxford's High Street and often took the opportunity to visit his mother. His wife, though, rarely accompanied him. It was a long time since Grace had last seen her sister-in-law, and she was startled to discover that Sheila – who was a year or two older than herself – was pregnant again. Her condition was concealed at first by the loose black coat which she wore for the church service and interment; but it became obvious when they all returned to Greystones for luncheon. How fortunate that Grace had resolved in advance not to mention the fact that little Tom had been born with a condition ascribed to his mother's advanced age!

Mrs Hardie, delighted to learn for the first time that she could expect to become a grandmother once more, insisted on taking Sheila upstairs to rest after the meal was over.

'Do you need a rest as well?' David asked Grace. 'It's not very long –'

'Oh, long enough.' She was surprised by the note of consideration in her brother's voice. Neither of the two of them ever made any direct reference to the quarrel which had split the family immediately after the war, but their usual attitude to each other was one of politeness rather than fraternal affection.

'Then if you feel strong enough – and if it's not too cold for you – perhaps we might take a walk in the grounds. The daffodils must be at their best now.' His manner made it clear that he had a particular subject to discuss.

'It was very bad luck about little Tom,' he said when they were alone. 'Especially since at your age I don't suppose you'll want to try again.'

'Don't make me sound as though I were seventy!' A remark which she would have accepted from Jay as a statement of fact seemed to emerge from her elder brother's lips as a criticism. 'After all, Sheila is older than I am, and she –'

'Yes, well, that was an accident. But at least we have three healthy children to reassure us that everything is likely to go well again.'

Grace nodded. 'I know what you mean. Yes, you're right, I'm too old.'

'You've probably been waiting to see how things turned out.

99

But now – I was wondering: have you made a new will since your marriage?'

'No,' said Grace. 'Nor before it. I may be long in the tooth for motherhood, but I'm a bit young for dying.'

'Accidents can happen at any age. And in the hands of anyone who could afford to maintain the house properly, Greystones would be a very valuable property.'

'Even so, since my affairs are so simple . . . There are rules, aren't there, about what happens if there's no will. My husband –'

'You mean that you'd like Ellis to become the owner, without thinking what might happen to Mother and Philip? Don't imagine that he'd necessarily let things go on as they were, because life doesn't work that way. In any case, the intestacy rules aren't as simple as that. If you died leaving a husband and son, that would be reasonably straightforward, I agree. But if you only leave a husband, other people have entitlements. Ellis might have to sell Greystones in order to distribute shares of the value of your estate, and to pay death duties. Where would that leave Mother and Philip? I won't offer to draw up something for you myself: it's not a good idea to do that kind of thing inside the family. But I do most strongly urge you to make proper arrangements. Greystones may be legally your house, but it has become the family home. You have a responsibility –'

'I'll bear it in mind.' Grace interrupted her brother and turned back towards the house. They were coming too near to that earlier argument in which she had refused to mortgage Greystones in order to save The House of Hardie from bankruptcy. 'Thank you for the reminder.'

She was rescued from further pressure by the sound of someone calling her name. Rupert, with Trish riding pick-a-back on his shoulders, was searching for her.

'Goodness, has term started already?' exclaimed Grace. 'I didn't expect to see you for another week or two.' Rupert's visits were always unannounced, but were usually confined within the weeks of the Oxford terms. 'Meet my brother, David. David, I don't think you've met Lord Rupert Beverley.'

'Another Hardie cousin? Good-oh: I collect cousins. How do you do? I must say first of all, Cousin Grace, how sorry I am to hear about your baby. I was here the day he was born, and I hoped he'd bring you a lot of happiness. It's rotten bad luck.'

'Thank you.' Grace didn't want to talk about Tom any more. 'But you didn't come here to say that.'

'No. I only found out a moment ago. I came to give your mother a piece of perfectly spiffing news.' His face, which he had tried to keep grave as he expressed his condolences, reverted to its usual grin. 'I'll leave her to pass it on to you. Don't let her kid you that it has anything to do with me. I'm only the messenger, that's all. And I've got to get back straightaway. Down you come.' He tipped Trish off his shoulders, depositing her on the ground in front of David's feet before making off with a last wave of his hand.

Grace, curious, went to find her mother. But Mrs Hardie refused to say anything until much later that day, when Jay and David and Sheila had left, Trish had gone to bed, and Ellis had excused himself to go and work in what was once the smoking room but had now been converted into a darkroom.

Philip, as always, sat in silence as Grace begged her mother to reveal the news which Rupert had brought.

'Dear Rupert. He likes to behave as though he's a bit of an ass, but I suspect that he's really quite sharp. Businesslike. He's been delving in my brother's papers. There's something that the lawyers who are supposed to be winding up his estate don't seem to have noticed until Rupert pointed it out.'

'What's that?'

'Well, as you know, my mother married when she was very young. My grandfather – the marquess who gave you Greystones, Grace – made a marriage settlement on her. That was quite usual in those days. After she died – in her early twenties, when I was born – the money stayed in a trust fund

101

for the benefit of Archie and myself. We should each have been given our share on our twenty-first birthdays. Archie took his, but I was never even told about mine. By the time I was twenty-one, you see, I'd married and gone off to China with your father and was in deep disgrace with my family.'

'Do you mean that your brother stole your share of the money?' exclaimed Grace.

'Not stole it, no. Simply never handed it over. He'd threatened that if I married without his permission I'd never receive another penny from anyone in the family and he didn't feel inclined to break his promise. So he simply held on to my share of the settlement. It's been sitting in some trustee account ever since, earning a little interest every year. I imagine that by the time he died even Archie had forgotten all about it, and no one else would ever have known.'

'So has it grown into a huge fortune? Millions and millions?'

'Nothing like that, no. It wasn't a great sum to start with. Just enough – or rather, half of just enough – to keep a well-connected young lady in ballgowns and French maids. But it's going to seem like a fortune to us.'

'To you,' said Grace; and Philip nodded his agreement. She hugged her mother in pleasure. 'You're to have a bit of luxury at last. Whatever it will run to. More help in the house. A cook as well as a maid, for a start.'

'I enjoy the cooking,' said Mrs Hardie. 'When I remember the terrible overcooked food we used to have, I couldn't bear to go back to it. But a housekeeper might be useful. Or a kitchen maid to do the dirty jobs. What I thought was, I could keep back enough of the capital to produce income which would pay wages. Then we ought to get the roof repaired before the attics get any damper. But as well as that I want to give you each a present. Grace is to go and choose the most beautiful piece of stone that she can find. And Philip, I want you to start the vineyard that you were talking about.'

Her son and daughter looked at each other incredulously. On the day, many months ago, when Andy Frith had suggested the suitability of part of their land for growing vines, they had discussed the possibility at some length. Their conclusion had been definite. They could not possibly afford the initial cost of preparing the land and buying the vines – and the stakes and wires and tools that would also be necessary. Philip, although saying as little as usual, had made it clear from his wistful expression how much he would have enjoyed conducting such an experiment had it been possible: but they had both agreed that it was out of the question, giving the idea no further thought.

'We won't discuss it any more now,' said Mrs Hardie. 'You may have changed your minds, of course. But if it still interests you, make an estimate of what it would cost to get going, and bring me the figures. I'll promise to tell you honestly if it's more than I can manage. But you've had such a bleak time, you two dears, these past years. I'd like to give you a treat – and I realize what you enjoy most of all is an opportunity to work even harder than before. Now Grace, dear, I think you should go to bed early. You've had a harrowing time this past month. I'd like you to wake up tomorrow morning and throw it all off. Start again. Get back to your work.'

Grace hugged her mother and went slowly upstairs. She had not yet returned to her tower room since her confinement, but would do so tomorrow. As she moved lethargically around the larger room which she had used for the past few months, there was a knock on the door.

TWELVE

It was Ellis who had come to see her, as anxious about her state of health and mind as her mother had been. 'All right?' he asked.

Grace nodded. 'If it had to end this way, I'm glad it's over.'

He took her hand. 'You're a brave woman. I've been admiring you. Not a tear all day. And not a tear even when you were told what was wrong with him. Yet that must have been devastating, after all those months of waiting, and so much pain.'

Grace was comforted by his touch. 'I'll tell you something that I've never confessed to anyone before,' she said. 'Not even to my mother. One of my brothers knew, the one who lives in Australia now, but he never told anyone either.'

She paused for a moment, gathering her thoughts and her courage.

'It was when I was about a year younger than Trish is now. My mother had another baby, Felix. He was premature; very small. That day I had a terrible quarrel with my other brothers. They killed my pet cat – hunted it, like a tiger. Shot it with a bow and arrow, and then beat its brains out, in front of my eyes. I think I went a little mad. I tried to see my mother, but no one would let me into her room. So when I found myself alone with the new baby, I knocked the cradle over. I only meant it as a gesture of bad temper, but he banged his head on the floor. It must have done some kind of damage. He grew up to be very good-looking – and very happy – but his mind was always that of a child.'

'And your parents never knew that it was your fault?'

'No. I was waiting to confess. I *needed* to confess. But immediately after it happened I was ill; and when I was better they told me that the baby had died because he'd been too small when he was born. That story wasn't invented to spare my feelings, because nobody knew . . . Anyway, I believed it. I genuinely didn't think, after that, that I'd done any harm.'

'When did you find out?'

'Oh, not for twenty years or so. When both my parents were abroad. Felix had been living in a sort of nursing home all those years. It might have made me feel guilty again to see him, I suppose; but it didn't. He was so contented; smiling all the time. I didn't see much point then in raking up the past. But when I was told about Tom . . .'

'You felt it was Mother Nature taking her revenge? Inflicting a punishment for a past crime?'

'That came into it, yes. But also – when I met Felix for the first time as a young man, I understood why my parents had chosen that name for him. The happy one. A fortunate child, because he would never have the understanding to feel despair or disappointment or anything of that kind. And Tom would have been like that as well. It would have been selfish of me to cry because I hadn't got quite the sort of baby I wanted, when he wouldn't ever have cried for himself. And as for today –'

She paused, trying to be clear about her feelings. She had never quite felt that the baby belonged to her. The midwife had taken him away as soon as he was born, and did not bring him back. At first Grace had been too exhausted to notice and when, later, she expected to feed him, she was told that her breasts were too small and that he would thrive better on a bottle. When he was eventually put in her arms, he lay without moving or smiling and she felt none of the love which she had expected to overcome her. She had never bathed or changed or dressed him, because he had been taken to hospital while she was still lying-in. All this might have been upsetting, but she expressed herself sincerely now.

'I decided years ago that I didn't want to have children. Tom was an accident, as you know. I'd have done my best to be a good mother, but –'

'But you're relieved that it's not going to be expected of you after all.'

'Well I'm sad, of course, about his death. But – yes, to be honest, it *is* a relief.'

'And when you were deciding that you didn't want to be a mother, all those years ago, were you also choosing not to be a wife?'

'Yes. I embraced spinsterhood as a vocation.' She laughed, suddenly carefree again after ten months of anxiety.

'So would you like to be released from marriage as well as from motherhood?' Ellis let go of her hand and walked across to the window, standing with his back to her.

'What do you mean?'

'I mean that we struck a kind of bargain, didn't we? What you were going to get out of it was a father for your child. You don't need that any more. Do you want to be free again?'

'Ellis, are you trying to say that *you* –?'

'I'm getting everything I could possibly want,' he said. 'Trish is being loved and cared for. She has the kind of happy family life that I could never have provided for her on my own. As for myself . . .' He turned to face her. 'Greystones is a country house which I can enjoy without being responsible for it. A house which my father built. A house where I feel welcome, where there will always be company and friendship. No, I don't want to change anything. All the advantage is on my side. I just want to be sure you realize that you have grounds for getting the marriage annulled if you choose to do so. Well, those grounds have existed all the time; but this is the moment when you might want to use them.'

There was a long silence. Grace tried to cast her mind back to the moment, years earlier, when at the age of twenty-two she had balanced the humiliation of being a spinster, left on the shelf, against the freedom to live a life of independence in

106

the house which she loved and owned – not caring that she would be poor, as long as she could devote herself to the creative work which brought her such satisfaction. Her decision had been definite and – as she thought then – final. Now Ellis was offering her a second chance to return to that kind of self-sufficiency. It was not a question to be answered lightly.

But although she was slow to speak, her answer was never in doubt. Because Ellis spent more than half his time in London, she still felt as free as ever; and when he came to Greystones she enjoyed his company and the excitement of feeling herself linked at one remove to London society and London art.

As for Trish, her presence was not a burden but a delight. Her enthusiasm for experiment was a constant pleasure; the kind of pleasure which baby Tom, had he lived, would never have been able to provide. She shared with her stepmother the ability to concentrate on a practical task, although the speed with which she discarded a finished object in order to move on to something else was alien to Grace's own attitude. She was intelligent and vivacious and, above all, affectionate. Even if Grace had been prepared to let her go, Mrs Hardie would have refused to relinquish her role as grandmother.

'We can't do without Trish,' said Grace, making a joke of the truth. 'And how shall I ever achieve a one-man show in London without my personal agent working away on my behalf?' Then she spoke more seriously. 'Your companionship means a lot to me, Ellis. I may not have known that I wanted it until I had it, but now I couldn't do without it. I suppose it is a funny sort of marriage, but it suits me. So if it suits you as well, I hope you'll stay.'

'Good.' He strode across the room to take her in his arms, kissing her cheek. It was unusual for him to touch her, but the pleasure revealed in both their smiles had more than a physical cause. They trusted each other to speak and believe the truth. It was a friendship rather than a real marriage; but a very special friendship.

Grace had a question to ask. She did not intend to let her conversation with David affect her behaviour, but could not quite dismiss it from her mind.

'Ellis, if anything were to happen to me, and Greystones came to you, you'd let Mother and Philip go on living here wouldn't you?'

'What do you mean, if anything happens? You're not feeling unwell, are you?'

She shook her head. 'A purely hypothetical question. I'd like to hear you promise.'

'I'll promise anything you ask me and yes, specifically, I'll promise that. But what you ought to do, Grace, if you're worried, is to make a will. You can set down exactly what you want to happen – and need never think about it again.'

'That's what David's been telling me. I've been trying to think why he should suddenly become so concerned.'

'I can tell you the answer to that. He wants to own Greystones himself one day – or if not himself, his children. I've noticed how he looks at us all. I don't think Trish bothers him much; a mere stepdaughter. But he can't be sure what you'd do about me. And of course when Tom was born, that must really have been a blow.' Only those members of the family who lived in the house had known that Tom would never have been capable of running the estate: his condition had been kept a secret from everyone else. 'It seemed to me at the funeral that he was pleased that your heir had died.'

'You're imagining things!'

Ellis shrugged his shoulders. 'It's none of my business,' he said. 'Greystones is your house and you must do whatever you like to protect its future. I don't want to know what you decide. But whatever I can do to keep it as a home for your mother and Philip would be done. That's a promise. Now you must get some sleep.'

'Yes. Thank you, Ellis. For being such a support and – and for everything.'

After he had left the room she paced up and down,

undecided. It would be sensible to go to a lawyer and safeguard the future of the house. The trouble was that she had no idea what she wanted to happen. If she tried to envisage how the life with which she was happy would continue, she was always part of it herself. She could not nominate an heir without first pushing herself out of the picture, and found this impossible.

Besides, it was ridiculous to start considering the possibility of her death so soon. All this business of making wills could wait for a few years. There was plenty of time.

1936

ONE

'I hear that you're starting to produce your own wine. English wine.'

Even the liveliest dinner party may experience a sudden break in the general conversation, and it is always into such a silence that the most embarrassing remarks fall. Every head turned towards David Hardie and awaited his answer.

The occasion was one of a regular series of dinner parties given by The House of Hardie for faithful or potential customers. How on earth had one of these – the secretary of a London club whose members were for the most part artists and musicians – managed to pick up such a piece of gossip?

'No, no,' David assured him with a smile. 'We only deal in the very finest wines, the most respected names. The country wine business can be left to ladies in embroidered aprons, working away in their own kitchens and drinking their own produce.'

'But the buzz is that this isn't a country wine. The real thing, they say. What are you going to call it? Hardie hock?'

'I didn't know you owned a vineyard,' said the guest on his right. To David's dismay, the conversation had become general.

'No, I don't. Not in any ordinary sense. The reference must be to an experiment which my brother is running on the family estate. He's planted half a dozen different grape varieties to see which of them, if any, will thrive in our climate. Without any encouragement from me, I can tell you. He's a botanist, interested in this sort of thing – and he's read about the Marquess of Bute's trials. Nothing will come of it, in my opinion – and even if he does produce a few bottles of wine, I certainly wouldn't stock them in The House of Hardie. This is purely my brother's hobby.'

It must have been Ellis Faraday who had started the rumour going. He was just the sort of chap who would belong to an arty club – a club whose members sat at a single long table, chatting to each other instead of preserving a gentlemanly silence over meals. David silently chalked up another black mark against his brother-in-law, who had made an early bad impression by enquiring whether The House of Hardie was not yet sufficiently profitable to restore to Mrs Hardie some of the income which had been necessarily withdrawn when it was near to bankruptcy. As though it were any of his business!

What his guests should be concentrating on at the moment was the 1921 Château d'Yquem. It was the finest dessert wine ever produced, in David Hardie's opinion, and he voiced that opinion firmly now in order to change the subject, which had touched an awkward nerve. A man in his position, the proprietor of a family wine business which had been in existence for over two hundred years, ought to be able to live in some style. It was expected of him, and he was reluctant to disappoint such expectations: that was one reason why he always entertained on his Pall Mall premises and never at home. He did not in so many words claim to be the owner of a large country estate, but a photograph of Greystones hung in the room which was used for dinners like the present one, and it was his habit from time to time to use phrases like 'the Hardie estate' or 'our country place' in a manner which he knew must create a false impression. This made it more difficult than it ought to have been to disown activities which in fact were completely outside his control.

These House of Hardie dinners were always a strain. The food must be good and everything about the wines chosen to accompany it – suitability, temperature and manner of service – must be perfect. David was host and salesman at the same time. All the guests knew that this was a selling exercise, yet both they and their host pretended otherwise. It was understood that he would bring to their notice the finer points of whatever they were drinking, but no actual business was done at the table.

The tension of the occasion made the food and drink lie heavily on David's stomach. When the last of his guests had departed he decided in the interests of exercise and fresh air to walk at least part of the way towards Baker Street, where he would catch his Metropolitan train. He set off from Pall Mall towards Piccadilly and Bond Street.

He was a good-looking man who held himself well and moved with a confident stride. From his father he had inherited a tall frame, strong features and dark hair and eyes. But there was one thing which Gordon Hardie had not been able to pass on to this one of his sons: the enthusiasm which had been so much a part of his character. David's dark brown eyes rarely expressed a lively interest in anything, but instead were dull, even uneasy. For David Hardie at the age of forty-two was a discontented man.

He would have found difficulty in specifying what it was about his life that disappointed him. He had a comfortable enough home in Harrow – although it was the wrong part of Harrow, at the foot of the hill instead of on the top. It had been a country house when he first bought it, of respectable size and set in its own grounds. But by now the surrounding fields had disappeared beneath rows of semi-detached villas and he found himself living in a suburb. This was something he did his best to conceal from his customers.

In other respects he should have had no complaints. His three elder children went to church every Sunday without protest and were, on the whole, well-behaved. Sheila was a good mother, a tidy housewife. His marriage had never been passionate, but it had run its course placidly for almost twenty years. Only since the birth of their last, unwanted, son had any problems arisen. Max proved to be an over-active baby who hardly slept at all. It had seemed reasonable that Sheila should move into a separate bedroom to spare her husband the disturbance caused by frequent crying in the night. Even her unwillingness to return as the boy grew older was understandable, for David shared his wife's wish that there should be no more 'accidents'. He might have been able to ignore the lack of warmth in his home life if his business career had brought him more satisfaction.

Had he made a mistake in leaving the law? As a young solicitor he had married the daughter of the senior partner, and his legal career seemed set fair. But as time passed he realized that he had no hope of advancement until his father-in-law should choose to retire. Trapped by the strength of his own expectations and Sheila's family feeling, he could neither look outside the partnership nor hope for senior status within it.

That was one of the factors which had persuaded him to take active control of The House of Hardie in 1929, after the death of Will Witney, its manager. He had not been trained for the task. His eldest brother, Frank, destined to inherit the business, had been killed in the war. Another brother – David's twin, Kenneth – had worked under Will Witney for a time; but his desertion from the army had made it impossible for him to stay in England. As for Philip, disabled by shell-shock and lung damage, he would never be strong enough to shoulder the responsibilities of running a business.

David had given the matter careful thought. The legal profession offered a safe career. The wine trade was risky – but for almost the first time in his life, he had decided to take a chance. Even more surprising was the fact that his reason was a sentimental one. David saw himself as the only member of the family competent to be a vintner. If The House of Hardie was to be saved, only he could save it. And then it would be inherited by his son, to continue through the generations for another two hundred years or more.

Neither his brothers nor his sister, as far as he could tell, understood that the strength of his family feeling was as great as their own. It expressed itself differently, that was all. The House of Hardie had been handed down from father to son through many generations and it was his responsibility to continue the tradition. Greystones, more recently, had become part of the family heritage as well. Had the house belonged to him, he would never have been as selfish as Grace in refusing to offer it as security for a necessary loan. It would be a long time before he forgave her for that – and yet she sometimes appeared to think that he was the one who was being unreasonable.

More than anything else, Greystones was the cause of his dissatisfaction with his life. It ought to be his one day. The present position was quite ridiculous. Grace had no money to keep it up, and for years had not bothered even to try. Since her marriage the house had recovered a trace of its old dignity, but it was still absurd that a mansion which could, with care, have preserved its grandeur, should be owned by a woman who spent her life in workman's overalls chipping off bits of stone or wood.

He was realistic enough to see that there was nothing to be done for the moment. But he had spent years drawing up wills and trusts and settlements and felt no sentimentality in accepting that even his own closest relations must die eventually and in considering what then would be for the best. Greystones ought to come to him.

It was Grace, in a sense, who had condemned David himself to a suburban existence. The House of Hardie maintained premises not only in Pall Mall but also in Oxford's High Street. As the owner of a firm of such antiquity and prestige, he would only need to move to Oxford to become a big fish in a smaller pond of high-class trades, instead of representing merely one of many minor businesses in London. But he could not afford to buy a property on the scale of Greystones, and it would be unthinkable to live in the city in something unpretentious while his sister was lording it up on Shotover Hill.

Had she had a scrap of generosity or family feeling in her

114

body she would have invited him to bring his family to live in the house when he made the move from the law to the business. Goodness knows, there was room enough for them all. Common sense told David that the arrangement would never have worked and that Sheila would have been horrified at the idea of moving in with her mother-in-law. Nevertheless, the offer should have been made.

All these resentments could be borne as long as his sister remained a spinster, for even someone as eccentric as Grace would have recognized that a family home must stay in the family, and his own children were the only members of a younger generation of Hardies. But her marriage to Ellis Faraday had wrecked that last hope. Sooner or later the house would become the home of the Faradays and no longer of the Hardies. There was no chance that David or his children would ever inherit it. It was a disgraceful business.

How often it happens that a name which dominates the mind for reasons of either love or hate by coincidence forces itself on the attention in a quite different context. David had crossed Piccadilly by now and was walking up Cork Street when he stopped in his tracks by a poster displayed in the porch of a gallery.

GRACE HARDIE
Recent Work

Astonished, he stared through the plate glass window. In the centre of the display area were a few of the immense shapes with which Grace had been amusing herself for years: carvings full of holes and twists, not representing anything recognizable at all. One of them at least he had seen in the walled garden at Greystones, used as a perch by birds on their way to attack the fruit. Surely no one would want to buy something so misshapen!

There were smaller carvings on view as well, mounted on pillars or in cases, and these he had not seen before. Curiosity prompted him to push at the door, but it was locked. A private view party must only recently have ended, for the gallery staff were collecting wine glasses and bottles and packing them into boxes. There was no sign of Grace herself – but one of the gallery's occupants was familiar. Sitting at the reception desk and talking with animation into a telephone was Ellis Faraday.

TWO

Nothing could have persuaded Grace to attend her own private view. Only after much persuasion from Ellis had she agreed to hold a show at all. After experimenting with her shapes for so long without any thought of selling the finished works, she feared that both her enjoyment and her style might be affected if she began, even subconsciously, to take into account what a buyer might choose to own.

In the end she was persuaded that she had almost a duty to contribute publicly to the new movement in sculpture, in order that the tastes of art-lovers might gradually be educated. It was flattering, too, to think that she might be recognized as a sculptor and begin to establish a reputation. So Ellis had won that part of the argument. But the idea of being present to watch dozens of people sipping champagne as they glanced at her works and passed on without buying them – that was a form of rejection which she could not have endured.

Since Trish had become a member of the household supper was taken early, at six o'clock, allowing Grace time for an evening session of work if she chose. She was in the studio, twisting a ball of clay into miniature shapes, when her mother came to say that the telephone was ringing.

Mrs Hardie, approaching her seventieth year, was not at ease with the apparatus, which Ellis had installed when he first began to look for sitters in Oxford; but Grace had become familiar with its use many years earlier, when she worked in the High Street shop. Most of the calls made to Greystones were either for or from her husband, and this one was no exception.

'Such an exciting evening!' Whether because of the excitement or merely the distortion caused by distance, Ellis's voice emerged at a higher pitch than usual. 'I'm phoning from the gallery because I can't wait to tell you.'

'Tell away, then.' It must mean that the private view had been a success. If that were the case, the credit must go to Ellis, for the show represented the end of a three-year campaign on his part. He had first of all devoted weeks to photographing her early works, whose large scale needed landscaped grounds to show them off at their best. He lit them dramatically so that the strength of the design was emphasized by shadows, and sometimes used the holes which were Grace's speciality as frames for a secondary subject.

The book which resulted, following fast on his studies of Patrick Faraday's buildings, established a reputation for Ellis himself. He was no longer merely a society portraitist: his new work was recognized as a form of art in its own right. But the book also achieved exactly the effect he had intended for Grace, arousing curiosity about this woman whose name nobody knew and whose work nobody had seen but who was producing pieces of such extraordinary power and originality.

Many of the photographs from the book would be hanging on the gallery walls at this moment to illustrate what was too big to be moved. The little maquettes from which her garden sculptures had developed were on show as well, together with four of the major pieces themselves. But Ellis had encouraged her to carve smaller pieces which could be displayed inside private houses; and it was when she had a sufficient collection of these that he had used his London contacts to arrange this one-man show. In spite of her refusal to attend, Grace was as eager to hear what was happening as he was to tell.

'Well, someone bought the Figure of Eight within five minutes of the door opening. He made such a fuss about how he had to have it that it built up an atmosphere even before other people had got their first glass of champagne in their hands. You know, a kind of nervousness. Are they going to

118

miss their chance if they stop to think? I tell you, Grace, it felt as though the work were giving off electric shocks. And of course everyone wanted to know why you weren't here.'

'I hope you didn't confess that it's simply because I'm a coward.'

'No. I've been churning out a story about how you never come to London because you're working obsessively away in the country. There should be one or two stories in tomorrow's papers about this mysterious, reclusive genius.'

Grace was not at all sure that she wanted to feature in newspaper gossip columns, but Ellis gave her no time to protest before rushing on.

'So two of the large pieces and five of the smaller ones have gone already. That's terrific for the first evening, Grace. And so many people expressed interest in one of the maquettes – the Breaking Wave – in spite of being told that it wasn't for sale, that I've said you'll get a bronze made of it, in an edition of twelve. That's possible, isn't it?'

'Yes, I suppose so.' Grace's breath seemed to have been snatched away by the speed at which things were happening. Making a bronze involved foundry charges, so she had never considered the process before; but if the edition were to be subscribed before it was made, she would welcome the chance to explore the possibilities of a new material.

'And there's another thing.' Ellis had not finished yet. 'Oh, hold on a second.'

'What's the matter?' asked Grace, as the pause lengthened.

'Nothing. There was someone staring through the window as though he wanted to come in. Looked rather like your brother David.'

'I don't see David as an art-lover. And he's never been able to make sense of my shapes. Did you say that *two* of the large ones had gone?'

'Yes. The Second Pregnant Woman is the other one. Bought by a chap called Lawrence Ley. He's whatever doctors are called who deliver babies.'

'An obstetrician?'

'Yes. I knew I couldn't pronounce it. Rolling in money, I rather gather, and has his own clinic. Anyway, I'll give you a blow-by-blow account when I get back. Look after yourself, Mysterious Recluse.'

'Are you coming here tonight?'

'No. Going to an all-night party. 'Bye.'

A sense of mystery did indeed shroud Grace's mind as she replaced the receiver, but it had nothing to do with herself. London was the mystery. A city packed, it sometimes seemed from Ellis's account, with exciting people who spent their lives not merely painting pictures, making statues, writing books or symphonies or poems, but talking about them as well at an endless succession of glamorous parties. Grace had no wish to live their sort of life, but the thought of being recognized by them as one of themselves, in a remote way, was heady.

Her marriage to Ellis had grown into a partnership. Each of them lived an independent life and produced independent work, but each of them at the same time had gained from the stimulus provided by the other. Tonight was the first great test of the partnership, and it seemed that it was a success. Grace was in a cheerful mood when she went to bed that night.

In the early hours of the morning, however, she was awakened from a deep sleep. Trish was shaking her shoulder.

'What's the matter?' Grace asked sleepily – and then, suddenly alarmed, 'Is there a fire?'

'No. But someone wants to talk to you on the telephone. It kept ringing, so I went downstairs. I knew you wouldn't be able to hear.' Grace's bedroom in the tower was far away from the receiver on the ground floor, and it was surprising that even Trish had heard it.

'Who was it?' she asked anxiously. No one but Ellis would need to phone in the middle of the night, and Ellis would know better than anyone else how unlikely it was that the ring

120

would be heard. Unless he was drunk. Was that it, that he was drunk?

'He wouldn't say. He asked for you and then he asked who I was and I could hear him talking to someone else and the someone else said "She's only ten." So the first person told me to go and fetch you and said he'd ring again in five minutes.'

It must be a hospital. Ellis had had an accident. What other explanation could there be? Grace's feet groped for their bedroom slippers and she was already pulling on her dressing gown as she made her way down the stairs. She picked up the receiver as soon as the first ring was heard and waited impatiently while the connection was made.

'Grace? It's me. John.'

Grace had a nephew called John, David's elder son. But why should he need to get in touch with her? And he would call her Aunt. Besides, the voice was familiar, although not attached to that name. It was Jay, surely, who was speaking.

'John?' she queried.

'Come on, big sister, wake up. I know it's a terrible time to disturb you, and I'm sorry. This is your brother John Hardie speaking, and I need your help.'

Yes, it was certainly Jay. 'Where are you speaking from?' she asked.

'I'm in a police station in London. I was at a party last night and the police suddenly decided that they wanted to take the names and addresses of everyone there. I haven't got a passport because I've never been abroad, and I haven't got a driving licence because I don't drive, and Mother's still got my birth certificate as far as I know, so I need someone to confirm that I am who I say I am. In other words, that my name is John Hardie and that my permanent home is Greystones and that I work in London as a clerk. There's an officer breathing down my neck at this moment, and if you can make him happy I shall be able to get bail.'

'You mean that you've been arrested?' But Jay had already

121

handed over the telephone. It was a policeman who asked Grace to confirm what he had been told.

This was not too far from the truth. Although Jay was never called anything but Jay, he had been christened John Archibald Yates Hardie. And in a sense Greystones was his only permanent address, because in London he lived in rented flats which he gave up whenever he was touring. Why he should want to describe himself as a clerk rather than an actor was more mysterious, but in the periods when he was 'resting' he took any work he was offered, and perhaps this was one of these times. Grace gave the information for which she was asked.

After the call was over, she sent Trish back to bed but herself remained by the telephone. As she had expected, Jay rang her again as soon as he was free from supervision.

'Thanks for being so quick on the uptake, Grace. The thing is, it was a big raid, and the newspapers are going to have a field day with it. They're bound to pick out the names which are best known. If I'd said I was Jay Hardie, actor, my photograph would have been on every front page tomorrow. As it is, there are enough other well-known people to keep everyone happy. No one's likely to be interested in a provincial clerk.'

'I don't understand what's been going on, Jay? What sort of a raid are you talking about?'

Jay did not reply at once, and when he did it was with a weary voice, as though he had hoped to avoid an explanation.

'There are half a dozen pubs in London which have a certain reputation. The police know all about them. But they turn a blind eye, as long as everything's kept discreet. If someone makes a complaint, though, they have to move in. That seems to be what happened tonight. They came along and found eighty men on licensed premises but outside licensed hours, dancing to quiet music for which there'd never been a licence. That's all they've got me for, and there's no defence. I shall plead guilty and get off with a warning. They've got bigger fish in their net tonight, and the charge will be indecent behaviour.

The trouble is that in the public eye all of us will be tarred with the same brush. That's why I want to –'

'What do you mean by indecent behaviour?'

There was a long pause.

'It's not like you to be slow on the uptake, Grace. There was dancing in progress when the police arrived, and all the dancers were men. I'm too tired to start giving you a lecture on homosexuality and the law. Why don't you ask Ellis to spell it out for you?'

'Ellis?'

'Ellis was at the party as well,' said Jay. 'Listen, Grace, will you drop a kind of hint to Mother? I don't know quite how you can put it; but just in case a policeman turns up on the doorstep and starts asking questions about John Hardie, I wouldn't want her to say brightly, "Do you mean Jay?" Look, I've had the hell of a night. Thanks for being such a brick with the police. And I hope that Ellis was one of the ones who got away.'

He rang off before Grace had time to ask any more questions. She continued to sit near the telephone in case her husband should also need to contact her, but must have fallen asleep in the chair. What awakened her, at half past four in the morning, was not the ringing of the bell but Ellis's return in person. He was moving stealthily, doing his best not to disturb the household, and was startled when she appeared in front of him in pyjamas.

They stared at each other unhappily. This should have been a triumphant meeting, with the success of the exhibition to be described and enjoyed once more. But already that was forgotten.

'Jay phoned,' said Grace. 'Did the police catch you?'

Ellis nodded. For a moment he seemed too upset to speak, but then burst out in fury. 'It was David. It had to be David. Damn and blast him!'

'What do you mean?'

'He must have followed me from the gallery. Someone told

123

me, at the party, that a friend of mine had arrived and was asking where he could find me. I did think it was a bit odd, because we don't use our actual names much, as a rule, but I can't say I bothered about it. And then about twenty minutes later I was in one of the small rooms and he, David, opened the door. He just stared for a moment and shut the door again. The police told me that they'd had a tip-off, mentioning me by name. It must have been him.'

'Why should he want to do such a thing, to hurt you?'

Ellis shrugged his shoulders and turned away, pulling himself wearily up the stairs towards his bedroom.

'Don't know why, but he's certainly succeeded. This will finish me. When I come out of prison, no one will want to know me. Can you imagine that any duchess is going to trust her daughter and her ostrich feathers to a jailbird's studio?'

'Prison!'

'Well, I shall fight it, of course, but I can't see much hope. It seems to be me they're gunning for.' He sat down on the bed, burying his head in his hands.

Grace hesitated for a moment, but the question had to be asked. 'What did David see when he looked in at you?'

'What usually goes on at parties? Well, of course, you never go to them. At an ordinary sort of party, with men and girls, if a man cottons on to the fact that the bedrooms are available, he picks up the prettiest girl he can see and disappears with her for half an hour. Nothing illegal about that. Expected behaviour. But if a man glad-eyes another man instead, they can throw the book at you.'

Grace blinked, unable to visualize the scene. Even if her imagination had been adequate, she would not have been able to believe it. What could men *do* with each other? But she did not like to reveal her total ignorance by asking. There was another and more important question to put instead.

'When the police came, did they see – well, the same things as David?'

'God, no. Puts you off your stroke a bit, a peeping Tom.

Specially when it's your wife's brother. Anyway, Alan scarpered straightaway. I'd have been gone myself in another couple of minutes.'

'Alan?' Grace queried. Alan was the name of the young man who acted as servant of all work in Ellis's London flat.

'Yes. Don't bother to tell me we were crazy. I know that now. When we have the opportunity to be private any time we want! It was the party atmosphere, I suppose. Goes to your head. This is rotten for you, Grace, having to listen to all this.'

'You did warn me,' she said. It was her fault, not his, if she had not completely understood. Had this been an ordinary marriage, with a normal marital relationship, she might well have felt disgusted and betrayed. But because he had been honest she was able to consider the situation as though it had nothing to do with her. It was on his behalf that she was dismayed.

'The police can't actually prove anything, can they?' she suggested. 'Not unless David were to go into the witness box, at least, and I shouldn't think he'd enjoy doing that.'

'They haven't precisely got a photograph of indecent behaviour in progress, if that's what you mean. But everyone at the party, probably, was there for the same sort of reason, so they can take intention and opportunity for granted. That doesn't leave them with much to prove. Juries don't approve of people like me. The benefit of the doubt has a strictly one-way meaning. I've let you down badly, Grace. I'm sorry.'

'You haven't let me down at all. You spelled it out quite clearly, when you were offering to do me a favour.'

'But it's spoiled everything for you. On this night of all nights, which started as such a triumph for you.' He looked up at her with tears in his eyes. 'I'll do everything I can to keep you out of this. Thank God you decided to use your maiden name for the show. There's no need —'

But Grace had other ideas. She said nothing for the moment,

because it was a matter to be discussed with lawyers. But it seemed clear to her that what Ellis needed more than anything else was a wife.

THREE

Jay Hardie's appearance in the magistrates' court was the star role of his acting career. The use of the name by which he had been christened could not have protected him had his face been recognized by any of the court reporters who spent their working lives in this sordid theatre. But by a curious chance he had first made a name for himself in a West End revue in which he appeared every few minutes as a bearded eighty-year-old. So successful was this impersonation that he was regularly engaged to play old men's parts. Often he had complained laughingly to Grace of the waste of his youthful beauty: for in his twenties his thick fair hair, smooth complexion, and the long dark eyelashes which framed his expressive eyes, seemed to have been created for youthful *ingénu* roles. But any part was better than unemployment. He took what he was offered and devoted his considerable talent to making each of his elderly characters different from the others.

Today, in the role of a thirty-six-year-old, he was unrecognizable. A currently fashionable oil had darkened his hair at the same time as sleeking it down. He held himself stiffly and had managed to acquire a suit carefully chosen to suggest that it was the Sunday best of someone whose usual dress was shabbier. The same subtlety was applied to the change in his voice. Far from being a caricature of the way in which a lowly clerk might speak, it seemed to reveal the effort required by a man who was speaking well but not naturally.

The case proceeded briskly and without the need for any untruthfulness on Jay's part. He agreed that his name was John

Hardie. He managed to demote Greystones to the status of a semi-detached villa by giving it as an address Number 1, The Ridings. He claimed, accurately, to be unemployed. He agreed that he had been present on the occasion specified in the charge, but in mitigation pleaded the assumption that the owner of the premises would have applied for the necessary licences for music and an extension of drinking hours. He was one of a batch of twenty who had been spared a charge of indecent behaviour by their swiftness to agree that they would plead guilty to a lesser charge, and they were bustled through the court in no greater time than was necessary for each to be fined.

Ellis's case was different, for it was he who had been specifically named in the anonymous tip-off to the police. His case was dealt with as speedily as Jay's, but for a different reason: he was sent for trial by jury at a higher court.

Grace knew in advance that this was going to happen. It had already been agreed between the lawyers that the prosecution would present a summary of its case, but without calling witnesses at this stage; the defence, entering a plea of Not Guilty, would reserve its evidence. She had hoped, all the same, that some miracle would cause the case to be dismissed; and so strong was that hope that she had come to believe it. Over a sad, silent lunch with Ellis she was forced to accept the reality.

'Well,' he said at last, with a deliberate effort of cheerfulness. 'I have a choice. I can get out of the country, or I can stay and fight the case. We'll talk about it over the weekend. In the meantime, it will be weeks before anything happens. We mustn't spend the time moping. Business as usual, as much as we can manage. I've no doubt I shall find myself suffering from a mysterious rash of cancelled appointments for sittings. I must think of a new subject for a book of photographs to keep myself occupied.'

'Party Clothes,' said Grace.

'What?'

'Party Clothes. What people wear to different kinds of parties. You've already got some of the most formal examples in your portfolio. A group of débutantes in their white evening dresses for the Queen Charlotte Ball, for example, and in court dress for their presentations. You could contrast that with a street party in the East End. There are bound to be lots of those at Coronation time. And little middle-class girls in velvet dresses clutching a present for the hostess. Fancy Dress at the Chelsea Arts Ball. Christmas parties and Hallowe'en parties and Guy Fawkes Night parties – oh, and Hunt Balls, with everyone in kilts.'

'But – yes, I see what you mean, and there would be some good contrasts; but what makes you think of a subject like that at a time like this?'

'Don't you see, Ellis, that's why you were at this particular party. Not your sort of scene really. But you had your camera with you, to get a shot of men dancing together. In their party clothes.'

The idea had only occurred to her while she was actually in the process of explaining it, but its possibilities excited her. Until this moment neither she nor Ellis nor his lawyer had been able to think of any defence at all. This one might stretch belief, but it was better than nothing.

'If I was only accused of being on the premises, that might run,' said Ellis slowly. 'But David will give evidence for the prosecution, and I can hardly claim that I was just setting up a scene for the camera when he opened the door.'

'I shall deal with David.' Grace stood up, pushing back her chair. 'It's too late to wish that that anonymous telephone call had never been made. But when it comes to the giving of detailed evidence, I don't intend to let my brother send my husband into exile. Leave David to me.'

'I don't want to be the cause of a family quarrel.'

'Oh, it's a long time since David and I were friends. I never forgave him for murdering my pet cat when I was six. And there have been other quarrels since then. I don't propose to appeal to him on grounds of fraternal affection. But I can offer him a trade.'

She made her way at once to the premises in Pall Mall where The House of Hardie had its headquarters. Several times, when she was a little girl, her father had taken her there and told her about some of the famous men who had passed through its doorway over the years. There was a large artist's sketchbook beside the reception counter, she remembered, containing designs for personal wine labels. Many of these had been scribbled by the customers themselves, before being redrawn by a draughtsman. The artistic efforts of men whose fame lay in other fields – Victorian prime ministers, Hanoverian generals – must be worth a good deal of money. But David had never considered selling them at the time when he had pressed her so hard to let him use Greystones as security for a loan.

She was shown straight up to her brother's office. As David rose to his feet he smiled as though he were delighted to see her and had no idea that her visit could be anything but a friendly one: but his dark eyes were wary.

'I want to know why you're persecuting Ellis,' Grace said without preamble, refusing his invitation to sit down.

'I don't know what you mean.' But his smile faded. He understood very well what she was saying.

'You made a telephone call to tell the police about that party.'

'I absolutely deny –'

'Oh, shut up, David. Ellis and I both know it was you. You mentioned Ellis by name, to make sure that he wouldn't get away, whoever else did. And you're proposing to give evidence, aren't you, about what was going on.' The brief synopsis of the prosecution's case that morning had mentioned a witness. It seemed a reasonable guess that it would be David – perhaps inventing a reason why he had hoped to speak to Ellis – who would describe the scene he had interrupted.

He hesitated for only a few seconds longer before indirectly admitting her accusation.

'It's for your sake, Grace. If you'd seen . . . It was disgusting! To think that my sister should be married to a beast like that! I thought you ought to realize . . . You have grounds for divorce.'

'Have I ever said that I wanted a divorce? You believed it would make me happy, did you, to see my husband in court on a charge like this? Thank you very much indeed. My marriage is none of your business, David. My husband's behaviour is none of your business. It's too late to turn back the clock and persuade the police that they never knew about the party. But you are not going to stand up in court and name him as a – as a pervert.' She had learned a new vocabulary in recent days, but was not yet at ease in using the words.

'And exactly how do you propose to stop me?'

'You reminded me a few years ago, on the day of Tom's funeral, that I ought to make a will. I didn't take your advice then. But I'm telling you now that if my husband goes to prison I shall go straight to a lawyer and make Ellis joint owner of Greystones during my lifetime, and heir to my interest in it when I die. Is that what you want to happen?'

'You're crazy,' said David.

'I'm angry.'

'And you think that's enough to make me withdraw my accusation, knowing that you could still take the same action the day after he's acquitted?'

'No.' Grace sat down in the leather chair which her brother had originally offered her, prepared now to discuss the matter more calmly. 'I don't suppose you told the police that it was your own brother-in-law you were shopping. The relationship will come out if you go into the witness box at the jury trial, of course, because our lawyers will suggest malice as one of the possible reasons why you were at the party yourself. But presumably until now you've been claiming to have recognized him after a glimpse on some public occasion.'

She paused, but David made no comment. 'Well, you could tell the prosecution lawyers now that, after seeing Mr Faraday in court, you no longer feel sufficiently sure that he was one of the two men in the private room. I'm not asking you to say that it was someone else. But they can't force you to give evidence against your will. And in return I'll make you a promise: that Ellis will never own Greystones. That's all you want to know, isn't it? That's why you want me to divorce him. You don't care whether it makes me happy or unhappy. You just don't want him to get his hands on the house.'

David also sat down, taking his time to consider the proposal. 'You mean that you will now make a will?'

'Yes.'

'And you'll bequeath the property inside the family?'

'I'm telling you what I *won't* do, David, which is that I won't leave it to Ellis. I don't have to tell you what I *will* do. I could leave it to the Cats' Home if I chose!'

There was a sudden dramatic silence as she spoke the words. She had meant them only as a cliché: the ultimate threat of cantankerous old ladies. But as she – and undoubtedly David also – remembered how their childhood quarrel had begun with David's bow and arrow shooting of her beloved cat, the threat seemed dangerously appropriate. Since she had not intended it that way, she continued in a mollifying tone.

'Well, I'm not suggesting that as a real possibility. My family feeling is as strong as yours. All I meant in that sense was that I could make a will on one day which would suit you and change it the next day without telling you. I'm not prepared to tie my hands for the rest of my life. But I am prepared, as part of a bargain, to give an absolute promise that Ellis will not inherit Greystones from me.'

David needed a few minutes longer, tapping his fingers together as he weighed up the proposal.

'Even without my evidence, he may still be convicted,' he warned her.

Grace let out the breath she had been holding, realizing that she had won.

'Yes,' she agreed. 'But we shall be able to tell whether you've kept your side of the bargain. And if you do, I shall keep mine.'

She stood up and made her departure with dignity, neither smiling nor thanking him. But once she had left the premises and turned the corner towards St James's Square she was forced to stop for a moment while she waited for the tension of her mind and body to relax. Her life had not prepared her for such encounters, and she was trembling with the nervous effort.

Well, that was one obstacle surmounted, and the price she had paid for it was insignificant. Ellis loved Greystones almost as much as she did, because it had been his father's first major work; but one result of the unusual circumstances of their marriage was that neither of them expected to share the other's life – or possessions – completely. When she told him what she had done he would be grateful rather than upset.

The next obstacle, however, loomed larger. There was still the trial to be faced.

FOUR

Ellis and Jay took Grace shopping before the trial. Ellis paid for her clothes, but Jay chose them. He saw himself as the producer of what would be a brief but vitally important scene set in the witness box. The first requirement was that she should be suitably dressed.

'I mean to say, you can't turn up wearing those awful overalls.'

'Well, of course not!' protested Grace. Her mother, out of the windfall from the Beverley estate, had made her a present of an outfit which she thought eminently suitable for London, but Jay rejected it at sight as too matronly.

'You may be nearly forty but there's no need to look it. You've got a marvellous complexion, good legs, a trim figure. What we've got to find is something which gives two impressions at the same time. You're a respectable married woman, living quietly in the country, with the sort of conventional opinions which would make you chuck Ellis out on his ear if you really believed he was guilty of the charge. But at the same time you're a desirable, sexy kind of woman to whom any man would like to come home in the evenings.'

'Tall order!' Grace laughed, knowing that she was neither of these things.

'You're not to run yourself down,' said her brother severely. 'I know just the right place.'

The expedition took a whole morning. There were stockings and shoes to be bought, and gloves and a hat. Grace, who only on the very hottest days was prepared to protect her head with a wide-brimmed straw hat, tried to protest at this last item but was overruled. A hat was part of her respectable image, just as a touch of lipstick should be applied to emphasize the other side of her character.

On the question of lipstick Grace was adamant, knowing that the contrast with her exceptionally pale complexion would make her look like a tart; but in every other respect she obeyed Jay's instructions. Ellis's sombre expression as he paid each bill in turn had nothing to do with the cost of the exercise. He would have preferred not to involve Grace at all; but she was determined to help him.

When he had completed his task as wardrobe master, Jay set to work on her lines, suggesting not only the words but the expressions on her face as she spoke them.

'And there's one temptation to be resisted at all costs,' he told her. 'If you're asked whether you disapproved of your husband going to a party with no women present, do *not* reply brightly that if he were to be invited to dine at the Athenaeum there'd be no women present there either but you'd think none the worse of the occasion for that. You'd be surprised how often people on trial think that sort of thing is funny, without stopping to reflect that the judge is bound to be a member of the Athenaeum himself.'

'It would never have occurred to me,' said Grace. 'But now you've put it into my mind, I shall hardly be able to resist it.'

'You'd better try. Now then, stand up, look attentively at Counsel when he's asking you a question, but then turn your head and look the jury straight in their collective eye.'

He was doing his best to prepare her for every possible trap and opportunity, but this coaching did nothing, for her hope that the charge would be withdrawn if its chief witness withdrew his evidence was not fulfilled.

Without it, however, the prosecution case was greatly weakened, and this was recognized in the decision to try five men at the same time, presumably in the hope that if a charge of indecent behaviour could be made to stick against one of them, the others -- merely because they were on the premises at the same time -- would be tarred with the same brush. Each of the five had his own team of defence lawyers, so that the courtroom was crowded when Grace at last took the stand. For a moment she was bewildered. But then she saw Ellis, soberly dressed in a well-cut dark suit, and smiled at him. Jay had instructed her to give just such a smile, but she had forgotten the instructions: it came from the heart.

She was appearing as a character witness. The main strand of his defence had already been presented. He had adopted her suggestion of claiming to have been present on professional business -- realizing too late that this would earn him the fury of the other defendants by labelling them as members of the illegal community which he wished to photograph. Now it was time to establish him as a happily married man.

In consultation with the lawyers it had been decided that Grace would take a risk. Ellis's own counsel would do no more than elicit a statement that she loved her husband, knew that he loved her, and did not believe him to be guilty of the charge against him. Only under hostile cross-examination would she play her trump card. The risk was that she would be treated gently instead of being submitted to a hostile cross-examination; but the prosecuting counsel played into her hands.

'Did you know, Mrs Faraday, that your husband was proposing to attend a party on the evening in question?'

'Oh yes. He always telephones if he expects either to be late home or to be spending the night in London, and tells me where he's going.'

'How much did he tell you?'

'He talked about it in terms of the photographs he was hoping to take.' Grace, having made the decision to lie, was lying with conviction. 'I remember he was afraid that the light would be dim and the atmosphere smoky.'

'He didn't mention the fact that there would be no females at the party.'

136

'I don't really remember. I would probably have been pleased if he did. It would have been reassuring to know that he wasn't going to spend the evening surrounded by beautiful women. But I don't suppose he thought it important. I mean –' Grace could not resist this, in spite of Jay's warning – 'he belongs to a gentlemen's club in London and often has meals there. But he doesn't bother to tell me every time that he'll be dining with other photographers and artists and that they'll all be male.'

'How much time do you yourself spend in London, Mrs Faraday?'

'Very little. My husband's main studio is there, because it's convenient for most of his sitters; so he has to spend part of each week in the city.'

'Where he is attended, I believe, by a certain Alan Jenkins?'

'Is that supposed to be significant?'

'That's the question I'm putting to you, Mrs Faraday.'

'Mr Prescott, if my husband were looked after in my absence by a pretty young maid, would you immediately suggest to me that I had grounds for divorce? Well, perhaps you would. If you start with a presumption of guilt, no doubt everything appears suspicious. All I can say is that I believe it to be quite usual for a gentleman's gentleman to be employed in a pied-à-terre.'

'I'd be glad if you'd confine yourself to answering my questions, Mrs Faraday.'

'I'm sorry. What exactly is the question?'

'Why do you not live with your husband in London?'

'Because as well as our London flat we have a large house in the country. I very much prefer country life, and he is glad to be able to join me there for three days a week or more. Besides, I feel that the country is a much healthier place in which to bring up a child.'

'A child?'

'My stepdaughter, Patricia. My husband has been married before and she is the daughter of his first marriage – but I love

137

her as though she were my own. We have an extremely happy family life.'

'You have, however, no children of your own, I believe, Mrs Faraday.'

This was the moment which Jay had taught her to milk for its greatest effect. But just as she was not acting when she first smiled across the courtroom at Ellis, so also now the tears which came to her eyes were genuine and she had to bite her lip to prevent it from trembling before she spoke.

'We have no living child, no, but –'

'Would you raise your head, Mrs Faraday. I don't think the jury can hear you.'

Grace swallowed the lump in her throat and looked straight at the foreman of the jury.

'We did have a child, the year after we were married. Little Tom. But he died.'

It was ridiculous. She was crying. These were real tears which trickled down her cheeks as she groped hastily in the new handbag for a handkerchief. And yet she had never wanted to be a mother. It seemed that she had acquired the talent which Jay had enjoyed since babyhood – to cross not only the line at which lies or pretences became acting, but a second line, where an acted emotion became real. Pulling herself together, she looked from face to face in the jury box.

'As you can see, I'm not young any more. It wouldn't be wise . . . So my husband is all I have, and we love each other very much. He can't possibly be guilty of –'

'That's all, Mrs Faraday, thank you very much.'

She stepped down from the witness box. Now there was nothing to do but wait.

The waiting seemed interminable. In addition to the prosecuting counsel's final speech, each of the five defending counsel had his say. Then the judge gave his summing up. It was unbearably long, repeating everything which had been argued. But one remark was enough to bring the light of hope back into Grace's eyes.

'In the case of the defendant Ellis Faraday, who appears to enjoy a happy and settled family life and to be well-regarded in his profession, you may consider, members of the jury, that the reason put forward for his presence on the premises is lacking in good taste, but that does not necessarily mean that you should disbelieve it.'

She could not resist a glance at their own barrister at that point, and was rewarded by an almost imperceptible nod. It was going to be all right. Surely.

FIVE

'Not guilty!'

The jury's verdict made Grace feel faint – almost sick – with relief. Outside the courtroom she paced impatiently up and down as she waited for Ellis to thank his lawyers. When he appeared in the corridor at last, she was so happy that she rushed into his arms.

It was a curious moment. Husband and wife they might be, but it was very rare for them even to touch, and even rarer to embrace. As he held her tightly, Grace was amused to think that she had almost talked herself into the gesture by the emotional force with which she had given her less than truthful evidence. It was a happy coincidence that at that very moment one of the jurors in the case emerged from the courtroom. He looked at the couple, hesitated as though about to speak to them, but then smiled and passed on.

Ellis laughed at the incident and then, drawing away, began to thank Grace.

'You were marvellous. I can't begin to say . . .'

'Ssh! Someone might hear. Come on. Let's go home.'

Home was Greystones: but the return was not an easy one, for both relief and excitement had to be as tightly concealed as had been the earlier anxiety. No mention of Ellis's arrest and trial had been made to the other members of the family. So he and Grace waited until they were alone, late in the evening, before discussing the case further. Once again Ellis expressed his gratitude.

'All the same,' he began; and then stopped, shaking his head.

'All the same what?'

'No. It's no good. How can I ask another favour of you, a huge favour, when I'm so much in your debt already?'

'No harm in asking.' Grace poured another glass of Philip's home-made apple and raisin wine, which they had chosen for their celebration.

'I can't stay in England.'

This was not what she had expected. 'Why not?'

'Too many people know the truth. The police, to start with. They failed to prove their case this time, but that will make them all the keener to pin something on me in the future. They'll be watching – and I'm not likely to be given the benefit of the doubt twice. There'll be no shortage of people willing to inform on me. The whispering's begun already. Someone in the gallery who knows that Grace Hardie is Grace Faraday has started to spread gossip. No one will dare print it so soon after the case, because my acquittal means I could sue them for libel. But –'

'I'm not ashamed –' said Grace heatedly.

'But I am. I'm not having you involved. That really is only part of it, though. I can't face the thought of being continually under observation, and I can't change my way of life either. That means that I've got to live abroad. And you see –'

There was a long silence while he forced himself to continue.

'I don't like to say it. I know how much it must hurt you. But I still love Alan. I don't blame him for running. It made it easier for me, in fact. But the thought that I might never see him again . . .'

'Where did he go?'

'To Spain. He's gone to fight for the Republic. A lot of our friends are in the International Brigade already.'

'Ellis, you're not going to fight!'

'No. I haven't any military skills to offer. I've been invited to go out as a war photographer. It's an offer which might have tempted me in any case. I've come to realize how undemanding it is to photograph débutantes all day. Or Oxford graduates.

All the time now, as I move around, I can see pictures to be created on film. It must be the same with you, getting ideas for carvings.'

'That doesn't send me off to the middle of a civil war, though. So you're expecting to meet Alan again in the middle of a battle, are you?'

'I can't count on that, but I can find out which front he's on and try to get there. Besides, I'm going to need the money. The judge didn't allow me costs, so I've got all the lawyers' fees to pay. The paper has offered part of my salary in advance. And my life will be insured. If anything happens, Trish will be all right.'

'I was wondering when you were going to mention Trish.'

'Well, that's the thing, isn't it? The favour that I hardly dare to ask. She's so happy here, Grace. She loves you all, and the house, and her school. I know you've got no obligation towards her. But if you would let her stay . . . Well, you'd have come to my rescue twice. I'd never be able to thank you enough.'

It was Grace's turn to be silent, and she made a face as she stood up. This was not how she had expected the day to end.

'I'll sleep on it,' she said. 'If anything did happen to you, Ellis, the insurance might pay bills, but it would mean that she would be here, without you, until she grows up. I need to think whether that would be right for her as well as for us.'

'It would happen anyway, if you took her on. You can't think of it as a contingency which would arise only on my death. I can't see myself ever returning to live in England. Not unless the law is changed, and that doesn't seem likely.'

'But if you made a settled home abroad . . .'

'Until now she's been only a child. Not realizing. But I couldn't let her spend her adolescence in a household consisting of two men. One way or another I shall have to make an arrangement for her. This would be the perfect one, because you're her stepmother and she already thinks of Greystones as her home. There would be a reason – a good professional reason – for me to go away, and an equally good reason for her to stay here. I'd come back to see her, of course, as often as possible. She'd never need to doubt that I loved her. Whereas if she has to start again somewhere she's bound to wonder.'

'So really you're asking me to adopt her? At the same moment that you desert the two of us.'

'Oh God!' said Ellis. 'I'm sorry, Grace. What am I thinking of? Forget I mentioned it. It's too much, I see that now.'

'It may not be too much at all. I only want to get it absolutely clear. There'd be no point in my agreeing to a fifty per cent solution and only realizing later that you wanted a hundred per cent. I'll tell you in the morning.'

At the moment of making that remark she feared that she might be condemning herself to a sleepless night, but the decision proved to be a quick and easy one. If Tom had lived, Ellis would have been at her side during these past three years, helping her to come to terms with the baby's limitations. Now he was offering her, as a gift, a different kind of motherhood. Trish, lively and intelligent, was everything that Tom could never have been.

More pertinent still was the fact that they were mother and daughter already. It was in large part due to Mrs Hardie that the little girl had so quickly found her place in the family, but Grace too took her for granted there. If she were to leave, there would be a gap. Had Grace been asked a day earlier what her relationship was with Trish, she would have said that they were good friends. But in court that day she had claimed to love her stepdaughter, and now realized that the claim was true. Ellis was only asking her to recognize a situation which already existed. And Greystones needed a new generation growing up in it if it was to remain a living home.

That was settled, then. But there was still another matter to be considered.

David had kept his part of their bargain. It was time for her to make a will. The temptation was very strong to bequeath Greystones to Trish. How furious that would make her brother!

Well, that would not be fair. Yet she was certainly not going to appoint David himself, or one of his children, as her heir. He had claimed to be worried about the position of their mother and Philip if his sister were to die early. She could deal with that by leaving Greystones to them. Accidents apart, they were not likely to outlive her, but they would be safe if they did. And then she could make another will later on.

With a sigh of satisfaction she fell asleep. Over breakfast she told Ellis that she would be happy to bring up his daughter, and to adopt her legally if he thought that necessary. And in the afternoon she went down the hill to Oxford and instructed a lawyer to draw up a will.

PART TWO
Trish

1939

ONE

'I wish, I wish, I wish, and what I wish three times comes true.'

Trish looked challengingly across the breakfast table. Her father, home on holiday, responded as she expected. 'What do you wish?'

'I wish I could go to boarding school.'

'What makes you think you'd enjoy that, for heaven's sake?'

'The *Magnet!*' explained Grace, laughing. 'What she really wants is to go to Greyfriars with Bob Cherry and Harry Wharton and Billy Bunter.'

'Well, I know it would be girls, but –'

'A school is still a school,' said her father. 'Latin and French and arithmetic.'

'That would be only part of the day. They play games half the time, and there are midnight feasts and pillow fights and all that sort of thing.'

'What a lot literature has to answer for!'

Grace shook her head in pretended distress. 'She just wants to get away from me, that's all. She'll be telling you next what a terrible life she has with her harsh stepmother.'

'Grace, you know it's not like that at all.' Trish had been invited from the start to call Grace and Philip by their Christian names, but had only recently begun to do so. Aged thirteen, she was battling to be recognized as an adult. 'Think how much more I'd appreciate living at Greystones with you if I only came home for the holidays.'

'Have you any idea how much it would cost to send you to boarding school?' asked Ellis. 'Not just the fees, but the uniform and all the special kit you'd need for those games you were

147

talking about. If only that bomb in Barcelona had fallen a little bit closer to me you'd have come into all the insurance money and could be doing anything you wanted. I'd better go out and find another war.'

It was the wrong thing to say when war was so near – and would affect them all so much more directly. Trish knew that he had just signed a new contract with the newspaper which had sent him out to Spain. Already he had set to work photographing air raid precaution drills, the digging of trenches in Hyde Park and the sandbagging of government buildings. It was not likely to be long before British soldiers were in France; and Ellis with them. Both the adults fell silent and Trish flung herself into her father's arms.

'You know I wouldn't want . . . You're not to go away again.'

'I must, I'm afraid. But at least we'll have had our holiday.'

Since the ending of the war in Spain Ellis had been making a living as a roving press photographer based in France. His war photographs – especially those of the air raid in which he had been wounded – had caused such a stir that the paper had kept him on its foreign staff, paying a generous retainer with bonuses for whatever material he sent back to London. Between assignments he returned to Greystones for at least a week in the Christmas and Easter school holidays. In the summer holiday he spent longer in England, taking his daughter away for a fortnight, just the two of them. They had returned the previous day from a camping expedition in Wales.

'How would Greystones survive without you if you were away all term?' asked Grace, obviously thinking that even boarding school was a safer subject than war. 'We need our slave. At grape-picking time, for example.'

'Let's go and see how the grapes are coming on.' Ellis seized the excuse to leave the breakfast table. They had had the room to themselves, for since her seventieth birthday Mrs Hardie breakfasted in bed; and Philip, who still rose at five every morning, was already at work.

Today he was hoeing in the vineyard, which was gradually growing in size. Mrs Hardie had tried to persuade him to buy a large number of vines with the money from her legacy; but he had preferred to tackle the new venture more cautiously. Investing first in outside labour to prepare the hillside for planting, and a generous stock of stakes and wire and tools, he had ordered only a hundred vines of each of five varieties to test which best suited the soil and climate. The Brandt and the Riesling Sylvaner had both done well, so he used the eyes of the prunings to propagate new plants. This year more than a thousand vines were expected to bear fruit, and the number would quickly treble as the younger plants matured.

So far he had managed with only home-made equipment and simple routines, but very soon now it would be necessary to acquire bigger and better machinery. Andy, who inspected progress each year while visiting his mother, assured them all that the traditional method of treading the grapes with bare feet, which did not crush the pips, was far better than the use of any new-fangled machines; Trish and Grace and Jean-Paul joined happily in this ritual, not caring that their legs remained stained a dirty brown for several weeks. But a wooden press was needed to extract the juice from the must after the first fermentation, and the small one which had been adequate at first would soon have to be replaced. More and more barrels and bottles and corks were needed every year; and more and more time for stirring, testing, topping up, filtering, bottling and labelling.

All this was far too much for Philip and Jean-Paul alone – especially as they were kept busy at the same time with the pruning, tying in and hoeing, and must not allow the normal fruit and vegetable gardens to be neglected. Already it had proved necessary to engage seasonal help, and more would soon be needed. Then there was the problem of selling in quantity. None of the family had any taste for business, and Philip was becoming anxious because his experiment was succeeding too well.

Trish knew too that he was worried by more than merely the new vineyard, for Grace had confided in her. For more than a year now the nightmares which had plagued him for years after his experiences in the Great War had returned. The Munich agreement had afforded only a temporary relief. He was sure even then, as everyone in the country was now, that war was inevitable; and war, to Philip, meant mud and gas and pain and agony of mind. Trish did not completely understand why he should be so upset, since it seemed unlikely that anything violent would happen at Greystones, but she did her best to cheer up the atmosphere by the brightness of her voice whenever she spoke to him.

'How's it going?' she called as, in company with Ellis and Grace, she approached the long straight rows of vines. They had all been stopped four feet from the ground. The leaves were dark and glossy. The fruit was swollen with the rain of late spring, and beginning to ripen in a summer generous with sunshine.

Philip straightened himself, leaned on his hoe and nodded his head to signify that all was well. His companion, in the next row, was more forthcoming.

'I think we have a bumper crop. And of best quality. I tell Philip, this may be a vintage year.'

Andy's second son was twenty years old and after seven years in England could pride himself on an idiomatic vocabulary. He returned home each year to celebrate Christmas and New Year with his family, but had made it clear after the death of his grandmother a few months earlier that he wished to stay on in the lodge cottage. He was cheerful and hard-working and did a good deal to prevent Philip from succumbing too often to his black moods. But for the first time now it occurred to Trish that if – no, when – war came he might feel his place to be in France. No wonder Philip was anxious.

The sound of an approaching motor car made them all lift their heads in surprise.

'It must be Rupert,' said Trish, and it was not long before

150

her guess was proved right. Seeing the little group on the hillside, he stopped in the middle of the drive and walked across to join them.

'Good morning, everybody. Good morning, Patricia.'

'Aren't I part of everybody?' asked Trish.

'Certainly not,' said Rupert. 'You're special. I know this is an ungodly hour for a call, but I've come to bear you all off to Castlemere for lunch.'

Philip and Jean-Paul shook their heads politely, as he must have expected, but the others recognized a sense of urgency beneath his usual light tone of voice.

'Something wrong?' asked Grace as they walked together up towards the house.

'The state of the world's wrong.' Rupert sighed. 'I've volunteered, of course. All those years in the OTC about to bear fruit at last. The second son doing his traditional duty. For King and Country. Well, I'm not complaining about that. Not the life I'd chosen for myself, but it's got to be done. But this morning –'

He stood still. Trish could see that he was distressed.

'A letter arrived this morning. The agent brought it in to discuss the details. In the event of hostilities – and I imagine that we can take that for granted – a girls' school is to be evacuated from the south coast to Castlemere. There was a sort of portfolio attached to the letter. Somebody trying to be helpful, actually, but the effect is chilling. Fifteen trestle tables will be delivered tomorrow for erection in the banqueting hall. A hundred and fifty iron bedsteads, a hundred and fifty horsehair mattresses, fifteen rubber mattress protectors for bedwetters. That sort of thing, on and on. Iron bedsteads in the state bedrooms! They'll pin timetables into the panelling and carve their initials on the library reading tables and light fires to cook sausages in their dormitories. Odd, isn't it? The prospect of being killed as a soldier hasn't got through to me at all, but the thought of Castlemere being invaded . . .'

'Better children than soldiers,' said Ellis consolingly. 'They'll

151

have teachers and rules to keep them in order. If it became an army billet you'd find cigarette burns and beer stains all over the place.'

'Yes, well, that's obviously what my father thinks. He's been arranging this behind my back. Knew how much it would upset me, so kept quiet till it was settled. None of my business, strictly speaking, I suppose. He reckons it's better to have a negotiated arrangement, with provision for compensation, than to wait and see what some billeting officer comes up with. But in my opinion there's nothing more wickedly destructive than a child. Am I right, Patricia? Anyway, I'm not in the mood for being comforted. Castlemere was not created to be a boarding school.'

'*I* want to go to boarding school,' said Trish.

Rupert turned to grin at her, throwing off in a second the gloom which it was so unusual for him to reveal.

'That's the solution, then!' he exclaimed. 'We'll put Patricia in as the family spy. With instructions to prevent or report all unseemly behaviour. The other girls would lynch her eventually, of course, but the message might get through first. Except that, come to think of it, she's a defiler of walls herself.'

He was referring to the flower-arranging scullery; one of many small rooms in the kitchen wing. Mrs Hardie had given her a paint box three years earlier and taught her how to use it, discovering with delight that Trish had a natural talent for the use of colour, although too little patience to practise drawing.

She was not, however, interested in watercolour, which was Mrs Hardie's favourite medium, but preferred the bright pots of poster paint which were available at school. So for her next Christmas present she was supplied with a set of these to use at home, and offered a set of white painted walls to decorate to her own taste. As in the case of the clay models which she invariably destroyed when they were finished, her pleasure was only in the act of painting rather than in admiring the finished result; so she continually washed the wall or put on a new coat of white paint so that she could attempt another mural.

She was tempted now to grumble that nobody took her seriously, but was sensitive enough to recognize that Rupert was genuinely upset, and so held her peace.

'Two reasons why I've rushed over today,' he said. 'One, so that you can all have a last look, a last civilized meal, before the barbarians arrive. The other's more specific – a favour. I know you're on holiday, Ellis, but I wondered: I really would like to have a record of how the house looks now. The family's been living in it for hundreds of years and there are paintings of the outside, of course, but hardly anything of the interior. I suppose we all thought that nothing would ever change.'

'You want me to photograph the interior?'

'As much as there's time for. The sort of thing you did in your book on your father's buildings. I realize it's too big a job to do with any completeness, but just anything you could manage. The clutter will start to arrive tomorrow, but we can insist that it's stored in the coach house. The girls themselves won't turn up until war is actually declared. There could always be a miracle, I suppose, but –'

'I'll do what I can,' Ellis promised. 'I've got all my old equipment here. It was too slow and clumsy for a war assignment, but it's just what this kind of job would need. If Trish is willing to act as assistant . . .'

'We shall all assist,' Rupert promised. 'I shall lug tripods around and the maids will open and close curtains and ply you with drinks and Grace will clap her hands and say Well Done. We'll put you up, naturally, for as long as you're prepared to stay.'

'You and the others had better go on ahead, then. I'll need to load my van and then stop on the way to stock up with film and plates.'

'The bills to be sent to us, of course.' Rupert's moment of emotion had passed and he spoke in a businesslike manner. 'And we shall pay your usual fee for your time and a set of the prints. If you come anywhere near to making a complete record, we could discuss the possibility of a book. I've been doing a bit of work myself on the history of the family and the house. But I suspect that from now on we're all going to have to live a day at a time.'

The truth of that remark was proved as they returned to the house. Mrs Hardie, flustered and unhappy, came hurrying out to meet them.

'Grace, there's a woman here to see you. I don't know what she wants. She keeps trying to make me agree to something, but I said she'd have to talk to you.'

'Yes, all right, Mother. I'll see to her in a minute. Trish, you go and pack some things so that you can stay on at Castlemere and help your father. Rupert, will you explain to Mother what you've just told us, and ask whether she wants to come this time.' Until now Mrs Hardie had steadfastly refused every invitation to return to the house which she remembered with such love from her childhood, but the prospect of change in the near future might make her grasp at a last opportunity. 'And Rupert, if this visitor ties me up for too long, you and Trish could go without me. You could start making a list of the photographs you'd like, in an order of priority. I'll come in the van.'

She hurried into the morning room. A tall, thin woman whose mouth turned down sourly at both corners stood up to greet her.

'Mrs Faraday? My name is Miss Hoare. I'm the billeting officer.'

TWO

'I *know* it's a big house.' After half an hour Grace was still arguing with the billeting officer. 'But not all of it is habitable.' Although the roof had been repaired recently after years of neglect, most of the attic rooms remained damp and musty.

'You said there were seven bedrooms on the first floor.'

'And five people living in the house. Besides that, I have a widowed aunt in her seventies who visits frequently and will come to live here permanently if things get more difficult. She knows that there's a room reserved for her.'

'Of the five people, you and your husband presumably share one of the bedrooms?'

Grace was tempted to say what she thought of such an impertinent question, but managed to control herself.

'No, we don't,' she replied shortly.

'Even so, we've established that you have one free bedroom, extra to your aunt's.' Miss Hoare spoke in a businesslike tone. Presumably she had a conversation very much like this one in every house she visited. 'It will be large enough, I imagine, to take two children.' She paused and looked Grace straight in the eye. 'We're not using compulsory powers yet, Mrs Faraday. Obviously these arrangements will work best when they're accepted willingly. But I hope you'll consider very seriously where your patriotic duty lies. You could offer two children safety and fresh air and care. Could you live with your conscience if they stayed in their slum homes and were killed in an air raid?'

Grace was tempted to remark that she would never know. But the first shock of the unexpected visit had been succeeded by a different kind of gloom. Over the past few days she had come to recognize the inevitability of war, but it seemed that she had not yet come to terms with its pettier consequences. No one would require her to die heroically in battle. But she could hardly expect her way of life to continue unchanged. They would all have to accept inconveniences. The arrival of two unwelcome young strangers would be only the beginning.

The ringing of the telephone gave her an opportunity to postpone any decision for a few moments.

'Excuse me,' she said, and picked up the receiver.

'Is that Miss Grace Hardie?'

'Yes, speaking.'

'You won't know my name, Miss Hardie. Lawrence Ley. But –'

'Oh yes, I do remember it. You bought one of my carvings from the 1936 show.' Ellis had been meticulous in keeping a register of purchasers, so that if he or anyone else decided at a later date to make a photographic record of all Grace's works in their new homes, they could be easily traced.

'That's right. The Second Pregnant Woman, it was called.'

'It's my husband who gives the work titles, for the sake of the catalogues. I just carve what I'm feeling without intending to represent anything. I hope you've been happy with it.'

'Absolutely delighted. And so are all my mothers.' It was a curious phrase, until she remembered that Dr Ley was an obstetrician. 'It's become a kind of superstition with them. I only found out recently. They stroke the statue when they first arrive at the clinic, and then everything will go smoothly.'

Grace laughed at the thought. She was aware of the billeting officer looking at her watch, but saw no reason to cut a pleasant conversation short for the sake of a less enjoyable one.

'I'll come straight to the point, Miss Hardie. I'm just about to open another clinic. In the country, so that the mothers can have their babies in complete safety and calm. I was wondering whether to move the statue. And then the thought suddenly occurred to me. If mine is called Second Pregnant

156

Woman, does that mean that somewhere there's a First Pregnant Woman, and if so, might it be for sale?'

'Give me a second to think about that question.'

It was a painful thought. Out in the grounds at this moment was a large stone figure which Grace had carved when she herself was pregnant. Although she had intended it to convey only her feeling of being swollen, heavy and lethargic, it had proved, unusually in her work, to be a representation of a human figure; a woman expecting a baby. As she first of all smoothed its curves with her tools and then ran her hands over the surface, she had used it – successfully – to come to terms with her impending but originally unwelcome motherhood.

So baby Tom had been born into love, as he deserved. But after his death she had banished from her sight the carving which would remind her only that the pregnancy had been a period of wasted time, to be forgotten as soon as possible.

Later, as a different kind of therapy, she had used the same shape as a starting point for a carving which produced a completely different effect. While paring down the heaviness of the body, she had also cut out of it a hole in the shape of a foetus. It was possible to look right through the hole when standing at the side of the statue, and the effect was to give this version a positive, tense strength which had been absent from the original. This was the version now owned by Dr Ley. Looking at the two carvings side by side when the exhibition was being planned, she had decided that no one would ever want to buy the first. But it still held unhappy memories for her: she would be glad if it were to go.

'The answer to both your questions is Yes,' she said. 'Considered as a work of art, the First Pregnant Woman isn't as good as the Second, in my opinion. But for your particular purpose, it might actually be better. It's not in showroom condition, I ought to say. It's been out in the open for five or six years, so of course it's weathered.'

'All the better. An instant antique. May I come and look at it?'

'Yes, of course. I wonder whether you'd be kind enough to telephone me again in a few days' time to make an appointment. I have someone with me at the moment, and I'm just about to go out to help my husband with a commission; altogether things are a little unsettled.'

'Of course. I'll be in touch, then. Thank you very much.'

For a moment after she had put down the telephone Grace did not move. Suppose she were to sell three large pieces each year, instead of holding them back in preparation for another one-woman show. Would that cover the cost of sending Trish to boarding school? But how would it be possible to get on with her work if there were strange children to be looked after?

It was time to return her attention to Miss Hoare.

'I'm sorry to have kept you waiting. But you must understand – that call was an example of it – that I have my own occupation. I don't suppose that's true of many of the married women you call on. Seeing a big house like this, you probably think that its owner spends her time picking roses or doing embroidery. Well, that's not true here. I work for at least six hours a day. That means six hours in which I can't be disturbed. And as well as that there are the hens and animals and the vegetable garden and the house to be looked after.'

There was a second interruption as Trish opened the door and waited politely until both heads turned towards her.

'Rupert and I are ready to leave now,' she said. 'Grandmother's not coming. Shall we wait for you?'

Although the billeting officer could not have realized it, this second interruption worked to her advantage. Rupert, that most unmilitary young man, was reconciled to becoming a soldier. How selfish it was, Grace told herself now, even to hesitate when her own duty was put before her so clearly. And at least she would be able to continue living in her own home. Rupert would have to endure the thought of Castlemere being desecrated in his absence.

'No. I'll follow on with Ellis,' she said. For a moment after

Trish had left she remained silent. Then, sighing, she made up her mind.

'All right, then, Miss Hoare. I'll take two children as long as they're of an age to look after themselves. They must be over eleven. I don't know where they'll go to school but it's bound to be a long walk from here, and no one in the household will be free to take them every day. Besides, I don't know anything about bringing up young children.'

'Your daughter must have been young once.'

'She's my stepdaughter. I had nothing to do with her in her infancy. I can only accept older children.'

'I'm afraid I can't promise that. It's an elementary school that's been allocated to this area. We've found classroom premises for them in Headington Quarry.' The billeting officer considered for a moment. 'Would you be prepared to take a mother as well, Mrs Faraday? Most people don't fancy the idea of having a stranger in their kitchen, and in a small house that's understandable. But in a place like this, you could probably make arrangements for them to have their own cooking facilities. It would mean a woman with a small child, and probably two other older children as well. But although there'd be more of them, they'd probably keep out of your way better.'

'I'll think about it.'

'Let me know then.' The woman stood up. 'For the moment I'll put you down for two, as old as possible.' For the first time in the interview, she smiled. 'I know I'm not the most popular visitor in the county at the moment, Mrs Faraday. But just imagine . . . The London docks are bound to be a target when the war starts, and not every bomb will hit the bull's-eye. Just imagine the effect if one demolishes a school in the East End, or a street in which children play. We have to get them away. And although you may feel it's going to be an upheaval for you, think how it will seem to the children! They won't understand why they're being taken away from their mothers and brought to a strange place. I can only make the

159

arrangements. We have to rely on people like you to provide a genuine welcome.'

It seemed ironic to Grace, who had decided twenty years earlier that she did not want to have children of her own, that at the age of forty-two she should now be expected to love someone else's. But she had managed it with Trish; and all her doubts were selfish ones. Greystones, she reminded herself, had been designed as a family house, the home of six children. She could not reasonably argue that it was unsuitable. In the next few days there was bound to be a good deal of talk about patriotic duty and this, without doubt, was hers. As they shook hands in parting, she managed to smile back.

'I'll do my best,' she promised.

THREE

'Grace! Grace, where are you? It's time we went.'

It was half past two on Friday, 1 September 1939, and all hostesses had been requested to collect their evacuees from the village hall before three o'clock. Trish had harnessed Brown Bess to the pony cart in case the family allotted to them had too much luggage to carry. But Grace, who was supposed to join her outside the stable yard, had not appeared.

Perhaps she had gone to her studio, meaning to do only some small job but quickly becoming absorbed and oblivious of the passage of time: that was something which frequently happened. Trish went inside the house and began to search it, calling her stepmother's name as she opened each door. Only after the third summons did Grace come running down the stairs, her face creased with worry.

'Hush, dear. Don't shout. Philip's not well.'

'Oh, sorry. I didn't know. What's wrong?'

'That stupid man who came this morning. Making us all put our gas masks on to show that we knew how to do it! Just the sight of the mask is enough to remind Philip of that awful day . . . I found it claustrophobic enough myself. And trying to breathe through it with lungs as badly damaged as his . . . He's collapsed in his bedroom and I can't get him to open his eyes. It frightens me, to see him so upset and struggling for breath. I've sent for the doctor. You'd better go down to the hall, Trish, so that they know we haven't simply forgotten. But explain that it's impossible . . . An invalid in the house . . . I can't possibly take responsibility for a family of strangers under these circumstances.'

'But then they won't have anywhere to go.'

'There must be someone else who could take them.' Grace sat down on one of the lower stairs and buried her head in her hands for a moment. After a little while she looked up again, sighing, and held out her hand to pull Trish down beside her.

'I know you think that all of us are being too gloomy about this. And not wanting to pull our weight. It's because it's the second time, you see. Philip is remembering how terrible it was to be fighting, and Mother and I are remembering how terrible it was to wait at home, wondering. The days when the telegrams came . . . People we loved, dead or wounded.' Trish could see that there were tears in her eyes. 'But at least, when it was all over, we thought it was finished for ever. The war to end wars, that's what they said. And now . . .'

'Ellis believes that it's going to be like Barcelona, but worse.' Trish's reason for mentioning her father's graphic description of the air raid in which so many civilians had died and he himself had been injured was not to increase her stepmother's gloom but to remind her of the reason for the present upheaval in the household. 'No one's likely to drop a bomb on a hill in the middle of Oxfordshire. But the family we're supposed to be taking will have come from somewhere near the docks. If they have to go back there and a bomb drops tonight, it will be all our fault.'

'We're not actually at war yet. Nothing will happen tonight.'

'All the same – to send them back home when they'll have to make the journey all over again to another billet is a bit mean, isn't it? Mrs Barrett and I will settle them in. And then we'll make sure that they keep to their own rooms.'

Mrs Barrett, who had joined the Hardies as a housekeeper, did not see it as part of her duties to wait on a family of evacuees, but she had willingly co-operated in the task of converting a scullery into a separate kitchen for them and the old servants' hall into their sitting room.

'Well, do what you think best. For a day or two I suppose

we can manage, to give Miss Hoare time to find somewhere else. But tell her today that it can be only temporary.'

Trish hurried away, anxious not to be late. Flicking the reins to start Brown Bess on her way down the hill, she considered with approval that phrase 'Do what you think best'.

Ever since her thirteenth birthday ten weeks earlier she had been considering how to make it clear that she was an adult member of the family now. The problem was that in a sense she had always been treated as an adult. Her lack of a mother meant that Ellis had never talked over her head in the usual grown-up manner, but even when she was quite small had discussed everything seriously with her and asked her opinion.

As for Grace, she had made it clear from the beginning that she knew nothing about children and found it easier to welcome her stepdaughter into the household on more or less equal terms. True, in the studio their relationship was one of teacher and pupil, but that was a matter of skill rather than age. True again, Grace was willing to play games – either seriously in front of the fire, or dashing about high-spiritedly in the open air; but these were occasions on which she seemed to become a child herself rather than condescending to someone who happened to be nearly thirty years her junior.

So there were no great issues on which to take a stand: no grounds for rebellion. On the day after her birthday Trish had taken a book into the drawing room, determined to share in the after-supper conversation of the adults instead of retreating to the desk in her bedroom to do her homework – only to find herself alone there, with the others having returned to their separate pursuits. Nobody ever told her that she must go to bed at a certain time, or stop reading and turn out the light. There was no question of anyone having to force her to eat up her meals, because they were always delicious. She was expected to do her share of work in the house and garden, but that in itself was a kind of recognition that she was strong enough and sensible enough to be useful.

Even Rupert, who was twelve years older than she was,

treated her almost as though she were a lady. When he called her by her full name or held doors open for her or asked her opinion on some question to do with Castlemere his voice was often teasing, but it was possible to hope that the teasing was itself a tease and that really he was behaving towards her as he thought she deserved.

Perhaps that was wishful thinking. Rupert was the most handsome man she had ever known, and the best companion, except for her father. All the other girls at school had pashes on one of the prefects or teachers, but Trish was in love with Rupert. No doubt that was just a pash as well: but whatever it was, it was powerful enough to make her blush and feel hot all over whenever he said something nice to her without putting the tease in his voice. But he was twenty-five. How could she expect him to wait for another four or five years without falling in love and getting married to someone else? And yet it did sometimes seem that he smiled at her as though she were seventeen already.

The only person who had ever treated her as a little girl when she *was* a little girl was Mrs Hardie, who found it easier than Grace to kiss and cuddle. But it had been Mrs Hardie who several months before her thirteenth birthday had told her that very soon now she would find that she was old enough to start having babies, although of course she mustn't dream of doing so for a long time yet and until she was married. And when, not long afterwards, the first sign of adulthood arrived, it was Mrs Hardie who showed her, as woman to woman, how to cope with it. So even to her step-grandmother she was not a child any longer.

Grace had told her to do what she thought best. It was a message of trust, which must be taken seriously. And as Brown Bess turned out of the lodge gates and into The Riding, Trish came to the first truly adult decision of her life.

She had asked to go to boarding school. For all the wrong reasons, because she thought it would be fun. She knew that the request had been taken seriously, because when her father returned from photographing Castlemere, she had heard Grace telling him about the man who wanted to buy her Pregnant Woman statue. It had not occurred to Trish that she ought not to be eavesdropping – because she knew about the statue already – until her stepmother had gone on to say that she thought boarding school fees could be afforded if they were really wanted. And someone must have written off or made enquiries amongst friends, for the past week had seen the arrival of three large envelopes which were carried away from the breakfast table unopened.

It would not be fair to bring a family of evacuees back to Greystones and then disappear somewhere else herself. It was not at all clear to Trish what the war was going to mean, but if her father was going to be in France and if Philip was going to be ill and Grace and Mrs Hardie both worried, then she must stay at home to help. And perhaps after all she had not really wanted to go, but only to find out whether her wish would be properly considered or merely brushed aside.

This train of thought carried her to the hall, which was crowded with villagers and the children they had come to collect. Miss Hoare stood in the middle of the crush, clutching a sheaf of papers as she called out names and marked them off.

Trish made her way through the crowd to announce her arrival and be given her family; but another woman claimed Miss Hoare's attention first.

'I can't be doing with this,' she said indignantly. 'Saving a little English kiddie from Hitler's bombs, that's one thing, but taking a nigger into my own home, that's quite another.'

'Not so loud,' said Miss Hoare, flustered. 'They'll hear you.'

'He knows what he is. I'll take one of them like I promised. The white one. But not the other.'

'They're brothers.' Miss Hoare spoke more firmly. 'It would be quite wrong to separate them.'

'Brothers! If those two are brothers, all I can say is that their mother's no better than she ought to be.'

'That may be so, but it's not the children's fault. Please keep your voice down, Mrs Goodwin.'

Trish looked with interest at the two boys who were the subject of this discussion, and who had certainly heard every word of it. It was true that nobody would take them for brothers. They were identically dressed, wearing long mackintoshes, with their gas masks, in cardboard boxes, slung across their chests by string. But the elder of the two was thin and sharp-featured. Beneath his straight brown hair, his face was long and unhealthily pale. The six-year-old who stood beside him, clutching his hand anxiously, was stockily built, with black curly hair. It was not fair, thought Trish, to call him a nigger, but it could not be denied that his skin was khaki. At any moment, she could tell, he was going to burst into tears.

There was no time to feel sorry for him, though, for Miss Hoare, looking round for some escape from the indignant Mrs Goodwin, had caught her eye. Trish announced her name and address and was led to the end of the hall, where two women in green uniforms were pouring cups of tea for the Londoners.

'Here you are. The family for Greystones. Mrs Jackson and Jimmy and Florrie.'

A stout woman with a runny-nosed two-year-old on her knee set down her cup and looked Trish up and down.

'About bleeding time,' she said.

Trish, who had intended to say something welcoming, was taken aback and had to make an effort to be polite.

'Can I carry some of your luggage?' she asked.

Mrs Jackson pointed at two brown carrier bags.

'Is that all?' said Trish.

'What d'you expect? Couple of bleeding cabin trunks?' She began to lead the way out of the hall. Bending to pick up the bags as they passed, Trish became aware of a strong smell. She looked at the billeting officer in dismay.

'It'll be all right,' said Miss Hoare hastily. 'It's bound to be an upheaval on both sides, but –'

'They smell,' said Trish.

166

'Yes, I know, dear, but – Look, if you take young children out of their homes at half past six in the morning and move them half way across London and then put them on a train with no corridor there are bound to be one or two accidents.'

'It's her more than them.'

'Just do your best to be sympathetic for the first day or two, there's a good girl, and I'm sure you'll settle down nicely together. Tell your mother –'

'My mother's got sickness in the house,' said Trish. She had not meant to pass on the warning that any arrangement must be considered only temporary, but was realizing fast that Grace had seen the snags of the proposed arrangement better than she had. 'She'll be wanting a word with you in a day or two. But she didn't want to let you down now.'

She turned to hurry after the Jacksons, who were standing outside and looking up and down the village street in bewilderment.

'Where are the bleeding shops?' demanded Mrs Jackson.

'The village shop's just round the corner there.'

'Proper shops, I mean. Woolies, that sort of thing. And the cinema. Where's that?'

'In Oxford.'

'That where we got off the train? That's miles away.'

'That makes it more of a treat. Here we are.' She smiled at the two children in as friendly a way as she could manage. 'Would you like to pat the pony on her nose? She's called Brown Bess.'

The little boy backed away nervously, whilst Florrie buried her face in her mother's skirt. As for Mrs Jackson, she was silenced for a moment by incredulity.

'You're expecting us to ride in a bleeding cart!' she exclaimed at last.

'You don't have to,' said Trish. 'I brought it to carry your luggage and because I thought the children might like it. It's got proper seats. But you can walk if you'd rather.'

'Aren't there any buses?'

167

'Not from the village to our house, no.'

With much effort and complaint the family was loaded aboard. More slowly than on the outward journey, Brown Bess began to plod uphill. As they turned in through the lodge gates, Trish pointed proudly. 'That's Greystones.'

The reaction was not what she had hoped for.

'My Gawd! Miles from anywhere! What am I expected to do with myself all day in a place like that?'

'Well, I suppose the same as you'd do anywhere, looking after children,' said Trish, her patience wearing thin. 'Cooking and cleaning and washing and mending, that sort of thing. You can help in the garden if you want to.' She realized the unlikelihood of this. 'But even if you don't, we'll give you fresh vegetables every day.'

'Jimmy won't eat no greens. Where's the chip shop?'

'I don't know. We grow all our own potatoes. They're much nicer than anything from a shop.'

'I'm not stopping here,' said Mrs Jackson. 'Turn this thing round and take me back.'

'But you can't –'

'I can do what I bloody well like. I'd rather take my chance with Mr Hitler than be buried alive out here. Get us back there while there's still time to get on a train.'

Just for a moment Trish hesitated. But Grace would be relieved and Miss Hoare would not care as long as she was not expected to find another billet for the family. 'Come on then, Bess,' she said, and pulled on the rein to turn round.

'It wasn't our fault,' she said to Miss Hoare twenty minutes later. 'We'd gone to ever such a lot of trouble. Making them a kitchen and somewhere to sit. And we were going to have a lovely supper. We killed a chicken specially, because we knew she wouldn't want to start cooking straight after arriving. But all they want to eat is chips.'

'Don't worry, dear. I'm sure you did your best. There's another one the same. It's difficult when they're not used to country ways. Go home and thank your mother very much for offering. I might have to call on her again, mind you. But –'

'What's happening to those two?' interrupted Trish. She pointed across the hall. By now all the unaccompanied children had been taken away except for the boys whom she had heard being rejected an hour earlier. Side by side they were sitting on a bench, the picture of dejection. The younger boy was slumped in exhaustion; his brother, silently, was crying.

'I'll have to take them home with me until I can find somewhere else. I couldn't persuade Mrs Goodwin to change her mind and keep her promise. I've walked them all the way up the High Street knocking on doors, in the hope that someone would take pity on them. The little one's too tired to walk any further. It's going to be a problem, but –'

'We'll take them,' said Trish.

Startled, the billeting officer turned to stare at her. At first her expression was one of relief, but then she shook her head regretfully.

'It's a different sort of arrangement, dear. They're on their own. It would mean looking after them. I know your mother was willing to provide accommodation, but I don't think –'

'When I tell her what she's been spared! That foul-mouthed smelly woman! She'll be glad. Well, anyway, it would be better than you having to walk them round the streets while you look for somewhere. If you find another place you can come up and tell them that someone else wants them. But it must have been horrid for them, hearing everyone say No.'

Without waiting for any further comment she walked across to the two boys.

'Hello,' she said. 'My name's Trish Faraday. Would you like to come and live in my house?'

Smiling, she put out a hand to be shaken. The younger boy, who had been half asleep, leapt to his feet and began to pummel her stomach with his small fists.

'Hoy, steady on, you young boxer!' she exclaimed. 'I was only trying to shake hands.'

169

'He thought you was going to 'it 'im,' explained his brother anxiously. 'Didn't 'urt you, did he?'

'No. What's your name?'

'I'm Dan. He's Brian.'

'I shall call him Boxer. Would you like a ride in a pony and cart?'

'He's awful tired,' said Dan anxiously.

'It's just outside.' Trish bent down and picked the little boy up. He was heavier than he looked, and she staggered for a moment before settling his legs round her waist. 'All right?' She rubbed his cheek with her knuckles in a friendly way and felt his face burrowing into her neck.

Miss Hoare came hurrying over to help.

'They've got some clothes here. Their mother's really made an effort. Pyjamas, even. But are you quite sure, dear, that your mother –'

'She told me to do whatever I thought was best,' said Trish. She had made her second grown-up decision of the day.

FOUR

'Where's that Boxer hiding, then? I'll give him such a boxing if ever I find him.'

The little boy, waiting to be found, hugged himself in pleasure as Trish circled the kitchen, growling like a tiger.

'Got you!' She pounced, pulling him out from underneath the table and embarking on the mock sparring routine with which every encounter between the two now began. 'Come on. Time to pick the sprouts for Christmas Day.'

'Don't like sprouts.'

Trish had known he would say that. Sprouting was a cold job on a frosty day, and he was too young to be allowed a knife. 'It's either picking sprouts or reading.'

'Reading, then.' He pretended not to enjoy his reading lessons with her any more than he liked being made to go out in the garden in winter, but she felt sure that secretly he wanted to catch up with the other children in his class. Trish herself, who had been a fluent reader before she was four, had been shocked to discover soon after the arrival of the two evacuees that the six-year-old could not even read his own name.

So in the old scullery which was now called Trish's Painting Room she and Dan had cut out little squares of cardboard and written a letter of the alphabet on each. To make a game of it, she painted bright pictures on scraps of paper. Boxer had to recognize what the picture was supposed to be, find the letters to spell the word and arrange them under the picture. The next day Trish took the picture away and he had to recognize just the word. It might not be the most professional

171

way of teaching someone to read, but they both enjoyed it.

They were in the middle of the game when Trish heard footsteps approaching, walking round the side of the house. She lifted her head, listening, and Boxer did the same. A young man in army uniform appeared and paused by the window, staring in. For a moment Trish was alarmed, but the little boy by her side began to bounce up and down in delight.

'Terry! Terry! Where's Dan, Trish? Dan, Terry's here, Terry's here!'

Dropping his handful of cardboard letters, he dashed towards the kitchen door. Trish followed more slowly and found him being tossed up into the air by the unexpected visitor.

'Go and tell Dan I'm here,' said the soldier, putting him down at last and watching him run off. He turned towards Trish. 'Didn't startle you, I hope. I'm Terry Travis. Dan and Brian's brother.'

'Brian? Oh yes, of course. I call him Boxer. Just as a joke, but he seems to like it.' She stared at him in a considering way. 'You don't look like their brother.'

He was a tall, thin young man – as Dan might perhaps be one day. But Dan's thinness, even after three months of good food, was of the skinny sort, whilst the soldier seemed to conceal a muscular strength inside his greatcoat. The real difference, though, was in his eyes.

Neither Dan nor Boxer was clever. They were not even curious about what things were or how things worked. Their first reaction when offered something new was always to say No. Trish herself was not clever in the sense of coming top in examinations at school, but she was always ready to be interested in a new subject or skill. She asked questions and listened to the answers; and she liked talking to people with lively ideas. She looked for this quality in their eyes – and Terry Travis's grey eyes were as alert as her own. As they shook hands she took an immediate liking to him. She had made friends with Dan and Boxer because she was sorry for them. Their brother was different.

172

Even his voice was different. Boxer and Dan dropped their aitches and swallowed the middle of words in a way which at first she had found hard to follow. Even now, it made it difficult to teach Boxer how to read words like hat and butter when he always pronounced them 'at' and 'bu-er'. But this young man had at some point made an effort to practise a more precise way of speaking. He answered her point in a straightforward way.

'Should have said half-brother. Same mother, different fathers. Me dad died when I was six. It knocked me mum to pieces in all sorts of ways. Money was one way, and wanting to have a man around was another. I didn't like it when I was a kid, but I can understand it now.'

Trish, who had had a woman-to-woman chat on the subject with Mrs Hardie soon after the arrival of the evacuees, nodded in a grown-up manner. 'Do come in, Mr Travis.'

'Terry,' he reminded her, stepping inside.

'Terry, yes. I'm Trish Faraday. I'm afraid there's no one around but me at the moment. My uncle's ill and my grandmother's gone to visit him at the infirmary and my mother's not to be disturbed while she's working. But there'll be plenty to eat for lunch, so I hope you'll stay.'

'Thanks. And look, before the nippers come back. When Mum came to see them a couple of months ago, Dan told her how it was you who brought them here when no one else would have them. It made her cry, hearing how they'd been treated. But you – well, thanks, anyway.'

'That's all right. We like having them.'

'All same, I expect you'll be glad I'm going to take them back.'

'Is that why you've come?'

'Yes. Mum's been miserable without the boys. She wanted them to be safe, but all that bombing they were expecting hasn't happened. And so many of the kids have drifted back already that they're going to open part of the school again in January. I've got Christmas leave. So she asked me to come and get them. We can all be together again.'

'They'll like that. But –' Trish's face clouded with disappointment.

'What's up?'

'We'd got a Christmas present ready for them.'

'Nice of you. Could I take it back with me, and give it them from you on Christmas Day?'

'I don't think it'll be any use in London. I'll show you.'

She led the way to the cellar door. It was closed by a bolt too high for the boys to reach – and in any case they had been told that they must never try to open the door because the steps down were steep and dangerous. Opening it now, she showed him a two-seater sledge.

'Our hill is marvellous for sledging and we always have snow in January,' she said. 'But –'

'You're right, I'm afraid. Not many hills in Bethnal Green.' He glanced at her in surprise. 'You made this here, yourselves?'

She nodded. 'Grace did all the wood part and the metal runners underneath. And I painted it.' She had painted it bright red, with the names Boxer and Dan in black, one on each side.

'You ought to show it them. So that they know all the trouble you've taken.'

'I could say we'd invite them back for a holiday some time when there's plenty of snow.' Even as she spoke, closing the door for safety's sake, Trish guessed that the cost of the journey would be too high. Mrs Travis had visited her sons just once, to satisfy herself that they were happy, but had made it clear that she could not afford to come often.

As Dan came dashing back with Boxer to greet his brother, Trish left the three alone while she went to tell Mrs Barrett that there would be an extra place needed at what she called lunch and the boys called dinner.

Fortunately for the comfort of the household, the housekeeper was too well settled into the life of Greystones to be lured away by the money on offer for factory work or the glamour of a uniform. It was ironic, as Grace often commented to Trish, that when – after so many years – the family income was once again sufficient to support an adequate staff, it had become impossible to attract girls into service. But women from the village were willing to come and clean by the hour. Mrs Barrett herself realized, as everyone in the family did, that Mrs Hardie was no longer strong enough to carry all the responsibilities which she had shouldered for the past twenty-five years, and was determined that the old lady should end her days in orderly comfort.

The midday meal was already in progress when Mrs Hardie returned from her visit to the Infirmary. Trish was interested to notice how fast and politely Terry sprang to his feet when she appeared, and was about to introduce him. But Mrs Hardie turned back towards the door as soon as she saw that Grace – who preferred to work through the daylight hours without interruption – was not seated at the table.

There was something different about her bearing. Until today, age had made no difference to the way in which she carried herself. As a young girl she had been forced by use of a back board to hold herself straight, and the effect of the lesson still showed itself in her seventies. But for the first time Trish noticed a stooping of the shoulders that was caused not so much by tiredness as by despair. Alarmed, she too rose to her feet.

'Grandmother! How's Philip?'

Mrs Hardie's lips trembled and for a moment it seemed that she could not speak. Then her distress was conquered by anger.

'Germans!' she said. 'Murderers! First Frank. Now Philip. Killed by the Germans as surely as though they'd held a gun to his head. Couldn't quite finish it off last time, so had to come back again for a second chance.'

The words were mumbled so that they could hardly be heard, but Trish understood their meaning well enough. She was about to run into her grandmother's arms, but Mrs Hardie shook her head.

'Not now, thank you, darling.' Still mumbling to herself,

she went out of the room. She had not even noticed that there was a visitor.

Terry, resuming his seat, looked questioningly at Trish.

'It must mean that Philip has died. Her son.' This was the first death in Trish's life and she had to struggle to control her tears. 'He's been ill ever since 1917. He was gassed. It made breathing terribly hard work for him. When the war started – this war – he almost seemed to decide that it wasn't worth trying any more.' It was the putting on of the new gas mask which had caused him to collapse, but there had seemed no reason for his continuing illness except his own simple decision not to fight it.

She could not expect a stranger to be interested in the death of a man he had never met. The news served only to hasten the departure of the three Travises. Terry helped Trish to pack up the boys' possessions. At the last minute she bundled all the letters and pictures into a bag so that Boxer could continue his reading lessons in his own home. When they were ready to leave, Terry held out his hand.

'Thanks a lot for all you've done,' he said. 'And you'll thank your mother and grandmother as well, won't you. I ought really –'

'I think it's better not to disturb them, considering. I'll tell them that you wanted to and I wouldn't let you.'

'Right, well then, thanks again.'

The house seemed very empty after the boys had left. In the weeks since their arrival Trish had regarded it as her duty to keep them amused outside school hours, since it was because of her that they had come to Greystones in the first place. With that occupation gone, she could not think what to do. Grace and Mrs Hardie would not want to be disturbed. Miserable, and unexpectedly lonely, she went in search of Jean-Paul.

He was in the walled garden, digging the area in which next year's vegetables would be grown. Trish watched without speaking as he worked his way in a straight line, thrusting in the spade with a regular movement and turning it as it emerged so that the earth fell in a series of humps.

'Shall I rake it smooth for you?' she asked.

He straightened himself, leaning on the spade, and shook his head.

'I leave it so for the frost to break up. You can make a bonfire if you like.'

He tossed a box of matches across to her and automatically she put out a hand to catch it. Burning whatever rubbish could not be composted was an occupation which she enjoyed, but she did not move immediately. Instead she stared at him as he returned to his steady digging.

How different young men were from each other! No one could be as handsome as Rupert, especially in his new officer's uniform; but Jean-Paul was good-looking as well in a healthy, outdoor way. Naturally he wore old clothes all the time he was working, but inside them he would be clean and strong. Rupert was serious at heart, although he tried to disguise this by perpetual joking and teasing. Jean-Paul was just the opposite: genuinely light-hearted, but able to put on an act of being older and more responsible than he really was.

Today's visitor had been different again: a responsible young man with lively eyes. Not well educated, but sharp-witted. Before his call-up, he had told her, he had run a market stall. The unusual thing about him was that, unlike the other two, he did not quite seem to have settled inside his own skin. Rupert and Jean-Paul each knew who they were and knew when they were putting on an act. But Terry Travis – though this could only be a guess – was in the middle of changing himself. He must once have looked as skinny and under-nourished as Dan and spoken as badly as Boxer. Army food might have built up his strength, but it must have been his own decision to change his voice. Not just the sounds of vowels and consonants, but a whole manner of speaking. And the change was still in progress. He had not decided yet what he wanted to be.

Ambition. That was the difference. Trish herself had no ambitions, but there was plenty of time for that yet. Rupert would never want to change his place in society because he was already at the top; his only possible wish – to have been born an elder instead of a second son – could never come true. As for Jean-Paul, he was happy where he was. But Terry Travis wanted to be someone else. Not because he was ashamed of being a market trader, but because he thought he could do better for himself. It would be interesting to meet him again in five or six years to see whether he had managed it. But that was not likely to happen.

Why was she comparing people like this when they had nothing in common except that she happened to know them? She interrupted her own train of thought and Jean-Paul's work with an abrupt statement.

'Philip's dead.'

This time Jean-Paul drove the spade hard into the ground before straightening himself to look at her.

'It was so serious? I didn't realize.'

'It's rotten luck, isn't it? I mean, he was only your sort of age when he went off to fight. Healthy and clever, with a good life to look forward to. All spoilt in a single moment. It must have been almost worse than dying, knowing every day of your life how different things might have been.'

'You're upset for him.' Jean-Paul pulled off his muddy gloves and gripped her hands tightly with his own.

Trish nodded, trying unsuccessfully to sniff her tears under control.

'He never talked much, of course,' she said, groping for a handkerchief and failing to find one. 'But I liked the way he sort of took me for granted. Grandmother always made a fuss of me, and that was nice; and Grace did deliberate things like adopting me, and that was nice as well. But Philip just behaved as though it was the most natural thing in the world that I should be around. And now he's not going to be around any more, and I, I . . .'

Unable to restrain the tears, she pulled the sleeve of her coat across her eyes. Jean-Paul's hug was comforting. After a little while she managed to speak normally again.

'We must keep the vineyard going for him. As a sort of memorial.'

'That will hardly be possible, Trish. The war –'

'Can't you manage it on your own?'

'Even if I were here, no, I could not. But I shall not be here. I have had my first papers already for the army. I wait only to be told when I must go, and where.'

'I didn't realize. What are we going to do?'

'If I have time to finish this digging, the earth will be ready. For one year at least it will be easy to grow as many vegetables as before. Mrs Faraday knows what must be done, from the time before I came here. And you are strong enough to help her now. I will ask to see if there is a boy in the village to come when I have to leave. We're all told that we must grow our own food if we can. But grapes – no one will have time to spare for grapes.'

'There's not so very much to do, is there? Philip always said that the pruning was the most important thing. I could do that, if you showed me how. A few weeds between the rows wouldn't matter too much.'

'Oh, the grapes could be grown, yes. But the picking needs many hands, and even that is only the beginning. The making of the wine needs skill and full attention. This year already, with Philip ill, it was too much for me. And each year from now on there will be more grapes, more work; and I shall not be here.'

'I could get some of the girls from school to help pick and tread.' Trish was thinking aloud. 'They'd think it was fun.'

'There's much more than that to be done. Go to the coach house now and listen to the fermentation. Every day I – or someone else – must top up the levels and – oh, there's too much to say. No one in England knows how to make wine. And no one cares. They think it's impossible. It can only be

179

done by someone who has Philip's enthusiasm and skill. You'd waste your time, Trish, just trying.'

Trish had been brought up to believe that nothing was impossible. Any kind of achievement, she had been taught, was the result of determination, willpower, commitment – the adults in her life used different words but all said the same thing. Any kind of failure, in whatever sphere it might show itself, had its roots in the mind. It was hard for her to accept that there were some physical obstacles which could never be surmounted.

Nevertheless, common sense told her that Jean-Paul was right. And in her own life she did not expect anything to last for ever. She painted pictures and threw them away. She made clay models and squashed them flat again. When she first came to Greystones and was offered a piece of land to be her own private garden, she had tended it for one season and then watched without caring as it reverted to jungle when she began to neglect it. How curious it was that she should feel the need to preserve what Philip had loved.

'It just seems terrible that everything he's done should die with him. As though he'd never lived.'

'That's what almost always happens. Except to people who have children, I suppose. Or people like Mrs Faraday, who leave behind things they've made. But most of us – we disappear!'

She handed back the box of matches and wandered away, trying to think her feelings straight. It wouldn't matter to her if she disappeared after her own death. But if other people disappeared, totally disappeared, out of her life while she was still alive, then she was being robbed of something she didn't want to lose.

'Greystones!' she exclaimed to herself, stopping in her tracks. A house could keep a person alive in memory. Someone who had lived in Greystones for forty years had become part of it. There were places – rooms and corners and chairs – which would always be Philip's, as long as other members of the family still lived there and were able to remember him.

Rupert felt like that about Castlemere, she recalled. That was why it hurt him so much to think of a crowd of schoolgirls running riot there. It was not just a house to him: it was his family's history. Trish had not exactly understood his feelings before, but now the sense of attachment to a place struck her with an almost physical pain. Already she had spent more than half her life at Greystones. She had become part of it, as Philip was part of it.

So the vineyard was not important. It would be sad if all that work had to be wasted, but wastage was no doubt a necessary consequence of war. The important thing was that Greystones must survive.

1940

ONE

Very often during the first five months of 1940 Trish wished that she had not abandoned her request to be a boarder. Life at day school was busy and pleasant enough, but she returned each afternoon to a home which had been drained of its normal light-heartedness.

Jean-Paul had received his call-up papers and disappeared. Whenever Grace was not busy carving she was even more busily working in the vegetable garden. If Trish came to look for her, whether to have a chat or merely report that she was home, she was handed a fork or trowel and set to work weeding or planting out seedlings; it was impossible to have a proper conversation.

As for Mrs Hardie, she seemed to be fading away. All her meals were carried to her room, and she ate little of what she was offered. Most of her time was spent turning the sheets of her portfolios of paintings, staring in silence at the faces of her children when they were young and at the sketches she had made during her honeymoon journey in China fifty years earlier.

So there was no one for Trish to talk to at home: nothing for her to do except homework and gardening. Nothing to look forward to, either. Easter was spent slogging away and nobody had even mentioned the possibility of a summer holiday. Life was boring, boring. At the age of not-quite-fourteen she had yet to learn that in the middle of a war boredom was greatly to be desired.

She did not bother to keep up with the news, so the sweep of events which culminated in the Dunkirk evacuation seemed to come out of the blue. Then the radio was rarely switched off. It became the focal point of the household, which abruptly ceased to be a collection of individuals who had forgotten how to communicate.

Once she understood what was happening, Trish was as much affected as her elders by the drama and anxiety. Jean-Paul might not yet be in France, but Rupert would certainly be involved. At this moment he might be standing in the sea to organize the lines of men who waited for rescue while German planes dropped bombs and raked the beach with machine gun fire. Terry Travis might be there as well, although Trish did not know enough about him to be able to envisage him as a soldier. Her father, as an accredited photographer, might even be recording the scene on film and in as much danger as the fighting men. Trish put out her hand to Grace and felt it gripped tightly.

'It'll be all right,' she was told. 'We'll soon hear something.'

This optimism was not immediately justified. For three days they heard nothing at all. Then, on the first Saturday in June, Rupert arrived at Greystones.

He was almost unrecognizable as the handsome, teasing young man who had waved goodbye to Trish at the end of her visit to Castlemere nine months earlier. His exhausted eyes seemed to have sunk into the black hollows of tiredness which surrounded them. As he waited for someone to answer the bell, he leaned his head against the doorpost, almost asleep on his feet. The taxi driver, obviously concerned about his passenger, lingered to make sure that there was someone at home.

Trish, returning from her afternoon walk with Mrs Hardie, was the first to see him and ran anxiously forward.

'Rupert! Rupert, are you all right?'

With what seemed an enormous effort he managed to smile.

'A bit tired. Greeted into England with a cup of tea and a travel warrant for immediate leave. The army trying to save on soap. Can't face Castlemere and Mother's in Scotland.

Wondered if you'd let me doss down here for the night.'

'Wait while I fetch Grace to help you.' Trish could see that he was on the point of collapse. Together they supported him, staggering, to the nearest bedroom. Mrs Hardie, meanwhile, drawing strength from the need to help, looked for the house-keeper. A returning hero ought not to be restricted to the five inches of bath water allowed to civilians, so the range must be stoked up.

Too exhausted to be aware of the luxury on offer, Rupert slept for fourteen hours. When at last he appeared for a meal, clean and shaved and wearing a set of Philip's clothes, he still seemed to be a stranger, wanting to talk and yet apparently unable to formulate the words; ravenously hungry and yet finding it painful to swallow.

Mrs Hardie – a stranger herself at the breakfast table – came to the rescue, as though remembering how once she had needed to coax her shell-shocked son back into life. Speaking gently, she patted and stroked her young cousin until without warning the floodgates opened and he began to describe the experiences of the past few days.

To the women, listening on the radio, the evacuation had been presented as a miracle, almost as a victory. Rupert painted a very different picture – one of horror and disgrace. Trish listened wide-eyed, and it was her obvious alarm which in the end brought the account to an abrupt end.

'Enough of that,' he said. 'That battle's over and lost. The next one will be in England. May I use your telephone, Cousin Lucy? I must speak to my parents. I sent them a telegram to say that I was safe and well, but they don't know where I am.'

'Of course, dear.'

He was away for some time, returning to report a lack of success. 'My mother's been up in Scotland with her sister for the past two months but left there yesterday. No one seems to know exactly where she is, but I've scattered messages around. I'm hoping she'll get one of them and phone me here. Would it be very rude if I went back to sleep while I'm waiting?'

'Much the best thing,' Mrs Hardie assured him.

He did not, however, return to the bedroom, but carried garden mattresses out into the shade of the oak tree – for the heatwave was continuing unbroken. At first he read, but after less than an hour the book fell from his hand. Trish settled down with a book of her own nearby, to be near when he awoke.

When Mrs Barrett came hurrying from the house to announce that there was a telephone call for Lord Rupert, Trish went quietly across to awaken him, picking up one hand and squeezing it gently.

His eyes opened and he smiled in his old way, as if the past few days had been banished from his mind.

'Beautiful Patricia. This is what we all dreamed of during the retreat – or would have dreamed if ever we'd been allowed to sleep. A beautiful girl to hold our hands and stroke our fevered brows.'

It was good to hear him teasing again and she was sorry to spoil the moment with news of the telephone call. Although he was still stiff as he rose to his feet, there was a spring in his movements to suggest that he had thrown off the nightmare of the past days. But when he returned to the garden twenty minutes later, his step was heavy with shock. Both Grace and Trish came hurrying to find out what the matter was.

'My father's dead,' he told them. He sat down on the mattress with his knees wide apart, burying his head in his hands. 'Apparently he tried to get to Dunkirk.'

'How?' Grace was astonished.

'He had a boat. Used to keep it in the Mediterranean. Sailed it back to England last summer, when he saw how things were going. Apparently, as soon as he read about the evacuation he sent for Murray, his old chauffeur, to act as mechanic and dashed off to get her – the *Beverley Belle* – shipshape again. Had a heart attack hauling her down to the water.'

'Oh Rupert, I'm so sorry.'

'Bad time for Mother. Hearing about him and not knowing about me.'

185

'Where's your brother?' asked Trish. She knew that he was a professional soldier and as likely as Rupert to have been in danger.

'He's just been posted abroad. We don't know exactly where he's going, of course, but since they've seconded him to the Indian Army it's probably Bombay or Singapore. At this moment he'll be somewhere in the Atlantic, surrounded by U-boats. I must go to my mother. I can't tell you how grateful I am to you all for taking me in. Tell Cousin Lucy that for me, will you, Grace? I don't want to disturb her rest. We'll meet again in happier times, Patricia.'

For once she did not make the usual protest that her name was Trish. Right from their first meeting he had refused to use the abbreviation because it was childish. Calling her by her real name had always been one of his teases – but there was something different in his voice today: a new kind of seriousness. Was he beginning to recognize that she was growing into the grown-up name?

No, she told herself, there was no chance of that yet. Although she was overwhelmed by the wish that he would kiss her, he would have no idea how much she loved him. He still thought of her only as a child. She nodded, faint with emotion but just managing to keep it under control.

'To happier times!' he repeated, rubbing his fingers affectionately against her cheek before hurrying into the house to collect his kit and phone for a taxi. Within half an hour he had gone.

TWO

Dunkirk might have killed the Marquess of Ross and exhausted Rupert, but Ellis emerged very much alive. In the chaos of the evacuation he had lost his own camera but had managed to attach himself to a film unit which had suffered casualties, and in a time of crisis quickly mastered the art of taking moving pictures. He telephoned from Dover to say that he was safe; then spent two days there filming the returning soldiers. By the time he arrived at Greystones he had had a bath and had caught up on his sleep.

Trish changed rapidly from a young woman hopelessly in love with a handsome hero to a schoolgirl delighted and relieved to see her father again. For the first time she noticed how differently he greeted Grace and herself when he arrived. For Trish he had a vigorous, cuddly hug, but for his wife only a smile. It was a warm smile, a loving smile, but it was odd, all the same, that they did not kiss. She stored the small question up in her mind to be considered later.

'You won't be going back to France, will you?' she asked her father when the first flurry of news had been exchanged.

'No, I don't think that would be a very good idea. Any Englishmen who get caught in France after it surrenders will be interned as enemy aliens. So, until the paper decides where it wants me to go next – or allows me to switch to being a newsreel cameraman – I hope you and Grace will put up with me here.'

He looked at Grace almost, thought Trish, as though he were asking her permission.

'Of course,' she said, laughing. 'It's about time you visited your own home for more than a few days at a time. But Ellis –' her expression became more serious again – 'what you said about enemy aliens. Will that apply to someone like Andy Frith? You know, Jean-Paul's father.'

'Depends what his status is. Maybe he's a naturalized Frenchman by now. I must say, if I were in his shoes I wouldn't hang about. But when you've got a wife and children and land, I don't suppose the choice is easy.'

They did not have to wait long before discovering what he had chosen. Only two days later a weary figure trudged up the long drive. It was Andy, asking whether he could stay in the lodge. His tiredness was of a different kind from Rupert's, caused not so much by lack of sleep as by hopelessness. He looked like a defeated man staring into an empty future.

'I'd thought to find Jean-Paul here,' he told Grace and Trish.

'Didn't you know he'd been called up?'

'Only that he was waiting for his papers. Letters haven't been getting through these past weeks.'

'Your farm's in occupied territory, I suppose,' said Grace.

'It's not a farm any more. Part of a battlefield. I watched the tanks roll over the land and I thought, "This is where I came in." And my wife –' He had to wait for a moment before he could speak. 'She was in the barn when it was shelled. The roof came down on her. Broke her back. She lived for ten days, but she'd never have been able to walk again. It was a good thing, really, that –'

Grace stretched out a sympathetic hand but then, to Trish's surprise, withdrew it without touching him and instead began asking questions about the rest of his family. Only after a few moments did a sudden thought seem to occur to her. She put her arm round Trish's shoulders.

'You haven't been up to the house since my marriage, have you? I suppose you've never met my stepdaughter, Trish Faraday. I should have introduced you properly.'

'Hello, Trish.' He shook hands with a formality which made her giggle. 'I've heard a lot about you from Jean-Paul.'

'You'll come back later for supper with us, I hope,' said Grace after she had fetched the keys of the lodge.

Andy shook his head. 'I've no appetite, thank you very much. Somewhere to rest, that's all I need for the moment.'

'But there'll be nothing to eat in the cottage at all.'

'I'll bring something down to you,' Trish offered. 'Just so that you have something handy when you start to feel hungry.'

Half an hour later she walked carefully down the hill carrying in one hand a jug of milk and in the other a basket containing not only bread and potatoes and rhubarb, but butter, honey, cheese and eggs. The occupants of Greystones had learned to be self-sufficient long before the war.

Looking through the window as she approached she could see Andy sitting at the kitchen table in an attitude of lonely despair. Grace had told her, when she asked, that he was not yet fifty, but he looked older. She kicked at the door with her foot, to save having to put her load down on the ground, and the pressure was enough to open it.

'Here you are.' She set the basket down on the table. 'And Grace said to remind you about the blackout tonight. The ground floor has got blackout curtains, but Jean-Paul used to go to bed in the dark, to save bother. And you're to come and ask if there are things you find you need.'

'You're very kind, all of you.' She could see that he was trying to smile, but failing.

'It must be horrid, having to leave your home.' She sat down to face him across the table, well aware that he did not want to chat, but feeling that it would do him good. Her comment, though, went too directly to the heart of his distress, and for some time he was not able to answer.

'You'll be able to go back when the war is over,' she added in an attempt at consolation.

'Shall I want to go back? When you see twenty-five years' work spoiled in a week, you think that only a fool would make the same mistake twice, stake his happiness on something so quickly spoiled.' He looked up at her, trying to explain. 'You know that people are going to die. Your wife or yourself, one of you's got to face bereavement one day. Doesn't make it any easier when it happens, of course, but it's, well, in the natural order of things. But land: you think that land will last for ever. For your own lifetime, anyway.'

He sighed.

'You don't make any other plans, that's the trouble. Just what's going to happen on the land next season. That seems enough. So when you haven't got the land any more, you haven't got anything. But no, I shan't go back. Even if it becomes possible, it will be for the boys to start all over again. So I don't know what I'm going to do with myself. Don't know at all. I never really liked France. My roots are here. But –'

He sat with his head bowed as though on the verge of tears. Trish stared at him with an intentness of which he was unaware.

'Did Jean-Paul tell you that Philip had died?' she asked at last.

'Yes. That was the last letter I got. Oh, I should have told Grace how sorry I was while I was up at the house.'

Trish drew in a breath to speak but then let it out again, wondering whether she would do better to wait. Patience was not one of her virtues, though. She put her elbows on the table and leaned earnestly forward.

'It was something I wanted to do, after he died. To keep the vineyard going as a kind of memorial to Philip. You know about the vineyard, don't you?'

'It was my idea. I sent the original vines.'

'Of course! Well, I asked Jean-Paul if we could keep it going, and he said not without him. But I got him to show me how to do the pruning before he went. The thing is, though, I didn't realize how much time it would take just tying the vines as they grow. And Grace expects me to spend hours in the vegetable garden. It's too much, really, just like Jean-Paul said it would be. If you're going to stay here, Mr Frith –'

'Oh, call me Andy,' he said. He tilted his head as he looked at her. 'Well, go on.'

'I was thinking of what you said about having a feeling for land, and wondering whether you needed to own it for that. Because you must know the Greystones land just as well as what you had in France.'

'Better,' he said. 'When you're a boy, you cover your territory in a different way. Get to know every twig and puddle. That's what I meant about my roots.'

'It's not my business, really,' said Trish. 'It's for Grace to say. But we need someone like you here. Everyone keeps telling us all that we should grow as much of our own food as we can, and at Greystones we do it more than most people, but it's terribly hard work now that Philip's dead and Jean-Paul has gone. And Grace really wants to spend more time on her carving and I ought to be doing homework though I don't specially want to, and so you see we do need you terribly badly.'

'But Grace might not want –' He checked himself and stared at Trish for a long time. His face gave no indication of what he was thinking.

'Let's go and have a look at these vines,' he said suddenly. 'See what sort of a mess you've been making of them. Just let me cover the milk, though.'

He set the jug down in a bowl of cold water to keep it cool, and covered it with the beaded muslin that his mother must once have used as a protection against flies. With the simple domestic action he seemed to shrug off a little of his depression, and he strode across the sheep meadow towards the vineyard with no trace in his movements of the heaviness which had earlier weighed him down.

'Well, most of this looks healthy enough,' he said approvingly, testing the firmness of the nearest stakes and wires. 'The Riesling Sylvaner's doing very well. But I see what you mean about the tying. Getting out of hand, isn't it?'

Trish nodded. Content now to leave him to make up his own mind, she stood still as he walked up and down the rows, patting away the tendrils which seemed to stretch out to touch him as he passed. By the time he returned to stand beside her again he had made up his mind.

'As you say, it's for your stepmother to decide. Or your father, perhaps, if he's the master here now.'

'Oh no!' Even as she laughed at the idea, Trish had time to notice the oddity of her surprise. It might have been considered normal for a man who married the owner of a property to consider himself its proprietor. But nothing in his behaviour had ever suggested that to be the case. 'No, my father's terribly fond of the house. It was built by my grandfather, you see. But gardening isn't his line, any more than it's mine. Greystones is still the Hardies' place.'

'Well then,' said Andy, 'why don't you tell your stepmother that you had this idea about putting me to work here and you realized that it shouldn't have come from you and so you didn't exactly ask me the question: but you got the impression that I'd be glad to help out if I was wanted. Well, more than that – that I need a roof over my head and I'm looking for a chance to earn it. Then it'll be up to her to raise the subject if she wants to, and if she doesn't there'll be no hard feelings.'

'I'll do it now!' exclaimed Trish, and began to run up the hill, pausing only to call over her shoulder, 'Don't forget the blackout!'

Ellis had returned from a day in London by the time she reached the house, so she was able to pant out her idea to both of them at once.

'What do you think?' Grace asked Ellis with a note of doubt in her voice which was surprising in someone who normally made all the decisions regarding the property without hesitation.

'How you feel about it is up to you,' Ellis replied. 'But speaking in a practical sort of way, I'd have thought it solved all your problems. And his. From what you've told me, his father was always more than a mere gardener, and the boy may well have inherited his loyalty to the land.'

192

'Not exactly a boy!' exclaimed Trish: but she understood what he meant.

'My only doubts would be about the vines,' Ellis suggested. 'To give him a free hand on the fruit and vegetables and general maintenance would be absolutely fine, I should have thought, but is it really worth struggling on with the vineyard?'

'I think that might be the attraction for him,' suggested Trish. 'I mean, that he'd do the donkey work for the sake of looking after the vines.'

'Could be. Well, we'd better let Grace sleep on it.'

It seemed an unnecessarily cautious answer to Trish, who could see no possible objection to her inspired plan. Why were grown-ups always so stuffy and slow to recognize good ideas? But by the next morning, although no one said anything directly to her, she could tell that a decision had been made. There was a change in the atmosphere, a lightening of the sky. She found herself excited by the atmosphere of coming and going and planning for the future. Greystones had come to life again.

THREE

'I'm in Oxford.' Sheila's voice over the telephone sounded breathless, almost secretive. 'David will be at the shop all day, but he doesn't need me hanging around so I wondered if little Max and I could come up for an hour or two?'

'Yes, of course.' Grace did her best to inject a note of welcome into her voice, although without any great success. There were very few people whose company, in her opinion, justified the loss of her working hours, and her sister-in-law was not one of them.

The two women had nothing in common. Sheila's only topics of conversation were her children and the affairs of the church which was not just a place of worship but also the centre of her social life. Her conventional mind made no pretence of understanding Grace's way of life and for a long time she had kept away in disapproval. But perhaps the advent of a husband and stepdaughter had made Grace more respectable in her eyes, for since then she had invited herself to Greystones several times.

Although she sought the invitation from Grace, it was Mrs Hardie with whom she and Max usually spent their visits. No doubt she would do so again today. And Trish must be somewhere around and could help to amuse them. With any luck half an hour's chat over a cup of tea would be enough to discharge the duties of a hostess.

The two visitors who were shown into the drawing room an hour later provided a startling contrast in appearance. Sheila, always a sturdily-built woman, had become stout since the birth of her fourth child. Max on the other hand was small for his age, and everything about his body was compact and neat. He was always on the move but – unlike Boxer and Dan, who during their stay at Greystones had tended to barge around noisily and clumsily – his movements were under control and even graceful. Everything about him – the back of his head, his chin, his ears, even his eyebrows – seemed to be more pointed than was usual. Grace saw him as an elf, who should be dancing on his toes round a giant mushroom instead of sitting politely in a drawing room.

'Could Trish take little Max out to look at the statues?' asked Sheila, almost before the first politenesses had been exchanged. 'The fresh air –' Her voice trailed away, but not before she had made it clear that she had something to say without her son listening.

Trish, who hated to be excluded from grown-up conversations, looked sulky for a moment but did as she was asked.

'It's about Max that I want to talk to you,' Sheila said, looking from Grace to Mrs Hardie after the door had closed. 'Everyone thinks that there'll be an invasion now. And that there's bound to be bombing before that – to knock London out, so to speak.'

Grace did not disagree, but as her mind leapt ahead to the possible point of this remark she had to fight to prevent her dismay from revealing itself in her expression. From David's point of view it might seem reasonable that he should control the affairs of The House of Hardie from Oxford rather than London, but if he thought he could come with his family to live at Greystones he would have to think again. 'Harrow hardly counts as London, does it?' was all she said.

'It's got railway lines. The main line to Scotland is only a quarter of a mile away from us. It could be a target. And bombs don't always fall exactly where they're intended to. David doesn't plan to move, and of course I must stay with him. John's in the air force and Lily's going to do her first year at college before she decides what sort of war work to do, and

Peter's away at school all term. But little Max – I don't know what to do for the best. He's too young just to be packed off with a crowd of other evacuees. I'd never have a moment's peace, thinking of him crying in bed, missing his home. And yet if he stays and the bombing starts and he's frightened or hurt . . .'

'You want him to come here,' said Mrs Hardie. 'Well, of course –' But she checked herself and looked at Grace, as Sheila was already looking.

'You had evacuees here before, didn't you?' Sheila reminded her. 'And if the bombing really does start, I suppose they'll ask you to have someone again. I thought you might actually prefer to have your own nephew rather than some strange child. And of course I wouldn't ask you until it actually became necessary. But for our peace of mind, just to know . . .'

Grace stood up and walked over to one of the drawing room windows. Outside, Trish and Max were playing a complicated game of tag which seemed to involve Max in climbing through the hole in the large stone sculpture which stood in front of the house. The boy moved like a gymnast – and indeed, as that thought entered her mind, he ran towards the sculpture, jumped as high in the air as if he had a springboard and turned a handstand over the stone. She blinked in surprise at his agility and smiled to see the gleeful expression on his face as he dared Trish to attempt the same feat.

There was nothing about his slight but athletic body or expressive pointed face which bore the slightest resemblance to his father's dark solidity or his mother's stout respectability. It was as though he were a changeling. To accept him into the household might expose her to a surfeit of visits from the brother she still disliked, but between those times there would be no need to be constantly aware of Max as being David's son. He would be himself. Dan and Boxer had proved that it was possible to have children in the house and survive. She smiled, making her acceptance a gracious one.

'Of course. We'd be delighted to look after him whenever

you feel it's necessary. I'll get a room ready for him so that you can phone up at short notice and send him here.'

'He should come before he needs to,' said Mrs Hardie, speaking with a more definite tone than had been usual in recent years. 'For a little holiday, with no sense of emergency. So that he'll know in advance which is his room and what sort of life he'll be leading.'

'That would be very kind.' Once again Sheila looked to Grace for agreement. Then she blushed slightly. 'I'm afraid – I'll provide a mackintosh sheet, of course – I'm afraid he does sometimes wet his bed still.'

'We're used to that. We had the same trouble with Boxer. He'd never been away from home before.'

'It happens even at home, I'm afraid. To tell you the truth, he and his father . . . I suppose it was because we thought we'd finished with having children. It was quite a shock, having to start again with a baby in the house. And when he became a toddler, that was even worse. He never seemed to sleep. Always on the go. I got tired, and David got irritated. And he, Max I mean, gets frightened when he's shouted at. David was always a good father to the other three, but he doesn't seem to *like* Max.'

Grace was hardly acquainted with her youngest nephew, who on previous visits had spent all his time with his grandmother. But as she listened to Sheila's comments she felt more and more interested in getting to know him.

'You have a chat with Mother,' she suggested. 'I'll go out and play with him for a little while, so that he feels he knows who it is who's inviting him for a holiday.'

There was a surprising element of satisfaction to be found in accepting the situation. Sometimes – although not often – Grace worried that her obsession with her own work and preference for her own company revealed an unnatural lack of family feeling. On such occasions she found it necessary to itemize her relationships with her brothers, for it was reassuring to remember that she had adored Frank, who was dead, had felt sympathy with Kenneth, who had run away for reasons quite unconnected with her, and had loved and cared for Philip until he too had died. As for Jay, her feelings towards him were almost maternal. It was only David to whom she felt cold, and to show affection to one of his sons would in an odd way help to prove that it was not as a brother that she disliked him but simply as a man whom she would never have needed to meet had they not been born to the same parents.

Odd, she thought to herself as she took Max's hand and led him off to be introduced to the hens and the sow, odd that she should think of herself as a free woman, untrammelled by family relationships, when in fact she was a daughter, sister, wife, stepmother and aunt.

She had made no effort to adapt her long, fast stride to the age of her companion. Max was neither running nor skipping in his effort to keep up. Instead, his feet moved rapidly in what was clearly a pattern which he had invented, occasionally crossing over and back again and incorporating little hops and jumps. He watched his own toes moving, concentrating on the effort to repeat the pattern correctly.

If there was one thing more than any other that Grace liked in a child, it was the ability to concentrate. Trish had it to a marked degree, although her periods of concentration usually ended in an orgy of destruction. Dan and Boxer had been quite different, needing continual stimulus and encouragement to keep them at a single task. It seemed to Grace that Max would prove to be more like Trish and herself. There would be no need for him to struggle against his aunt as he had to struggle against his father. It might take a little time to find what exactly it was that he was so anxious to encourage in himself, but she would succeed in the end through sympathy.

'Would you like to come and spend a little holiday here with me, Max?' she asked. 'We'd love to have you.'

FOUR

The blitzkrieg which had been so confidently expected and feared began on the night of 7 September 1940. Two days later Max Hardie arrived at Greystones for what had been described to him as a second holiday.

On the last Sunday in September, nine months after he had taken his two half-brothers away from Greystones, Terry Travis brought them back again.

Trish was enjoying an hour of freedom when she heard the bell ring. It was part of her weekend duty to keep Max amused. But Sheila had been anxious that his Bible education should not be neglected, and since no one in the Greystones household was a churchgoer or prepared to undertake the long walk to take him to Sunday School at the Quarry church, Mrs Hardie had undertaken to spend an hour each Sunday morning reading and explaining Bible stories to him.

At the sound of the bell Trish came downstairs, just in time to see Mrs Barrett going in search of Grace while the three visitors stood in the hall as if uncertain of their welcome.

When she first glimpsed Dan and Boxer a year earlier, they had been frightened and unhappy, and they were frightened and unhappy now. But on that first occasion it had been clear that, although poor, they were well cared for. The boys themselves and their clothes had both been clean and neat. The same could not be said today.

As though realizing that he was under observation, Terry looked up and smiled.

'Look, there's Trish,' he said to the boys.

She ran down to hug them, but they shrank nervously away and Boxer put his thumb in his mouth and began to suck it.

'You can't do that,' said Trish. 'You're a big boy now. You haven't forgotten me, surely.' She was hurt by their reaction, and by the fact that Terry's attention switched towards Grace as soon as the door from the studio opened.

'I'm very sorry to disturb you, Mrs Faraday, but I wonder if I could have a word. Without Dan and Brian listening.'

'Of course. Trish will look after them.'

But Trish, put out by the lack of warmth in their greeting, wanted to be part of the conversation.

'They can go and explore,' she said. 'See if all the pigs and hens and things are still there. Off you go. You know where to look.'

Reluctantly they let go of Terry's hands, but within only a few seconds could be heard shouting excitedly outside.

'Come and sit down,' said Grace. 'Is this more than just a social visit?'

Terry nodded unhappily.

'You'll have read in the newspapers about the bombing.'

'Of course, yes. It sounds terrible.'

'Yes. I've been in barracks, out of it all. It doesn't seem right that soldiers should be safe when civilians are getting killed. Well, our mum's one of the casualties. She was hit the night before last. Killed outright.' He swallowed the lump in his throat.

'Oh, I'm so sorry. Very sorry indeed. The boys weren't hurt?'

'They were in a shelter when the bomb fell. There's been a raid every night this week. According to one of the neighbours, Mum had settled them down for the night at eight o'clock, so that she wouldn't need to wake them up when the sirens went. She went back to the house for something, since nothing seemed to be happening. I don't know why she was still there when the raid started. But it got a direct hit.'

'How awful!' said Trish. 'No wonder they look so miserable. Who's looking after them?'

'They spent yesterday in a school hall with all the other families who had lost their homes. I was given compassionate leave to decide what to do. There's no choice, really. They'll have to be evacuated again. They understand that, and they know they haven't got a home any more.'

'But they're frightened at the thought of being sent away to strangers?'

'Yes. And upset about Mum, of course.'

Trish could see what was coming, and so no doubt could Grace.

'I realize that it's an awful lot to ask, Mrs Faraday, but would you be willing to take them back again? It would be all official, if you would. You'd get the billeting allowance, just as if they'd been here all the time.' He made a face, criticizing himself. 'I shouldn't ever have taken them back to London. I can see that now, but it seemed safe.'

'What will happen if they don't come here?' asked Grace.

'They'll be sent off to Wales in a party leaving tomorrow. A lot of the kids drifted back to London when nothing seemed to be happening, but they all understand that they can't stay any longer. It's terrible, what's going on there. And we've no family outside the area. It would mean a lot to me, Mrs Faraday, to know that they were here where they've been happy, where I could be sure that they were being kindly treated. But of course I do realize . . .'

His voice began to fade away into uncertainty. Until that moment he had spoken in the positive manner of someone putting forward the only possible solution to a problem. It was perhaps only now that he did indeed realize what he was asking.

'I can guess what Trish will want,' said Grace, smiling at her. 'But I have a young nephew here already and I must have a word with Mrs Barrett before I give you an answer. It would be easy for me to say Yes, but I wouldn't be the one to tackle the extra work. Why don't you and Trish take the boys for a walk? You must all stay for lunch anyway.'

'That's very kind of you.' But he looked dejected as he followed Trish outside. 'She's going to say No, isn't she?'

'What makes you think that?'

'That business about asking Mrs Barrett. People like you don't *ask* their servants: they tell them. That's only an excuse.'

'I don't know what you mean by "people like us".'

'Rich people who live in big houses, that's what I mean.'

'People like me who live in houses like this are treated as slaves!' said Trish. 'If you knew what I had to do before I go to school every day!'

'Sorry. I didn't realize you were one of the oppressed masses.' For the first time since his arrival at Greystones he laughed without any trace of anxiety on his face and the natural liveliness of his eyes returned. Boxer and Dan came running to join them, already feeling at home again – proprietorial, even, as they introduced their brother to the animals and hens.

'Dan and Boxer will be junior slaves if they come back here. I hope you realize that,' Trish said to their brother. 'We had them harvesting onions almost as soon as they arrived here last time – and there's a new crop ready now.' A thought struck her, and she turned towards the younger boy. 'But perhaps you're not Boxer any longer. Have you gone back to being Brian again?'

'Boxer,' he said. 'I like being Boxer.' He put his fists up to show that he had not forgotten how he and Trish used to spar. Terry, confirmed in his belief that his brothers would be happier here than anywhere else, was becoming more light-hearted with every moment that passed, but his anxious expression returned as he saw Grace coming towards them.

She was quick to put his mind at rest.

'Mrs Barrett will be delighted to have your brothers back,' she said. 'I've just telephoned the billeting officer to make sure that there would be school places for them; there's no problem there either. And apparently the WVS issue welfare bundles to people who've been bombed out, so we can apply for some clothes and even toys immediately. There's a form which you should get filled in in London and stamped to certify that the house has been destroyed. That will help the boys to get new ration books and more clothing coupons. And you'll need to register the loss of furniture even if you don't propose to replace it straightaway.'

She was interrupted by the sound of a Red Indian war cry as Max was released from his grandmother's boudoir. His period of imprisonment had left him full of energy and as soon as he reached the grass he did three cartwheels in succession before noticing the visitors.

'This is Max,' said Trish. 'He's an evacuee as well, but Grace is his aunt. Boxer and Dan are going to be living here too, Max, and this is their brother Terry, who's brought them.'

Max's expressive eyes indicated alarm and even resentment that other boys should have come to share his holiday, and there was a grudging note in his voice as he said 'Hello.'

'It'll be nice for you to have someone to play with,' said Trish, reassuringly. 'I wonder if Boxer can do cartwheels as well as you. Have a go, Boxer.'

But the two London boys were shy. Perhaps they too had felt proprietorial on their return and now were equally resentful that the territory was to be shared. Grace interrupted the awkwardness with a brisk conclusion to what she had been saying earlier.

'Anyway, we'll be very glad to have you living with us again, Dan and Boxer. Do you want to have the same bedroom as last time?'

The two boys nodded.

'Right. Go and collect your things to take up to it, then. Max, you go and help Mrs Barrett with her pastry. She's making a big apple pie for us all, and I expect there'll be enough over for you to cut out little tarts. Trish, open all the windows of the bedroom and give it a good airing, will you?'

'Yes, ma'am. This moment, ma'am.' She led the way indoors and upstairs, with Terry following behind. 'You never saw their room when you came to take them away, did you? It's an odd shape, because it was planned for twins, so they could each have a bed in these sort of alcoves and then share the middle of the room for playing.'

Opening the door, she made a face at the musty smell, and hurried to open the windows as she had been told.

'When the house was built, there were maids to light fires in all the bedrooms,' she told Terry. 'But now there's no heat upstairs at all and the rooms get damp if they're not used. But we'll warm the mattresses and sheets and things.' She looked critically round the room. 'It's a bit shabby, isn't it?'

'Doesn't look as if it's been redecorated since the day the house was built,' agreed Terry. He walked across to the window and tugged at a peeling tag of blotched and yellowed wallpaper. A long triangle of the paper came away from the wall, bringing with it lumps of plaster.

'You're spoiling it!' exclaimed Trish indignantly.

'Not much to spoil. It's all damp. There'll be bad trouble with the wood if you're not careful.'

'It certainly doesn't look very cheerful. I could paint it, though. On top of the wallpaper, as long as you don't make any more holes in the wall.'

'Make things worse, that would.' Terry took a penknife from his pocket and stuck it into the skirting board. 'Not too bad,' he admitted. 'Tell you what, Trish. If your mother wouldn't think it an impertinence. This time I've only got as long as it needs to settle the boys, but next time I get an ordinary leave I could come here, if you'd have me, and strip the walls down and replaster and put on an undercoat. Then you could finish off the painting – and add pictures, if you wanted to, like you did in that little room downstairs.'

'D'you know how to?' asked Trish. 'How to plaster walls, I mean.'

'I was apprenticed to a builder when I was fourteen. Only lasted a couple of years, because I got the chance of a market licence. So I didn't finish serving my time, but I can turn my

204

hand to most things around a house. Anyway, couldn't look much worse, could it?'

'Suppose not. Well, we'll have to ask Grace. But I should think she'll be pleased.'

She chose a private moment to put the question, because she had a comment to add on it.

'It would be nice to have the room looking smart, wouldn't it?' she suggested. 'And besides, I don't suppose Terry's got anywhere to go for his leave now that his house has been bombed.'

'We can't act as a welfare refuge for the whole of the East End,' said Grace; but she did not say it as an objection.

'It would be different for Terry, with his brothers here already and wanting to see him whenever they can. I expect that's why he wants to do some work here, to feel that he could earn his keep.'

'I was only teasing. Yes, of course he can come. And we shall be very glad of his help.'

As it turned out, he was able to write less than four weeks later to give the date of a forthcoming leave. Trish asked Grace for some money and took the boys down to the covered market in Oxford to choose material for curtains. On their return, she set them the joyously messy task of stripping the wallpaper off their room while she went to find Mrs Hardie.

'I wondered,' she asked, 'whether you could show me how to make curtains.'

Mrs Hardie, who in recent months had grown vague and listless, looked at her more sharply than usual.

'What you mean is, you wonder whether I would make curtains for you.'

'Yes,' admitted Trish. 'Not for me, though. For Dan and Boxer. Because Auntie Sheila brought all the things to make Max's room look bright and homey – the rug and counterpane and curtains and the lamb for putting his pyjamas in -- and he's got his own toys. But Dan and Boxer haven't got anything at all. I want to make the room a bit more cheerful.'

'Have you got the measurements?'

Trish produced a drawing she had made of the window and the curtain rail. 'I showed this to the market lady and she said how much I'd need, to allow for shrinking. There are blackout curtains hanging there already, which would do for lining.'

'I'll see what I can do,' promised Mrs Hardie. 'But you'll have to thread the needles for me.'

'Oh, thank you. And there's something else. The walls are going to be painted this time, not papered, and I thought it would look more interesting if the two alcoves were a different colour from the rest of the room to make them look sort of deeper.'

'A good idea.'

'But the thing is, I don't know which colours will make them look deeper and which will flatten them out again. And ought they to be quite different colours, or just different shades of the same thing?'

'I remember soon after you first came here, I gave you painting lessons, and that was what I wanted to teach you – how to use colour to suggest distance or contrast and all that kind of thing. All you wanted to do was to slap pillar-box red around.'

'I was only little then,' Trish pointed out. 'You were trying to show me quite difficult things and I didn't understand. If you'd try again, I'd listen this time. Because I can see that some colours go together and some don't – but only when I *can* see them, if you know what I mean. Mind you,' she added honestly, 'I still do like pillar-box red. If Terry has time to do the walls of my room when he's finished the boys' I shall paint the walls bright white with the outlines of black shapes on it – squares and circles and things – and clusters of little red dots inside them. I can see exactly how I want it to look, although I don't know whether I'll be able to do it neatly enough.'

Mrs Hardie looked startled by the prospect of such a transformation of the house which had been her home for forty years, but raised no objection. Some of the old life returned to her eyes as on cold winter evenings she used her own paintings as illustrations of how colour could be mixed and used. Failing eyesight prevented her from any longer producing the detailed flower sketches which had once given her such pleasure, but she opened her paint box again to give her young pupil practical illustrations of primary and complementary and contrasting colours.

'Did you know,' Trish asked Terry when he arrived for the second of his leaves. 'Did you know that shadows aren't really grey at all? Or at least, not necessarily. If you screw your eyes up and look you can see that they're a bit yellow and a bit blue and a bit of all sorts of other things.'

'You painting shadows all over the walls, then?'

''Course not. Come and look at my room.' He had left it, at the end of his previous leave, ready for her to decorate.

'It's not quite right,' she said critically. 'I wanted the white to be all smooth, with no brushstrokes showing, but I couldn't get it like that. And there's more black than I meant, because sometimes the brush wobbled and then I had to make the whole line thicker. But it's not bad, is it?'

'Not what I'd call restful,' suggested Terry. 'All those red spots. I'd feel as if I was sleeping inside a bad case of measles!'

'Who wants to be restful now? Anyway, I can do it all again next year in different colours if I want to. You know what I'd like to do, Terry? I'd like to go right through the house making every room exactly the right colour for the person who lives in it. I mean, I'm a black and white with splodges sort of person. Grace's room ought to be just white, plain white. Mrs Barrett is a cheerful orange and brown. Ellis is blues and greys. And Grandmother is pale pink and pale green.'

'What about the house? Doesn't that have a colour of its own?'

That was a new idea to Trish, who had been thinking only of the bedrooms which were a manageable size. She knew that even in the most slapdash manner she could not tackle the high entertaining rooms. She considered the point for a moment, recognizing that when moving from one room to another there should not be too many shocks to the eye.

'They're right already. My grandfather wrote it all down when he designed the house. Red for the dining room and the library. Pink and green for the drawing room and the morning room. I suppose that's why I think those colours are right for Grandmother. It's just all the porridgy bedrooms that need changing.'

'Sounds to me as though you're going to be an artist when you grow up.'

Trish stared at him in a puzzled manner. There was something wrong with that remark, although it took her a moment to think what it was. Then she worked it out. In Rupert's company, or Jean-Paul's, she could not pretend to be an adult. They had known her since she was six, and felt themselves to be of a different generation. But although Terry also was a few years older than she was, she felt on equal terms with him. They were meeting on her territory, so that his self-confidence as a workman was matched by hers as a hostess. It was a shock to be reminded that he too might see her only as a schoolgirl.

'I'm grown-up already,' she said with a touch of indignation in her voice.

It was not true, of course. She just felt that it ought to be. If only the years would fly, fly, fly.

1944

ONE

'How did it go?' When Trish arrived home from school Grace, unusually, was waiting to welcome her. Dan and Boxer also came running to hear her news as she put her bicycle away in the coach-house.

'Well,' said Trish. 'Considering that it's inhuman to expect a person to spend midsummer day in an examination room and considering that it's an extra form of torture if it happens to be that person's eighteenth birthday and considering that it's completely ridiculous that a person who only wants to go to art school should be expected to know all about history and Shakespeare and that sort of thing, it wasn't too bad.'

Grace, who had been treated to her stepdaughter's views on the Higher School Certificate at frequent intervals during the past two years, smiled in relief.

'I think it'll be all right,' said Trish. 'I'm only required to pass. No nonsense about credits or distinctions. Anyway, it's all over. No more exams. No more school, even, if I happen not to feel like it.'

'Will you stop going then?' asked Boxer. At twelve, he had two more years of education to endure and would certainly leave earlier if he could.

'No. The last three weeks should be rather fun. No proper lessons. Is there any more *real* news?'

The invasion of France had begun a fortnight earlier. She was torn between excitement at the prospect of victory at last and anxiety about her father. Ellis was in almost as much danger as the fighting men whose exploits he was recording on film.

209

'More of those pilotless bombs falling on London,' Dan told her. 'But it sounds as though everything's going all right in France.' It was the fourteen-year-old who most regularly listened to the radio news and moved coloured pins and flags over the large map which hung on the wall of the boys' bedroom. 'I moved Rupert today,' he added. Trish had made tiny figures of the soldiers in whose fate they were all most interested and had fastened them to the heads of drawing pins. 'There's a postcard for you. From Rome, I think.'

'Rome! Why didn't you tell me?'

'It's only just come.' But Trish did not wait to hear. Already she was running out of the stable towards the hall.

Rupert was her most faithful correspondent. Jean-Paul, who had joined the Free French army, wrote mostly to his father, enclosing only messages for Andy to pass on to her, and Terry was not a letter-writer at all. Until a month earlier he had been stationed near enough to Greystones to enable him to spend every leave there, and felt this to provide sufficient contact with his brothers and their hosts. But for two years Rupert had sent her long letters from the North African desert. Sometimes she felt that they were not exactly addressed to her as an individual, but were merely words that he needed to put on paper, with the choice of recipient to be decided later. But since he did so often choose her, she had no complaints about that.

For several weeks now there had been silence, which was eventually explained by news of the landings in Italy. The announcement of the fall of Rome had been made only a little while before that of the Normandy landings. If Rupert was safely in the city, it must surely mean that the worst was over for him.

Grace caught up with her while she was reading the card for the second time.

'Trish dear, there's something I want to ask you about. I had a telephone call from my brother today.'

'Uncle David?'

'Yes. It's about Max. Apparently one of these flying bomb things came down in Harrow yesterday.'

'Was Max hurt?'

'Oh no, no. It was in the next street, I gather. Though the blast caused damage over a wide area. All the windows at the back of the house were blown out. More important than that, Sheila had another of her heart attacks. The shock, I suppose. It sounds as though she'll be all right, but obviously David's worried. The thing is –'

'He wants to send Max back here?'

Unlike Boxer and Dan, who had stayed on at Greystones regardless of conditions in London, because they had no home, Max had been shuttled about between Harrow and Greystones in a way which had done his education no good.

For the first eighteen months after the start of the Blitz in September 1940 he had been permanently in Grace's care, attending the village school with Dan and Boxer and visited by his mother once a month. By the time the raids eased off enough for him to return to his parents, he had become so attached to his new home that he was returned there for each of the school holidays. Trish suspected that this was his mother's way of protecting him from his father's discipline. A new wave of bombing brought him hastily back to the country in January 1944, but by the beginning of the summer term this too seemed to have come to an end and once again he had returned home.

'Well, it would be ridiculous for him to stay there while there's still danger. And with Sheila in hospital and David at work all day . . .'

There was a note almost of apology in Grace's voice, as though she was aware of Trish's ambivalent feelings towards Max. Trish herself hardly understood her own lack of enthusiasm for this particular visitor. It had something to do with the confidence with which he took his place as a member of the family, making it clear that Dan and Boxer, unlike himself, did not really belong, but were being allowed to stay as a favour because of the special circumstances.

211

Max was a mother's boy and had transferred his need to be cuddled and spoiled from his mother to his grandmother on the first day of his arrival. Even Grace, who had never been a kissing or hugging kind of person, seemed to recognize his need to be petted. Trish regarded herself as being the champion of the two East End boys whom she had chosen to bring into the household, but perhaps it was on her own account that she had been a little jealous when Max first came to stay.

But it was her birthday, her exams were over and the sun was shining. 'Yes, of course,' she said cheerfully. 'When's he coming?'

'Not till later this evening. He went to school as usual. David only decided to ask me after he'd heard the doctor's report on Sheila. They'll catch the 6.20 from Paddington. Trish, you'll have a chat with Mother about your exams, won't you? You know how interested she is in all your news.'

Trish would have preferred to dismiss the subject from her mind, but she nodded dutifully.

'I'll do it now. D'you know where she is?'

'Boxer's just gone to help her outside. She'll be in the walled garden.'

Stuffing the postcard into the pocket of her school blazer, Trish set out to find them – but was diverted by the sight of a young man of about her own age striding up the hill from the lodge gates. He was wearing civilian clothes but had a kitbag slung over his shoulder. She paused to see what he wanted.

'Hi, there,' he said in a voice that sounded American – or was it perhaps Australian? 'I'm Gordon Hardie.' He set down his kitbag and held out a hand.

'How do you do? I'm Trish Faraday.'

'And you don't know who I am?'

'Should I? I'm only adopted into this family. There are probably Hardies all over the world waiting to bob up here and I wouldn't know any of them, so don't take it personally. Are you looking for anyone in particular?'

'Mrs Lucy Hardie, my grandmother.'

'I'll go and find her. Would you like to wait inside or do you prefer the sunshine?'

'I'll take what passes for sunshine.' He sat down on the kitbag with his long legs stretched out in front of him. 'Hey, is that a toy vineyard you've got over there? I didn't know such things existed in England.'

'There aren't many and ours is the best. We make a scrumptious white wine. Hang around till October and we'll set you to work here. Clever of you to recognize it. Most people don't.'

'My grandfather out in Australia started one of his own fifty years ago. 'Spect it'll be mine one day. Mind if I take a look?'

'Go ahead.' Trish set off in the opposite direction to look for Mrs Hardie.

She found her, as Grace had suggested, in the walled garden, standing at the far end of the strawberry rows as she set Dan and Boxer to work. It was a tradition that Trish's birthday should always be celebrated with a strawberry tea from what was usually the first picking of the year.

'You've got a visitor,' she called cheerfully as she approached Mrs Hardie. 'From far-off parts. Mr Gordon Hardie by name.'

'Gordon? Gordon! Gordon, where are you?'

Mrs Hardie took a single step forward and then stopped, clutching her arms to her chest. A harsh rasping sound emerged from the back of her throat. Then she began to move again. It was difficult to tell whether she was trying to run or merely overbalancing, toppling forward. Whichever it was, she made no attempt to approach Trish along the gravel path, but took a step forward between two rows of strawberries.

The ground was rough with lumps of earth which had been turned up by the hoe and had since baked hard in the sun. Trish could see what was going to happen a second before the fall occurred. Lucy Hardie was a tall woman and in recent years inactivity had made her heavy. She crashed awkwardly on to one side without having time to put out an arm to break the fall. Then she lay still.

Trish froze in horror, her hands flung up in front of her eyes:

knowing what she ought to do, but unable to move. It was Dan and Boxer who ran to find Grace.

An hour later Mrs Hardie had been taken off to the Infirmary in an ambulance and Trish lay sobbing on her bed. The brightly-painted walls which as a rule gave her such pleasure seemed inappropriate to the day, so that she had pulled the blackout curtains across to darken the room. Grace, coming to look for her, opened them again.

'Pull yourself together, Trish,' she said. 'Accidents happen. They can't always be helped.'

'It was all my fault,' said Trish miserably, dabbing her eyes. 'It must have been. But I don't understand why.'

'Dan told me what happened. He didn't understand either. But I can guess what it must have been.' Grace sat down to explain. 'When you said that Gordon Hardie was here, Mother must have become confused, thinking you meant her husband. I don't suppose it even occurred to you that it was the same name.'

Trish shook her head. 'When she shows me paintings and things, she always calls him "Mr Hardie". And to you she says "your father". I think I did know that he was Gordon, if I'd thought about it. But –' She sat up and swung her legs over the side of the bed. 'He's been dead for years and years. How could she possibly imagine –?'

'We can't all think rationally all the time. The real trouble is that she never saw him die. He went off on an expedition to China, looking for new plants, and simply never came back. For a long time she hoped that he was still alive somewhere. In the end she went out to China herself to look for him. That trip did seem to satisfy her that he was dead. But I've no doubt in her heart of hearts she went on hoping that there might have been some mistake, that one day he might walk up the drive out of the blue. So when she heard his name spoken – it wouldn't have been fright or shock that affected her. Joy, rather. Which means, of course, that there'll be disappointment to come.'

'Is she going to be all right?'

Grace hesitated. 'It's too soon to say. It does seem to have been an awkward fall. The doctor thinks she may have broken her hip. She'll probably have to stay in hospital for some time.'

'Old ladies die of broken hips, don't they?'

'Not directly, no. Sometimes it makes them more likely to catch pneumonia, and *that*'s dangerous. But in hospital she'll be under observation all the time. The real answer is, I don't know. Whatever happens, you're not to blame yourself. It was an accident. As for Mother, when she finds out who *this* Gordon Hardie is, it will cheer her up no end.'

'Who is he, then?' asked Trish.

'His father is my brother Kenneth. One of the twins who shared the room that Dan and Boxer have now. I've just been trying to find out how much Gordon knows about his father, and he seems to have been told the truth, so there's no harm in my telling you. Kenneth was a conscientious objector in the first war – or rather, he applied to be one, but was refused permission and conscripted instead. He had a terrible time in the army. In the end he deserted. So he's always felt that he couldn't return to England – and he was so badly treated that he never *wanted* to return. It's been hard on Mother, losing touch. He went with her on her trip to China, but she hasn't seen him since.'

'Did they write to each other?'

'It's one of the things that's most hurt her – and that young Gordon's arrival will heal. All we've ever had from Kenneth is a Christmas card sent to Greystones every year; and he never puts his address on it. I think perhaps there were years when he simply didn't have an address. He worked on ships for a bit, and then he drifted around Australia looking for gold. Perhaps he was ashamed of what he was doing – or perhaps he simply never realized that we didn't know how to get in touch with him and thought *we* were ashamed of him. Anyway, now we can learn all about him and his family. Mother will be very happy. As for you, it's still your birthday and we have a young

guest to entertain. So give yourself a wash and brush-up and come and have tea.'

'Yes.' Trish stood up. 'All the same, Grace – I am most terribly sorry.'

'I know you are. And it must have given you a fright. But you're not to blame yourself any more.' Grace walked over to the wardrobe and opened it. 'Get out of your school uniform and into this.'

She threw a sleeveless cotton dress on to the bed and then stared at it with an expression of such dismay that Trish was alarmed.

'What's the matter?' she asked.

TWO

Grace pulled a face.

'How awful of me!' she said. 'I should have arranged a party for you today.'

Trish could not help laughing. 'You've *never* had a party for me,' she said.

'Never?'

'Never. It's simply not something you do. I shouldn't think you've ever had a party for yourself, have you?'

Grace sat down again and considered the question.

'It's odd,' she admitted. 'The first war caught me at just the age that this war has caught you. And it was a much gloomier war, somehow. So many men being killed. Even if we'd wanted to have parties and dances, there were hardly any young men in England at all. But on the whole we didn't feel like that sort of thing. Life was too unhappy. It seemed wrong.' She was silent for a moment, remembering the time when she had worked in the family business, hoping for letters but never expecting invitations. 'So my mother never arranged any kind of social début for me. I didn't miss it at the time. But I suppose it had the effect that I've never been interested in social life.' She looked up at Trish. 'But that doesn't excuse me for not making an effort for you. The end of exams, nearly the end of school, your eighteenth birthday. We should most certainly have had a celebration. Perhaps –'

Trish interrupted her firmly. 'I've had marvellous birthday presents from you all. I'm just about to hog all the strawberries and I happen to know that Mrs Barrett has made a special cake.'

'It's not good enough. Company is what makes a celebration.'

With a heavy sigh Trish prepared to reveal a secret.

'I wasn't going to tell you. But if you're going to go around feeling guilty, I suppose I'd better say. A party today wouldn't have been any good anyway, because the people who are taking science haven't finished their exams yet and they're all busy swotting. But I shall be celebrating my birthday on Saturday. In the plant room. I hope you don't mind.'

The plant room stood away from the house. It had been built for Mrs Hardie's husband to carry out his hybridizing experiments near to one of the glasshouses and well removed from his boisterous family of children.

'I chose that so that you wouldn't be disturbed by the noise. Everyone's bringing some food and we shall all eat each other's. I cleaned the room out last Sunday.'

Grace stared at her in astonishment. 'Have you done this before?' she asked.

'Yes. Each of the past three years. It's not that I want to have parties specially, but if I go to other people's then they expect to be asked back. Keeping it secret was all part of the fun. Everyone was told the way they'd got to sneak up without being seen. It's always been warm, so we could have games and treasure hunts and that sort of thing in the wood. I never told you any fibs about it. I always said that I was going to a party, and I was.'

Grace absorbed all this in silence.

'What a rotten mother I've been to you,' she said at last.

'You're not to say that sort of thing. Did you mind about your mother not having parties for you?'

'No.'

'Well, then. Why should I mind?'

'We're different, you and I.'

'You've given me everything that it's possible to give,' Trish said. 'Having fun is something that a person – anybody – has to arrange for herself. Because as you said, we're different, and different people want different things. What I liked was having a *secret* party. You couldn't ever have given me that, could you?'

Lost for words, Grace stood up again. Before leaving the room she pointed to the dress she had thrown on to the bed. 'Make yourself pretty,' she repeated.

The telephone was ringing as she went downstairs. It would almost certainly be for Trish, but she answered it all the same.

'Aunt Grace?' Max's voice was pitched high with anxiety and indignation. 'It's me.'

'Hello, Max. I'm looking forward to seeing you this evening.'

'Well, that's what I'm phoning about. I've only just got home from school and Father's phoned to say that I'm to be ready to leave in an hour. I know it's not your fault, but it's beastly unfair of him making me go tonight, when he knows how important tomorrow is. Nobody else is running away from the doodlebugs and I can look after myself perfectly well and it isn't because I don't like coming to Greystones because you know I do but he's doing it on purpose just to be horrid and I won't go.'

'Steady on, Max. I don't know what you're talking about. Start again at the beginning and take it one step at a time.'

There was a gulp at the other end of the line as the eleven-year-old struggled to accept his instructions.

'Father says I'm to come back to Greystones because of these flying bombs and because Mummy's had to go to hospital.'

'Yes. He phoned me a couple of hours ago. We're always delighted to see you here; you know that.'

'Yes, well, I like coming as well, but I could come tomorrow evening instead so that I could take the exam first. I mean, he's not even letting me have proper time to pack or anything. He's rushing me off specially so that I won't be able to take it. And I've worked for it all year and –'

'Slowly, slowly. What exam are you talking about?'

'My dance grade. You remember, you fixed for me to go on having lessons when I came back to Greystones in January, so that I could keep up.'

'Yes.' Grace was beginning to get his drift. It was she who had realized soon after Max first arrived at Greystones in 1940 that her nephew was a natural gymnast and she had made use of this talent to combat the six-year-old's homesickness, searching out a Saturday-morning class in which he could receive training and providing a variety of ropes and bars in the grounds of Greystones for him to practise his exercises.

The therapy proved successful. One of Grace's strongest beliefs was that everyone needed to enjoy an overwhelming enthusiasm for something, and she had congratulated herself on hitting the target for Max with her first shot.

Trish had been given the duty of escorting him to his class, and had formed the habit of taking Dan and Boxer to a children's film show in a nearby cinema instead of waiting in the hall. Because the matinée lasted longer than the class, it was Max who was kept waiting, and he soon became interested in the ballet class which came next on the timetable of the community hall. Grace never knew how many weeks elapsed before he asked whether he could join in, because during that first term no request was made for the payment of a fee. Little boys who actually wanted to learn ballet were apparently as rare as gold dust, and one enthusiast could be used to persuade others that at least they would not be alone; so the teacher preferred not to risk parental discouragement by asking for Max to be officially enrolled. Only when Grace was invited to the end-of-term concert did she realize that her nephew, from the unlikeliest of backgrounds, had recognized his own true talent and enthusiasm.

It had caused trouble, of course. When he returned to London his indulgent mother was willing to let him do anything he wanted. But David, whose instinct was always to say No to his youngest child, was predictably horrified at the thought of any son of his prancing about on a stage in tights. Grace could well believe that David was seizing a plausible opportunity to act spitefully and disappoint his son.

'This exam is an important one,' said Max, impatient with the length of silence. 'Miss Berry thinks I might get distinction. But if I'm not even allowed to take it . . . It's at ten o'clock. I only need the morning. Oh, he's here! Please do something, Aunt Grace.'

The line went dead. Unauthorized telephone calls were doubtless yet another source of argument in the David Hardie household. Grace hardly hesitated for a moment before making a return call to her brother's number.

'David? Grace here. Thank goodness I've caught you before you leave. Look, David, can you put it off for a day – bringing Max over, I mean. We're in a state of complete chaos here and I need a little time to sort myself out.'

'What's happening?' David's voice was cool but not suspicious.

'Three things all at once. It's Trish's birthday, and I forgot . . . I didn't arrange . . . Well, I've got to do something urgently about that. And then Kenneth's son has just turned up without warning to stay.'

'From Australia!'

'Yes. To join up. But the real thing is, Mother's had an accident.'

'Mother? Is it serious? If she's ill, that's all the more reason why I ought to come at once.'

'No, not now. There'd be no point. She's got to have an operation and she won't be allowed visitors at once. I'll phone you at the office tomorrow, David, and let you know. I'll be glad to help you out by taking Max tomorrow, but I simply can't cope this evening. I'm sorry.'

In the five years since Dan and Boxer first arrived on the scene, Grace had discovered that she was perfectly well able to cope with any kind of domestic flurry; but the lack of sympathy between her brother and herself meant that he would take her words at face value without suspecting a conspiracy. It would be up to Max to make good use of his reprieve. Grace smiled to herself as she put down the telephone.

THREE

Trish, meanwhile, was obeying Grace's orders to make herself look pretty. In the matter of clothes rationing, as with food, the inhabitants of Greystones hardly knew that there was a war on. Mrs Hardie seemed never to have thrown any of her clothes away, and had willingly cut them up and used the material to keep up with the pace at which Trish had outgrown everything she owned over the past four years.

It was amazing what a difference the change of clothing made. In her severe blue uniform dress, with its white collar and cuffs, she had been merely a schoolgirl. Now, when she looked in the mirror, she saw an attractive young woman. Her breasts were small and her hips narrow, but by pulling the belt of her dress tight she was able to add curves to her figure. The need to revise had so far this summer kept her out of the sun, so that her oval face and long, slim arms were pale, without any of the stripes which in normal years indicated what length of sleeve she had worn for working in the garden.

Last of all Trish pulled off the ribbon which tied her long hair neatly at the back of her neck, as school regulations demanded. Her hair was very straight, which was bad, but very blonde, which was good. She brushed it vigorously and then spun round like a dancer, so that both hair and skirt swirled high before settling back into place. Even on a day of guilt and tragedy, she found it hard to remain subdued for long.

Tea had already started, although the strawberries were being kept for her arrival. The new visitor leapt to his feet as she came into the room and stared at her appreciatively.

'Transformation scene!' he exclaimed. 'I always thought we

had the prettiest girls in the world in Australia, but now I'm not so sure. Hey, I'm sorry to hear that my grandmother's crock.'

'Crock?' asked Trish, puzzled; but Grace interrupted to change the subject.

'I've been waiting until Trish arrived to ask you, Gordon, how you come to be here.'

'Worked my passage. Don't know that I'd have been so keen if I'd known how many U-boats were lurking in the Atlantic, but we came through OK. I wanted to enlist in the Old Country, 'stead of at home. Sort of making up for Dad, see?'

'Did he approve of that – of you enlisting at all, I mean?' asked Grace.

'Yeh. He explained it to me, as much as it could be explained, what happened before. There was something about him and his brother killing a cat, when they were only kids.' He looked across the table at Grace. '*Your* cat.'

Grace nodded but added no further information.

'Set up a sort of block, he said, so that he couldn't bear the thought of killing anyone else at all. Wasn't specially that he disapproved of war. That was the problem, I gather, when he asked for exemption. If he'd been a Quaker or something like that, he might have got away with it. But being a cat-murderer wasn't a recognized category. Mind you, I reckon he has his doubts, looking back, on whether the last war was worth fighting. But this one's different, he says, and I think so too. A fight against wickedness. So he was all for me joining up. It was my idea to do it here.'

'You'll stay at Greystones, I hope,' said Grace. 'Treat it as your home while you're in England.'

'Thanks a lot.' He made no pretence that he had not expected the invitation. Instead, he turned his attention from Grace to Trish. 'There's a dance on in Oxford tonight,' he told her. 'To celebrate midsummer, the notice outside the station said. How about it?'

'Well, I don't know.' Although it was easy to see that Grace

224

wanted her to accept, Trish was taken aback. She and the rest of the sixth form had organized dancing lessons for themselves after school, but had never used their new skill for anything more adventurous than the dances which were arranged once a term with a nearby boys' school. The embarrassment of these occasions, when the girls huddled shyly at one end of a hall and waited to be picked out by a boy from the other end, had not filled her with much enthusiasm for the activity. And was it right that she should enjoy herself on this day of family disaster?

'Aw, come on,' pressed Gordon. 'It's my birthday. Got to have someone to celebrate with.'

'Your birthday?' Trish's eyes brightened with interest. 'It's mine, too. I'm eighteen. How old are you?'

'Seventeen and eleven-twelfths,' he told her, and before she finished laughing she had agreed to go.

Oxford was almost a foreign city to her. School in Heading-ton and the house on the hill were enough to fill the whole of her ordinary life and she made the journey down into the city only to go shopping or to the cinema or to take Max to his classes. As they cycled across Magdalen Bridge and along the High, with Gordon wobbling uncertainly on his borrowed bicycle, she pointed out the family shop, with the name of Hardie above it in gold Gothic letters, but was ashamed of her inability to answer his questions about the colleges they passed.

'You reckoning to study here yourself now you've finished with school?' he asked as they dismounted.

'Not at the university; heavens no. I'm not nearly bright enough for that. I want to go to art school. It would have been in London if things had been normal, but as it happens the college has been evacuated to Oxford. So I'll go on living at home.'

'You don't have to join the army?'

'I have a choice. I can start a course if I want to, but if the war goes on I'd have to cut it short and join up. Everyone thinks now, though, that the war will be over soon.' She watched as he studied the unfamiliar currency in his wallet and bought their tickets at the Town Hall.

To her relief, she quickly discovered that she was a better dancer than Gordon. At least she knew the steps – although this proved to be a mixed blessing, since he made no attempt to follow the rules, but merely jigged energetically on the beat.

'Look,' he said at last. 'I know I'm no good at this, but you have to follow me. Otherwise we'll spend the evening saying sorry to each other. Come in closer and go wherever I go.'

He tightened his grip. Trish had never been held so close before and was stiff at first. But once she was able to relax the movement became fun. They swept round the floor, laughing at the couples who more staidly and correctly concentrated on their slow, slow, quick-quick slow.

'You got a boy?' asked Gordon as the evening approached its end. 'I mean, pretty girl like you, you'll have a lot of boys noticing you, but is there a special one?'

'I don't know.' The answer sounded silly, but was true. 'They're all fighting, you see.' But even when they came home, would any of them – Rupert or Jean-Paul or Terry – think of her as their special girl? Rupert in particular was so much older. Trish herself might be grown-up at last, but Rupert must be thirty. He would have other girls, women; of course he would. She herself could never hope to be more to him than some kind of relation: a kid cousin.

'All older than you, then?' said Gordon astutely.

'Yes. Yes, they are.'

'What you need's a chap your own age. Well, a month younger's neither here nor there. Agree?' And suddenly, in the middle of the dance floor, he was kissing her.

'Gordon! People will see!' she exclaimed, twisting away from him.

'That's the idea. The male as hunter. Establishing territory. Telling the rest of the world to keep its hands off.'

'I may not want the rest of the world to keep its hands off,' she said indignantly. 'For heaven's sake, I've only known you about six hours.'

'Sorry, ma'am. What's the waiting period for a first kiss? Remembering that some of us have got a war to fight and can't hang about. Shall we say six hours and five minutes?' They were walking back to their chairs by now; he stopped and kissed her again.

'You can't expect stuffy Pom manners from a brash Aussie,' he said. 'I just want you to know that I like you.'

'It's time we went home,' said Trish.

'Another hour yet.'

'I've had quite a day,' she said. It was true: she felt emotionally drained. 'Birthday, and exams, and Grandmother's accident.'

'And now a strange young man rushing you. Sorry. But you don't really mind, do you?'

She turned her head to stare at him, thinking how odd it was that he should be so obviously not English in spite of the fact that he came of English stock. There was a looseness about his limbs, making him seem at once strong and relaxed. His grin was wider and his gaze more direct than any other boy she knew – as though, like Trish herself, he believed in having fun: not waiting for it to be offered to him, but setting out to make it happen.

He put out a hand to take hers. The touch made her body tingle with excitement. Was this what was meant by falling in love? At one time or another she had thought herself to be in love with each of the three young men whose names had come into her mind when Gordon asked her if she had a boy. But probably what she felt for Rupert was a schoolgirl crush. And Jean-Paul and Terry were just good company. She liked working beside them – on the land with Jean-Paul, in the house with Terry – talking only occasionally; just happy to be with them. But neither of them had ever made her feel hot and cold at the same time, as Gordon Hardie was doing.

227

He was waiting for an answer. She looked at him with a gaze as direct as his own.

'No,' she said. 'I don't mind.'

FOUR

Trish arrived home from school the next day to find that the household had increased still further in size. Jay, it appeared, had arrived soon after breakfast – and not merely for a short visit to see his mother. When Trish went to look for him she found that he had taken possession of his old bedroom and had already filled all the storage space it contained with the extensive wardrobe essential, he always claimed, for an actor. Books and photographs covered every available surface and there was still one trunk unpacked on the floor.

'Are you coming to live here?' she asked.

'Try that again with a different inflection. "Darling Jay, can it be true that you're coming to live here! Oh, goody, goody!" Well, I do seem to be in need of a new base. London is becoming just the teeniest weeniest bit unpleasant again. Not that you'd realize that. Living here, you –'

'Don't know there's a war on.' Trish finished the remark in unison with him. 'Are you talking about these pilotless planes?'

'Flying bombs,' said Jay. 'Doodlebugs, people are calling them. A toy name for something very nasty. You can hear them coming from a long way off. A horrid gritty noise.' He gave an imitation of it. 'As long as the noise goes on, you're all right. Then it stops. If it stops directly overhead, you're still all right because the beastly thing will glide a bit further on. But if it stops before it reaches you, you're not all right at all. The show closed last night. People simply stopped coming.'

'I suppose you can't really blame them.'

'No. Ever since the Blitz we've been starting the evening performances much earlier than in peacetime, so that people didn't have to cope with the blackout and could get home before the night raids started; but the doodlebugs are coming over in daylight. So the final curtain has descended.'

'Bad luck.'

'Well, mustn't complain. I've had one great piece of luck in my life. Born in the right year. Just too young to fight in the first war: just too old to be much use in this one, since my ENSA tours hardly rank as active service. And I shan't be unemployed for long. The management's trying to set up a provincial tour to keep the company together. But if I don't need to be in London, there doesn't seem much point in paying rent for a flat which may be blasted into little bits at any moment.'

'Terry thinks this is the time to buy the place you live in, instead of paying rent,' said Trish. 'Or at least, that's what he thought when the Blitz was on. While prices are low because lots of people in London want to sell and get out and most people think it's crazy to buy. If the house doesn't get bombed, it will be ever so valuable after the war, he says, because there won't be enough homes to go round. And even if it does get bombed, you'd have the land and the compensation. Terry says that if he had any capital at all, that's what he'd do, buy houses and then sell them again later.'

'Terry will be a millionaire one day, no doubt about it,' said Jay. 'But there's a difference between a house and a flat. There's no way I can get my hands on the land underneath my flat. Anyway, I haven't got any capital, any more than Terry has.'

'I thought actors earned hundreds and hundreds of pounds.'

'Then you thought wrong. I find no difficulty in spending everything I earn. And unemployment and destitution are always just round the corner. So it's just as well that I have a loving sister who'll make sure that I never lack a roof over my head. Long life to Grace, that's what I say!'

'How's Grandmother?' asked Trish. That ought to have been her first question.

'Hasn't come round after the operation yet. Grace and I

went down this morning to sit with her, but she didn't know we were there. Sister promised to phone us as soon as she starts to wake up. We'll go down again in any case in an hour or so. We've arranged to meet David there.'

'But how *is* she?'

'Honestly don't know, my duck.' But the lightness had disappeared from his voice. 'The doctor seems to think that she may have had a slight stroke just before she fell – in fact, that that was *why* she fell. They won't know for a bit how much that's affected her. It'll be a little while, either way, before she's running around again. Grace is thinking of turning some ground floor rooms into a bedroom and sitting room for her if necessary. And I suppose she'd need a downstairs bathroom as well.'

'There ought to be more bathrooms anyhow,' said Trish. 'I don't know how you managed when you were all children.'

'That's because you don't know what it's like to be waited on. The roaring coal fire in the nursery, with the bath towel warming in front of it. The tin bath filled with kettles of hot water by a succession of maids. And Nanny ready to soap your back while you played with your ducks. Bliss. Growing up is a great mistake.'

'I'll go and help Grace choose,' decided Trish. There was nothing she liked better than changing rooms around, and for half an hour they discussed possibilities together. The morning room, which was the ground floor of the tower, would be ideal as a bedroom, but was too small to act as a sitting room as well.

'No point in making up our minds yet awhile,' said Grace at last. 'It may turn out that a bedroom's all she'll need. Have you had tea yet?'

'Not yet. Where's Gordon?'

'Finding out how to enlist. Don't look so horrified! He doesn't expect to be press-ganged straight away. He needs to know what the procedures are – and what choices he may have. I tried to suggest to him that the British Army might

231

not suit him too well. I can't quite see him saying "Yes sir, no sir" to someone he'll regard as a stuffy Pom.'

'That must have set him back a bit, when he's come all this way specially.'

'Yes. Well, I discovered that he can fly a plane – and make repairs to it, as well. He's used to visiting his friends and neighbours by air where you might get on your bike. It's not easy to get into the RAF, I don't think, but he'd be better qualified than most volunteers and he might find it more congenial if they'd have him. He should be back soon.'

Trish waited for him with a mixture of impatience and shyness while Grace and Jay made their second journey to the Infirmary. Would he want to kiss her again? Did she want him to? Yes, she did. It was odd, when she thought about it now, that neither Jean-Paul nor Terry had ever kissed her; although neither of them, as far as she knew, had any other special girl and each of them was in a way 'interested' in her. As for Rupert, he planted kisses on her forehead or cheek when they met and parted, but only in a cousinly way. Was Gordon treating her as an adult because he had not known her as a child? Or had she unconsciously given him some kind of signal that she was ready for a flirtation?

No, not a flirtation. She was eager for something deeper than that, and Gordon had sensed her eagerness. She hoped he would not be too quick to disappear into the armed forces.

He returned, by chance, only a few moments after his aunt and uncles came back from the Infirmary. David and Grace had gone straight into the house but Trish, watching out, was disappointed to see him introduce himself to Jay and accept the suggestion of a walk.

Max had arrived as well, trailing behind the others. Trish saw his eyes brighten at the sight of the two long ropes which hung from a branch of the cedar tree. Originally fastened there for Dan and Boxer to climb, they were close enough together for a boy to grip one in each hand. Setting down his suitcase, Max gave a little jump on the spot and then ran with long, high strides before leaping into the air and grasping the ropes higher up than Trish would have believed possible. He swung his legs until they pointed straight up in the air above his head, and then pushed himself off the ropes in a somersault, taking pains to keep his balance steady after landing.

She found his agility incredible. Even more extraordinary was the fact that he showed no interest in what he could achieve on the ropes or bars. Gymnastics was simply one kind of exercise to help him develop strength and balance. All he wanted to do was to dance. Though Trish did not go as far as David in disapproving of such an ambition, she did secretly consider it to be rather cissy. But remembering her manners as a hostess, she went outside to welcome him.

'How did you get on with your exam?' she asked. Grace had confided the situation to her.

Max's pointed face creased with mischief. He gave a little run and leapt into the air, his body turning while his toes crossed each other more quickly than Trish could count.

'Jolly well,' he said. 'All my jumps went right. Where's Boxer?'

'Playing cricket. I'll look after your case if you want to join in.'

For the time being, she left it in the hall and took her sketch pad and pencil and a pair of scissors into the library. If Mrs Hardie were to need a ground floor room when she returned home, the library would be almost as suitable as the morning room, and far larger – large enough to be divided into two sections. True, it did not get the early morning sun; but there would be plenty of afternoon brightness. Since Philip's death, nobody ever looked at the books which had once been Mr Hardie's, for neither Trish nor Grace was a great reader. There could be no objection to moving some of them in order to make room for a bed.

Indeed, perhaps two of the heavy bookcases could be turned at right angles to the wall to cut off a sleeping cubicle, with the wide space between them leading to a comfortable sitting room. The solid backs of the bookcases could be covered with some kind of fabric and used to hang a few of Mrs Hardie's watercolours so that she could see them from her bed. After pacing out the size of the whole room, Trish sat down on the steps which were used to reach the highest shelves of books and began to sketch an outline of the room and cut out the shapes of furniture to arrange on it.

So engrossed was she in the task that she was not immediately aware that Grace and David had come into the drawing room. There was a corridor running round the edge of the internal courtyard of Greystones to give access to each of the downstairs rooms, but every room was also connected with its neighbours directly by means of double doors. To reach the library, Trish had walked from the hall through the drawing room, and had left both sets of doors open behind her.

There was a quarrel in progress. Even without hearing the words, the tone of the two raised voices told her that. Trish moved quietly towards the wide doors with the intention of closing them, but realized that the action would draw attention to her presence and perhaps make two angry people even angrier. The right solution was to make her way out into the corridor, but curiosity proved to be too strong. Standing still against the end wall of the library, she began to eavesdrop.

'It only goes to prove what I've always said.' David, in the middle of some argument whose subject she would have to work out gradually, was in a state of fury. 'I can't think what possessed anyone to give a house like this to a *girl*.'

'I take it you don't hold me responsible for that, since I was only one year old at the time.' Grace's voice was calmer, but icy.

'But you have the responsibility now to take proper care of it. For goodness' sake, Grace, don't you know anything at all about death duties? Suppose you had died a month ago, and Mother today, do you realize what would have happened? The family would have had to find an enormous sum of money to pay the duty on the value of Greystones when you died, and then within a few weeks would have had to pay the same sum all over again. Since none of us has got that sort of money, or anything like it, the only way it could have been paid would be by selling the house. Is that really what you wanted to happen?'

'It was never likely that I would die before Mother.'

'That's what wills are for, to deal with the consequences of the unlikely as well as the inevitable. Any lawyer would have told you what a mess you were getting yourself into.'

'You were the one,' said Grace – and she too was growing angry now – 'who was concerned lest Philip and Mother should lose their home if anything happened to me. I promised that I'd guard against any danger of that, and I took the necessary steps.'

'I assumed that at least you'd have the sense to take advice. You could have set up a family trust, for example. I don't consider that you kept your promise in any proper sense of the phrase. I did you a big favour and I remind you that you're still under an obligation to keep the spirit of your promise as well as the letter.'

Grace sighed so heavily that Trish could hear it in the next room. When she spoke again the anger had gone out of her voice, which was low and unhappy.

'This isn't the right time for this kind of discussion. We ought not to be quarrelling now. I must go and find Trish and tell her.'

Tell her what? Trish guessed what it must be, and could not understand why she had not realized at once.

'Grace, Grace!' she called, hurtling into the drawing room at such speed that she might well be assumed to have only just run the length of the library. 'How's Grandmother?'

Grace, who so rarely gave caresses, opened her arms in an embrace. No further words were needed to tell Trish that Mrs Hardie was dead.

1945

ONE

'Is it all over now?' asked Trish, coming late to breakfast. Germany had surrendered on the previous day and everyone at Greystones had listened to the radio all evening in the hope of hearing the official announcement of the end of hostilities. For some reason this had been continually postponed; but surely, with Hitler dead and Italy officially out of the war, there could not be any last-minute snags.

'All over bar the shouting.' Gordon, on leave after three months of training with Bomber Command, had also treated himself to a morning lie-in. 'Churchill's going to have lunch at Buckingham Palace. Due to make a broadcast at three o'clock. And then – when I say shouting, shouting is what I mean. What say you and I go up to London and join in?'

'Yes, let's.' Often during the past few years Trish had wished, in a sort of way, that she lived in London. Obviously it would not have been nice to be bombed or to live in a house with all its windows blown out or to queue for rationed food and have nothing but that to eat at all. But for the past five and half years the capital had seemed to enjoy a very special atmosphere of romance and excitement. Compared with London, Oxford was dull.

No one she knew had died in battle. Jean-Paul had been wounded and taken prisoner; but his injuries were not serious. Not a single bomb had fallen on Oxford and she had never gone hungry, although there were times when she sighed for the taste of an orange or banana or swore that she never wanted to eat rabbit again. In a sense she hardly deserved to celebrate a victory to which she had contributed so little – but to join the crowds might help her for the first time to feel part of the excitement she had missed. 'I'll go and tell Grace,' she said.

On the way across the hall she passed Dan and Boxer sitting on the bottom stair.

'Is the war over?' asked Dan.

'Any minute now. You should be looking excited. Isn't there going to be a party at school?'

'Yes, but –'

Trish stopped, sensitive to their anxiety. 'But what?'

'What's going to happen to us? All the other 'vacuees have gone home already.'

It was a question which deserved serious consideration. Trish knew that the boys' only relatives, apart from Terry, were an uncle in Australia whose address no one could remember and an aunt who had lived next door and had lost both legs in the same raid which killed their mother.

'I'll ask Grace,' she promised. She was sure she knew what the answer would be, but it was too important a matter to risk a guess.

Grace, who took no notice of public holidays, was working in the studio, rolling pieces of clay between her hands in the abstracted manner which was always the prelude to a new piece of work.

'Preparing a victory piece?'

'No. Unless – I suppose you might say, this is what the victory is over; why it was worth while fighting.' She pointed to a maquette on the work bench.

Trish could see that the small clay figure had only just been completed, and knew better than to touch. She stared, startled, at the emaciated man, little more than a skeleton. He represented, almost certainly, one of the victims of the camp at Belsen, which had been discovered and liberated a few days earlier.

'It won't be a figure, of course, by the time I finish working on it,' Grace explained. 'I shall use just the rib structure, probably, as the basis of a shape. A symbol. I see it in metal.

237

To give the impression of a cage. Do you think Gordon knows anything about metal-working? It's not something I've tried before.'

'I expect so. Gordon knows something about most things.' But Trish's voice was abstracted. The tiny figure horrified her, yet she was unable to take her eyes off it. 'Grace, no one will buy it! How could anyone possibly live with something like that?'

'It will be a piece for a museum.'

Grace never discussed the commercial aspect of her work. Trish was aware that she was preparing for a large exhibition to be held as soon as the war was over; in addition, private buyers came to the house from time to time after seeing some earlier piece of work. And very often when Ellis came to Greystones he brought with him magazine articles which mentioned Grace Hardie in the same sentence as Barbara Hepworth.

Trish found it difficult to believe that someone so unpretentiously hard-working could apparently be acquiring a public reputation. But as well as the indications that the work was admired, there were more material signs of success. Money, which had been a major anxiety when she first arrived at Greystones, seemed no longer to present any problem. Ellis's contribution to the household and the Beverley money which had come to Mrs Hardie late in her life and passed to Grace after her death had each played a part, but could not by themselves explain Grace's frequent references to her new affluence.

The war made it difficult to find servants, either for the house or for the land; but when any became available, there was money to pay them. The still-modest nature of the household bills was caused by the shortage of anything to buy rather than lack of cash. Trish's own college fees were paid by her father, but it was Grace who, without being asked, had discussed her need for a personal allowance and fixed it at a generous figure.

So perhaps it was true that she was becoming important and producing the kind of sculpture which might be admired in museums. Trish studied the emaciated figure with a different eye – although it still made her uncomfortable to look at it.

With an effort she remembered why she had come, and passed on Dan's question.

'What's going to happen about the boys?' she asked. 'They're worried about whether they're going to be taken away.'

'Of course they're not.' Grace slapped a new piece of clay on to the work bench and began to beat the air out of it. 'They'll stay with us until Terry is demobbed and can tell us what he plans to do.'

'Will you invite him to live here as well?'

'He won't want that,' said Grace confidently. 'An ambitious young man, in my opinion. Doing odd jobs around the house here was a nice way of paying for hospitality, but he'll want a place of his own, if I know anything about him. Anyway, as far as Boxer and Dan are concerned, this is their home until Terry tells them differently. Tell them that straightaway, will you, and I'll say it again this evening.' She laughed as though surprised at herself. 'I never saw myself as a kind of foster-mother, but it's nice that people want to stay on. I've already had Max here in tears.'

'Crying? What about?'

'Because he'll have to go home soon. Mind you, it's not me that he doesn't want to leave; it's his ballet class. He doesn't believe that his father will let him keep on with it – and I should think he's quite right about that.'

'Couldn't you invite him to stay on? I mean, since he and Uncle David get on so badly it might suit both of them, not just Max.'

Grace shook her head. 'I ought not to split up someone else's family. And his mother will want him back, even if his father doesn't. It sounds as though she's living an invalid life these days, frightened of having another heart attack – and his brothers and sister have all left home by now. I shall suggest to David that it's not a good idea to move him in the middle of term. That will give him until July, but after that . . . I feel sorry for him, but I can't interfere unless David asks me himself, and he's not likely to do that.'

'I can see his point of view,' said Trish. 'It's an awfully peculiar thing for a boy to want to do, isn't it, dancing? And a very unHardie-ish thing.'

'I don't think it's peculiar at all. As for whether it's un-Hardie-ish –' She laughed, turning her clay-smeared hands outwards for inspection. 'Look at Jay. And look at me. I wouldn't say that my life has been exactly what's expected of a young lady born into a good class of trade. You never knew my father, but he had the same kind of –' She searched for the right word.

'Enthusiasm? Obsession?'

'Something more than either of those. He had to earn his living as a wine merchant, but what he really *was*, in his heart, was an explorer. A sense of vocation, I think that's what it is. Something that I inherited, and so did Jay, and now Max. Each in a different field, but with the same kind of certainty and determination and dedication. So you might almost say that Max is more of a Hardie than his father, who merely earns a living.'

'I'd forgotten about Jay. Yes, I suppose –'

'I see great resemblances.' Grace picked up another piece of clay and began to mould it between her fingers. 'The same kind of self-absorption. I suppose it's always rather selfish, this sense of vocation thing. You're so sure of what is right for yourself that you don't have much time for considering other people. It wasn't so obvious in Jay as a boy, because his vocation was always to be somebody else, and that was amusing. All Max's ambition is directed on himself. That's probably why you don't like him as much as Dan and Boxer, because they're ordinary boys with time to be friendly.'

'I never said I didn't like him.'

'I can tell. I expect he can as well, but it's a part of that

240

kind of selfishness not to care. I remember –' She paused for a moment, perhaps to collect the memory accurately. 'I remember very clearly something that Jay said when he first became aware of his own vocation. He'd have been a year or two older than Max is now. Happiness, he said, is when what you are is the same as what you do. He knew that he *was* an actor, but he didn't know at that point whether he'd be able to spend his life acting. I thought it was quite a good definition for a thirteen-year-old to produce. I was in my twenties before I proved it for myself. Max has got there young. He knows what he needs for his own happiness, and he's frightened that he may not be allowed to have it.'

'If you think that, then oughtn't you to let him stay?'

'I've been making a few enquiries. What I'm told is that it's very important for a girl who wants to be a ballet dancer to start young and keep up the training without a break. But for some reason it's easier for a boy to start later – to start right from scratch, if necessary. As long as he has a natural talent and is strong and fit he could leave it until the age of fourteen, or even longer. So all these lessons which Max has had already are a kind of bonus, but it won't ruin his life if he has to take a break.'

'And later? When he *is* fourteen.'

'We can jump that hurdle when we come to it.' But Grace's smile was mischievous. 'I've never been afraid of quarrelling with David. Max's best chance is to keep his mother on his side. But if that fails, I've told him he can rely on my support when the crunch comes.'

'For someone who hasn't got children of her own, you're very nice to other people's.' Trish was tempted to give Grace a hug, but knew that this would not be appreciated. 'Right, then, I'll go and tell Dan and Boxer that they're not going to be turned out into the May snow. Gordon and I are going to London, Grace. To see the king. And mill about generally.'

'What time will you be back?'

'Do I have to say?' Of course I don't, she thought to herself:

I'm nearly nineteen. But old habits died hard. 'There could be a sort of party atmosphere going on till late. I wouldn't like to be tied to catching the last train home. Gordon will look after me.'

She turned away, not anticipating any dispute; but was called to a halt.

'Just a minute, Trish. Close the door, will you?'

TWO

What an ominous ring there was to that last phrase. When Trish was a little girl, it had often been the prelude to a lecture. Puzzled, she did as she was told. As she turned back towards the work bench, she was astonished to see that her stepmother's face, usually so pale, was flushed with embarrassment.

'Trish, dear,' Grace said with an effort. 'It's a long time since we talked about this sort of thing. I've never felt I needed . . . I mean, you've always been very sensible. But . . .'

'But what?'

'I want you to promise –' The words came out in a rush. 'I want you to promise me that you won't do anything which could leave you with an illegitimate baby.'

Now it was Trish's turn to flush. 'Why on earth should you think –'

Grace, having jumped the first hurdle, was able to ease the conversation by speaking in a more casual tone of voice.

'I know that you're very fond of Gordon. And he is of you.'

'Yes. But we've never –'

'No, I'm sure. What I'm trying to say is this. You're grown up now. You feel yourself to be an adult. But anyone, of any age, can take themselves by surprise and find themselves being swept off their feet. I'd go further than that, in fact. It happens to everyone once. Sensible people learn from the experience and are careful the second time. But it's terribly hard to guard against the first time, when your feelings may be much stronger than you ever expected.'

'Did it happen to you, getting swept away?' asked Trish curiously.

'Everyone. And the reason why I'm saying this now is that today will be dangerous. You'll be part of a huge crowd. There'll be a kind of atmosphere – well, that's why you're going, isn't it? And it won't seem the right kind of occasion to worry about train times. You'll find yourself there for the night and the crowds will drift away and one of you will begin to think "Why not?" It happens so easily, Trish, and once the idea starts it's so difficult to stop.'

Trish was silent because she was reluctant to put her thoughts into words. This was something which had got to happen sometime. Why shouldn't it be today, with Gordon? She found herself becoming angry with Grace for forcing her to consider her attitude in advance in a cold-blooded way instead of enjoying the emotions as they came. The older woman had no difficulty in guessing how she felt.

'It's not worth it, Trish. People think that just once isn't much of a risk, but for some reason the first time seems specially likely to produce a baby. You must wait till you're married. You're sensible enough to understand that, while you're looking at it rationally. It can ruin a girl's life, being landed with an illegitimate baby.'

'Gordon would marry me.'

'Gordon's only eighteen, and he won't be planning to stay in England much longer now. Far too young to want to settle down. The sort of marriage that starts with a shotgun wedding never quite escapes from the feeling that one partner or the other has been trapped.'

'Well anyway, of course I don't intend to do anything silly.'

'I'm sure. All I'm asking is for you to turn that into a promise. Just for the next twenty-four hours. Your own resolve to yourself might get swept away in a general mood of celebration; but if you make a specific promise, from you to me, I know you'll keep it.'

'I promise,' said Trish, although there was a note of sulkiness in her voice. But as soon as she emerged from the studio her feeling that the day had been spoiled was swept away by the sight of Gordon in his uniform.

'Might as well make it clear that I won the war personally,' he grinned. 'You nearly ready?'

'Not quite. We'd better take a picnic meal with us, don't you think? I'm just going to see what Mrs Barrett can spare.' All her ebullience returned as she ran off to the kitchen. This was going to be a day to remember.

Even the train journey to London proved to be part of the celebration. Undergraduates were not allowed to leave Oxford during term without special permission from their tutors, but it looked as though almost the whole student body would be fined or sent down if the rules were to be enforced today. There was a good deal of singing and every Union Jack flying within sight of the track provoked a burst of cheering. Trish and Gordon were as noisy as the rest.

Only one moment of seriousness interrupted their gaiety.

'You'll be able to make plans now,' Gordon suggested. 'Difficult to think ahead, isn't it, in wartime, knowing you're likely to get pushed around. What are you going to do when –'

'If you say "when you're grown up" I shall never speak to you again. I'm grown up now.'

'I know that. When you've finished at college, I meant.'

'I don't know. I don't even know whether I'm going to go on with the course. There's so much dull stuff. Drawing from plaster casts. I'm not really interested in drawing. I tell myself that it's a necessary skill, a kind of basic foundation, but I don't enjoy it. I like sloshing colours about, and I seem to have picked the wrong teachers for that.'

'I was asking a more general question. Do you see yourself in five years' time, say, as an artist?'

'Yes,' said Trish emphatically. 'Some kind of artist. Not the sort who sits in front of an easel painting rectangular pictures, though. That's the problem, in a way. I can't quite visualize what it is that I want to paint, and so I don't know whether I'm going the right way about learning how to do it. But you're right about the end of the war making a difference. Grace will let me live in London now, I'm sure. And then I shall feel that I'm in the swim of things at last. I mean, I know how lucky I've been to be brought up at Greystones, but it's a sort of backwater, if you see what I mean.'

'It doesn't seem to worry Grace.'

'I think Grace is a genius,' Trish said seriously. 'All these marvellous things she creates just come out of her own imagination. She could do them anywhere, wherever she happened to be. I'm not like that. I need to have new experiences bouncing off me all the time so that I can choose to grab one or two of them that interest me and see what I can do with them.'

'Reckon you're right, then, that London is the place for you. It's not likely to seem a backwater today. The centre of the world, more like.'

He leaned over to kiss her on the lips as the train pulled into Paddington. The undergraduates in their compartment cheered their approval as loudly as if they had seen another Union Jack. It was that sort of day.

The hours passed in a happy jostling. The only time silence fell was when Big Ben chimed three o'clock and the dense mass of people in Whitehall listened over loudspeakers to the Prime Minister's announcement that the war in Europe would end at midnight.

The cheering turned into singing. To the strains of 'Land of Hope and Glory' Trish and Gordon were carried by the tide of bodies into Trafalgar Square. They held hands tightly in order not to lose each other in the crowd.

'Buckingham Palace?' Gordon suggested. But they were not the only ones who had decided to visit the royal family, and the Mall was so crowded that it was hardly possible to move.

'We could go along Pall Mall,' suggested Trish. 'Let's call on The House of Hardie.'

The shop was closed, of course, but they paused for a moment in front of its unpretentious entrance. Gordon laughed.

'You could say this is responsible for my existence!'

'How d'you mean?'

'Well, when my dad first arrived in Australia he bummed around prospecting for gold, without ever finding anything to make a fuss about. Time came when he needed a job if he was going to eat, and he was told my grandfather was looking for labour. First thing he was asked – well, the *only* thing he was asked – was whether he knew anything about growing grapes or making wine. Shouldn't think he'd ever pruned a vine in his life, but he pitched in strong about how he'd been brought up in this great family wine business. Got the job and went on to marry the boss's only daughter. Which is how he comes to own a vineyard.'

'And you'll own it one day.'

'Unless I do something so crazy that I get the boot. But that won't happen.' They began to walk along the street again. 'Something I've noticed. People who have money – cash – like to jiggle about with their wills. Always thinking of something new they could do with it. This week it's Auntie Jane, next week it's the cook, next year it could be the local orphanage. Seems to be part of the fun, imagining someone's pleasure and someone else's disappointment. But people who've got land, property, are different. They want to know for sure who's going to inherit, because they're spending the whole of their own life working for that person. My dad works like a nigger clearing new land and planting it, digging irrigation systems, all that lark. Doesn't make sense, really. He can live well enough on what he's got. But he wants me to have more than he had. That's his pleasure. If I were to say to him one day, "Sorry, Dad, but I'm going to be an opera singer or something and I don't want the land," it would break his heart. What would be the point of anything for him?'

'I hadn't thought of it like that,' said Trish. 'I've never wanted to inherit anything. Because first of all someone you love has to die. And because it seemed – well, greedy, I suppose – to want what belongs to somebody else.'

'Some people *are* greedy. You have to look at your own feelings straight. I know in my case that it gives my father pleasure to know that in thirty years' time I shall be walking between the vines he's just planted. Holy cow, look at this!'

From the top of a flight of steps they stared down at a carpet of heads. The carpet was both moving and singing.

'The hokey cokey! Come on, in we go.' Together they ran down the steps and joined the huge snake of dancers.

The movement brought them at last to the front of the palace. They cheered the king and queen and the two princesses on the balcony, they sang and danced, they cheered the king and queen again.

By ten o'clock they had been on their feet for eight hours and retreated, exhausted, to sit on the grass in Green Park.

'When d'you think you'll go back to Australia?' asked Trish.

'Dunno. This could be the snag about coming over here to join up. The Jap war isn't over yet, so the Aussie brigades may be sent back straightaway. But if the British work on the first in first out system, I'll be well down the list. All the same, it's soldiers on the ground, not aeroplanes, they'll need to occupy Germany. The ability to drop a bomb in the right place won't be in much demand. They might decide that there's not much point in paying me to hang around.'

'You'll be glad to go?'

'Glad and sorry both.' He turned his head to look at her. 'Glad to get home to my own personal backwater. But sorry to leave you, Trish.'

'Sorry enough to consider staying? You might take over the Greystones vineyard.'

'That's only a toy project. A sideline. Not a full-time job for a man. One of these days you're going to find yourself ditching it. I remember you told me you wanted to keep it going in memory of my Uncle Philip. But that's not good enough. A vineyard's not like an ordinary farm. It isn't enough just to hoe it and prune it and tie it and spray it. You have to, well, love it. My dad, he can't think of anything else. But no one has room for more than one enthusiasm like that. Grace has got her carving and you're going to have your painting. Unless Andy takes it off your hands, you're going to find it a burden.'

'That's why it would be so marvellous if you'd take it over. As something to do while your father is still in charge of his own property.'

Gordon shook his head. 'It doesn't work like that,' he said. 'He let me go because coming here was something I wanted to do. But he's not trying to keep me at arm's length until it's time for me to take over. He's working for me and I must work for him. Kind of partnership.' He leaned across and kissed her on the lips, pressing her back until they were both lying on the grass. 'I really am sorry, Trish. I love you, you know that.'

'Not enough,' said Trish, struggling with a wish to cry.

'Maybe you'll come out to Australia one day.'

'Maybe.'

Now, when it was too late to take back anything that had been said earlier, she realized that this conversation could never have been more than a summing up. Without realizing what she was saying, she had made it clear on the train that she would find as little stimulus in an Australian backwater as she would in Greystones. And now he was telling her in so many words what Grace had warned her of already: that he was not yet ready to think of marriage.

She flung her arms round his neck, pulling him down closer as though the strength of her embrace could hold him in England. At first he kissed her as passionately as she could have wished, pressing his lips against her face and neck until she was gasping with the wish to surrender to him. But almost as though he was aware of the promise she had made to Grace – and knew that she needed help if she were to keep it – he drew away, sighing with the effort.

'Wouldn't be right when I'll be going so soon,' he muttered, almost to himself. 'Reckon we ought to be getting back.'

Looking at her watch, Trish saw that they could catch the

last train. She stood up and smoothed down her frock. Out in the street the crowds were still noisy, singing to the sound of accordions or mouth organs. But the park was a quiet place of whispers. She held Gordon's hand tightly as they made their way between couples who for the rest of their lives would remember VE-Day for the beginning of a love affair rather than an end.

In the train going home, Trish sat close to Gordon. Her head pressed against his shoulder; his arm squeezed her waist. They did not speak. There was something bitter sweet about their recognition that soon they would part and might never see each other again. It was in keeping with the mood of the day, the ending of the war. For almost six years people had been talking about what they would do when the war was over, and now it was. A new era was starting, and part of its thrill lay in the fact that Trish had no idea what it might hold for her.

So, as the train clattered through the night, she found herself happy and sad at the same time. Peace would bring homecoming, and 'home' meant something different to everyone. Gordon would go to Australia: Rupert and Jean-Paul and Terry would come back to England. Max would return to Harrow. She herself could choose to leave a house which had become her home simply because her father had married its owner. A new life was about to begin.

THREE

Now that the war was over, Ellis returned to Greystones. Unsure what direction his own career should take, he set himself to the task of organizing a new exhibition of Grace's sculptures.

This proved difficult, for the triumphs and disasters of war had inspired her to work on a heroic scale. There was no London gallery which could display more than one or two of these pieces or provide them with an appropriate setting.

It was Terry, a natural salesman but unencumbered by any knowledge of the traditional methods of selling works of art, who came up with a solution. He appeared without warning on an afternoon at the end of May, his head dramatically turbaned by a bandage which covered one eye and ear and wound round his forehead.

'My luck ran out,' he announced. 'After five years without a scratch! Still, at least it's going to get me an early demob. I've got a medical board next week, but I've seen the doctor's report. No more marching, no more drill.'

'But does that mean that there are going to be permanent effects?' asked Grace anxiously.

'Looks like it, yes. Hasn't done my left eye much good.' He grinned at his brothers. 'Shall I wear a black patch and look like a pirate? Good thing Jerry hit something I've got two of. How's everything here?'

Accepting his wish to change the subject and keep the conversation cheerful, Grace told him about Ellis's efforts to arrange a selling exhibition for her.

'He's up in London again today,' she told him. 'But he doesn't seem to be having much luck.'

'You should make the customers come here! Let them walk round the grounds. See the work as it should be seen. You could turn the studio into a gallery for a day to show off any small pieces.'

The idea was so simple – and so perfect – that Grace's first reaction was to clap her hands. Then she made a face.

'Nobody would come. There's a recognized area in the middle of London for buying works of art. It's hard enough to get them even as far from Bond Street as Chelsea. Oxford would be well out of bounds.'

'I shouldn't think many people enjoyed shopping or selling in London when the bombs were falling.' Trish was quick to support Terry's idea. 'I mean, habits must have been broken. Just because we're getting back to ordinary life again now doesn't necessarily mean that it has to be 1939 ordinary life. And something that's made to stand out of doors will never look right inside.'

'But even so –'

'Charge them to come, that's the answer,' said Terry. 'If you send out invites, they'll wait to see how they feel on the day and probably decide it's too much trouble. But get the word around that the Grace Hardie Sculpture Park will be open for only one day, or two, and that admission will be limited, and you'll have them climbing over themselves to get in.'

His voice changed as he went into his street market patter. ''Urry, 'urry, 'urry, ladies and gents. Your last opportunity, your *very* last opportunity to pick up a bargain. Only ten pieces of sculpture remaining, ladies and gents: 'urry, 'urry, 'urry. It's not just the price that can't be repeated. You'll never see goods of this quality on offer again. And every one different. A u-nique bargain just for you. Yes sir, you on the left there. Only the first fifty ticket-holders can be lucky, ladies and gents, so 'urry, 'urry, 'urry while stocks last. Do it right,' he said more

252

seriously, 'and you'll find you've got a waiting list for tickets a mile long.'

All objections were swept aside as Terry's enthusiasm gathered way.

'What's there to lose, anyway? You're saving yourself transport costs and the risk of damage. You own the land and the studio so there's no rent to pay. You'll have to fork out on publicity – but there's no gallery to take a rake-off so you're quids in with the first sale.'

The enthusiasm was infectious. 'We'll all help,' said Trish. 'I'll print some posters. I can use the college litho stone. Ellis could do catalogues, with a photograph on the front and a plan on the back.'

'The catalogue could act as the ticket,' Terry suggested.

'Right.' By now Trish was bubbling with eagerness.

'What about us?' asked Boxer.

'One of you could check that everyone who comes has a catalogue and sell him one if he hasn't. And the other would have to sit in the studio as a sort of guard, to see that nobody nicks the smaller stuff. Max and I could sell glasses of our own wine.' Too late she realized that Max would probably have left Greystones before any exhibition could be prepared, but thought it tactful not to correct herself.

'Charge a bit more for the catalogues, give a glass of wine free and have the bottles on sale for anyone who likes the taste,' said Terry. Grace looked surprised by the authority with which he spoke, but Trish accepted the suggestion at once.

'Yes. And we could keep changing places, so that it wouldn't get boring. Why don't we all go out now and work out a route to put as a dotted line on the plan, so that everyone would see everything and always get the first glimpse from the best angle?'

'Steady on,' pleaded Grace, but already the three boys were running to find pencil and paper. Laughing at the speed with which Terry's spark was catching fire, she went outside to keep them company and form her own opinion. Trish was about to hurry after them when she remembered Terry's wound.

253

'Can you manage a walk?' she asked.

'Get a bit dizzy if I turn my head too quickly. They tell me that'll go when I get used to being one-eyed. I'll be OK if we take it slowly.'

She took his arm as they strolled, ready to support him if he should need it, but trying to make the gesture a natural one. 'Is it going to be all right, Terry?'

'Depends what you mean by all right. I'll have to get used to looking like a freak. But then, I never had any ambition to be a film star. Don't see why it should interfere with my plans for the future.'

'What are they?'

'I've decided to make my fortune,' said Terry, grinning at the simplicity of his ambition. 'Dan and Boxer have had a chance here to see what it's like to be happy and well-fed and safe. I'm not going to put them back into the slums. And if ever I have kids myself, I want to bring them up in the sunshine.'

'And will it happen as easily as that, just because you've decided?'

'Will it heck! But people *do* make fortunes by working hard. And the deciding to do it is half the battle. The only snag is, I want to be honest and I want to be useful. That's tying both hands behind my back.'

'How are you going to set about it?'

'Not sure. I'll start from the fact that I know how to buy and sell. Bigger scale, that's what I need. Sell a pound of potatoes and you count the profit in farthings. I've got to think of something big – big price, big profit. Trouble is, you've got to have money before you can make money. Getting started, that's the problem. I'm waiting for a bit of inspiration – a brilliant idea for working on a large scale.'

'You'll get it,' said Trish confidently. 'Just look what you came up with for Grace, without any warning. Genius! I do like people who have good ideas.'

'And I like people who appreciate good ideas.' They smiled

254

at each other, but almost at once Terry was serious again.

'I'm not ever going to forget what you've done for the nippers,' he said.

'It's nothing to do with me. Grace had a baby son once, you know. If he hadn't died, he'd have been pretty much the same age as Boxer. I expect –'

Terry interrupted her with a shake of the head.

'She doesn't care about kids,' he said. 'I don't mean that she's against them specially. She just doesn't want to be bothered. *You* chose to have them here, and it was because of you they were allowed back. I wouldn't want you to think that I don't realize.'

'No need to be sloppy about it,' she told him. 'When do you think would be a good time for the sculpture day?'

'July's too soon. August, people will be on holiday. October, you'll be busy with the grapes. September.'

'September,' agreed Trish. 'And perhaps you'll be out of the army by then.'

Another of her friends managed to secure his release even earlier. Rupert arrived at Greystones only a week after Terry had returned to his convalescent hospital.

'I'd had enough,' he announced. 'So I looked down the list of special demobilization schemes to see what I qualified for. The only one which seemed remotely possible was immediate release for all parliamentary candidates in the general election. I persuaded a group of worthy citizens to nominate me, and here I am. I ought to be knocking on constituency doorsteps at this moment, but I wanted to knock on yours first.'

'You mean you're going to be a Member of Parliament?' Trish exclaimed. 'How marvellous!'

'I didn't say that. I had to sign a statement that I was a candidate. I didn't have to guarantee to win.'

'But you will. How could anyone possibly vote against you?' Rupert at thirty was even more handsome than Rupert at eighteen. Although he claimed to be the most unmilitary of men, five and a half years in uniform had stiffened his posture and added authority to his speech. And she knew that ever since his time at Oxford he had had a serious interest in politics as well as history. 'But – are you allowed to sit in the House of Commons if you're a lord?'

'Patricia, Patricia! Didn't they teach you anything in that school of yours? My father sat in the House of Lords. My elder brother will take his seat in the House of Lords as soon as he's repatriated from the Far East. But mere second sons, whatever handle they may be given as a courtesy, are common as –'

'Dirt?'

'I was going to say as common as you.' He laughed, and Trish put out her tongue at him.

'Have you had any news of Miles?' she asked. She knew little about Rupert's elder brother, except that he had been taken prisoner by the Japanese soon after the fall of Singapore.

'One Red Cross postcard in three years. Every morning now when I wake up and thank God the war is over for me, I have to remind myself that it's still going on for him.' He was silent for a moment, shaking his head unhappily. 'We've no idea what his state of health is, but at least he was still alive four months ago. Julia seems to be coping quite well, but it's killing Mother by inches: too little news and too much rumour.'

'Who's Julia?'

'Miles's fiancée. They got engaged the night before he sailed. Bad timing, in my opinion. If he'd popped the question a week earlier, they might have managed to get married and apply themselves to producing an heir. As it is, she's had a miserable time staying faithful to someone who for all she knows might not be coming back. Wondering whether he's still going to want her if he does. Wondering how much he'll have been changed by what he's gone through.'

'Horrid,' agreed Trish. 'Have you met her?'

'I met her on leave in Alex. Mother wrote to tell me she was there. In the ATS. No time to mope while the war was on, but this last bit of waiting is harder for her to cope with.'

Trish searched for a change of subject, realizing how much

this one upset him, and realized only as she spoke that she was touching a second tender nerve.

'Have you been back to Castlemere yet?'

Rupert shook his head. 'We couldn't ask the school to move out in the middle of term. And I don't want to see it swarming with girls in gym slips. I shall wait till the end of July. With Miles out of action and Mother on the edge of a nervous collapse, it looks as though I shall have the job of dealing with everything – so you may get an urgent summons to come and hold my hand. Will you come?'

'Of course.'

'And what about a bit of electioneering before that?'

This time Trish hesitated. 'My term hasn't finished yet, either,' she said. 'And besides – which party are you standing for?'

'What a question! The party of enlightened self-interest, of course. Do you realize what the socialists will do to a family like mine if they get power, as I fear they may? Don't tell me that you've turned red in my absence, Patricia.'

'I don't know what I am,' Trish admitted honestly. 'I mean, until a month ago I'd have said that I was against inherited wealth, just like Labour. But now, although I still think people shouldn't be allowed to inherit great fortunes, I agree that the ones who already own a bit of money or land ought to have a voice in saying where it goes. So you see –'

'I see that you have got your knickers in a twist. It will be interesting to discover how you extricate yourself from that position. In the meantime, I agree that you wouldn't be wholly reliable as a Conservative canvasser. I shall have to ask Julia instead.'

Trish was conscious of an odd stab of jealousy at the casual suggestion. If anyone was going to be his daily companion during the campaign, it ought to be herself. Would it really matter so much if she were to spend two or three weeks repeating Rupert's opinions rather than her own? But she had missed her chance. It was necessary to remind herself firmly that she had no right to be possessive about him – and that the unknown Julia was safely engaged to Miles.

'I do hope you get in, all the same,' she said.

'Thank you. And there's something else.'

'Yes?' she asked as he showed no sign of continuing.

'I was waiting for the sound of a plaintive violin, followed by the strains of a Hollywood heavenly choir. It doesn't seem to be forthcoming, so I suppose I shall have to speak without accompaniment.'

'The suspense is killing me.'

'I only wanted to comment on the fact that when I went off to war you were a child.'

'You've seen me since then,' Trish pointed out.

'Yes. But still as a schoolgirl. And now – the conquering hero returns and finds that you've – well, grown up.'

It was not the most romantic of declarations, but it was enough to warm Trish's heart. She lowered her eyes, trying to recall to her face the demure expression that he would have remembered from 1939.

'Decent of you to notice,' she said.

FOUR

If Brian was Boxer, there was no doubt that from now on Terry would be the Pirate. During his convalescence he had been assigned to an army demobilization course on book-keeping and business methods, and since then had been busy with mysterious projects in London. But in the last week of August he arrived at Greystones in order to help with the sculpture exhibition – no longer bandaged, but wearing a black eye patch.

'Don't really need it,' he told Trish, pulling it away from his face to reveal that his eye, although useless, was normal to look at. 'But I fancy it. People'll notice me. Right, now I'll be guinea pig and see if your plan will take me round the route.'

They walked together through the grounds.

'Good way of doing the paths, this,' Terry said approvingly. 'Whose idea was it?'

'Andy's.' The lawns of the terraces and flower gardens were always kept tidy. But instead of struggling to get the larger area which was to be on show into immaculate condition, Andy had mown wide approaches to the sculptures, leaving the wildness of the grass on either side to emphasize the smoothness of the mown area and persuade visitors to approach each piece of sculpture from the angle chosen by Grace to show it at its best.

'It's going to be open for four days, not just one,' Trish told Terry. 'Ellis has been doing marvellously on publicity. On Thursday there's to be a preview. He's got someone from the radio coming down to do an interview with Grace and to talk

259

about the exhibits. And art critics from the newspapers as well.'

'So when do the buyers come?'

'Friday and Saturday. We're using your idea of selling catalogues in advance. And doing what you said about limiting the numbers, though Ellis has been taking the names and addresses of anyone he turns away, so they can always be invited privately afterwards. And he thinks that some of them will just turn up and demand to buy catalogues at the door, so he's allowed for that. I've been making Dan and Boxer practise giving change. They're terribly quick at it. I'm surprised, because their school reports are never up to much.'

'It's the result of being descended from generations of market traders,' said Terry, smiling as though it were a joke and yet speaking seriously. 'Mum had a stall up to the start of the war. I can do much more complicated sums in my head, and faster, than I can on paper. Talking of moving fast, there's one thing I've got to tell you. Just been having a word with Dan and Boxer about it. I've got somewhere for us all to live.'

Trish was pleased and disappointed at the same time. 'We'll miss them,' she said.

'Nice of you to say so. But we can't expect you to put them up for ever, and school begins on Tuesday. Besides, you won't be here yourself so much, will you, if that art school of yours goes back to its old place in London.'

'Tuesday!' Trish exclaimed. 'You mean you're going straight off after the weekend. You won't just disappear, will you, Terry?'

''Course not. Might need you to put a coat of paint on the flat for us. Where do we go next?'

He was concentrating on the sculpture route, and again Trish felt a kind of disappointment that he should apparently be able to break the connection with Greystones so easily. But perhaps that attitude was necessary to persuade his brothers that the return to London was natural and inevitable. Although still troubled by the thought of their departure, she tried to follow Terry's lead and concentrate on discussions of the opening arrangements.

From the moment on Thursday when newspaper photographers began to arrive, the success of the adventure was assured and, at least to start with, the system operated smoothly. On Friday and Saturday there were never more than thirty people in the grounds at any time, and the amateur band of helpers had no difficulties in dealing with them. Grace was available to talk about her work, whilst Ellis talked business.

Sunday, however, was different. A feeling of guilt at turning her own garden into a shop had led Grace to offer an extra afternoon's opening to a charity. They were all totally unprepared for the response. September 2nd was a warm, sunny day and it seemed that half the population of Oxford had decided to combine a country walk with the chance of exploring an estate which was usually private. Art-lovers who had learned of the show too late to apply for catalogues took the opportunity to see the sculptures after all, so that once again Grace and Ellis were kept busy in the studio.

The charity provided its own gatekeepers to collect entrance money – and this was just as well, since it freed the other members of the household to patrol the grounds. Charity or no charity, Andy was not prepared to allow anyone to do more than admire the vineyard from a safe distance. Jean-Paul was on duty in the walled garden, whilst Dan and Boxer, Terry and Trish kept on the move, discouraging visitors from touching the sculptures with sticky fingers or from breaking off pieces of plants to take home. Jay had taken a deck chair to the heart of the serpentine garden originally created by Philip, ready to surprise any plant thieves who thought themselves unobserved.

It was when the crowds were at their largest that Trish caught a glimpse of someone who was certainly not a sightseer, and who even as a potential patron would have chosen a quieter day to call. Rupert, dressed for riding, was looking round with a bemused expression on his face. Deserting her duty, Trish hurried towards him.

'What on earth is going on here?' he exclaimed. 'Has the Revolution begun?'

'It's for charity.' But Trish's quick explanation only made him shake his head incredulously.

'How can Grace stand it? So many people trampling around. Are they in the house as well?'

'Only the studio.' Originally designed for Lucy Hardie and her watercolour painting, this had a direct door to the garden; so visitors were able to enter it without going through the rest of the house.

'It would drive me up the wall to have so many strangers invading my privacy. Well, I won't stay. I've been spending a couple of days with Julia and realized it was within riding distance. Just come and say Hello to her, and then we'll be off. I can see that this is no moment for a tête-à-tête.'

Trish had not until then realized that Rupert had arrived with a companion; but now, as she turned to accompany him, she saw a slim young woman in her late twenties standing beside the fence to which two horses were tethered.

So that was his brother's fiancée! Trish put a hand on Rupert's arm to hold him back. 'Before I meet her, have you had any news about Miles?' The war against Japan was over at last.

'He's alive, thank God,' said Rupert. 'Mother heard yesterday. That's why I went over to Julia's place, to tell her. But he's not fit enough to travel yet. Suffering from malnutrition and two separate tropical diseases. All the same, there've been times when we feared the worst – so yes, we're all very happy.' They walked on again. 'Julia, meet Patricia Faraday. Patricia, this is Julia Lloyd-Jones.'

'Trish,' said Trish, shaking hands. 'Rupert's just told me about Miles. I'm so glad. I know how worried you've all been – and for such a long time.'

'Yes, it's a great relief. Marvellous news. We're not going to let ourselves get frightened by the medical report.'

'We have to let Patricia get back to control her perfectly frightful crowds,' Rupert said. 'But before you go, you promised to come and see what's happened to Castlemere? Would the day after tomorrow be any good?'

'I'd love to come. Oh, and Rupert, congratulations on your magnificent victory! Have you taken your seat yet?'

'Yes, I went up on the 20th, with all the other new boys. To sit in impotent opposition while the country goes to the dogs. The Labour lot even sang the Red Flag in the Chamber, would you believe? But we mustn't have a political argument. No doubt you're gloating over the result.'

'Not really. I thought it was rather ungrateful, as a matter of fact, after all that Churchill's done. Oh, just look at that boy climbing through the hole!'

'Why else does Grace carve holes if not for them to be climbed through? But I mustn't distract you from your police duties. See you on Tuesday, then.'

Trish watched as he and Julia swung themselves up into their saddles and rode away. Then it was time to return to crowd control.

It was an exhausted group of people who gathered for a drink of home-made lemonade or wine that evening half an hour after the last of the invaders had left. But Grace, flushed with the success of the venture, was more animated than Trish ever remembered seeing her before.

'I need to make a short speech,' she said. 'To thank you all for your help and hard work. I've suddenly become a rich woman!'

'Don't let it go to your head,' Ellis warned her. 'Remember that it's six years' work you've been selling. You won't be able to replace it in five minutes. You need to divide the total by six to work out an income.'

'But I've kept alive during those six years,' Grace pointed out. 'I refuse to be sensible and cautious about this. When all the buyers have paid for what they've chosen, for the first time in my life I shall have money in the bank that I've earned myself and that isn't earmarked in advance for something dull like repairing the roof. It seems the right opportunity to distribute one or two rewards.'

'Oh goody!' exclaimed Jay. 'It's certainly been a very arduous afternoon, guarding your property from a deck chair.'

'Those who live as family are expected to work as family,' said Grace, laughing. 'Bad luck, Jay. Nothing for you except a big thank-you. Andy, I'd like to call down at the lodge for a chat later this evening, if I may. Boxer, will you come to the library with me? And Dan afterwards.'

Within only a few minutes the two boys were back, eager to show their brother what they had been given. Dan was waving a ten shilling note, while Boxer clutched a handful of silver coins.

'You're to go next,' they said to Terry before dashing up to their bedroom with their fortunes.

'A pound for me, d'you think?' he guessed. 'Since I'm bigger than them.' He was smiling as he went out of the room; but when he returned his face was pale with shock.

'What's the matter?' asked Trish, fearing that he must have been given bad news of some kind.

'Nothing's the matter. I'll say nothing's the matter!'

'Well, tell me what's happened, then.' By now the two of them were alone.

'She's given me a cheque. For ten per cent of the sales. And there'll be more to come later, when the bronze editions have been cast. Because it was my idea, she said. But it's much more than an idea is worth.'

Trish shook her head. 'There's nothing more valuable than an idea. That's what starts everything off.'

'Well, what she said is that if she'd sold through a London gallery it would have taken forty per cent, so she reckons she's got all that to give away. Ellis doesn't want any, except to pay the exhibition bills. Jean-Paul's going to keep the money from selling the wine, and Mrs Barrett's having whatever she took for refreshments. And there'll be something for you; you're to go in next. But –' He looked unbelievingly at the cheque in his hand. 'I haven't even got a bank account!'

'You'd better hurry up and open one, then. What will you do with the money?'

'Get stock. Premises, even. You can make a good living from a market stall but to take a step up you've got to have capital. I thought I'd have to wheedle it out of a bank and be saddled with interest payments. But now . . . ! This was what I really needed, to make a start. Grace said she wanted to see me doing well. But it's crazy. I mean, we owe her; she doesn't owe us.'

'She's not interested in money,' Trish told him confidently. 'But she *is* interested in people being able to do what they specially want to do. And she knows how hard it is, starting.'

'Maybe she's going to set you up in business as well then!'

But Grace, smiling as Trish went into the library, was more practical than that.

'I imagine the Slade will be going back to London now that the war's over,' she said. 'You'll need a more generous allowance for living there. Ellis will discuss that with you when you've got some idea of what your expenses will be. The first problem will be to find somewhere to live. You'll have to put down a deposit and pay the first month in advance; and you may want to buy things to make the place more homey. So you'd better have a lump sum ready.' She pushed a cheque across the table.

'Oh Grace, you are generous. You oughtn't –'

'I've given more to Terry – because I think he needs it more. But I really do appreciate all the hard work you put into the weekend, Trish. It's not just the money. In fact, that's not important at all, except as a practical sign of how people see my work. But it's been wonderful to have people coming and enjoying what they see. It's not something I ever expected to happen. And Ellis has just been showing me an article in the *Observer*. It makes me feel – well, important.'

'And so you are.'

'It's not something that's easy to imagine, while I'm hammering away here on my own. Yesterday in particular was quite a day. So a few thank-yous seem to be in order.'

'Terry's thrilled to bits,' Trish told her. 'Are you doing something for Andy as well, or shouldn't I ask?'

'It's something he and I have got to talk about,' Grace told her. 'I don't even know whether he wants to stay in England, or whether he'd like to go back to France and start again from scratch on the farm there. But if he *does* stay, he ought to be offered a more formal arrangement. What I have in mind is to offer him a tenancy of the vineyard. So that if it makes any profits, he can keep them. And he could have a few acres extra to that to make a small-holding.'

'You ought to keep the land at the bottom of the hill in your own hands,' said Ellis, who had been sitting quietly at the other end of the room with the papers relating to the sculpture sales in front of him.

'Why?' asked Grace.

'If the Morris works want to expand again at the rate they were going before the war, you could get a good price for the fields on the far side of the wood.'

'I don't want to see a factory going up in our grounds!' exclaimed Grace, horrified.

'Then you need to keep full ownership of the land in order to protect it.'

'I suppose you're right. Anyway, Andy wouldn't want the wood. He may not even be interested in taking over the vineyard. But he seems enthusiastic enough. I haven't got either the skill or the time to give it proper attention. I want to concentrate on my own work. It's all very selfish.'

'It sounds very generous to me,' Trish said.

'Well, you know.' Grace looked serious for a moment. 'My brother David is always on at me about wills and things, and I suppose there may be a pleasure of a sort in thinking who's going to enjoy my possessions after I'm dead. But there's a much greater pleasure, it seems to me, in making presents while I'm still alive and watching people smile and tell me how generous I am! I know that I can't do that with the house, and – to forestall what Ellis is bursting to say – I also know that the house can't continue to exist without the land. But I see absolutely no point in hoarding anything else.'

'That way lies ruin,' said Ellis; but he was smiling.

'I shall rely on Trish to keep me in my old age. Right, Trish?'

'Half my stale crust will always be yours,' Trish assured her. 'And talking of stale crusts, d'you think there's anything for supper?'

'Let's all go and see.' Mrs Barrett was enjoying an evening off, but had probably left a salad prepared.

As Trish led the way towards the kitchen, she smiled to herself in satisfaction. She would be sad to say goodbye to Dan and Boxer, whom she thought of almost as brothers. But on Tuesday she would see Rupert again and before too long would be able to leave home and make a life for herself in London.

London! She was going to become a metropolitan person at last: the very thought made her feel sophisticated. And in the meantime she was part of a happy family, which would still be there whenever she wished to return to her home. It was all too good to be true.

FIVE

In the nineteenth century the ninth Marquess of Ross had been at some pains to ensure that that new-fangled invention, the railway, should not be allowed to spoil the view from Castlemere or disturb the pheasants by crossing his estate. So when Trish dismounted from the train for her visit, she found herself being led to a long, low open coach bearing the Beverley coat of arms.

'How splendid!' she exclaimed. 'Is this a governess cart?'

'Certainly not,' said Rupert. 'Don't you know a phaeton when you see one, ignorant girl?' He helped her up before flicking the reins to start the chestnut on its way. 'It was Mother's idea, when petrol rationing first came in, to see what we'd got in the coach-house. And in the stables – all those horses eating their heads off and getting fat for lack of exercise while Miles and I were away. There was a certain amount of protest to start with, I'm told, but they soon got the hang of it. Rather more quickly than I'm learning to cope with petrol rationing. I'm sorry to have inflicted such a journey on you instead of nipping over to pick you up as usual. This time last year, if I wanted to go anywhere I simply hopped into a tank.'

'Just what we civilians always suspected,' laughed Trish. 'The army simply didn't know there was a war on!'

'Well, I'm certainly learning fast about the hardships of peace. Just wait till you see Castlemere!'

'Is it very bad?'

'Yes.' He was no longer smiling and was less chatty than usual as they rattled first along the road and then through the huge park which surrounded his home.

From a distance, nothing seemed to have changed. It was still a fairy castle, a French chateau improbably set down in the middle of the English countryside. But as they came close and Rupert slowed the horses to a halt, Trish gasped in dismay. The moat had always been one of the glories of Castlemere, a smooth ring of water on which swans were accustomed to float. Now, however, the house was surrounded by nothing but a wide, muddy ditch.

'The headmistress had it drained because she was afraid that one of her little darlings might fall in and drown,' Rupert explained. 'Simply refilling it would be no problem. It was designed to be fed by a cutting from a stream to which the water returned lower down. That was why it was never stagnant or smelly. It would be easy enough to unblock the dam. But unfortunately it seems that six years of being allowed to dry out for the first time ever have done unexpected things to the foundations. It's going to cost a small fortune to make them good before we can risk letting the water back.'

'Isn't the school liable for that sort of expense?'

'I've been living with the contract for the past month until I could recite it in my sleep. I'm afraid my father wasn't too well advised. At the time, of course, he may have seen it as a patriotic duty rather than a business negotiation. Or else a way of avoiding army occupation, which might have been worse. There are clear categories of damage which have to be made good. And there are clear exclusions, for fair wear and tear, which are left on our plate. But there's a terrible fog in between. If the school sent its handyman to set the stream flowing through the moat again – as they were on the point of doing when our agent pointed out the risks – they could claim that they were leaving it as they found it. I suspect that the lawyers are going to have a field day before it's all sorted out. And that's only one out of dozens of problems. Come and look inside.'

Trish's last visit to the great house had been in 1939, when her father took a portfolio of photographs of the interior. She had seen the rooms very much as they must have been when the house was first built, filled with the furniture which had been sent over from France as a bride's dowry, curtained with elegant silk draperies, and with expensive rugs and carpets on the polished parquet floors. But since then all the best furniture had been put into store. As Rupert led her first into what had once been the marquess's study, she was not surprised by the bleakness of the empty spaces or the ugliness of the thick blackout curtains. But he gave a sigh as he waved a hand towards the panelled walls.

'They used this as a sort of reading room for the older girls. Equipped it with their own tables and chairs and brought in a couple of old bookcases which they picked up at a country sale. Now we find that the panelling's infested with woodworm. The whole lot will have to come off the wall so that it can be treated. *They* say it must have been there already. I claim that they must be responsible. But the truth of the matter is that a house like this needs loving care, which a temporary tenant isn't interested in providing. Do you remember the Chinese room?'

Trish nodded. It was a small room which took its name from the beauty of its hand-painted wall covering and the intricate carving of the gilded mirror frames.

'Well, for a couple of centuries maids have been going into that room every morning to pull down a blind, and returning three hours later to let it up again. They may never have known why they did it. It was just a regular duty. That room was one that the school undertook not to use, because the danger of damage to the wall paintings was so great; so how, they cry, can we possibly hold them responsible for the fact that a four-foot strip of the paper has completely lost its colour? All they did, in the interests of opening a window one day to air the room, was to draw back the curtains and forget to close them again afterwards. Six years of sunshine, and the room will never be a perfect work of art again. How do you send in a bill for something like that?'

'I'm so sorry,' said Trish. 'You must be terribly upset.'

Rupert looked at her with the serious expression which she was more and more often nowadays catching on his face.

'Yes, it is upsetting, because I love the house,' he said. 'But I'll tell you what's almost worse, though I don't know if it will make sense to you. I've always known that Castlemere would never belong to me. To be a son living in my father's house, that was all right; that's natural. But to be a brother, living in Miles's house, that wouldn't do at all. So after the pater's death, I told myself that Castlemere was no longer my home. I might come back for the odd visit, but the first thing to do after the war would be to find a home of my own. I could have managed that all right. Clean break. All this, putting things right, ought to be Miles's job.'

'But now Miles isn't here.'

'That's it. We heard this morning that he's been put on a hospital ship. But it doesn't sound as though he'll be in any state to get down to business for some time when he gets home. And there's too much that can't wait. A socking great bill for estate duty after my father's death, for a start. Two million pounds.'

'Two million!' gasped Trish.

'They value the property, you see, without taking into account whether or not we have any assets apart from the property itself with which to pay.'

'I see.' Trish remembered the occasion on which she had overheard David quarrelling with Grace. He had made exactly the same point about death duties. 'What will you do?'

'Mother's been battling on that front while we were both away. But it's been a worry to her, and we were supposed to settle within five years. We shall have to sell some land. Even if I don't actually *do* anything, I must have some solutions cut and dried, ready for when Miles returns.'

'You're probably better equipped to do it than he would be even if he were here.'

'Maybe so. But it's hard, all the same, to have to devote

271

every waking thought to Castlemere and know that sooner or later I shall have to tear myself away for a second time.'

'What about Julia?' asked Trish.

'What about her?'

'Well, if she's going to become the chatelaine, couldn't she —?'

'I did have a word with her about that,' confessed Rupert. 'At the party we had to celebrate winning the seat. She put forward what seems a very balanced point of view. She's longing for Miles to come home, and she still regards herself as engaged to him. But they haven't seen each other for five years. He might not be interested in her any more. "I don't want him to marry me merely because it's the gentlemanly thing to do," she said. I admire her for that. But it means that she's not prepared to jump the gun in any way. So, for the moment at least, it's down to yours truly.'

Throwing off his sombre mood, he flung an arm round her shoulders and hugged her affectionately, grinning in the way she remembered from the old days, before the war. 'With a little help from my friends!' he exclaimed. 'I can't tell you how marvellous it is to see you, and looking so happy and pretty. In the desert, you know, I used to conjure up my own mirages, remembering people as I used to see them and trying to imagine what they might be doing at that particular moment.'

'Was I on the cast list?' she asked, happily anticipating the answer.

'Starring role. Except that I didn't manage to grow you up quite enough in the imagining bits. It's good to discover that not all the surprises are rotten ones. Well, Mother will have luncheon waiting for us in the dower house at one. Before that, I want your advice on what to do about redecoration.'

'I don't know anything about decorations.'

'Yes, you do. Those marvellous rooms you've done in Greystones. Not,' he added hastily, 'that I quite see the drawing room at Castlemere painted in black and white with red spots. But you have an eye. Don't deny it.'

Shaking her head to disclaim any expertise, Trish allowed herself to be led through a series of stately rooms. She did her best to close her eyes to the discoloured patches on the walls which could be covered once again with the paintings now stored, and to the tatty light shades, ludicrously small, which would be replaced by the original chandeliers. But it was easy to sympathize with Rupert's depression at the sight of scratched parquet floors and lines of dirt or grease to show where school furniture had been standing against the walls.

At Castlemere even the bedrooms were larger and grander than most people's drawings rooms, but many of them were now scarred by blackened dents – caused, no doubt, by iron bedheads banging against the wall during one of the jolly pillow fights for which Trish herself had once pined.

'I see what you mean,' she said when the tour was over. They were both silent as they returned to the phaeton for the drive across the park.

'And you see,' sighed Rupert, 'there are two separate problems and each of them is a killer. Money, first. No one ever believes that a family like ours could be strapped for ready cash and yes, before the war we did manage to cover running expenses out of rents. But there was never much in hand for extraordinary expenditure like this, and now we're faced with the death duties too.'

'And the other?'

'The other problem is that even if we could afford to buy, the goods aren't there to be bought. I mean to say, if I have to hand over sixteen coupons to buy myself a new suit, what would they expect for hundreds of yards of silk to hang on the ballroom wall?'

Trish resisted the temptation to inform him that furnishing fabrics were unrationed, for he was quite right in principle. Shops stocked only with utility fabrics and wallpapers would certainly not be able to offer expensive imported silks.

'Come on, Patricia. I need your advice.'

'I don't see that you can do more than draw up a list of

273

priorities,' she said. 'If the death duties have got to be paid, and if the damage to the foundations could have worse effects if it's left untreated, presumably those must come at the top of the list. The entertaining rooms ought to be restored eventually to their original state; and since that's impossible now, they'll have to come at the bottom. That will put them on Miles's and Julia's list of problems.'

'But I ought to do something practical. Or at least have firm proposals to make. At the moment I don't feel that the house belongs to us at all. It's as though the invaders have destroyed the – oh, I don't know what the right word is: the atmosphere, the ambience. I need to make some gesture to show that Castlemere is ours again.'

'I'd start with the bedrooms,' said Trish. 'They've been altered from the original state already, haven't they?'

'True. My grandmother gave them a great doing-over to make them suitable for Edwardian house parties.'

'So it wouldn't do any harm to redecorate them unambitiously now. You could always put them back to the eighteenth century later on. If I were you –' she spoke with the confidence of someone who had acted as Terry's assistant while he worked at Greystones – 'I should strip, make good and paint. Pale country colours. Because probably there isn't the right sort of wallpaper around, and paint is cheaper, as well as being easier to cover later, and flat colours look better for hanging pictures on.'

'Just what I needed!' exclaimed Rupert, squeezing her shoulders for a second time. 'Someone decisive. We'll go back this afternoon and look at them again. And you can tell me what colours would be best.'

Trish shook her head. 'Julia will want to choose for herself,' she said. 'And your mother would like to be consulted, I'm sure. But actually I think you need professional advice. For an ordinary sort of house someone like me can play about and learn from mistakes. But everything here is on such a large scale that you can't afford to waste time on second thoughts.

You ought to look for someone who knows exactly how to make a room look smaller or larger or lower or higher, and what goes with what. Besides . . .'

'Besides what?'

'Well, you know me, always wanting to change things.'

'You mean you'd want to burn all the Louis Quinze furniture and fill the drawing room with Bauhaus designs!'

'Not that, of course. I wasn't talking about the grand rooms. I do recognize that a house like this has always got to look like a house like this. But even with the bedrooms, looking at them through Miles's and Julia's eyes would be a big effort for me. Whereas people who do it for a living presumably start by finding out just what their clients want and then providing it.'

'I suppose you're right,' agreed Rupert. 'But if I find someone like that, I'd still appreciate it if you'd come round with me and him. Or her.'

'As someone else – like you – who's never going to live in the finished result?'

'You've hit it. To remind me that there's a life outside Castlemere. The world of the second son.'

His arm was still round her shoulders and now he turned her to face him, holding her close as his mouth widened in a warm smile and his eyes danced with the light-heartedness which she remembered from before the war. Trish found herself stirred by his closeness and pleased at the invitation. Often during the past few weeks she had regretted not helping Rupert in his election campaign. Now he was offering a second opportunity of working companionship.

She smiled agreement. 'Though I'll be in London during term time,' she reminded him.

'So shall I, Monday to Friday. And hoping to find someone there to be frivolous with. All those years in the army, looking forward to a bit of carefree social life, and now I'm up to the neck with family business here and the affairs of the nation in Westminster. What I need more than anything else is an art student who'll invite me to Bohemian parties and let me take

275

her out for the odd meal in return. It's well known that all art students live on the edge of starvation. Are you on?'

Pulling her even more closely towards him, he kissed her lightly on the lips. Often in the past he had kissed her cheek or forehead, but this was the first real kiss.

It was over in a second, before she had time to put her arms around him and tell him that she loved him. Perhaps it was part of being frivolous that he should pretend a kiss to be only a careless gesture, of no significance. She must show herself to be a sophisticated adult, a London art student, by accepting it as lightly as it was offered.

'I'm on,' she agreed.

SIX

Trish had left her bicycle at Oxford station. As a rule she found the four-mile ride back to Greystones steep and tiring, but today the pedals seemed to turn without effort. She was strong and confident and unusually conscious of the whole of her body, instead of just the artist's eye that observed and the hand that drew. She was in love.

Gordon had not yet left England, but she had forgotten him already. Forgotten, too, was the schoolgirl crush which she had had on Rupert for almost as long as she could remember. She had thought she loved him before; but now, overwhelmed by the true emotion, she recognized her years of childish adoration for what they were. Her real love for him dated from today.

It was because Rupert's attitude towards her had changed that she could recognize the change in herself. He was seeing her now as an adult, an equal partner. Before too long he might begin to think of her as a lover. Had they been strangers, he would have kissed her more passionately today. It was because he was already accustomed to hug her affectionately that such a small change as a kiss on the lips instead of the cheek or forehead was really an important gesture. For almost the whole of her life she had been waiting for the moment when Rupert would love her, and at last it had arrived.

She did her best to conceal the nature of her happiness as she made her way to the studio, intending only to put her head round the door to announce her return. But Grace, standing at her work bench, demanded to be told the day's news and – always sensitive to other people's emotions – seemed to guess at once that the day had held some special significance.

'How's Rupert?' she asked. 'And Castlemere?'

'Castlemere's awful.' Trish described its neglected and depressing condition. 'I suppose it will start to look better when all the pictures and furniture are back in place. But Rupert's terribly worried about money. For death duties and repairs and redecoration, everything.'

'And how is Rupert apart from that?' Grace had not seen him during his brief Sunday visit.

'Oh, fine. Not as jokey as he used to be before the war. More serious. But probably that's only because of all these responsibilities. Once Miles gets home . . .'

'He – Rupert, I mean – must be at least thirty now,' said Grace. 'And whether or not he managed to enjoy being in the army, he must have the feeling of having lost six years out of his life – of having to start again, in a sense, at a rather more advanced age than usual. It's understandable that he should be serious.'

'Yes.' Trish searched for a question which would change the subject. Only when she heard herself speak the words did she realize how much she was giving away.

'Why did *you* leave it so late to get married, Grace?' she asked. 'I mean, it's not unusual for men to wait till they're thirty, but for a woman . . . Was it all because of the first war?'

'No. From choice.' Grace turned back to work as she talked, cutting and bending thick wire to form an armature. 'I had the chance to marry – I was engaged – when I was your sort of age. But I ran away. For all the wrong reasons, at the time. But, as things turned out, with the right result. If I'd had the sense to sit down when I was nineteen and work out how I wanted to spend my life, I might well have come up with exactly what I've got. As it is, things have fallen into my lap. I've been lucky. Not something one can count on. Nobody ever takes advice on this sort of thing, so I've never bothered to give it. But I do feel quite strongly that it's important for anyone of your age to start off by settling what she wants to do with her life before even considering who she wants to do it with.'

'I don't get you,' said Trish.

Grace put down the wire cutter and studied the skeleton she had made with a critical eye for a moment. Then she gave Trish her full attention.

'Right, let's get personal, then. You're a very attractive girl, and any moment now you're going to be loose in London and under siege from any number of young men. If you very sensibly recognize, as you did with Gordon, that love without marriage holds pitfalls, sooner or later the idea of love inside marriage is going to seem extremely tempting. All I'd say is, don't let yourself drift into marriage just because you see everyone else of your age doing it, without first stopping to think whether a particular marriage would suit you.'

'How do you mean?'

'Well, if all you want is to sit at home and bring up babies, then falling in love is as good a start as any other. But you may feel that you've got more in you than that – and a good many husbands actively dislike the idea that their wives should work. That means that if you've set your heart on having your own career, you must either decide not to marry or else look for a husband who'll back you in whatever you want to do. And whose way of life is compatible with it. Marry a farmer, and you'll be expected to work as a farmer's wife. You can't expect to combine that with managing a bank, say.'

Trish laughed at the idea of herself as a bank manager, but she saw what Grace meant.

'You're saying that I ought to marry a way of life rather than a man.'

'I didn't mean it to sound as cold as that. Just to be aware what way of life goes with the man, and see whether you'll be happy with it.'

'Suppose I just want to paint. Well, I do. I could do that with anyone.'

'Then you need to consider your own character. As a rich man's wife you might use financial security to achieve exactly

279

what you wanted without needing to please the market; or you might lose incentive and just produce the occasional watercolour to give to your mother-in-law. Marry a poor man and you could find yourself either spurred on or commercialized by the need to sell your work – or forced to give up in order to earn a living some other way.'

'How very complicated you make it sound!'

'Well, it's a big thing, Trish. An important time of your life, with choices to be made which may have consequences far beyond what you realize at the time. Some girls have neither talent nor ambition. It may not matter what they do. And some girls – like me in my twenties – have such a strong sense of vocation, whatever it's for, that the idea of marriage is always going to take second place. All I'm saying is that it's just as important to know yourself as it is to know a man you might fall in love with.'

'You make it sound as though it's possible to stop yourself –'

Grace interrupted her. 'Of course it is, if you put the brake on early enough. You found that out for yourself, with Gordon. You didn't want to spend the rest of your life on a vineyard in Australia and so you let him go.'

Trish was silent for a moment. Had it been her decision or Gordon's that their brief romance should never be anything more than that? It was true, though, that the parting had not broken her heart.

'So you thought all this out, years ago, and decided that you'd rather be a sculptor than an ordinary wife.'

'No. I told you, I was lucky. I'm trying to persuade you to be more sensible than I ever was. And I'm sure you will be. But you know, these films you enjoy so much in the cinema. So often they seem to finish with a man and a woman getting married, as though that were the end of something, when really it's only the beginning. You've had a childhood life here at Greystones and that's coming to an end, one way or another, whatever you decide to do in the future. You have a period of freedom ahead. On the day you get married you'll start a new way of life, from which it will be extremely difficult to escape and which it may not be easy to change. So it's important not to make a mistake.'

'Noted.'

Grace laughed, but then raised her eyes to look steadily into Trish's.

'I like Rupert enormously,' she said, with a directness which made Trish flush. 'Nothing I've just said was intended as any sort of warning in that direction. Although –' As though surprised by her own thoughts she bit her lip and began once more to work on the armature, pressing clay around the wire. 'Although there is one big difference between you. You're a creator, I think, like me – and at the same time, wicked girl, a destroyer of creations. Always looking for something new. Rupert is a preserver. He's in love with Castlemere. Something you should never forget.'

'Castlemere isn't his home any more.' Trish made no attempt to contradict her stepmother's assumptions. 'It's like you said earlier, he's got to start from scratch now, making a new life. So anyone he marries will have a hand in the making.'

'Yes. Well.' Grace smiled at her affectionately. 'Thank you for listening so patiently and letting me perform my stepmaternal duty. I was sure even before I started that I could rely on you to be sensible.'

Trish grinned back. 'Trush Trist,' she said.

SEVEN

The view of Castlemere in winter was even more beautiful than in summer. Snow smoothed the gentle contours of the park, outlined the bare branches of the chestnut avenue and clung to the northern side of each pencil-sharp turret roof.

'It's ridiculous!' exclaimed Trish, who had been invited over for the day as soon as the Christmas vacation began. 'A French chateau in the middle of England. The idea that any ordinary person should actually *live* in it –'

'Is becoming more and more remote,' said Rupert, drawing to a halt in the Morris which, chosen for the modesty of its petrol consumption, was so inappropriate a vehicle for someone who had always enjoyed sleek and expensive cars. 'It's a totally impossible situation. Almost all the indoor servants have disappeared. Moved away, married, discovered the delights of earning a factory wage and living within reach of a dance hall. Even if we could get them back, they'd want higher wages than we could afford to pay. And a house like this is entirely dependent on servants. Dozens of them.'

'Grace and Grandmother and Philip managed without at Greystones, before Ellis and I came along.'

'By acting as servants themselves and closing up most of the house. Three of them working non-stop to keep themselves warm and fed in only half a dozen rooms. Greystones may be a large house by ordinary standards, but Castlemere doesn't come into ordinary standards at all. We need a small army of housemaids carrying buckets of coal just to stop the house freezing up, let alone to keep it warm.'

'Perhaps you should have let the school stay on for one more winter.'

'Perish the thought!'

'Then what *are* you going to do, Rupert? Or I suppose I should say, what is Miles going to do?'

Rupert switched off the engine. 'Let's get out for a moment,' he said. They stood side by side in the peculiarly intense silence of a snow-smothered landscape. 'This is something you need to know before you see Julia. What Miles is going to do is to die.'

Trish, aghast, turned her head to look at him and saw that he was near to tears.

'I thought, when you said he was back in England –' she began.

'Yes, we all hoped that since he'd managed to survive so far, proper treatment would pull him through. But – those bastards, Patricia! You've read about what went on in the camps on the Burma–Siam railway.'

Trish nodded. Like everyone else she knew how many prisoners of war had died while in Japanese custody and had seen pictures of the walking skeletons who had been rescued at the end of the war.

'If it had only been starvation, malnutrition, he might have been pulled through. But – we've had a visit from one of his fellow-officers. In pretty bad shape himself, but coming round. He told us that when the Japs discovered Miles had a title, they went out of their way to humiliate him even more than the others. More beatings, worse duties. At his last camp he had to clean out the latrines. Almost everyone had a bug of some kind. He picked up all of them, on top of the vitamin deficiency that he already had on his own account. His whole system's destroyed. The doctors say that it's his liver that's going to kill him, but if it doesn't, something else will.'

'Oh, Rupert! Is he still in hospital?'

'We had him brought home three days ago. He told the doctors that he wanted to die at Castlemere. He knows, of course. I think he's known all the time. He just kept himself alive by willpower so that he could see his home once more. There was nothing more the hospital could have done for him except keep him comfortable. We've got a team of three nurses. They think he might just make Christmas.'

'I'm so sorry. Oh, darling, I'm so sorry.'

It was the first time she had used the endearment, and Rupert responded to it by taking her in his arms. She hugged him tightly, kissing his cheek, and felt his body shuddering with the need for comfort.

Only afterwards, as they returned silently to the car, did one consequence of what she had just learned occur to Trish. With his elder brother dead, Rupert would inherit the title and the estate. His wife would be the Marchioness of Ross.

Rupert's social life when Parliament was sitting was at the mercy of the Whips, but during the ten weeks of Trish's college term he had spent several evenings with her. Twice he had taken her to the theatre and once as his partner to a private dance. For her part, Trish had invited him to a dinner cooked by herself and her flatmate for half a dozen of their friends, and had also persuaded him to come to her college's end-of-term dance. On all these occasions they had been in other people's company, of course, and Rupert had seemed amusedly aware that he was assumed to be Trish's boyfriend, going out of his way to act the part. Trish herself, joining light-heartedly in the flirtation, had hoped that it was only the act which was being acted.

He had never spoken of marriage. Nor, indeed, had he ever attempted to engineer a private session in which he could tell her that he loved her. So she had been careful to keep any such thoughts out of her own mind. Only now, realizing that his whole future was about to change, was she tempted to wonder what her own part in it might be and to ask herself whether – if she were to be asked – she would want a title to be a marchioness.

The very idea seemed ridiculous; and yet in practice it might

284

be far from funny. Would she enjoy living in a house which resembled a museum? A marchioness would be expected to live in a particular style. She would have to behave and perhaps even to dress in a particular manner. To judge by Rupert's mother – who would most certainly disapprove of Trish's lack of pedigree if asked to consider her as a daughter-in-law rather than a remote and only adopted cousin – those particular manners would not be at all to Trish's own taste. And Rupert as a marquess might prove to be a completely different kind of person: serious and backward-looking.

Grace had given her a warning about just this sort of thing. Trish had promised to consider it seriously – and indeed, she was considering it seriously at this moment. Or rather, she was trying to; but in fact she could think of nothing but Rupert's closeness in the car and how much she loved him. If two people loved each other then everything else, surely, would come right. In a surrender of common sense she put a hand on his thigh and was rewarded by the smile with which he acknowledged her sympathy.

Happy again after the moment of doubt, she looked down as they drove across the bridge and exclaimed in surprise, 'The moat!' The great house was once again surrounded by water.

'Yes. The work was so urgent that we had to get it done first and wonder how to pay for it afterwards. And Julia's family chipped in. She has a nice old-fashioned father who believes in dowries and wedding settlements and had the generosity to recognize that he who pays quickly pays twice. I'll show you the other thing we've managed.' He parked the car and led the way into the house, taking her straight to the drawing room.

Everything was back in place: carpets, curtains, furniture and pictures. Anyone who looked hard enough could see the shabbiness of scuffed floors, worn paint on the window shutters and frames, a grey tinge to the plastered and painted ceiling. Nevertheless, the first impression was a splendid one, as though the war had never happened.

'Squalor all round, but it cheers the heart to have made just one gesture,' Rupert told her. 'Well, two, actually. We rushed to get this ready for Miles to see, and we also prepared one of the state bedrooms. Tester bed, magnificent draperies, all terribly grand. To give old Miles a proper send-off. But what he wanted, it turned out, was the room he had as a boy. Hasn't had a coat of paint for ten years, but he doesn't seem to mind. Matter of fact, I don't think he's seeing too well. Julia's up with him at the moment. She'll join us for our luncheon after he's had his. He sleeps most of the afternoon.'

Trish did her best to conceal her disappointment that she and Rupert would not be spending the day alone. 'Are we going to go round the house again?'

'Yes, if you're still interested. We've been writing down a few ideas for getting everything back to rights. Not that we shall be able to start for years. If – no, I must learn to say when – Miles dies, we shall be faced with a second lot of death duties within six years. It doesn't bear thinking about. I've got a lawyer looking into it already. I mean, it seems to me that he's as good as been killed on active service. But I don't know what will happen.'

'You could charge people to look round the house,' suggested Trish.

'What!' Rupert made no attempt to disguise his horror.

'Well, look at this room. It's as good as any picture gallery or museum of furniture – better, in fact, because everything belongs here. If you're going to put back all the rooms as they were before and as they've been for hundreds of years, I'm sure people would love to look round.'

'Well, I wouldn't love to let them. Just remember that day I came over to Greystones! Hundreds of people milling around! No privacy. And it would be a hundred times worse inside the house. Besides, to charge money –! Our housekeeper was always allowed to show visitors round when we were away and I think she made quite a nice extra income from the tips they gave her; but I hope we haven't sunk that low yet.'

'The other thing would be to invite some sort of organization to share the building with you. Something more appropriate than a school. I mean, one of the girls in my form at school went off to do something called a Brides' Class. Learning to cook and arrange flowers and appreciate art and make curtains, all in a terribly high-class way. Just think what people would pay if they could do that sort of thing in surroundings like this. And then half the house would be kept warm and –'

'Steady, steady.' Rupert, laughing, took her arm and led her out of the drawing room. 'I should have remembered, you're the girl who's always bursting with outrageous new ideas.'

'Not so outrageous.' It seemed to Trish a very practical suggestion.

'Well, we'll ask Julia over lunch what she thinks.'

'Is Julia going to marry Miles before – before –?'

'No. That's something they've talked out between them. He says he wants to wait till he can walk to his wedding. He knows it won't happen, but he's putting on an act.'

'It must be an awful time for her.'

'Yes. She's been marvellous. Not just to Miles, but to Mother as well. You can imagine . . .'

'But if –' Trish hesitated, not sure how to phrase her query.

'If what –?'

'If she's not going to come and live here after all, I'm surprised that her parents should have put in the money for the moat. And I wouldn't even have thought that she'd want to be involved in restoring rooms that weren't ever going to be hers.'

It was Rupert's turn to hesitate briefly, as though he were not sure how to explain.

'Well, she's having to act a part in a way. I think I told you, when she first heard that Miles was still alive, she wasn't going to hold him to his engagement if he wanted to be free. But as soon as she saw him, she realized how important it was that he should be able to rely on her. It wasn't clear straightaway that he wasn't going to make it. She wanted to give him hundred per cent support. I suppose you could call the money a gesture to assure Miles that he was going to pull through and get married.'

Trish frowned slightly to herself. This hardly seemed to square with Miles's acceptance of his approaching death. 'Even so –' she began, but was interrupted by the arrival of the subject of their conversation.

'Ah, Julia. You remember Patricia.'

'Of course. You survived that open day, then.' The frown of strain on Julia's face was smoothed by her smile. Neatly dressed in blouse and skirt, she brought with her an aura of businesslike calm. Trish found it easy to imagine her as the ATS officer she had been for the past five years: giving orders, in control of a situation.

Trish herself felt far from under control. Everything about the conversation throughout luncheon and during the afternoon seemed to leave her as an outsider. When she foolishly mentioned Egypt, the bout of reminiscence which followed was a reminder that Julia and Rupert had met there and – it appeared – had together travelled to visit the antiquities of the Upper Nile during weekend leaves. When politics came into the conversation it became clear that Julia had not only helped Rupert to canvass but was now assisting him to prepare a subject for his maiden speech. They had friends in common. They rode with the same hunt. Trish tried to persuade herself that Rupert was talking in this way merely to give moral support to someone who was living through a difficult time, but with each moment that passed she could feel a kind of panic in her throat rising to choke her.

They walked round the house together. Julia could identify all the family portraits in the long gallery. Julia was as shocked as Rupert had been by the damage and shabbiness resulting from the school's occupation and had clear ideas of how each room should be restored. Why didn't Rupert stop her? Why didn't he point out that there was no need to keep up the act while Miles was not present to see it? Trish looked at him appealingly and saw that he had eyes only for Julia.

Self-respect told Trish that she must leave as soon as was decently possible, without allowing any hint of her feelings to show, but both her pride and her strength failed her. It came as a last straw when, after Julia had disappeared to see whether Miles was awake, Rupert announced that they were to take tea with his mother. So he was not prepared to be alone with her for even this short time.

'Tell me first,' said Trish. 'Are you and Julia —?'

She was unable to finish the question, because even to complete the thought was unbearable. She was asking only in order that she might see Rupert grin in the old, carefree way before taking her into his arms and saying that of course it would never be anything but him and Trish. But instead his mouth moved in an odd way, as though he was trying to control an unsuitable smile.

'That's not a question to be put or answered in the circumstances,' he said.

'You're going to marry her. As soon as your brother's dead, you're going to marry her!'

'Patricia, you mustn't —'

'I'm not Patricia!' she exclaimed furiously. 'Patricia is the name you gave to a little girl when you pretended that she was a grown-up lady. But only pretended. Patricia has always been a child in your eyes, hasn't she? Well, I'm Trish. I've always been Trish. And Trish has grown up and is not prepared to be patronized any longer.'

'I've never patronized you. We've always been good friends, however old you were and — oh, my God!'

He stared at her in dismay as he understood what she had given away, and she felt herself beginning to flush. Not a slight, pretty blush of faint embarrassment, but an angry red flush which burned her cheeks and spread round her neck. Furious with herself for revealing her feelings in the first place and confirming them by this uncontrollable reaction, she turned away from him.

'I can't stay for tea,' she said. 'I have to get back to Greystones. Could someone ring for a taxi?'

EIGHT

The snow which had made Castlemere beautiful brought an appearance of desolation to the Oxfordshire countryside. On the previous occasion when Trish had made this railway journey back to Oxford the sun was shining and she had sung aloud for happiness; but today the unheated train was chilling and there was winter in her heart.

If only she had kept her stupid mouth shut! What was the point of asking Rupert about Julia when she was already sure what the answer would be? All she had needed to do was to keep quiet, and Rupert would never have known how she felt.

Was it really that which was hurting, she asked herself severely – not the fact that she had lost Rupert, but the humiliation of allowing him to discover that she had wanted him? No; it was not as simple as that. The loss and the shame were equally unbearable, and to them must be added anger with herself for so hopelessly misunderstanding his feelings.

Whatever he might say, he still saw her as a child. The twelve-year gap in their ages might not have mattered if they had met for the first time as adults. And had he been only six years old himself when he became friends with her at the same age, they would have grown up together and he would have recognized that she was a woman as soon as he knew himself to be a man. But as things were, she would never be able to catch up and it had been silly of her to try.

Well, it had been a lucky escape. The woman who became Rupert's wife would be acquiring not just a husband but a run-down house and a parcel of financial worries. Who in her senses would choose to live in a museum and devote her whole life to maintaining it in the manner to which it was accustomed. 'Not I,' said Trish aloud to the empty compartment; whistling in the dark.

Grace had given her a warning. It would not be too hard to pretend that she had observed it and had taken the initiative in backing away from a way of life to which she was temperamentally unsuited. She could at least spare herself the indignity of having it generally known that she had loved and lost. If anyone were to express sympathy, she would cry, and she was determined not to cry.

By the time she reached Greystones she had succeeded in bottling up her feelings of anger and shame. Such control would not survive close questioning, so as she went to look for Grace to report her return, it was a relief to hear from a distance that she was talking to someone. That would make it easier to withdraw quickly in order not to interrupt a conversation. She opened the drawing room door.

'I'm home!' she said – and found that she was in the middle of a battle, which her arrival did nothing to interrupt. Grace and Jay, facing each other across the sofa, could both see her, were both aware that she could hear what they were saying, but they seemed unable to control their anger even for the moment it would take to say hello.

Quarrels of any kind were a rarity at Greystones. Trish herself sulked from time to time if she could not have her own way, and during the war years Dan and Boxer and Max had not always done what they were told at once and had to be reprimanded. On such occasions it was Grace's habit to state an opinion or issue instructions in a calm but firm voice and then to walk away immediately, making it difficult to rebel when there was no further opportunity to protest in words. Only on the infrequent visits of her elder brother David was she likely to become involved in heated argument, and even then any loss of temper was always on David's side. To hear her shouting was a rare occurrence indeed.

'I won't have it going on under my own roof,' she said. She

had turned her head briefly to register Trish's appearance, but did not allow it to soften her expression. 'One of you will have to go. Or both.'

Jay, who even off the stage was always acting, whether by playing the fool or by expressing opinions through the voice of some invented character, seemed to have been caught without a script. Or perhaps, unlike his sister, he preferred for once not to have an audience. Trish needed no further invitation to depart. 'I'm home,' she repeated quietly, and left the room at once.

The oddness of the atmosphere was enough to banish her own unhappiness briefly from her thoughts as new questions and anxieties swirled around her mind. Grace had always seemed especially fond of her younger brother. He had by now managed to find a flat in London, but his room at Greystones was always available to him at weekends or between productions. What could have happened to make her so furious – and Jay so unusually subdued? Was it, she wondered, reaching her bedroom and changing into casual clothes, something to do with the fact that Jay was a queer?

Brought up in adult company, Trish had always been mature for her age. Her upbringing was nevertheless a sheltered one. Not until she left school and began to learn about life from her fellow-art students did she become aware that not all young men wanted nothing better than to find a nice girl and marry her. And even after she had absorbed this piece of knowledge in a theoretical way it had taken the outspoken Gordon to point out what she had not realized for herself: that Jay Hardie was, as he contemptuously put it, a pansy.

At the time she had seen no need to have a view about this. Jay was entitled to his private life and actors were not the same as ordinary people anyway. What bothered her now was the mention of a second person. Had Jay managed to smuggle some unauthorized visitor in without the rest of them knowing? No; he couldn't possibly have kept it secret, and it didn't fit with the phrasing of Grace's ultimatum.

There was Max, of course. A whole term of having his youngest son at home again had been enough to refuel David Hardie's irritation, and Grace's offer of a week's holiday at Greystones before Christmas had been gratefully accepted. But Max was only twelve. Even if he had somehow become involved with Jay, surely nobody would suggest turning him out of the house.

But who else could she have meant? A possible answer insinuated itself uneasily into Trish's mind. But it couldn't be? Could it? Her own father?

Trish did not remember her mother. As a little girl she had had no experience of living as a member of a family, of observing how people behaved when they were married. She had accepted without question the arrangements which were made when she moved into Greystones. Only much later had it occurred to her that it was unusual for a husband and wife to have bedrooms which were not only separate but a long way from each other. But by that time her father was mostly living abroad, for reasons of work which he explained to her and which she believed. What a naïve little girl she must have been!

So what was actually happening? One of the unpleasant things about being told the facts of life when she was twelve had been the picture it conjured up of her father and the unknown woman who was her mother doing what was necessary to begin her own existence. Now a different picture struggled to take shape in her mind – but with less success, because she was unable to imagine exactly what might take place. She felt as though a trapdoor had opened beneath her feet, plunging her into the unknown. Already she was feeling let down by Rupert. If even her father was not what she had always thought, was anyone to be trusted?

Above all, she was conscious of a deep disgust. In her art classes she was often set to draw the male figure, but it was made of plaster, hard and white and lifeless, bearing no resemblance to soft, moving human flesh. But now the figures of two naked men with the faces of Jay and Ellis took possession of her imagination and would not be dismissed.

It couldn't be true. Her father would tell her that it wasn't true. She stood up and rushed out of the room, calling his name.

NINE

Ellis was in his bedroom, with the door open. As Trish looked in she saw that he was packing a trunk.

It was too much to bear. For a moment she felt unable to breathe.

'Where are you going?'

Ellis looked up, smiling as though nothing were wrong.

'A new venture,' he said. 'A chance to make a film. What I've always wanted to do. Not as a cameraman; as director. It's a big moment for me.'

She could tell that he expected her to run into his arms and hug him in congratulation, as she would have done when she was a little girl; but instead she stared at him coldly.

'Can't you go on living here?'

He shook his head. 'I need to be nearer to London and the studio. Especially the studio. The film-maker's day starts at five or six in the morning. It'll be much easier if I'm on the spot.'

'Then can I come and live with you?' asked Trish. 'It would be silly for me to go on paying so much for digs if you're going to have a place.'

It was a test. She did not expect him to agree, but that did not lessen her disappointment when he shook his head.

''Fraid not, love. I shan't be as close to the centre of London as all that, and it's likely to be a fairly rackety household. I shall be working a long day; eating in the canteen or in restaurants; that sort of thing. I'm not proposing to go in much for home comforts.'

'Why didn't you say anything before? Have you only just decided to go?'

'I'd intended to wait until after Christmas. The shooting won't start for a bit yet. But I'm realizing already that the preparations – blocking out the scenes, working out the camera angles, that sort of thing – are as important as the actual filming. It will be an advantage to have the run of the studio at a quiet time, with no one about, so that I can concentrate. I'll come back for Christmas dinner and present-giving, of course.'

A few days earlier Trish would have taken his explanation at face value. Now she recognized the excuse for the evasion it was. For how many years had she been kept in the dark about the real reasons behind whatever arrangements were made? 'Is Jay going to live with you?' she asked.

The smile faded from her father's face. 'What do you mean?'

'Are you and Jay going to set up house together? I suppose what I mean is, are you and Jay in love with each other?'

Still clutching the pile of shirts which he had been about to pack, Ellis sat down on the edge of the bed.

'What has Grace been saying?' he asked quietly.

'Nothing special. She hasn't needed to. I'm just asking you –'

'You must be careful what you ask, Trish. What you're suggesting is against the law. People get sent to prison for that sort of thing.'

He was silent for a moment, but Trish's silence was stronger.

'Most girls' fathers would simply tell them not to be impertinent,' he said after a moment or two.

'I'm not a child any longer,' she pointed out. 'And most girls' fathers don't –'

He interrupted her abruptly. 'Shut the door, Trish.'

She did what she was told and then sat down, waiting.

'This is a serious matter. You have to regard it as a secret. From anyone at all. Do you promise?'

'Promise.' She was reminded of her childhood tongue-twister: Trush Trist. But this was no time for jokes.

'Jay has been living dangerously,' Ellis told her. 'Going home with people he hardly knows, for a night or a week. Picking young men up, just as when he was younger he used to be picked up himself. It's an appalling risk. There's the danger of blackmail every time. And he's getting too well known now to hide behind an assumed name.'

'You do things differently, do you?'

'Yes. My friend Alan and I have lost touch. He stayed behind in France when I left. But until then – well, I suppose you could call it a sort of marriage. What I wanted – what I still want – is a settled life. Emotional security rather than a series of adventures. It's the same choice that a girl like you has to make between marriage and a series of flirtations or affairs. I think Jay may be ready to settle down. He's going to have the leading part in my film. Setting up house together while we're shooting will be good for the work and will give us a chance to see whether we want to make a permanent arrangement. Discreetly.'

'And what about Grace?' exclaimed Trish.

'Grace has always known what sort of man I am. She's a very unusual woman, Grace, and it's suited both of us to have an unusual kind of marriage. I think she must have realized that Jay was the same kind of man as I am, but she may have managed to put it out of her mind. What has upset her today is something Max saw and told her about. I think she feels that Max is rather like Jay in some ways, and she's afraid that when he grows up . . . I've tried to tell her that if that's his nature it will show itself whatever anyone says or doesn't say, but she finds that hard to believe. She'll be all right again tomorrow.'

'But you're leaving.'

'That would have happened anyway and I probably shan't stay in England for very long. I've never cheated Grace.'

'You've cheated me,' said Trish.

'No. I'm still your father. I love you more than anyone else in the world, and I always have. Nothing's changed. A lot of girls have fathers who are unfaithful to their wives with other women, over and over again. That has nothing to do with their feelings for their daughters, any more than this has. I've never lied to you. I may not have spelled everything out when you were too young to understand.'

'That's the same as lying. And I wasn't too young to understand five minutes ago, when you were still doing it.'

'The truth can be a burden. Confess it now: wouldn't you have been happier never to have guessed? But the reasons I gave for living in France, for example, were true reasons. Just not the whole truth, that's all. Come on, Trish. Tell me we're still friends.'

He stood up and came towards her, holding out his hands; but Trish shook her head and backed towards the door. Ellis did not pursue her.

'Have a word with Grace,' he said. 'When I told you to keep the secret, I didn't mean from her. If she can be reasonable about it – and affectionate – surely you can, too.'

'She's as bad as you are. Pretending. For years and years, always pretending. Making me believe that she was a normal stepmother, that I was part of a nearly normal family, when all the time, all the time . . .' For a second time that day she found herself choking on her disappointment.

'Don't be silly, Trish. The fact that I've been less than an ordinary husband to her means that she's been far more than an ordinary stepmother to you. She chose deliberately to be your mother because she loved *you*, not because she loved me.'

'I don't believe you,' said Trish. 'She hardly knew me then. I don't believe anything you or Grace have ever told me. I'm not staying here to be treated like an idiot child.'

She went straight to her own room and began to pack. One suitcase for whatever she would need for the next couple of weeks, and two others to contain everything else she owned. All her painting things were in London already. She was kneeling on the last of the three, pressing it down to close, when Grace came into the room.

'Trish, dear, you mustn't flounce off in a huff like this. I've been looking forward so much to having you back here for Christmas. You surely don't want to spend the vacation all alone in London. Your landlady –'

'I shan't go back there. Why should you have to pay out for an appendage of someone who isn't even a proper husband?'

'You're not to say that. If I've had an uncustomary sort of marriage, that's my business, not yours. All the same – sit down for a minute and listen to me.'

Trish sat down on the suitcase, whilst Grace began to walk up and down the room, pausing at the window to look out.

'Well?' asked Trish as the silence lengthened.

'It sounds too simple to be believable, but it's the truth. The companionship and support and affection which your father has given me for the past thirteen years has been exactly what I wanted. No more, no less. You have to believe that.'

'If that were true, you wouldn't be throwing him out now.'

'He's going because he has a job to do.'

'With Jay.'

'Yes. With Jay. If Ellis and I are both happy with the situation, it isn't for you to go into a tantrum about it.'

'You weren't being happy when I came home an hour ago.'

'I was angry with Jay, not with Ellis. He was flaunting their relationship in a way which was disturbing Max and would have upset you. I didn't want you to find out –'

'No! Keep Trish in the dark; that's all that matters. I don't care a damn what you and Ellis do or don't do together. All right, it's none of my business; that's why I'm going. You've had thirteen years of companionship and affection. I've had thirteen years of being lied to and made to believe that everything was different from what it really was and I've had enough.'

Had it been the only shock of the day she might have been able to bear it. But she had suffered once already from an inability to realize what was going on in front of her eyes. In that case it had been all her own fault. Rupert had not deliberately tried to deceive her but had simply been as blind to her feelings as she was to his. She had no right to be angry

300

with him. But she had every right to be angry with the two people whom she should have been able to trust.

'Go away,' she said furiously. Only by giving her anger full rein could she prevent herself from bursting into tears. 'Just go away.'

TEN

Trish was squatting in someone else's squat. As squats went, this one was positively cosy. A land mine a year or two earlier had damaged almost every roof in an Islington square, but the tightly-packed terrace houses had held each other up. Some of the walls nearest to the blast had cracked, but all were still standing. The top floors were unusable, of course, but at ground level the rooms were dry.

The usual occupants were neither down-and-outs nor political protesters. They were fellow-students of hers who had failed to find accommodation in London at a rent they could afford. All of them had gone home for Christmas, but she knew how to get into the house and how to operate the illicitly-connected electricity. It was tempting to settle herself in and stay, since she had as much right as they to be there – in other words, no right at all. But this would be unfair. She proposed to use their premises as a base only while she made the house next door habitable.

Before the bomb fell all the residents of the square had been tenants, not owners. Most of them had moved away, but those who remained proved to be friendly, glad to welcome more life in the area: someone who might join in the battle against rats. Trish found herself offered cups of tea, advice, and a selection of battered saucepans and cracked mugs, together with information on where she might find equipment abandoned by earlier squatters – a paraffin stove and a small electric cooker which would be invaluable if she could find someone to wire it in.

There was another source of booty. Workmen had begun to

make repairs on the far side of the square. She went to see what they had thrown out, and was soon in possession of a mattress which was damp but serviceable, a battered kitchen table and two chairs with the right number of legs. There was a large sofa in the house already, presumably because it was too large to move. Within three days of her arrival her new home was beginning to look furnished.

The hard work of sweeping out the debris from the blast and carrying buckets of water to clean up the two ground-floor rooms exhausted her energy. Time passed unnoticed until suddenly it was Christmas Day.

Awakened by cold, she rose early and set out to look for a public telephone. Her resentment had burned itself out, but she still felt let down by the way she had been treated. Leaving home had been only half a gesture of independence. The other half was staying away, proving that she could look after herself: and a good way to prove that was to make a voluntary return for one day only, refusing all invitations to stay, even for a single night. Such a visit would have the secondary advantage of enabling her to have a hot bath, which she would not be too proud to refuse.

Even to herself she did not express her intentions in those terms. Instead, she allowed herself to feel sorry for Grace. Ellis and Jay, evicted from Greystones, would no doubt be happy enough with each other's company over Christmas and Max, back at home, would be enjoying the company of his sister and brothers. It was wrong that Grace should be left all alone on a day which she would have expected to be a happy family occasion. It was Trish's intention to wish her a merry Christmas and agree to come back for the day as though nothing had happened.

It took some time to find a call box in working order. By the time she dialled the number, Grace would be just finishing breakfast. She listened as it began to ring.

There was no answer. She rang off and tried again in case there had been a fault at the switchboard. The harsh buzzing went on and on. Mrs Barrett was nervous of answering the telephone, but would certainly have alerted her mistress to its ringing had she been in the house. She must have been given the day off. And as for Grace herself – might she have had an accident of some kind? It wasn't likely. Much more probable was that she was treating Christmas Day as an ordinary day and had already retreated into the studio, where the bell could not be heard.

More disappointed than she liked to admit, Trish put down the receiver. To make the journey and arrive without warning or invitation would be a confession of defeat, and she was not defeated. But the day stretched bleakly in front of her. There was no snow here in London to cover the dirty streets. There was no one around to provide even an impersonal nod of greeting. Behind the closed doors and curtained windows children would be opening their stockings, but they had not yet emerged to play with any new treasures.

She would have had a stocking of her own had she still been living at Greystones. 'Until you're twenty-one!' Grace had said firmly when she once wondered aloud whether she wasn't becoming too old for that sort of thing. It would have been filled with food treats and new paints and brushes. Grace would have made something out of clay or carved a puzzle or – but Trish shook such thoughts out of her head. She didn't care about such childish things as stockings herself, but was sorry that Grace had been deprived of the pleasure of giving and being thanked.

Wandering aimlessly through the empty streets, she found herself passing an ugly building labelled Public Baths. Perhaps she had noticed it before, but if so had assumed it to be a swimming pool. Now, looking more closely at the schedule of services, times and prices, she discovered that it would provide her – although not until after Boxing Day – with the hot bath which she badly needed. The promise of cleanliness made her immediately feel more clean. Her eyes brightened, her footsteps lightened as she set herself to make new plans.

By the time she returned to the square she had decided how to spend the day, if she could find the right materials. It was easy to break into the four houses on which the builders had been working. Yes, there were pots of paint and a selection of brushes. It wasn't stealing, she told herself as she picked up as much as she could carry; only borrowing. Most of the tins had already been opened and she would return everything except a few inches of paint before the holiday period was over.

The selection was not an inspiring one. House decoration, like everything else, was confined in a utility mode. There were two kinds of white paint: one for ceilings and the other for woodwork. There was cream for walls and black for gutters, and a variety of undercoats: white, grey and dark red. The one unopened tin was the most exciting: a daffodil yellow paint which was perhaps intended for a front door.

Back in her own squat, she sat down on the large sofa and stared at the wall which faced her. Most of it was covered with a wallpaper patterned with roses, but at both top and bottom lumps of plaster had fallen away. Had Terry been here, he would have made it all good, but there was an easier way to deal with the damage. Half closing her eyes, she allowed the triangular shapes of missing plaster to transform themselves into sharply pointed mountains. A graceful crack provided the skeleton of a willow tree. The damage higher up could be hidden under clouds.

If only the owner of the unpainted front door had chosen green instead of yellow! But even as she sighed, a study in grey and black and white began to form before her eyes. A Chinese landscape, but formalized until it was hardly identifiable as a landscape at all. So touches of the red metal undercoat would serve to indicate what ought to be green. The sun could shine on it from one corner, sending down daffodil yellow rays.

It was quite wrong to mix so many different kinds of paint, of course. The finished effect would probably be ridiculous. But it could only have a temporary life and planning and executing it would be fun. The first necessity was to obliterate the wallpaper roses.

Their colour proved to be stronger than the white of the ceiling paint, and two coats were needed to cover them. While she waited for the first to dry, she squared out a design which could be enlarged to the size of the wall. Although she wanted the work to emerge spontaneously, that much preparation was needed so that she could use bold brushstrokes with no second thoughts.

One of the boring things she had been taught at college was perspective, which now proved not to be boring at all. She used it to increase the size of the tiny room by opening up a vista, allowing a river to wind between the mountains of damaged plaster and away into the distance. By the time the light faded on Boxing Day, only the yellow sun was missing from her picture wall, and for good measure she had slapped white paint over the other three walls so that there was not a rose to be seen.

For two days she had hardly been aware of hunger, content to nibble at raw carrots and cabbage, but now she was starving. Returning to the next-door squat she raided her friends' small stock of tins. Unlike the paint, though, these could be replaced. Early the next morning she set out to shop.

ELEVEN

The street market behind the Angel was already crowded when Trish arrived. She was carrying her ration book, but quickly realized that no one here would demand it. The knowing looks of the stallholders were intended to give the impression that their goods were black market, but the solitary policeman patrolling the streets showed little interest. No clothing coupons were required for the army surplus blankets which were just what she needed; nor was she expected to hand over any 'points' for battered tins of food. Almost certainly these had been condemned as unfit for sale, but what did a few dents matter? Carefully picking the least damaged, she was just about to pay for half a dozen tins of baked beans when she heard her name being called and looked around to see who it could be.

It was Boxer. He was standing on a wooden box about three stalls away. She made her way towards him with her fists pumping like pistons in their old greeting.

'Hold on a tick,' he said, for he had serious business in hand. A crowd was already gathering around his table, which was loaded with cardboard boxes. He was selling china tea sets which he claimed to be export rejects. A non-stop patter flowed from his earnest, high-pitched voice as he waved a specimen cup in the air.

'Well of course they're seconds, ladies and gents. Who asked if they were seconds? Of course they're seconds. 'Ow else would you expect to get a pattern as pretty as this on your tea table. If you're 'appy with plain white china then go away and don't get in the way of them as knows a good thing when they sees one. If I'd 'ad these 'ere a week ago, ladies and gents, I'd 'ave been asking a tenner for the set so's you could give Granny a real treat this Christmas, but they're late and so you're lucky and yes, of course you can take a look but it's a fiver if you drop it. Now then, ten pound a set these are worth, but am I asking ten pound? No I'm not. Am I asking eight pound? No I'm not. Am I asking six pound?'

The crowd joined in. 'No, you're not.'

'But that's the limit, ladies and gents. A bargain's a bargain and if I go any lower there'll be a riot, fighting in the street, because I've only got ten of these boxes and I can see fifteen, twenny of you feeling for your money already. Only the first ten's going to be lucky. Best export reject, a fiver the set for the first nine but the sky's the limit for the last one.'

''Ere, guv. One for me!' With amusement Trish saw that the hand which was waving a five-pound note belonged to Dan.

'Thank you, sir. One for the gentleman. Only nine to go and the last one makes its own price. Don't be left standing, ladies and gents, while a bargain slips past yer eyes. Best export reject!'

Alerted by Boxer's shout, Dan came to stand beside Trish as soon as he had completed his purchase.

'I take it that goes straight back into stock,' she said laughing. 'When do you produce another set of only ten tea sets?'

'Not for two hours. All this crowd'll have gone by then. But they know there are plenty more, whatever old Boxer says. Not doing too badly, is he? It's my stall really, him being still at school, but I let him have a go in the hols to see how he gets on. You living near here, Trish?'

'Yes. Squatting. Just came down to pick up a bit of food.'

'We've got a trolley. Tell us what you want and we'll bring it round. Save you lugging heavy stuff home.'

'Right.' She gave him a ten-shilling note. 'Just tins of things that don't need cooking, only heating up. You could eat some of them with me.'

'About two o'clock then, after the market closes and we've

cleared up.' He wrote down the address and went back to his own stall to supervise Boxer's salesmanship.

When the time came they arrived together, pulling a trolley laden with tins and vegetables.

'Should keep you going for a day or two,' said Dan. 'Six bob change.'

'Dan, you can't – I can't possibly –' But she did not pursue the protest, realizing just in time that after accepting so much during their years at Greystones it was giving them pleasure to make a small return.

'Know how to get the best price, don't we?' said Boxer proudly. 'Always things going cheap after the market closes, and we do each other turns.'

'Well, thanks a lot. It's marvellous. What shall we eat now?'

They lunched on Spam and tinned peaches, washed down by a bottle of Tizer. 'A feast!' exclaimed Trish. 'Tell me, how's Terry?'

'Having the time of his life, old Terry,' Dan told her. 'Buying and selling. He's got a nose for it, finding people with something to sell. He's big in parachutes.'

'Parachutes? Who wants a parachute now the war's over?'

'Anyone who wants some nice undies without coupons. They're made of nylon, see, or silk. You buy a great big triangle and cut it up and make a petticoat or something out of it. All on the level – 'cos like you said, no one needs parachutes any more. It's the factory wot's selling them off. And army surplus, that's a big thing – warm stuff and no coupons.'

'So Terry has a stall as well as you, does he?'

Dan shook his head. 'He's got a shop. With a warehouse at the back. He buys bulk – things that have gone wrong in the factories – and sells to market traders like me. You can't go in ordinary, like, and buy just one of anything. You have to get it by the dozen. He makes me pay like anyone else –' Trish could tell that this was a sore point – ''cos he says it's the only way to learn about making a profit.'

'How did he manage to get hold of a shop?'

309

'He used that money Grace gave him, and his demob gratuity, to buy a bomb site with a shed still standing. He did the selling out of that to start with, while he and some mates and Boxer and me put a shop up in the front. We're going to build a flat on top of it soon's we can get some more bricks. He's on a winner, bound to be. Everyone wants to buy things but there's nothing you *can* buy except when there's something wrong with it and then the people who make it don't want anyone to know where it came from. I mean, he bought two prefabs last week because the transporter skidded off the road and they got bashed, but they're all right except for some dents. We're going to keep one of them and he reckons he can auction the other for as much as he paid for the two.'

'He must be a good salesman.'

'Anyone can sell, he says. It's finding something to buy that's the hard work. Well, we gotta get back. I help him out, afternoons.'

'It's been marvellous to see you.' She hugged them both vigorously. 'And all this food is my best Christmas present.' My only Christmas present, she might have said, but she had given no hint of her strained relations with the rest of her family. 'Give my love to Terry. And I'll see you again in the market, I expect.'

Cheered by the meeting – and the generous stocking of her larder – she set to work to finish her wall painting. She saw that her first idea for the daffodil paint would be disproportionately bright. Instead of a full sun high in the sky, she painted just its narrow curve rising from behind a mountain, and began to speckle in the rays with tiny dots. So well did they cheer up the scene that she scattered them more widely, making each almost too small to distinguish. The wall changed character in front of her eyes. Could she have started again – and with a more reasonable choice of materials – she would have done it all differently. Nevertheless, she was pleased with the effect when at last she stood back to look at the finished result.

'Not bad,' said a voice from the narrow hallway.

She turned, startled. Terry was sitting on the bottom stair, his hat on his knees.

'Terry! How long have you been there?'

''Bout half an hour. Didn't like to interrupt. You were going at it just like Grace does.'

'Yes.' Trish had had the same thought herself. It was from Grace that she had learned how to concentrate so completely on a task that she was not conscious of anything else. There was a difference, though. Grace would never have felt the urge to scrub the whole thing off as soon as she had finished.

'The lads told me about seeing you.' Terry stood up and came into the room. His finger went up to touch the black patch which covered his left eye, checking that it was in place. 'I can offer you something better than this, Trish. And all on the level. No wondering when someone's going to kick you out or pinch your stuff. Did they tell you about the prefabs? You could have one of them.'

Trish took her time about answering. If the offer had come from Grace or Ellis, she would have spurned it, determined not to accept a favour or be patronized. But from Terry it was in every sense on the level. Like Dan and Boxer with their overripe vegetables and dented tins, he was seizing the opportunity to show gratitude and repay a debt. It would be childish as well as churlish to refuse, and she was not a child any longer.

'I'd want to pay my way,' she said.

'Sure. Give me something to sell, and I'll sell it for you.'

'Even pictures?'

'Pictures, yes, easy, as long as they're cheap. Walls even! But we'd like to have you as a neighbour anyhow.'

Trish grinned. 'You always were one for having good ideas.'

'And you were always the girl who recognized a good idea when she heard it. Coming, then?'

She smiled in happiness and relief. There had been moments during the past few days when she had feared that she might in the end be forced to ask either Grace or Ellis for help in staying away from them, but now she felt safe. She had earned

Terry's help and would continue to earn it. They could build a kind of partnership in which they would both have brilliant ideas about what she could produce and he could sell.

'I'm coming,' she nodded. 'Thanks a lot.'

PART THREE
Separate Lives

1947

ONE

'Oughtn't you to be at school?' asked Grace; but she did not speak the words unkindly, for her youngest nephew was in a pitiable state.

This February of 1947 was the coldest month that she remembered in the whole of her life. January's snow had frozen into bumpy ice, making it impossible to cycle and hazardous even to walk up and down the steep approach to Greystones. The chill of the air outside pierced through to the bone. Max wore no gloves and his navy-blue school mackintosh had little warmth in it. He had walked, it seemed, all the way from the railway station. His face and hands were blue with cold and his thin body shivered uncontrollably.

Even Grace, who as a rule was hardly aware of the temperature, had been forced in recent weeks to surround herself with stoves in one corner of the icy studio if her hands were not to stiffen and become useless. In the evening a log fire would provide cosiness, but at this moment, in the middle of the morning, the only reliably warm place in the house was the kitchen. She led the way there now and put a pan of soup to heat on the hotplate before repeating her question. 'Oughtn't you to be at school?'

'I've run away.' So violently was Max still shivering that it was hard to hear the words. 'Not so much from school. From home. I'm never going back there again. Not ever.'

'What's the matter?' Grace sat down on a stool close to him and began to massage his icy hands. The thirteen-year-old had spent a week of the Christmas holiday with her and he had not been happy then, because his mother had died three weeks

315

earlier. For Christmas itself he had been invited to stay with his married elder brother, and had seemed cheerful enough when he left Greystones. What could have happened?

'It's the scholarship,' he said. 'To ballet school. I went in for it a year ago and they offered me a place and a bursary. Fifty pounds a year. It's hard enough even to get a place, but to get money as well . . . ! Father wouldn't let me take it. Because of Mummy being ill and wanting me at home, he said, but that wasn't the real reason.'

'And has the school renewed the offer now?'

He shook his head, his teeth still chattering. 'They don't hold anything over. You've got to take it when it's offered. But I went in for it again this year. Father wasn't going to let me, but I told him the wrong date purposely and I got Miss Berry to take me. I didn't think I'd got a hope, because I haven't been able to practise properly. But they have this thing that after you've done your audition piece one of the teachers gives you a kind of lesson in something new and they look to see whether you can do it. I was all right on that.'

'So you got another offer? Here, drink this.' She poured some of the hot soup into a mug and pressed his hands round it.

'The scholarship,' he said. 'The top scholarship! I never dreamed . . . It means that all the teaching would be free. I'd only have to pay the eating and sleeping part of the fees. It's a boarding school, you see. It has to be, because you spend hours every day at dancing class, but you have to do ordinary school work as well. I thought Father would be pleased at least that I'd done so well.'

'No, you didn't,' said Grace. 'You knew he'd be furious. You and your mother have been deceiving him for years, trying not to let him find out that you were still having lessons.'

There was an odd moment in which Max, who had been on the point of tears, gave a gulp as if to control an urge to laugh.

'But it's not fair!' he exclaimed. 'John and Peter both went to boarding school when they were thirteen and Lily only didn't go because she's a girl. He paid *all* the fees for them, and I only need half of them. And he says my school work's terrible and I know it is, but it would be better there because we'd all be the same and the teachers would understand.'

'So what did your father actually say?'

'The letter from the school came this morning.' Now Max did break down and cry. 'I thought it was the best thing that was ever likely to happen to me in the whole of my life. I mean, the top one! It's what everyone in the whole country wanted, and I got it.' He stopped, gulping back his sobs before he could continue. 'He always thinks that I'm no use at anything, so I really did hope that he could feel – well, proud, you know.'

'But what did he say? Stop blubbing. That soup's got quite enough salt in it already.' She refilled the mug, keeping her back turned for a moment longer than was necessary so that he could dab his eyes dry.

'He said that I was to understand once and for all that no son of his was going to earn a living as a ballet dancer. There was a family business waiting for me to go into and it was about time that I buckled down to my school work and passed exams in something useful. I thought he hadn't understood properly so I told him again that I'd got the top scholarship and he just said "I forbid you to go" and tore the letter up. But I grabbed it, so I've still got it. And then I said that the scholarship was offered to me, not to him, and I was going to take it, and he said that if I thought he was going to pay the rest of the fees for that kind of school I could think again.'

'May I see the letter?' She fitted the torn pieces together on the kitchen table. 'Well, congratulations, Max! It's a wonderful achievement. You must have worked very hard and it's marvellous for you to know that someone outside your own teacher recognizes that you've got talent.' Grace was not accustomed to gush, but it seemed to her that a little praise for her single-minded nephew was overdue.

317

'I'll go to Russia,' said Max sulkily. 'In Russia you don't pay anything at all at ballet school. Anyway, I'm never going home again. And if he makes me give up the scholarship, I'll kill myself.'

'No, you won't,' said Grace. 'And no one can make you give up the scholarship. Go and find some writing paper now and bring it back here into the warm. Thank the school for its offer of the scholarship and say you have great pleasure in accepting it. You'd like to take up the place at the earliest possible opportunity; when would that be? And ask them to address any future correspondence to you at this address.'

'But the other fees?'

'One thing at a time. It may be that your father will change his mind when he realizes that he can't change yours. After all, it's going to be lonely for him without anyone else at home.'

'He doesn't see me even when I'm there. He comes home late, and if I'm in the sitting room he sends me upstairs to do homework. If it's going to depend on him –'

'There are other possibilities. We may find that the school has some kind of fund to help people in your position. If not, you'll just have to ask your aunt to help you, won't you?'

'Would you really, Aunt Grace? And let me live here in the holidays?'

'Don't pretend that you've only just thought of the idea,' said Grace, laughing. 'That's why you've come here, isn't it? You realize, of course, that if I offer you a way of disobeying your father he'll probably never speak to me again.'

Max looked at her anxiously. 'Do you mind that?'

She tried to control the expression on her face. It was disgraceful that she should not care whether or not her brother broke all contact with her – and even more disgraceful that the thought of angering him gave her pleasure.

'I'll survive. Do you want your old bedroom?'

'Just to start with.' Max had stopped shivering. The colour

was returning to his cheeks and the liveliness to his eyes. 'But after that, I think I ought to sleep in a different room every holiday. All those bedrooms, with no one taking any notice of them!'

Grace laughed aloud. It had never occurred to her to feel sorry for a lonely bedroom. But then she looked at Max seriously.

'One thing we ought to get straight before we start, Max,' she said, addressing him as though he were an adult. 'Usually when you've been here before for more than a few days you've had Dan and Boxer to play with, or Trish to keep an eye on you. But now there's only me and Mrs Barrett. And I'm not going to change my habits to fit in with you. If I did that, I'd soon get fed up and wish you weren't here. I'm used to doing exactly what I want exactly when I want without bothering about other people's plans. It's a thoroughly selfish way of life, but I'm too old to change it.'

'You're not old!'

'I'm nearly fifty,' Grace told him. 'Old enough to be set in my ways. What I'm trying to say is this. You complained that your father never kept you company. Well, probably I shan't either. It won't mean that I'm cross with you or don't like you. Just that I'm used to being on my own and it won't occur to me to change. Trish had to get used to that when she was quite a little girl. I can give you a roof over your head and I'll pay out whatever is needed to make you the greatest dancer of your generation, but I'm not offering to be a mother to you. We shall be leading separate lives here. Do you understand?'

Max nodded. 'I know what you mean about a selfish way of life. Father says that I'm selfish, thinking of nothing but myself. But it isn't really me, it's what I think I could do with myself if I had the chance. It's just the same as you, isn't it, except that you've made your chance already.' He held out his hand. 'I'm ever so grateful to you, Aunt Grace, and the first time I dance at Covent Garden I shall get you a seat in the royal box.

But I'm used to looking after myself. I'll try not to bother you ever. Separate lives!'

At first solemnly and then smiling at each other, Grace and her nephew shook hands on the promise.

TWO

Guessing correctly that David would be out at lunch, Grace made a telephone call to his office and left a message to tell him of Max's whereabouts. Even the most unloving father would presumably be disturbed if he found that one of his children had disappeared without trace. There would be a quarrel later on, when he learned what was going to happen, but the prospect caused her no anxiety.

What a toss-up it was, this business of having children, she thought to herself as she put down the receiver and returned to the kitchen to advise Max on the drafting and spelling of his letter. David should count himself lucky that he had produced three conventional offspring before the arrival of the boy who was to nurse such an unlikely ambition. For a moment her thoughts flickered over the memory of baby Tom, who would have been just a few months older than Max if he had lived, but she pushed the memory away and instead considered another baby. Only that morning, she had received a card announcing the birth of a daughter to the Marquess and Marchioness of Ross. Rupert had married Julia three months after his brother's death, and they had wasted no time in starting a family. Lady Anne Beverley had been born with a title and a place in society already attached to her. As they bent over their first-born's cradle did her parents realize that hidden somewhere inside that tiny and helpless human being must already lie the seed of an independent personality?

A rattling and bumping outside the kitchen door interrupted her thoughts, announcing Andy's arrival with another sledge-load of logs. There was no work to be done on the frozen ground, so for the past three weeks he had worked with axe and saw to refill Grace's wood store as well as his own. On an impulse she opened the door and called to him.

'Max is here to stay,' she told him. 'Come and have a meal with us tonight, and share our fire afterwards. Only fair, since you've chopped all the wood for it.'

'I'll do that. Thanks.' He came regularly to Greystones for Sunday lunch, but during the rest of the week they rarely met. He liked Max, and sympathized with his ambitions.

'All I ever wanted to do as a boy was to grow things,' he said that evening as they came to the end of a candlelit meal – for the freezing weather and a national fuel shortage had combined to force electricity cuts. 'So I was lucky. No one ever tried to stop me, except the army. Even if you don't get what you want in the end, I reckon it's important to have a try. Otherwise you can spend the rest of your life moping about missing your chance. I've seen it happen. Good luck to you.'

'Thanks a lot.' Max was hardly recognizable as the shivering, tearful boy who had arrived that morning. He was still wearing his school uniform, for he had brought nothing else with him, but his face was flushed with happiness and the warmth of the log fire and a single meal seemed to have put weight on his thin frame. He had always been much stronger than he looked, but now his strength showed in the confident set of his shoulders.

After an exhausting day he went early to bed, leaving Grace and Andy to relax on either side of the fire. At least, Grace was relaxed. Andy was unusually restless.

'Something I wanted to ask you,' he said suddenly. 'Is Ellis ever coming back?'

Ellis's first film had been an immediate success. In the starring role Jay had conducted what could only be described as a love affair with the camera, and his performance brought him the offer of a Hollywood contract. His reluctance to travel to California without his friend resulted in a contract for Ellis too, and they had left England for a new life together.

322

'I doubt it,' said Grace. 'Not to Greystones, anyway.' It had proved easier to be tolerant of her husband and brother when they were no longer under the same roof, and they had parted good friends, her loss of temper forgotten. She and Ellis had been useful to each other once, but that stage of their lives had come to an end. There was no need to continue the pretence of being husband and wife, but divorce offered no advantage to either of them. Ellis's absence abroad would not make the slightest difference to his own way of life or hers, whether as husband or ex-husband.

'That's what I thought,' said Andy. He leaned forward in his chair and took hold of her hand – a hand as hard as his own, for they were both labourers in their own ways. 'That's why I want to ask you . . . That time before, when you sent me away, it was because I was married. And by the time I came back *you* were married. But we're both free now, more or less. I still love you, Grace. And to have you so close . . . Don't send me away this time.'

He was on his knees in front of her, burying his head in her lap for a few seconds before pulling her down to lie beside him on the carpet. At first he did no more than hold her tight, kissing her face and neck and murmuring words that she could not hear. Then she felt him start to unfasten her clothes – not tearing at them in a passionate rush as had happened by the boulders all those years ago, but carefully and slowly, pausing every now and then to stroke the new area of skin he had exposed.

There was a moment, when at last she lay naked, in which she felt anxious. Suppose Max were suddenly to reappear for some reason. It was just such an unexpected encounter which had led to her furious banishment of Ellis and Jay. But within seconds it was made clear to her how anyone could be so indiscreet, for the rest of the world ceased to exist as she felt herself pressed hard down on to the carpet, smothered, aroused, loved.

Andy was gasping, groaning, calling her name, while Grace

herself was conscious of a bubbling sound at the back of her throat. It was the sound of happiness, she realized, as her body stretched and arched, her legs imprisoning Andy as effectively as his weight imprisoned her. Then silence fell, broken only by the cracking and spitting of the logs on the fire.

'We're right for each other.' Andy turned on to his side, moving her with him so that they need not separate yet. Grace murmured her agreement. More than thirty years had passed since the kisses of first love had taken them by surprise, but their bodies were still firm and strong. The physical effort needed for her carving had saved her from becoming either fat or scraggy as she moved into middle age. She was as tall as Andy. Their toes touched, playing with each other while their lips met in another kiss.

When, very much later, Andy at last dressed and let himself out into the freezing night air, she lay for a long time without moving, watching the patterns made by the glowing logs and ashes and warmed from within with a contentment which she had never expected to experience. It was unbelievable that anyone should find her desirable. Unbelievable, but marvellous. Her hands moved over her body, feeling it as Andy had felt it. She stroked her skin with the very tips of her fingers and cupped her hands over her breasts.

Such small breasts! The current fashion, set by Hollywood film stars, was for a quite different shape. Trish – who was perfectly proportioned – had been heard to wish that she were better endowed. But Grace's figure had been fashionable in the generation of her youth and she could have dressed elegantly if she had ever been prepared to abandon the overalls in which she worked. She was not accustomed to examine her own body and surprised herself with the discovery that her breasts were not soft and fleshy, but firm and muscular. Yet Andy had loved them and that was all she cared about.

Stretching her body like a cat, she thought happily about Andy. Once upon a time they had wanted to marry, but he would not suggest that now. He knew her too well, recognizing that her need for solitude was more than simply a working practice. And he too valued his independence. It would suit them both that they should continue their separate ways of life by day. But at night . . . From now on, how different the nights would be.

THREE

'You're invited to a party,' said Trish. It was lunchtime in The Shed and even Terry, who worked an eighteen-hour day, was taking a brief break from the task of opening bales of army surplus stores.

'When? Where? Why?'

'I am about to come of age,' Trish told him with as much dignity as could be mustered by someone who was wearing paint-smeared overalls at least three sizes too large. 'Grace proposes to mark the occasion with a twenty-first birthday thrash at Greystones. Lunch and silly games. Crazy croquet. Batty badminton. Preposterous putting.'

'I thought you told me once that Grace never gave parties.'

'No more she has until now. This is to make up for a lifetime of neglected birthdays. All I have to do is provide the guest list. And you and the boys come at the top.'

'Accepted with thanks. I'm glad to hear that Grace has forgiven you.'

Trish opened her mouth to argue, but then changed her mind. *She*, not Grace, was the one to do the forgiving, in her opinion. She had not allowed very much time to pass before apologizing to her stepmother for the manner of her departure from Greystones eighteen months earlier, but there had been no reciprocal expression of regret for the way in which she had been deceived for so long about the marriage which wasn't really a marriage at all. Because of this, the reconciliation had not been quite complete. Trish was a welcome visitor but no longer a warmly loving stepdaughter, always ready to confide her secrets. Long before this approaching twenty-first birthday she had become an adult with a private life which she saw no need to discuss.

'Does she know yet?' asked Terry, as though following her train of thought. 'About the college, I mean?'

Trish shook her head. Towards the end of her second year at art school she had begun to find it more fun to take part in some of Terry's enterprises than to attend classes. The teachers wanted to turn out budding Rembrandts or Renoirs and she had failed to discover one with any sympathy for her own style of work.

'I'd better tell her before the party, so that it doesn't spoil the day, because I suppose she'll be expecting me to get some kind of diploma. Still, she never had any kind of teaching herself, except from an old stonemason who taught her about stone, and look how well she's done without it! She'll understand.'

'Hope you're right. So what have you got to show me today?' Once a month Trish was expected to amaze him with something outrageous.

'A real winner. Two in fact. Come outside and see. You remember those doors that Boxer got from the bombed houses on the Roman Road site?'

Terry nodded. Boxer, discharging himself from school a little before what he called his prison sentence expired, already showed in his eye for a bargain that he was a credit to his half-brother's training. The doors which he had saved from the swinging ball of a demolition contractor needed only to be sanded down and re-stained to attract a good price at a time when building materials were in short supply. Trish had been working secretly on two of them and now displayed the results with pride.

As so often when confronted with Trish's work, Terry fell about laughing. One of the doors was shining with fresh red gloss paint, applied in the dots which had become her trademark. By looking carefully it was possible to see that a scattering of black dots amongst the dark red made the shape

327

of a sinister intruder intent on picking the lock. On a second door she had painted an interior inside a wood-coloured frame. It depicted a hall so lifelike that a casual observer might believe himself to be looking through an open door.

'Boxer and I did all the preparation properly,' she assured Terry. 'So anyone who's tasteless enough to want just an ordinary door only has to put another coat of paint on.'

'Why d'you always think that people will want to paint over your work?' asked Terry. 'It's marvellous as it is. Are you going to do the others? Because if so, we'll hang on to one of these for a bit and take orders.'

Terry had abandoned his early idea of using the shabby warehouse as a wholesale depot and selling individual items only from the brick building at the front of the bomb site. All goods now were displayed in The Shed and could be bought in any quantity, although always cheaper by the dozen. Part of the excitement of the operation was that no one knew from day to day what would be on sale. It was Dan's task to persuade customers that the most unlikely objects were highly desirable, so that someone who arrived in the hope of finding a pair of Land Army boots might leave as the proud possessor of a mahogany lavatory seat.

Dan still rented a weekly stall in three different street markets and a gaudy poster by Trish which he displayed there, detailing the week's bargains at The Shed, was the only form of advertising found necessary. It was word of mouth which brought most of the customers in – that and the knowledge that, unlike the blackmarket spivs who were here today and gone tomorrow, these young salesmen would still be there the following week and could therefore be trusted.

Trish was in charge of sales during Dan's three market mornings, but for the rest of the time she was free to devise her own embellishments to the stock. She and Boxer had their own float for buying objects which could be improved. They had recently acquired ten wooden boxes, old and dirty but solidly made, of the kind used by boarding school boys for tuck, and for her next project she planned to pattern these with wooden soldiers or teddy bears to be sold as nursery toy boxes.

'Who else will be coming?' Terry asked her when he had completed his inspection of the painted doors. Trish, who had already forgotten their earlier conversation, looked puzzled until he added, 'To your twenty-first.'

'Oh, mostly Slade people. Some girls from school. All on double tickets, so to speak. Some of my schoolfriends are married already, and presumably the others will have boy-friends.'

Terry opened his mouth as if to say something, but paused, putting his hand up to touch his eye patch, in a way which suggested that he had thought of a different question. 'Will your father be there?'

Trish shook her head. 'He wrote to explain. He's earning a fantastic salary. If he comes back to England the tax man will take most of it. So if I want to see him I shall have to go out to California for a holiday. But I confidently expect that guilt at neglecting his only child will lead him to cough up a generous present of money. If he does, Terry, would you let me come into partnership with you? In a proper, businesslike, legal way? I might be able to put up enough to buy another site somewhere, in a different part of London, so that we can expand.'

'Once we do that, we're in a different kind of business,' he pointed out. 'Employing staff, for one thing. Perhaps splitting ourselves up to make sure that the branch is properly managed. So I'm not so sure about that part of it. But for the rest – well, perhaps you'd better wait until you see what your father comes up with. If he's not prepared to face the tax man, I don't suppose your Uncle Jay will want to either. Will you have any other family at the party?'

'Max is getting a weekend off school. And Rupert and Julia are coming. And Andy and Jean-Paul. Not that they're exactly family. But then, since I'm not a Hardie, none of the others are either.'

'Not any of the David Hardies, then, except Max?'

'I don't think Uncle David's on speaking terms with Grace at the moment. But John and Peter and Lily have been invited.'

'They're not likely to turn up if it's going to annoy their dad, are they?'

'You never can tell. I remember something I overheard once, when Grace and Uncle David were quarrelling. He thinks that he ought to own Greystones really.'

'He can't expect that he ever will.'

'Not while Grace is alive, no. And even if she died before him, she wouldn't leave it to him. But he might hope that she'd do her duty to the family and leave it to one of his children.'

'Get you. You mean that they'll be under instructions to suck up.'

'Well, to keep in touch, anyway. So they might come. We shall have to wait and see.'

FOUR

Not for the first time, Trish congratulated herself on choosing the right day of the year on which to be born. Although the early-morning clouds had been slow to clear, by the time the first guests arrived soon after noon the June sky was clear, the breeze had dropped and the sun shone with a proper birthday brightness. Mrs Barrett, with two helpers from the village, had produced a luncheon of pre-war magnificence, as though food rationing had ended overnight. Andy had provided a generous supply of his own white wine, and this helped to ensure that the afternoon of games, to ridiculous rules devised by Grace and Trish together, ended in animated shouting and uncontrollable laughter.

Very soon a buffet tea would be ready, to be carried into sun or shade according to choice, but already the party was beginning to split into small groups or pairs. Jay's present – which he had asked Grace to buy for him – had been a radiogram. Placed by an open window, it was providing the music for a few dancing couples on the terrace. Like Trish herself, almost all her girl friends had rushed to surrender their clothing coupons for a New Look outfit and their full, calf-length skirts swayed gracefully as they moved.

'How nice it is to see girls looking pretty again,' said Rupert, coming to stand beside Trish for a moment, but without suggesting that they should join the dancers. 'And especially my hostess, the prettiest of them all. But I'm afraid we must slip away now. Her Majesty the Tyrant requires her mother's attention at six o'clock. Thank you for a marvellous party. A wonderful relaxation.'

'Grace did all the work,' Trish pointed out. 'I'm just one of the guests. And I must thank *you*, both of you, for your lovely present. Much too generous, but thank you very much.'

How odd it was that she should be able to exchange such formal, unfelt politenesses with someone who once had so deeply thrilled and disappointed her – for Rupert's reference to her prettiness was no more likely to be sincere than her own gush over the birthday present.

They had given her a small leather case, with her initials tooled in gold, containing silver-lidded bottles and jars for beauty preparations. Trish, who rarely wore any more make-up than lipstick, could not imagine why they should have thought that such a gift was appropriate. It must have been Julia who bought it and presumably it represented the sort of thing which Julia herself had liked at the age of twenty-one. Rupert would have known better. What an odd consequence of marriage it was that someone should hand over even his friendships to his wife.

In other respects the day had been a good one for presents. Grace had greeted her merely with a birthday card, but promised that there would be something ready to be taken home when the time came to leave. Of all the guests, only Terry had not offered any sort of gift. Trish guessed that he, like Grace, planned some kind of surprise. From the way he kept nervously lifting a finger to touch his eye patch, she surmised also that he was not sure whether she would like it. She went over to join him as soon as Rupert and Julia had left.

'I've got something to tell you,' she said. 'Let's go and walk in Philip's garden.' All the gardens were Philip's in a sense, but particularly associated with him was the twisting grassy path which curved between flower beds and encircled some of his sister's sculptures; the garden which he had laid out when he was still suffering from the effect of shell-shock. Trish had always treasured its seclusion. When she and Terry sat down on the grass together at the furthest end of the walk, they could be sure that no one could interrupt or overhear them without giving early warning of an approach.

'I had a letter from my father this morning,' she said. 'He sent it early, to be safe, and asked Grace to keep it till the day. It's just what I expected: money. A lot of money. All the earnings from the film he made in England, except what he spent before he left. Apparently he can't transfer the money to America because of exchange controls, and he doesn't need it anyway because they're paying him the earth out there, so I'm to have whatever's in his special bank account straightaway and there'll be more if the film goes on playing. To set myself up, he says, so that he doesn't have to think of me starving in a garret. And that's exactly what I want to do, if you'll help me.'

'What? Starve in a garret?'

'No, idiot. What I was saying the other day. I would like to invest in Terry Travis. If you'd have me. In a partnership or a company or whatever the proper way is. Putting capital in and taking an income out.' She did her best to speak in a business-like way, while knowing nothing about the organization of business. 'I mean, I want to go on doing the sort of things I'm doing with you, because I enjoy it so much. But it would be fun to feel that I was helping to build the firm up, that I was more part of it. What do you say?'

'I can think of quite a lot to say. Mostly along the lines that you're a marvellous, generous girl and that I'm certainly never going to let you get away from The Shed, so that you're bound to win any arguments in the end. Shouldn't think this is exactly what your father had in mind, though. You ought to find someone to give you advice, independent advice.'

'But would you like it, me coming in with you? Would it be *possible*?'

'Can we leave that question for a moment while I put another question to you? Change of subject, but connected, sort of.'

Although impatient to hear her own proposition accepted, Trish waited to hear what he had to say. But the words did not come quickly. Once again he fidgeted with his eye patch.

'I haven't given you a birthday present yet,' he said at last.

'I noticed. Guessed why, as well. I'm betting that somewhere back at the yard there's some filthy, disgusting, unsaleable object which you're going to confront me with as a treat, a challenge for transformation.'

Terry shook his head. 'I want to offer you a choice,' he said. 'I mean I could give you a pair of trousers in a tasteful shade of WRAF blue, size 8 and guaranteed to make you look forty round the hips. Or a wool-lined flying jacket to add the final touch of elegance to your New Look.' He was doing his best to make a joke of it, but could not conceal his nervousness. 'What I really want to give you, though, is me.'

'You?' Trish must have looked puzzled for a moment, for he continued in a rush.

'I know I've no right to ask; you being brought up in a posh place like this, comfortable, plenty of space, enough money, and me starting off in a slum and not out of it yet. Not educated like you, either. Not used to your sort of manners and the way you do things. But one day I'll have as much money as your people, I promise you. I'll work until –'

'Hold it,' said Trish. 'You were the one who wanted to change the subject. So we're not meant to be talking about money now. What *are* we talking about? In words of one syllable, because I may have got School Certificate but I'm still a dumb blonde beneath it all.'

'I want to marry you,' said Terry. 'I always used to think that getting on and making a fortune was more important than anything else in the world, but it isn't. What I need is you. I want you to want me.'

'You've never even kissed me!' exclaimed Trish. She couldn't help laughing. 'I mean to say, there are intermediate stages. One doesn't usually move straight from the employer/slave relationship to that of husband and wife.'

'I was scared of frightening you. When I first found you in that squat you were so – so – well, you didn't want any kind of relationship with anyone at all, did you? If I'd pushed myself

334

on you, you'd just have run away. And anyway, you were in love with that handsome Lord Rupert then. I'm hoping that's worn off by now. As for the intermediate stages, we can get through those quickly enough.'

He proved his point by leaning over to kiss her, pressing her back until she was lying flat on the grass. Entering into the spirit of her laughter he began by kissing her lightly, decorously, before moving to lie more closely beside her. The kisses became harder, wetter; his tongue filled her mouth. Any minute now – but then, abruptly, he rolled away.

'Better not spoil your nice new dress in front of all your guests. But you have to believe –'

'I believe you.' Trish, still flat on her back, stretched her arms above her head in a gesture of blissful happiness. No one had ever kissed her like this before. No one had ever wanted her like this before. And yet Terry had not swept her off her feet. In some way she counted this to his credit.

'So will you –?'

'I don't think I'm interested in getting married.' She sat up, clutching her arms around her knees. 'I'm not terribly impressed with what I've seen of marriage. It doesn't keep people together who want to walk out on each other, so what's the point? Much better to stay with someone just because that's what you both want, rather than because the rules say you must.'

'Are you saying –'

'Twenty-one and still a virgin,' she said. 'It's a terrible burden. If you're offering to relieve me of it, I accept with enormous pleasure. The next time we have a quiet moment. I shall be happy to live with you. I want to be your partner in every possible way. But as for a wedding ceremony – thanks, but no thanks. It doesn't count for anything except as a notification to friends and relations.'

'Funny,' said Terry. 'I thought your sort of girl –'

'My sort of girl?' Trish felt a spurt of anger. 'My God, Terry, what do you think my sort of girl is? My sort of girl has a homosexual father, a deserting mother who's never sent me as much as a birthday card, and a stepmother who is a genius but has probably never had a sexual relationship in her life – and if she did, it might just as well be with the dustman as with anyone else. I'm the sort of girl who doesn't know how normal people live. Maybe you'll be able to teach me. But to start with, I'd prefer it to be my way. It doesn't mean that I don't love you enough, Terry. It's just that if ever you decide to move off, I'd prefer you to do it without drawing blood.'

'A long engagement, then. Could we call it that? So I can make an announcement. I want to tell everyone that I belong to you.'

His phrasing – when almost every other man she knew would have wanted to announce that she belonged to him – touched Trish almost as much as his kisses. She flung herself into his arms.

'You see why I wanted to ask my question before I answered yours,' said Terry after a while. 'Yes, of course we'll be partners, in business like everything else. But you won't need to put money in for that. What would be nicer would be to buy a proper house. I don't like to think of someone like you –'

'Stop that!' said Trish severely. 'Stop that for ever. I'm not a sort of girl and there's no someone like me. I'm just me.'

Terry nodded his acceptance of the command. 'You've always had space round you,' he said, defining what he had meant. 'Gardens. Big rooms, with walls you could paint. I want to get you out of that prefab, but it would be even more cramped if you moved into the flat above the shop. So –'

'Would there be enough?' asked Trish.

'Plenty. We'd have the money from selling the prefab as well. And there are lots of houses, decent houses with a bit of war damage or a lot of neglect, which people are frightened of taking on because they need so much doing and it's so hard to get the materials. I've got my eye on one already. I was going to borrow, but –'

'We'll go and see it tomorrow.' Trish scrambled to her feet and held out a hand to pull Terry up beside her. It was time

to return to her other guests. 'Oh Terry, it's going to be fun.'
The guests, she decided as he kissed her again, could wait for
a moment more.

FIVE

Unaccustomed as she was to giving parties – or, indeed, to attending them – Grace felt confident that this one was going well. The food and drink had been properly appreciated; there had been just enough organization of the games afterwards to prevent the afternoon from becoming aimless; and it was right that now, after tea, Trish's friends should be left to enjoy the peacefulness of the gardens and the heat of the sun in whatever way they chose. But where was Trish herself?

Grace had glimpsed her, almost an hour earlier, strolling with Terry, and now a familiar anxiety began to nag. Where had they gone? What were they doing? Once before she had given her stepdaughter a word of warning and advice and, so far as she knew, it had been heeded on that occasion – but did Trish still remember it? With a considerable effort Grace reminded herself that Trish had come of age. The time for interference was past. But she was glad when David's eldest son came up to interrupt her worrying.

'Can I bring you anything more to eat, Aunt Grace?'

'No thank you, John.' The young man resembled his father too closely for Grace to find him likeable. He had the same strong Hardie features, the same dark hair and brown eyes, the same serious expression. Yet he had been a good-mannered little boy who had grown up to become a hard-working businessman, applying himself conscientiously to the family firm which he would inherit one day. She could tell now from his earnest look that he had something else to say to her.

'We all – Lily and Peter as well as myself – want to thank you for being so good to Max. It was rotten for him at home after Mother died. Well, even before that. Father was never fond of him.'

'I suppose he was a bit of a mother's boy right from the start.'

'It wasn't just that. They let him know that he was an accident, that they hadn't intended to have another baby. I think that's an awful thing to do. I get on all right with Father myself, but I'm on Max's side about this. And then, Mother was so determined that there weren't going to be any more accidents that, well, you know, she moved into a separate bedroom, and Father behaved as though that were all the baby's fault. So he was ratty with him all the time. I'd have offered to look after Max myself after Sarah and I got married, but it would have been difficult, working in the same office as Father. Although he didn't like having Max at home, he was furious when he left.'

'I can imagine. Anyway, he's no trouble here. I made it clear when he came that I wasn't going to be a second mother to him and it seems to me that even in a few months he's become much more independent. Boarding school is just what he needed.'

'He's lucky to grow up in a place like this. Father talks about his childhood here a lot. Harrow's rather different.'

'Yes.' Grace had guessed that at some point during the afternoon her eldest nephew would put in an oblique plea to be considered as the heir to Greystones and she did not intend to make any comment on his prospects. Fortunately they were interrupted by the subject of their earlier conversation. Max was looking for Trish.

'I've got a dance to show her. I made it up specially. Everything's ready, but I can't find her anywhere.'

'We'll send out scouts. Dan and Boxer, run round shouting her name as loudly as you can, will you?'

Within a few minutes she answered the summons and arrived hand in hand with Terry, looking reassuringly cool and un-crumpled. But there was something different about the two of them, all the same. Grace's eyes noted it even while her lips were explaining what Max had in mind.

'A birthday dance? Terrific. I bet not many people are offered anything like that.'

'It's not just for your birthday,' Max explained. 'It's for your room.'

'Oh, so I'm not good enough to have a dance, only my room!'

'I went round the house in the Easter holiday. Sitting in each room and trying to think what sort of music was right for it. And your room was one of the easiest, because of the way you've painted the wall.'

'You mean you're going to dance black and red spots?' asked Terry teasingly.

'You'll see. I've put the record on the radiogram.'

While the scattered guests were assembled with shouting and hallooing, Max changed into a sleeveless white vest and a pair of long baggy black trousers, tied tightly at the ankles. He set the record going, stood still while the first vigorous chords were played, and then, pointing his feet neatly, embarked on a display which began as a kind of hornpipe, quickened into a vigorous Cossack dance and ended with a series of leaps and cartwheels which owed more to gymnastics than to dance. Merely watching him made Grace feel breathless, but as the record came to an end Max himself was able to steady his balance and stand still once again in perfect physical control.

Grace thought the performance a piece of showing-off; but it suited the party mood and was greeted with cheers and applause. It also served as a finale to the party. Two by two Trish's friends began to drift away, until only the birthday girl herself and the three Travises remained, preparing to travel back to London together in Terry's battered van.

'Time for me to give you my present,' said Grace.

'The party was present enough.'

'Nonsense. Come this way.'

She led them all to the coach-house and watched Trish's face as she opened the double doors.

'A car! For me? Grace, you shouldn't!'

'I hope I've chosen right,' Grace said. 'It was difficult. I did wonder whether you might like a sporty two-seater, but then I thought you'd want to drive Terry and the boys around sometimes, so a saloon seemed more sensible in the end. Andy told me which models were supposed to be more reliable. My only contribution was to decide that it ought to be red.'

'It's marvellous! The whole day, and then this.'

Grace found herself being hugged and kissed. She had never encouraged Trish to display affection for her, even as a little girl, but today she was glad to be assured that they were still friends. 'You have got a licence, haven't you?' she checked.

'Oh yes. I share the driving of the van.' Unexpectedly Trish blushed. 'I'm going to share a bit more than that in future. The whole business. Terry's going to let me be a partner in the firm. A working partner.'

'Is he indeed? And what's the firm going to be called? The Shed?'

'We haven't had time to think –' began Terry, but Trish was ahead of him.

'We ought to call it TT for Terry Travis. And for Trish-Trash, which will be my contribution. And Tempera Transformations as well.'

'What does that mean?' asked Dan, wrenching his attention away from the car.

'Painting walls as a fun thing. Tempera is a way of painting on plaster, and Tempora gives an impression of something temporary, so whichever way you spell it, it's appropriate.'

'What a lot of Ts,' Dan said, and Trish swooped on the comment.

'That's it. Why don't we call the business Tease?'

'Because it would make any customer think that we weren't going to deliver, that's why not,' answered Terry, laughing. He turned towards Grace and looked her steadily in the eye.

'There's one more thing that TT stands for, though. The thing that matters. Terry and Trish.'

Grace did not need Trish's second flush to understand what he meant. She was tempted to ask whether they had marriage in mind, but bit the question back. Terry, who had done his best to act as mother and father to his two young half-brothers, could be trusted to act responsibly by his own standards if not by society's. Besides – the thought of Andy came into her head – who was she to act as a guardian of morals? Instead, she turned towards the new car and stroked her hand along the roof.

'Take it gently for a little while, won't you?' she said. 'These things need to be run in.'

As the car and the van made their cautious departure down the steep, winding drive, Andy was already hard at work returning chairs and tables to their proper places in the house. Grace went to help, but was waved away.

'You've done enough for one day. Sit down and put your feet up. Lady of leisure, like.'

She found herself glad to obey. A social day had proved to be far more tiring than the same number of hours spent hammering a chisel into stone. After a visit to the kitchen to thank Mrs Barrett and her helpers, she flopped, exhausted, on to a sofa.

Andy joined her there later, and they dined off left-overs before making their way early to bed.

'Why don't you stay?' she asked later, when he began to dress again. As long as he was there, lying beside her, she could keep her mind off Trish.

He shook his head. For some reason it was a point of honour with him always to return to his own home. 'Love you, though,' he said, bending over to kiss her again.

Grace raised her hand to stroke his skin, so brown and freckled where the sun had caught it, and the rest so soft and pale. 'Love you, too,' she said. Neither of them was accustomed to be passionate in words.

342

After he had left she began to stroke her own body, prolonging the night by feeling her skin as Andy had felt it. It had become a soothing habit, but on this occasion, as her hands curved over her breasts, she felt her throat tightening with anxiety. Were Terry and Trish now, at this very moment . . . was he hurting her? Was she happy?

Stupid, to put such unanswerable questions to herself, but no doubt all mothers shared to some extent in the tension of a wedding – or not-quite-wedding – night. Her hands tightened. Her fingers pressed down into her breasts, exploring the muscles as though she were studying anatomy, prodding until it hurt. That was when she discovered the lump.

The room had been quiet before, but suddenly it was as though the sound of a roaring, shouting crowd had filled the air with noise before being abruptly cut off. A different kind of silence. Dead silence. With her eyes now wide open in the darkness she pressed her probing fingers hard down again.

It was the tiniest of lumps, insignificant, unimportant. Probably it was nothing but the beginning of a boil, a minute spur of bone, a small and hitherto unnoticed muscle – or so she tried to persuade herself. But Grace's fingers were the tools of her trade, able to identify a knot in a piece of wood or a flaw in a stone even when neither was visible on the surface. They knew what they had found.

1951

ONE

The year began badly. Even before she opened the thick brown envelope Grace felt sure that it contained unwelcome news.

It was not every day that the postman needed to extend his delivery round to Greystones, and as a rule those letters that he did bring revealed their source at a glance. There had never been any mistaking Max's handwriting on his compulsory Sunday-afternoon letter from boarding school; but now that he had joined a touring ballet company they kept in touch by telephone. A twice-yearly correspondent had taken his place. Grace's brother Kenneth, after many years of silence, had learned from his son how much the family in England longed to have news of him and an air mail envelope bearing an Australian stamp now arrived regularly on her birthdays and at Christmas time. On other air mail envelopes, edged in red and blue, a Los Angeles postmark indicated that they carried news from the Californian expatriates, Ellis and Jay.

Trish preferred to chat on the telephone, but another correspondent was the agent who had taken over the handling of Grace's work from Ellis. He came to Greystones every two or three months to see her new pieces and discuss possible sales, but his cheques always arrived in envelopes with bright green borders: green for good luck. There was nothing like that today to keep company with this grimly official communication, which she opened with foreboding.

The council, she read, wished to inform her of its intentions with regard to the area marked in red on the enclosed section of the ordnance survey map. Mrs Faraday would doubtless be aware that it was intended eventually to encircle the city of Oxford with a ring road, some sections of which were already in use. Plans were now being drawn up for the building of the eastern section, and a valuation officer would be happy to attend at the property to discuss the land which would be required and to negotiate its purchase. Should it not prove possible to come to an arrangement by mutual agreement, the council would seek powers of compulsory purchase.

Grace was so disturbed that she could hardly focus on the details and had to read it all through again. The long thin rectangle of red on the map enclosed the stream which ran through the lowest point of the Greystones estate, part of the wood on one side of it and an area of open ground on the further side. Was it really possible that this could be snatched away without her consent? And if that did happen, her land beyond the road would be cut off from the rest, so that she would really be losing far more than the designated area.

There was a lot to think about, but it would have to wait, because she had a New Year's Resolution to keep. She had promised herself that before the first week of January ended she would see a doctor.

As a child she had suffered regular bouts of ill-health. She now knew them to have been caused by asthma, but at the time her breathless, chesty wheezing had been assumed to be bronchial. It was because the swampy air round the riverside house in Oxford where she was born seemed to have brought her so near to death that Greystones had been built for her on a hill. Even after the move she suffered occasional attacks, but when it was realized that these were triggered by exposure to specific irritants, like horses, she had learned what to avoid and grew into a strong, healthy adult. No doctor had been summoned to the house on her behalf since the birth of her baby almost twenty years earlier.

All the same, Dr Murray, who had taken over the practice in Headington Quarry just before the war, was no stranger. The children had all had their share of childish ailments and accidents. The doctor smiled in recognition now as she entered his consulting room.

'How are you, Mrs Faraday?'

Grace was not one to beat about the bush. 'I feel very well,' she said. 'But I have a lump in my breast.'

'We'd better have a look, then.' He motioned to her to go behind a screen and waited while she took off her blouse and vest. 'Which side?'

'The right.'

'Put your hand on my shoulder, will you?' He did not need to ask exactly where to feel. Three and a half years earlier Grace had needed to probe deeply with her fingers before becoming suspicious, but within the last few months it had become easy to trace the outline of the lump beneath the skin which dimpled above it. She looked straight ahead as, pinching it gently, he measured it with his fingers, first in one direction and then the other. Next, with a firmer touch, he pressed into her armpits.

'Any other swellings or discomfort anywhere?'

'No.'

'Get dressed again, will you, Mrs Faraday.'

By the time she emerged from behind the screen he was writing his notes, but looked up with a serious expression on his face.

'When did you first notice it?'

'Some while ago now, but it was tiny then. It's just in the last few months that it seems to have been growing at a great rate.'

'I wish you had come to me straightaway. Or even a few months ago.' He reached forward to the telephone.

'Just a moment,' said Grace. 'What are you going to do?'

'Make an immediate appointment for you at the Radcliffe Infirmary. No point in my giving you a fuller examination here when they'll just do it all over again when you get there.'

'What will they do?'

346

'Blood tests. X-ray. And a biopsy on the lump itself to find out whether it's malignant.'

'Do you have any doubt about that?'

Dr Murray looked at her steadily.

'It's the strongest possibility. You realize that yourself, don't you? If it were smaller, we could hope that it might be a cyst, easily and permanently removed. But from what you say about the rate of growth . . .'

'So what you're saying is that they'd cut out the lump, discover whether it's malignant – and then what?'

'The biopsy is normally done very quickly, while you're still under anaesthetic. If carcinoma is confirmed, it would be necessary to remove the breast. It's a very safe operation. Nothing to be frightened of.'

Grace had known what he would say, but still felt herself paling. She was determined, though, to press the discussion to a conclusion.

'And would that be the end of it?'

'We would hope so.'

'But suppose our hopes are not realized. What's the worst case, Dr Murray? I mean, people die of breast cancer. If the operation itself is a minor one, what else goes wrong?' She could tell that he was reluctant to answer. 'I'm not going to let anything happen until I understand why. I have to rely on you to tell me the truth. I realize that I've been foolish and that I shall have to pay for it. I must know what the price will be.'

He hesitated a moment longer before giving in to her determination.

'If you had come to me when you first noticed a tiny lump,' he said, 'then I could have given you a more optimistic opinion. But as it is . . . What happens, you see, is something called metastasis. The cancer doesn't confine itself to the lump that you can see and feel. The malignant cells start to spread through the lymph nodes and into the bloodstream. They cause other tumours to grow. And whereas it's easy enough to operate on the breast, there are other parts of the body where it's more difficult. That's why it's urgent that you should attend the Infirmary as soon as possible.'

'Do you think that this process you describe may already have begun?'

'Only a specialist with all the proper test equipment can answer that question.'

'Let me have your guess, then. The balance of probabilities.'

'It would be grossly irresponsible to hazard an opinion without having any evidence.' But for a second time he submitted to her wish for a truthful answer. 'All I can say is that the consultant will be bound to ask you whether you have lost weight recently. Or noticed any unusual tiredness or lack of strength.'

Grace considered the hint in silence. She had no idea how much she weighed now or had ever weighed, but certainly she had noticed a loss of strength in recent months. It was one of the reasons why she had at last plucked up the courage to come to the surgery.

The previous year, with a particular carving in mind, she had acquired a large piece of rosewood. She knew before she set to work that it was harder than the walnut or oak which she chose as a rule, but was appalled, when she embarked on the process of roughing out the shape, to find how often she had to stop and rest. In the early stages of any large carving it was necessary to spend hours at a time hitting a large gouger with a mallet until most of the outside was cut away and an approximation of the final shape was left. This had never caused her any problem before.

She had wondered at first whether the lump itself, and the swelling under her arm, was distorting her action and putting an unusual strain on her muscles. And if that was not the answer, it had seemed reasonable to accept that, as she grew older, she was bound to become less strong. But now it appeared all too probable that Dr Murray's suggestion came nearer to the truth. She stood up, pushing back her chair.

'I'd like to think about it,' she said. 'Please don't phone the Infirmary just yet. I'll be in touch with you again.'

Dr Murray also stood up. 'You come here to ask my opinion and you must understand what it is. You are in urgent need of treatment and it would be foolish of you to waste any time before taking it.'

'I've been foolish already.' Grace managed to smile. 'When I've delayed for so long, a day or two can't make much difference.'

'When the tide comes up against a barrier of sand, there is one second when it's restrained, another second when the first small wave trickles over or through, and only one more second before the tide sweeps on and covers it completely. The point of no return in your own case could fall between one day and the next.'

'I'll be in touch,' Grace repeated. 'Thank you very much, doctor.'

The walk from the village to Greystones was uphill all the way, but it was a journey which she had been making without effort for fifty years. Today, though, her legs felt heavy and her body lethargic. She walked slowly, wearily, back to the house and into her studio.

The piece of rosewood, clamped to her work table, seemed to look at her reproachfully. This was a piece of work which she had intended to enter for a competition. The subject was political prisoners, and Grace had envisaged the hollowed-out shape of a skull, with slits cut out of its casing to reveal something – its shape not yet decided – struggling to escape through what would resemble prison bars. All possibility of finishing it in time for the competition had already vanished, but that did not mean that she intended to abandon the project.

Marking in charcoal the next area to be cut away, she then poured a few drops of oil on to her oilstone and selected the right chisel. Automatically – for this was part of every day's routine – she began to sharpen the chisel, moving its cutting edge over the stone in a figure of eight pattern; pressing it down, turning it over, checking with her fingers rather than her eyes that no burr remained. When satisfied of its sharpness she transferred it to her left hand and leaned forward to pick up a leather-bound mallet in her right.

She never completed the action. Checking herself in mid-movement, she stared at the chisel. It was an old one, its handle darkened by years of use. Only the edge was silver-bright, razor-sharp: she could not take her eyes off it.

Setting it carefully down, she turned her head to look at the rows of tools which hung neatly in their wooden racks along the wall. In the rest of the house Grace was untidy, and at first sight the studio often seemed the greatest mess of all; but she had always been meticulous in caring for the instruments of her trade. Stone-cutting tools, wood-carving tools, and the oddly-curved pieces of wire and bone with which she worked on the clay originals of her bronzes – all were in good order.

It was the knives which she studied now. A surgeon would pick up a knife like this and slice through her flesh as easily as she sliced through clay. The clarity of her vision made her shiver, although not with any imagining of pain. After all, she would be unconscious. Why then had she postponed for so long the visit which for three years or more she had known must be urgent? Was it sheer cowardice or had she subconsciously wanted to be told that she had come too late?

Abruptly she turned and hurried out of the studio, up the stairs, into the bathroom. Locking the door, she pulled off her clothes and stood naked in front of a looking glass. She could see herself only from the waist up, but that was enough.

Rarely even as a young girl and never in the past thirty years had she concerned herself with the look of her body. Was it beautiful or ugly, glamorous or ordinary? She didn't care. She had always accepted what she was born with, and hard physical work had kept it in good shape.

Until now. Already the lump was visible, beginning to distort the shape of her breast, and soon, presumably, it would

350

be larger still. But to lose the breast altogether would be a distortion of a different order. A mutilation. An amputation. What would Andy think? She shrugged the question away as soon as it entered her mind. She did not care what Andy thought. Only her own feelings mattered.

As she tried to imagine herself with one side of her chest flat and scarred, she was surprised to realize how consistently she had valued symmetry in her work. The holes she carved were usually circular or oval and even when, as often happened, they twisted round between one side of the sculpture and the other, the effect was always one of balance. Symmetry satisfied her eye because it was natural; and the prime example of natural design was the human body.

Anyone with an ounce of common sense would laugh her out of the proposition that since her body was, in a way, a work of art it was better dead than mutilated; but it must have been an underlying feeling of that kind which had kept her away from the doctor for so long, and had sent her to him at last not because she was alarmed but because she was already sure that the time for surgery had passed.

It was a certainty which Dr Murray had said nothing to dispel, and no one could turn the clock back four years. Calmly, not frightened yet, Grace dressed herself again.

TWO

Dr Murray called at Greystones later on the day of Grace's visit to his surgery. Although she had half expected him to come, she made no apology for the fact that she was wearing her working clothes as she offered him a cup of tea.

'It's a problem now, with the health service,' he said. 'The pressure of so many people queueing in the waiting room. You probably felt it as much as I did. Our conversation was one which ought not to have been hurried. I didn't feel that we'd brought it to a satisfactory conclusion.'

'Sugar?' asked Grace.

'No thank you. I feel a responsibility, you see, for making certain that you see a consultant as soon as possible.'

'The responsibility is mine, surely.'

'Well, not entirely. I can't be expected to know that a problem exists until you tell me; but once I *do* know, it's a failure of duty on my part if I don't see that you have the best possible treatment.'

Because her earlier uncertainty had disappeared, she was able to smile. 'I hadn't realized that a patient could be accused of damaging her doctor's reputation as well as of self-neglect.'

'I don't think you understand –'

'Of course I understand. I've decided, though. I'm not prepared to undergo surgery which may come too late to do any good.'

'But you can't know whether that's the case until you've had the tests. And just think, Mrs Faraday – I've been to your open days here. I know your work. Not many people have the talent to create beauty. You're only, what, fifty-three? There should be many years ahead of you to make more of these wonderful carvings. You owe it –'

She smiled for a second time. 'You're not suggesting that I have a duty to art to stay alive?'

'Well, yes I am, if you put it like that.'

'I can't agree with you. I work because I like to work – because I *have* to work. It's as necessary to me as breathing, and I did it long before it even occurred to me that anyone else might want to see what I produced. That necessity will die with me. I don't care what anyone else thinks. I'm told that the value of my work will rise as soon as I'm dead, so in the interests of my heirs –'

'It's not a joking matter, Mrs Faraday. This can be a distressing illness. If there's any chance of preventing it, that chance must be taken. You mention your heirs. All those young people –'

'Are grown up now, leading their own lives. I have no dependants. I don't have to consider anyone but myself.' But the anxious expression on the doctor's face made her, ridiculously, feel sorrier for him than for herself. 'Well, all right then. I'll go down to the Infirmary and have the blood tests and X-rays that you suggested. If – to use your own metaphor – they show that the tide has already broken through, that will be that, won't it? If it hasn't, if there's still something to be gained by surgery, then I'll think about it again. But I don't want the biopsy, not at this stage. I've read stories of women who go into the operating theatre just for a test and come out without a breast.'

'That couldn't happen without your consent. May I use your telephone, then, to make an appointment at once? And I'll write a letter for you to take with you.' He was happy to accept a half victory.

They both thought they had won, she realized as the doctor left: he because he had pressed her into the approved channel, she because her body told her that it was already too late. But **what sort of a triumph was that?**

For once she felt no wish to return to the studio. The whole day had been wasted. She had been unable to force herself to continue with the woodcarving and instead had played aimlessly with clay, breaking off small lumps and pressing them into a shape in the hope that some kind of inspiration would arrive to tell her what she was trying to make. It was not the way she usually worked, and the result brought no satisfaction.

The ringing of the telephone came as a welcome distraction. Max was calling from Manchester, where his company was performing.

'Aunt Grace, you know we're coming to Oxford in three weeks' time.'

'Certainly I do. I've bought my ticket already.'

'Well, I wanted to ask you about digs.'

'You'll stay here with me, surely. I'm expecting you.'

'Thanks a lot, yes, that'll be lovely. The thing is, though, digs are awful places, you know. People write sentimental twaddle about landladies with hearts of gold welcoming the same actors back each year, but really they have scruffy houses and stupid rules and expect you to eat at times which are impossible for a dancer. I wondered if I could bring some of my friends to Greystones as well. We'd look after ourselves, buying food and cooking it and everything. It would be marvellous just to have the freedom and the space and no one to nag.'

'How many of your friends?' asked Grace cautiously.

'Well, of course, everyone would want to come. It would be difficult to choose. What's the most you could bear?'

Grace had a ludicrous vision of the complete cast of *Swan Lake*, in costume, queueing for the bathroom every morning. 'Six,' she said firmly.

'Couldn't we manage just a few more? We really would do everything – make the beds and all that. And the house needs a bit of life going all through it. All those rooms on the top floor where the servants used to sleep! Nobody ever goes in them nowadays.'

'For good reason,' she told him. 'The beds up there are damp and probably rotten and we haven't enough bed linen anyway. Six, including yourself, is my final offer.' It was necessary to be stern with Max sometimes. He was not a scrounger: just too generous. 'But you can invite the rest up for a party one day if you want to,' she offered as a consolation.

'Thanks a lot, Aunt Grace. You're a brick.' From his tone she suspected that he had got just about what he anticipated. The pips hurried him into ringing off.

Max off-stage was such an ordinary boy – or rather, by now, young man. The transformation in him when he danced was unbelievable. Grace had attended the final performance given by his class at the ballet school – the performance which had brought him the offer of a place in the touring company. She did not know enough about ballet to judge his technique, but she could recognize artistic concentration when she saw it, because it was something she had developed in herself. It had taken her many years, but Max seemed to have been born with it. From the moment of his first entrance as Romeo he had dominated the stage, and not merely because of the importance of the role. Even when he stepped back into the crowd and stood motionless to watch Juliet pass, Grace had found it impossible to take her eyes off him. Whereas his uncle Jay had always known himself to be an actor but never imagined that he could become a star, Max was a star from the start and knew it.

When she first became aware of his talent, Trish had decided that David could not possibly be his true father and, since Sheila was too Christian and conventional to have a liaison outside marriage, declared that he must be a changeling. But Trish had never known Max's grandfather, Grace's father, who was as tall and strong as Max had grown to be. Gordon Hardie had startled his parents by running away to sea while still a schoolboy, and even after returning had disappeared again to hunt for rare plants on the other side of the world. David had claimed The House of Hardie as his inheritance, but it was

355

Grace and Jay and Max who had inherited the single-minded resolve to pursue their vocations in spite of all family or social disapproval.

Max's cheery voice on the telephone put the doctor's visit out of her mind, but there was that second piece of bad news to think about. Picking up the map sent by the council, she let herself out of the house and stood looking down the hill.

The light of the short winter day was already beginning to fade, and in the dimness the estate looked well-kept. Or perhaps it was the season rather than the light which allowed an impression of neatness. When the grass and the weeds stopped growing each year, it was possible to tidy the land and pretend that it would remain tidy. Not until May would the vegetation surge exuberantly out of control once again.

Andy, at the end of his day's work, saw her standing there and came to join her. Without speaking, she handed him the letter and the map and waited while he strained to study them in the dusk.

'Can they do this sort of thing?' she asked. 'Take the land, I mean, even if I refuse to sell.'

'Wouldn't be surprised. This lot reckon they can do anything they like with other people's property.'

'This is from the council, not the government.'

'It's the government that gives the powers to the councils. I saw you walk past this morning looking upset. Wondered whether you were ill. But it was this, was it?'

Grace nodded. She had not yet decided whether to tell Andy about the lump. 'I was certainly upset at first when I read the letter. I felt that I'm the guardian of the estate and ought to fight for it. But now I'm wondering: would it really matter? This wouldn't affect your bit of the land. And Greystones isn't like Castlemere, depending on the estate for its revenue. The wood down there keeps my fires going, but that's all. If the timber which they'd have to fell were stacked up it would probably do me the rest of my life. The bottom meadows are hardly visible from the house and they've had other people's sheep on them for thirty years. And you could argue that since I can't keep all the land I own under control, it might actually be a good thing to have less of it.'

'Trying to look on the bright side, are you?'

'Mm. All that those acres of land really represent is space: a barrier between me and the rest of the world.'

'That's not something to be sneezed at, if you're going to lose peace as well as land. There's going to be noise from cars and lorries. Before long, people will want to build houses along the side of the road, or factories even.'

Andy paused, struck by a new idea, and studied the map closely for a second time. 'Seems to me you ought to see a lawyer, Grace. Get some professional advice. The road will probably come whether you like it or not, but you might be able to do yourself a bit of good by bargaining. This parcel of land at the bottom is more than twenty acres. It wouldn't be any use to you once it was cut off from the rest. So it wouldn't do any harm to have houses built on it. Better for *you* to get them built. Bring you in a nice bit of money, that would.'

'We don't need money.' She could easily live just on the income which came from the land: Andy's rent for the vineyard, the grazing fee for the sheep and the sale of fruit and vegetables. But in addition to this her sculpture fetched what she considered to be absurd prices, and she had invested her small inheritance from her mother. Since she was no longer responsible for Trish's expenses, and spent very little on herself, her savings accumulated. The fact that she had become wealthy did not tempt her to alter her frugal way of life, but it was something to bear in mind during a discussion of this kind. She thought about it for a few minutes.

'I suppose you're right. It would be best to keep any development in my own hands.'

'That's where the bargaining comes in. You have to get all sorts of permissions before you can build. But if you were to save the council time and trouble by agreeing to sell the strip for the road voluntarily, like they're hoping, they might agree to let you do what you want with the land on the other side. I really don't know whether or how you could get away with that sort of deal, but a good lawyer ought to be able to fix it for you.'

Grace sighed at the thought of letting the wood go without a struggle. 'You're right, I suppose. One can't afford to be sentimental about a place just because we played there as children. And there would be plenty of land left. When you think how most people have to live . . .' She turned her back on the wood and looked at Greystones. 'It's only a house, after all.'

'But *your* house. Your home.'

Grace was not ready to share the secret that it might not be hers for much longer. But the thought, bringing together the two main events of the day, reminded her of something else. She had made a will many years earlier because David insisted. When circumstances changed, she altered it without seriously considering that its provisions would ever come into effect. She must have believed then that she would live for ever, but she knew better now. Decisions must be made which would change other people's lives.

'Yes,' she told Andy as though still talking about the road. 'Yes, I must see a lawyer.'

THREE

'Good morning, Michelangelo!'

Startled by the sound of Rupert's voice and the unheralded appearance of someone she had not seen in the four years since her coming-of-age party, Trish turned her head away from the wall she was painting.

'Rupert! Bring a chair over here so that I can see you while I go on working. I can't stop, because the plaster will dry out, but I've almost finished.' She continued to paint as she spoke. Her subject was a garden seen through a pair of wide French windows, also painted. Not an imaginary scene, but a view of Philip's serpentine garden at Greystones, winding into the distance.

'Don't I recognize that?' Rupert had found a chair, but before sitting down he stepped right and left to study her work from different angles. 'Not quite your usual style, is it?'

'Oh, it's not for myself. Not for long, anyway.'

'Oh? When I phoned The Shed, Terry told me that you were at home, here. Are you going to sell the wall or the whole house?'

'The house. All my homes are temporary.' She stepped back to consider whether a slim juniper tree was satisfactorily finished before picking up a new set of brushes. With a few broad strokes she blocked in the shape of one of Grace's sculptures and then began to apply the shadows and highlights which would make it appear three-dimensional.

'We have this system, you see,' she explained. 'We buy some crummy old house and move in and do it up and then sell it and buy another one. You'd be surprised how many people simply can't see the potential in a house if it's less than perfect. But set it in front of them all ready to be lived in and they'll pay a small fortune for it. Especially if it's got one of my walls inside. They've become a cult thing. I take commissions to do them on their own, extra to the house sales, so people who buy the houses seem to feel that they're getting one free.'

'What a restless life you must lead!'

'I like it. Boring, living in the same place all the time.'

'Don't you ever think about going back to live in Greystones?'

Biting her tongue with concentration as she created a hole in the sculpture with dark lines, Trish couldn't speak immediately. But she shook her head. Oddly enough, Grace had put the same question to her only a few months before. It was not the first time that she had been asked indirectly whether she would like to be the eventual owner of the house, or so it seemed. On an earlier occasion she had left her answer vague, believing that it might give Grace pleasure to imagine her living there one day. The more recent enquiry, although casually framed, had demanded a more definite response.

'I'm not really a country girl,' she said to Rupert as she had to Grace. 'That feeling of Mother Nature waiting to smother you if you take your mind off her for a second! And I wouldn't ever want to be *possessed* by a house, like Grace at Greystones and you at Castlemere. I mean, what you merely buy, you can sell.' A house inherited would carry the burden of being a house which must be cherished and eventually bequeathed. Poor Rupert was caught in exactly that honey trap. 'How's Castlemere?' she asked.

'Sinking oh so beautifully under the weight of debts and tax and deathwatch beetle and dangerous wiring and inadequate heating.'

'Isn't there any sort of grant you can winkle out of the government?'

'Oh yes. A very generous one, I don't think. If we spend money on repairs we can put in a Capital Expenditure Tax

360

claim against our Schedule A assessment. The catch is that we have to find the money before we can spend it, and we don't get it back in cash, only in tax relief on our income over the next ten years. This government simply doesn't care what happens to a house like ours. They don't see it as part of the national heritage. To them it's a symbol of privilege. They close their eyes to the fact that for hundreds of years it's been the centre of a community, giving employment, encouraging craftsmanship. If we go down, a lot of smaller people will go down with us.'

'This government can't last long,' said Trish. The general election earlier in the year had returned Labour with only a slender majority.

'Our lot may not be much better. We can't lay ourselves open to the charge of looking after the most privileged of our own kind first. So I've finally decided to surrender to what I've been fighting for years. We're going commercial.'

'You mean, opening Castlemere to the public?'

'That's one option, but not one that's as simple as it sounds. It would need a huge investment to put the house in order and make the contents secure before we could take a penny in admission charges. I've only just, this week, decided to do *something*. I haven't yet decided what. Any other ideas?'

Trish came to the end of her prepared section of wall, sat back on her heels and wiped her hands on her apron.

'There's nothing I like better than making suggestions for other people to do something about.' She was silent for a few moments, thinking. 'You might not need to open the house regularly or to the public generally. You could hire it out for special occasions. And capitalize on the fact that Castlemere looks so French. Get dress designers to have fashion shows there. Find out if anyone's making a film set in France, and suggest that you could provide a more convenient location. Encourage people to run courses there in speaking French or appreciating art or antique furniture. Let it out for wedding receptions or grand balls or chamber concerts. You could have performances of plays or operas which were written for the French court. Choose the plays which are being set for exams, and schools would bring their sixth forms along. I had to do Molière's *L'Avare* for Higher, and never had a chance to see what it looked like acted.'

'My, my!' Rupert patted her hand appreciatively. 'Julia's reaction, whenever I raise the subject, is along the lines of "over my dead body". But you come up with more suggestions in the first two minutes than – you wouldn't like a new job, I suppose? Castlemere promotions manager?'

'Sorry. Not my line at all. Organizational ability nil. Chucking ideas around is one thing. Doing the donkey work is quite another.'

'Don't run yourself down. You're a marvellous girl.' He paused as though struggling to hold back words which in the end proved too strong to restrain. 'I should never have let you go.' The intensity in his voice, which until then had remained light and teasing, startled Trish, and so did the tightening of his grip on her hand. She was tempted to comment that he had never exactly had her, but was allowed no time to interrupt. 'I should have realized that I needed someone like you to stop me getting stuck in a rut. Is it too late, Trish? For you and me?'

It would have been easy to reply at once, but more than just the wish not to be unkind made her pause. Once upon a time those words would have made her heart turn over. Now they only made her sad – sad for Rupert.

'Yes, it's too late,' she said at last. 'You've got Julia and I've got Terry.'

'I'm not sure that I have got Julia. Not for much longer, anyway. And you – you're not married to Terry.'

'Good as.'

'It can't be the same, otherwise you *would* marry him.'

'What's the point of someone like me getting married? If I had any sort of tribal instinct, yes, then I would, because babies deserve to have two parents. But I haven't, and that's that.'

'Don't you ever want to have children?'

'Everything I've ever created I've sold, given away or thrown away. I couldn't do that with a baby. And I don't want to get involved in the inheritance game. Acquiring, passing on.' She looked Rupert steadily in the eyes. 'I suppose you could say that I'm living as a loose woman, but really I'm very strait-laced about marriage – other people's marriages. Your babies certainly deserve to have two parents, Rupert.' In the five years since their marriage Julia had given birth to three baby girls. No male heir – was that the reason his marriage was breaking up?

In the silence which followed, Rupert was the first to drop his eyes. His face showed his disappointment. Trish searched for something to say that would be light and casual, a definite but friendly change of subject.

'Tell you something I *could* do if you go commercial. Stock you up with souvenirs. So that everyone who visited Castlemere could buy something to take home. Did you see my Domes at the Festival of Britain?'

It took Rupert a moment to withdraw his hand. Then he shook his head. 'I went to the exhibition of course, but I don't remember –'

'Well, they were for children mostly. Big sheets of cardboard, printed in colour. You cut the shape out and glued it in place and found yourself with a miniature Dome of Discovery. There were little windows to look through, with something different to be seen through each one. And as well as that I made a Festival stencil and printed it on the backs of children's blouses and shirts. People like to have some kind of memento of a visit, and if it's useful, all the better. So whatever you decide to do at Castlemere, you ought to have a shop.'

'Terry's still running The Shed, I gather?' Rupert stood up and moved away, pretending to study the painted wall from a distance.

'Yes. He's worked out a theory of shopping. Based on how fed-up people are with having to queue for everything they want and then being bossed around by rude shop assistants. I

363

don't suppose you ever go shopping for food yourself, but it's awful. If I go to our local grocer and want to buy butter, bacon, and cornflakes, I have to queue at three different counters. So as soon as food rationing ends, he's going to develop the system that he already uses for clothes and household things. Fill the shelves and let the customers help themselves instead of asking for each item individually and waiting while it's fetched.'

'People like service,' said Rupert doubtfully.

'Maybe they do in villages, where they know the shopkeeper and are glad of a chat. But in the towns, they just want to make their own choices and buy things as quickly as possible. Well, we shall find out one day whether you're right, or Terry. No point in starting until there's enough to sell. But we have a lot of fun working out the best way to organize it. I draw designs and Terry scouts around looking for sites with lots of houses around and no decent shops.'

'Yes, I can see you're having fun. I only wish I were. Well, Trish, I didn't really come here intending to say any of this. I wanted to ask you whether you'd seen Grace lately?'

'Not for . . .' Trish had to stop and think. As a rule she reckoned to visit Greystones every five or six weeks, but the Festival had been such a commitment that the present gap must have stretched for longer than that. But they had kept in touch by telephone. 'We've talked, but I can't have seen her since Easter, I suppose. Six months; heavens! Why do you ask?'

'She invited us all over to tea on Sunday. Pretending she wanted to see the girls. But I know she hasn't any real interest in small children. It was all a bit mysterious. I had the feeling that it was money she wanted to talk about.'

'She's not short, is she?'

'No, it seems to be the other way round. She wanted to find out how things stood with me, and whether she could help. But the thing is, Trish, she's ill.'

'How? Did she say?'

'Not a word. She didn't have to. You've only got to look at

her face. I know she's always been pale, but now she's gone grey. Not just her hair: her skin as well. And she was terribly tired. She admitted it, which isn't like her. It was the oppressive weather, she said. I think she's stopped working.'

'She can't have!' Grace not working was Grace not living. Trish froze as the implication struck home. 'I'll go down tomorrow,' she said.

FOUR

At first sight there seemed to be nothing out of the ordinary. The door of Greystones was never locked during the day. Letting herself in, Trish went first, as usual, to the studio and – as usual – found Grace working there. Rupert had been wrong about that, then. She was sitting down; that was the only difference.

'It's me,' Trish announced. 'With apologies for long absence. I've come to see how you're getting on with the skull. But –' she moved nearer – 'you don't seem to be getting on with it at all. It's positively dusty. Tut!'

'Abandoned.' Grace did not turn round at once. 'Just a moment, Trish dear, while I get this right. The skull, I fear, will never be finished. I seem to have developed a phobia about knives. Can't bear to cut into wood or stone in case it screams at me. Nothing could be more inconvenient for a sculptor. Luckily, there's clay. There, that's done.' She turned slowly on her swivel chair and smiled. 'Glad to see you, Trish.'

Round her dark eyes were black circles of tiredness. All the flesh seemed to have vanished from her face, leaving the colourless skin crumpled. Her cheeks had fallen in, making the cheekbones appear gaunt and over-prominent. Her body, too, had shrunk inside the familiar overalls. Before leaving London Trish had promised herself that she would show no reaction; would pretend that all was well, however justified Rupert's warning proved to be. But now that the moment had come, she could not hold back a gasp. 'Oh Grace, why didn't you tell me?'

'Nothing to tell.' That was what the old Grace would have

said. But this Grace merely shrugged her shoulders. 'Nothing to be done about it,' was what she said instead. 'And I almost hoped that you wouldn't ever see me like this. It's an odd sort of pride – feeling afraid that the sight of a miserable old hag will drive out the memories of all the happy years we had together.'

'You let Rupert see. You deliberately invited him.'

'There's a difference. I like Rupert, but I love you.'

The old Grace would not have said that either. Hardly ever in the past had she expressed her feelings in words. Trish rushed forward to embrace her.

'You're too thin. You're not eating properly. Mrs Barrett ought –'

'It's not her fault. I've no appetite. And what's the point, anyway?'

'What is it, Grace?' She asked the question although she was already sure of the answer.

'Cancer.'

'Where?'

'I should think everywhere by now. In the blood, being pumped around. Rather like something dirty or sugary in the fuel tank of a car, moving through the tubes for a time until it reaches the engine and stalls it. You're not to be upset, Trish. I'm on terms with it.'

'I'm coming back to live here. You can't stay here alone.'

'Two answers to that. The first one is that I like being alone. Always have; you know that. Living or dying, no difference. The second is that in fact I'm not alone because I have Mercy.'

'What do you mean, you have mercy?'

'My nurse. A marvellous name for a young woman, isn't it? Dr Murray found her for me, when I refused to go into hospital. Her main job is to push pills or stick needles into me at all hours of the day or night. To keep the pain away. Sometimes I make her stop, when I want to be sure of being clear-headed, but it's nice to know that she can always start again. She keeps me comfortable and bullies me into eating. And in her spare time –' Grace's mouth widened slowly into a skeletal grin – 'in her spare time she models for me.'

'I didn't think you ever used models.'

'Never have before. Started for her sake, really. She simply didn't know how beautiful she was. Shouldn't think she'd ever looked at her own body. Religious family, very strict.'

'I'm surprised she agreed to model, then.'

'Under instructions from the doctor to do anything to make me happy. But there are limits. I let her keep her knickers on. Look behind the screen.'

Trish moved the screen and pulled off the damp sheet which covered a clay model. Half life-size, the nude figure stood on tiptoe, her body strained backwards in a curve, with her hands, above her head, pointing down towards her heels. The design resembled one of Grace's abstract shapes, but there was nothing abstract about the tight round buttocks which were balanced by the firm round breasts.

'That's marvellous!' she exclaimed sincerely. The tension of the piece was breathtaking. 'But it must have been a painful pose. So stretched.'

'I've exaggerated it, of course. Odd how the beauty of the human body never occurred to me before. Female body, not male. This is supposed to be unfinished. Very important, the doctor says, for someone who's dying to have something which must be completed before she goes. Apparently it's the best way to keep alive. So I go on fiddling with this. Paring it down and smoothing it again. My Mercy gets thinner every week. But really she's finished. Ready for the foundry.'

'I don't know how you can talk like this.' Trish was in tears.

'I'm glad, after all, that you've come to give me the chance. I wrote you a letter, not posted yet. To say how lucky I've been to have you, and all that. And to tell you what's going to happen to everything afterwards. Wouldn't want you to be disappointed in your inheritance. Let's go for a walk.'

'Are you strong enough?'

'Mercy bullies me into a stroll every day. Wait for me outside the front door, will you, while she wraps me up. I feel the cold more these days.'

Trish dried her eyes and did as she was told. As she let herself out of the studio, she heard the tinkle of a hand bell. When Grace came out to join her she was carrying a walking stick in one hand but not appearing to rely on it. Instead, she took Trish's arm and they began to walk slowly down the drive, following its zig-zag bends instead of taking the customary short cuts.

'Would you like to stop and rest?' Trish asked after they had covered a third of the descent.

'In a moment. Andy has put a seat for me just a little lower. At a viewpoint I specially like. I remember – it's the first clear memory of my life, when I must have been about three years old. My father put a blindfold round my eyes and carried me up the hill, piggyback. Then he stopped and took it off – and there was Greystones, brand new. "A palace for a princess," he said, and I was to be the princess.'

This speech, taken slowly, a sentence at a time, brought them to the seat which Grace had mentioned. Trish helped her to sit down, and herself turned to face the house.

'That's right,' said Grace. 'Take a good look. I don't suppose you'll be invited back very often once David moves in.'

Grace expected a violent reaction to her mischievous remark; and she was not disappointed.

'David? Grace, you're not going to give the house to *David*!'

'Aren't I? Sit down, Trish. I asked you before whether you wanted it yourself. Perhaps you didn't take the question seriously – or thought it would be tactless even to envisage a time when I might not be here myself. So I asked Terry as well.'

'He didn't tell me.'

'He didn't need to. Mainly what he said was that it was none of his business what I chose to do, and that whatever you'd already told me was likely to be what you honestly felt. But what came out of the conversation strongly was that he sees it as his responsibility to provide you with the sort of home that you deserve. I think he'd feel he'd failed, in a way, if he merely moved into the house where you grew up. It would be different, he said, if you had a great sentimental tie to the place, as Rupert has to Castlemere; but you haven't, have you?'

'All the same!' Trish's astonishment was still on the boil. 'If I'd known that the choice was between me having it and David having it, I might not have been so honest. Grace, you don't even *like* him.'

'That's not the point.' Grace shivered a little and pulled her coat more closely round her. 'I shan't be here when he takes over, so my likes and dislikes hardly matter. The only important thing is that you don't want the house and he most certainly does. I'm a great believer in the need for ruling passions to be indulged. And I'm not in fact making him a gift of the house.'

'But you said –'

'I couldn't resist teasing you. Let's talk it out. No need for any polite hypocrisies any more. I've had to give proper thought to making a will, and I don't see any point in using legacies to pay off old scores. If I try to imagine the future at all, I want to see it as a time in which everyone's happy. And a house is always a special case when it comes to inheritances. I could have forced it on you, I suppose, as a token of affection, but then I'd have had to live with the thought of you selling it to strangers. That was the reason why I'm not leaving it to Rupert either.'

'Rupert!' For a second time Trish's voice expressed astonishment, but on this occasion the element of disapproval was absent. No doubt she merely thought it extraordinary that there could have been any idea of bequeathing Greystones to someone who had such a grand home of his own already.

'He's terribly short of money, poor fellow. And all because of Castlemere. If he sold it, he could become a rich man overnight. Buy a house in Mayfair, make a political career for himself in the House of Lords, live in style. Castlemere is his millstone. Another case of a ruling passion.'

'Which for that reason you think should be indulged?'

Grace did not answer the question directly.

'When I think how happy my mother was at Castlemere as a child,' she said, '– and when I remember how she was expelled from the family for marrying a Hardie – it amuses me to think that a Hardie might help to keep the Beverleys afloat. He and I talked about it a few days ago.'

'He told me. The conversation seems to have jerked him into action. As though he'd be ashamed to take your money without doing something positive at last to make Castlemere pay its own way.'

'He's going to have the residue of my estate; the cash. And all the sculptures still in my possession, except for the ones in the serpentine garden; they ought to stay. I suggested he might start an open-air sculpture park around the moat at Castlemere,

371

so that the house would act as a background without necessarily having to be open to the public. If he wanted to go commercial, he could sell other people's work from there. But certainly he could sell out the editions of my bronzes. That should bring him in quite a bit. Greystones would be no use to him, though, except to raise more cash by putting it on the market. So as far as the house was concerned, I had to sit down and think who might wish actually to live in it.'

'You don't have to tell me now.'

'I'd like to. I don't want there to be any unpleasant surprises. David will be surprised – pleasantly – but that's all. And as I just said, I'm not giving the house directly to him. He's to have a life interest, so he can move in and give himself the airs of an owner. But after he dies or whenever he renounces it, it will go to Max.'

'Max.' This time Trish's comment was neither amazed nor disapproving.

'Max loves the house. In a very peculiar manner, I must say. He wanders all round it when he's here, in the same way that I used to as a child. Letting the atmosphere soak in. He adored showing it off to all his friends in the ballet company. He seems to see it in terms of music. I confidently expect that in twenty or thirty years' time there will be a Greystones ballet choreographed by Max Hardie. But there's no point in saddling him with it straightaway. He couldn't afford to maintain it and while he still has his stage career he wouldn't be free to live in it anyway. But he'll be glad to know that he has a home waiting for later in his life – and one in which he can live in some style, if he chooses.'

She stood up, staggering slightly. It was always at such moments that she felt weakest, and she was grateful for Trish's grip on her arm as well as the nods of assent which indicated approval of her decision.

'I wouldn't want you to think that it was the house or nothing for you, and that you're not getting anything,' Grace continued, steadying her balance before setting off again.

372

'I don't –'

'I know you don't. But I do. Let's go on down.' They began to walk very slowly. 'Andy will get the lodge and the freehold of the land that he's leasing at present. As for your father, he won't be mentioned in my will, Trish, but he knows why. He got himself into a scrape years ago, and I had to make a rather peculiar bargain to get him out of it. So he's not going to make a fuss or be hurt by being ignored. Now then, stop here a moment.'

They had reached the near edge of the wood. Grace looked round for something on which she could sit and found the stump of a tree.

'I don't feel quite up to stepping over brambles,' she said, 'but if you carry on down the side of the wood a little way you should come across a red pole, and then a T-shaped marker further on.'

Trish explored as instructed, returning to report success.

'I told you about the plan for the road, didn't I?' asked Grace. 'I made the council surveyor mark out the area they're asking for. The red pole is one of my own markers. Andy put in a dozen of them for me, along the boundaries of the land I'm giving to you. Not as a legacy. The deed of gift has been signed already. There'll be getting on for thirty acres to do what you like with after you've lost whatever they take for the road. It would be too complicated for Max to be faced with all the negotiations with the council. Much better for you to take possession straightaway and fight your own corner.'

'You think I'm just the person to cope with that kind of complication, do you?' Trish's voice was teasing, but Grace could tell that beneath it she was close to tears again. She kept her own voice businesslike.

'I'm confident that Terry can. When are you going to marry him, Trish?'

'Well –'

'I know you're a great one for throwing things away, but you oughtn't to leave a man who loves you wondering whether

373

you'll discard *him* one day. It's not very kind to leave him in purgatory. Not that I'm a good one to preach about marriage, but what I'd really like is for this to be a wedding present. A kind of dowry. Let me spell out just what it is that I'm making over.'

She felt in her pocket for a piece of paper on which she had already sketched a plan.

'We're here,' she said, pointing, as Trish came to stand behind her and look over her shoulder. 'This nearest strip of woodland would stay with the house, to screen off the traffic and act as a sound baffle. The next strip would be yours, running alongside what's going to be the ring road. You might be able to build on it one of these days, but there's no permission for that at the moment. Then there's the strip which the council needs.'

'It seems very wide, just for a road.'

'They're talking about having two lanes for each direction, divided by a wide area of grass and with more grass on either side of the road. My lawyer has been negotiating a sale. He's got all the papers; everything's pretty well settled, except that the council doesn't want to pay until it's got all the land along the route tied up and is ready to start work. In return for our co-operation, we've got a declaration that the meadows on the far side of the road can be developed – because of course they'll be completely cut off from the house. That's where you're going to make your fortune.'

She tried to raise a hand to feel in her pocket again and found that she lacked the necessary strength. 'Fish out the city map for me, will you?'

Trish opened it and found the section which showed Shotover, Headington and Cowley.

'Now then, just look at this. There's this huge area of the car factories: Morris Motors and Pressed Steel. They keep expanding and they want more workers. There's this other area which has been filled in by houses for the factory hands. But there's no more room there, and not enough homes. Put a new housing estate on the meadows and you'd be doing other people a service, as well as yourself.'

'But I don't know anything about housing.'

'Terry does – or could soon learn. Anyway, you could always sell it straight on to a speculative builder. Land with building permission is a gold mine. But if you do that, I suggest you keep a site in the centre and build one of these big new shops that Terry's always talking about.'

'A self-service one, you mean?'

'That's right.' Grace circled the area with a finger. 'All the people who live here already are miles from any decent shops and there'd be a captive market in the new community. Another public service.'

'You've really been thinking about this, haven't you, Grace?'

'I have to do something to pass the time, and it's a challenge. Even when you know that you haven't got long, thinking about what will happen when you're not here is a bit of an effort. Satisfying when it works, though.'

With a different sort of effort Grace stood up, exhausted.

'You stay here,' Trish ordered. 'I'll bring the car down the drive to take you back. You mustn't try to walk up the hill.'

'In a moment. There's something I want to look at first, while I'm here. In case it's the last time I manage to get down.' She took Trish's arm for support again and leaned on the walking stick too as she indicated that she wished after all to plunge into the wood. 'Stupid to be so wobbly, isn't it? Something to do with these pills I have to take, I suppose. It should be somewhere about here.'

'What should?'

'Two pieces of slate.' Grace pointed to an area beneath a large beech tree where the ground was covered with leaves and brambles. 'Have a look round there for me, would you? They're pointed, the shape of a cat's ears, stuck into the ground.'

Trish picked up a fallen branch and used it to lift the brambles and probe the area beneath. 'Got them!' she called at last. 'Shall I bring them over to you?'

375

'No. Leave them where they are.' Grace made her way slowly across the rough ground until she was able to look down at the two black triangles – much smaller than she had remembered them. 'They were put there as a headstone. The dearest friend of my childhood is buried there. My cat.' She had to search her memory for a moment before coming up with the name. 'Pepper, he was called, because his fur made me sneeze. David shot him with a bow and arrow.'

'Is that why you've never got on with David? Did it begin that day?'

'Yes. It was the day I discovered how to hate and how to mourn. A six-year-old body bursting with misery and fury.' With her stick she touched each of the two slates in turn. 'And yet I ought to be grateful to David, I suppose, because something began for me that day. That was when I first found out that shapes could be used to express emotions – the biggest discovery of my life, though it was a good many years before I realized it.' Her expression suddenly lightened. 'So perhaps it's fair after all that David should be rewarded with Greystones. If it hadn't been for him, I might never have found my vocation.'

'You're a Pollyanna,' said Trish.

'What's that?'

'You gave me the book yourself, don't you remember, when I was about ten. Pollyanna was so determined to see the good side of everything that when she was given a pair of crutches for Christmas out of the charity box, she didn't cry at getting something so useless. She was just happy that she didn't need to use them.'

They laughed together. Then Grace buried the past by prodding the dead leaves of many winters back to conceal the pieces of slate.

'I'll accept your offer of a drive back up the hill,' she said. 'Come and find me by the boulders.'

Walking even more cautiously without Trish's helping hand, she made her way alongside the stream before lowering herself

376

gratefully to the mossy ground of the clearing. There she leaned back against one of the huge boulders and stared at the other. Short though it was, this excursion had been too much for her. It was almost impossible to recall the feeling of strength which she had taken for granted until a year or two ago – striding out on walks, hammering for hours at her carvings.

The boulders brought other memories, and these were what she had come to indulge. By these great rocks, rubbed smooth during the millennia of glacial movement, she had first fallen in love with Andy and later wept for the loss of him. Here, many years later, their love had been consummated. Here too she had brought her aunt to mourn a dead lover.

More importantly, it was here that, while searching for some way in which to express her grief after the death of her eldest brother, she found consolation in carving a memorial to him from the fallen branch of a tree. The two pieces of slate on Pepper's grave represented the instinctive reaction of a six-year-old to death, but it was within the atmosphere created by these ancient boulders that as an adult she had begun her life's work.

How peaceful the clearing was. Soon, if the council had its way, traffic would be thundering only a few yards away, but for the moment there was no sound to be heard except the thudding of her own heart. No birds sang and even the nearby stream moved in silence. So quiet was it that she could hear Trish starting the engine of her car at the top of the hill.

Grace lay back, waiting. She stretched her arms backwards, attempting to encircle the boulders; but they were too large. She had to be content with the feel of the stone – smooth in shape but rough in texture – beneath her fingers. Sighing with satisfaction, she pressed harder, as though pulling herself backwards into the centre of the stone.

The dull ache inside her body which nowadays never left her was sharpened by the effort into pain; but this was almost at once washed away by a more sinister sensation. She had suffered haemorrhages before and so was able to recognize that this was another; but for the first time Mercy was not on hand with the necessary medication to check the flow. There was a pill in her pocket now, if she could reach it: she was never without one. Instinctively she brought her arms forward, preparing to search her pockets for the tiny pill box. Then, restraining herself, she sat still.

What was the point? By quick action she might secure for herself another few weeks of life. But the sculpture which she had always known would be her last work was finished. More importantly, she had had the necessary chat with Trish, bringing to a satisfactory end the relationship which had brought her so much happiness. Trish would be all right. Greystones would be all right. Grace leaned back peacefully, listening to the sound of the car as it wound its way down the drive. Then the engine stopped.